IN ALL DIRECTIONS

IN ALL DIRECTIONS

James Bowring

Matador
5 Weir Road
Kibworth Beauchamp
Leicester LE8 0LQ, UK
Tel: (+44) 116 279 2299
Fax: (+44) 116 279 2277
Email: books@troubador.co.uk
Web: www.troubador.co.uk/matador

ISBN 978 1848765 481

British Library Cataloguing in Publication Data.
A catalogue record for this book is available from the British Library.

Typeset in 10.5pt Aldine401 BT Roman by Troubador Publishing Ltd, Leicester, UK

Matador is an imprint of Troubador Publishing Ltd

Printed in Great Britain by the MPG Books Group, Bodmin and King's Lynn

To Polly, Sarah and Jonathan

CHAPTER 1

Departures

The smell of breakfast hung tantalisingly in the air. It permeated the distant recesses of the kitchen and, through the half-open kitchen door, wafted gently into every crevice and nook of the house.

Susan Fuller was wearing a voluminous full-length dressing gown over an equally voluminous nightdress. She was standing by the cooker, carefully inspecting the contents of the sizzling frying pan. Although she became convinced, long ago, that Dave, her husband, had a lead-lined stomach and, although her catering skills were not greatly stretched by his unadventurous, if substantial, dietary requirements, she always made sure that all food was properly prepared and cooked the way Dave liked it – hot and abundant. A few well-aimed and vigorous prods with a wooden spatula assured her that the contents – a gargantuan assortment of fried eggs, rashers of bacon, sausages, mushrooms and tomatoes – had been cooked to her satisfaction. She turned off the cooker and emptied the contents of the frying pan onto two plain, slightly chipped, china plates, loading rather more onto one than the other.

She carried the plates a few steps to a small, battered and rickety wooden table in the corner of the well-used kitchen and placed them, with an emphatic clatter, onto the table. As she did so, she called over her shoulder towards the half-open door.

"Breakfast's ready, Dave!"

She then went back across the kitchen, grabbed the kettle and started to pour boiling water into two large mugs of coffee. Having stirred them thoroughly, she picked them up and was moving back to the table when Dave came into the room.

Dave was a stocky man, not especially tall, with a frame that was once muscular but now tended towards corpulence, largely as a result of many years of trencherman activity. Beneath the grey stubble and short-cropped wavy hair, his face had a ruddy complexion and his eyes had a mischievous sparkle. He approached the table, rubbing his hands together with obvious relish.

"I'm ready for this," he added as if either of them was in any doubt.

Initially, Susan hadn't paid too much attention to Dave's routine arrival, but suddenly the reason for his surreptitious visit to the local market earlier in the week had become all too apparent. He was wearing a loud, floral-patterned Hawaiian-style shirt, with a proliferation of blues and yellows in garish patterns.

Although Susan was not normally an advocate of subtle understatement, as her own exuberant style of dress bore witness, her distaste for Dave's latest fashion statement was immediate and obvious. She slammed the mugs of coffee onto the table, slopping them both, and sat down heavily, opposite him.

"What the… What the hell is that you're wearing?"

Dave stood up proudly, stuck his ample chest out – not quite as far as his ample stomach – and strutted ostentatiously around the kitchen.

"It's my new shirt. Do you like it? I thought it would put us in the holiday mood!"

Pleased with himself, he sat down, picked up his knife and fork and started to attack his breakfast with gourmand-like enthusiasm. Susan, meanwhile, fixed him with pale blue eyes that had instantly become icy cold and unblinking. It was the kind of look, her special disapproving look, that she reserved for those occasions when Dave's natural effervescence, or profound lack of mature judgement, became just a little too much to endure. It was the same disapproving look that she deployed sometimes at work when her boss, whoever that happened to be at the time, showed less than fulsome appreciation of her secretarial skills of which she, though not necessarily her boss, was inordinately proud. It was one of the reasons that she preferred, and seemed better suited to, temporary work.

"What do you mean 'holiday mood'?" she demanded crossly. "I mean … Just look at yourself. We're going on a coach trip around Europe, not a trip to Waikiki bloody beach!"

Dave was an ebullient character, often endearingly so, occasionally irritatingly so. This quality, linked to a juvenile sense of fun, normally made him good company to be with, in a loud, brash, unsubtle sort of way. But, in certain circumstances, his high spirits could easily bubble over into a kind of volatile passion that could make him angry and, in his youth, occasionally violent. He was not normally one to react placidly to criticism or reprimand – he disliked figures of authority as a matter of principle – but the passing years had started to mellow him and Susan's resiliently firm influence had had a limited calming effect on him. These days he knew that, when she nailed him with one of her withering looks, the game was up and all privileges, such as they were, were under threat of withdrawal. That didn't mean, of course, that he couldn't act a little hurt when it suited him.

"You don't like it then? That's a shame because I've three more in my suitcase!"

"Dave, Dave! It's a coach tour. Think of the average age of the people who normally go on these kinds of coach tours. The most adventurous colour most of them wear is beige. Look at the weather outside. It's raining! I mean do you want to look a complete prat?"

Dave adopted a dejected expression of theatrical proportions. "OK, OK, I'll go and change. But I'm finishing my breakfast first."

"OK, but don't be too long. Remember you're doing the washing up while I'm getting ready. Still, I suppose you'd better make the most of it. This'll be the last decent breakfast you'll get for a couple of weeks."

Dave had started to devour his substantial breakfast at a voraciously rapid pace. Suddenly he stopped, holding his heavily laden fork halfway between the plate and his mouth.

"Blimey, I'd forgotten about continental breakfasts. I ask you, what kind of breakfast is a croissant for a working man. And those thin strips of tasteless cheese; and those little individually wrapped portions of spread with odd pictures on them. You never know until you open it whether it's going to be chocolate spread, strawberry jam or peanut butter. Ugh!"

Susan watched with some distaste as a piece of bacon fell

from Dave's fork and settled precariously on the edge of his plate. It was clear that her holiday was not going to be full of new and exciting culinary delights.

"So you'll be sampling the full range of continental cuisine while we're on holiday then?" she asked sarcastically.

Dave had continued eating vigorously, if not especially tidily.

"That's right. Any restaurant will do for me as long as it's got a big yellow "M" outside it."

A dripping piece of egg yolk dropped from his fork as he raised it to his mouth, this time landing on the front of his shirt and sliding slowly into his lap.

"I suppose there is one good thing about that shirt," Susan offered after a moment's exasperated silence. "At least you can't see the egg stains on it."

★ ★ ★

In readiness for the journey, Barbara Khan had tied her long, glossy, black hair back and had dressed for comfort in her well-worn jeans and navy blue sweatshirt. She came downstairs, left her suitcase in the hall and paused briefly. This was the moment that she had been dreading. Over the past two or three weeks, the gradually rising anticipation of her imminent holiday had been increasingly tempered by the knowledge that this moment would inevitably arrive.

Her father was a very proud man, though not in any kind of showy, ostentatious way. Deep down, he was immensely proud of the way his diligent hard work had provided a comfortable, safe and decent environment for his family, and had earned him respect in a multi-cultural society where tensions of various kinds were often not far from the surface. But more than that, he was especially proud of his wife and his daughter and he loved them both dearly.

No matter how hard he tried, however, his cultural roots were so deep, and his attitudes so entrenched, that he found it difficult to approve of the sort of freedom that his daughter craved and that most of her contemporaries enjoyed. The family was a close one and a loving one and, as Barbara grew up, she always tried to avoid potential conflict by not openly challenging the status quo, often drawing back from her strong instinct to question her father's authority and rebel against his attitudes. As a result, there were times when she felt stifled and inhibited. She rarely strayed out of her comfort zone, or his for that matter, and her rebellions, such as they were, were small, subtle and trivial. Perhaps, she told herself, that was why when she did occasionally stray, accidentally or deliberately, into unfamiliar situations, she could quickly become stressed and panicky. But she was also increasingly coming to realise that, unless she did challenge him, unless she broke some of his arbitrary rules, unless she deliberately thrust herself into new and challenging situations, she was never going to know what she was capable of achieving.

So this was it. She took a deep breath.

As she expected, her father was sitting tidily and upright in his favourite armchair, reading his newspaper. Some dark tea, in a porcelain cup, nestled firmly on a matching saucer, which, in turn, rested neatly and symmetrically on a lace mat on a small, well-polished, mahogany coffee table. The room was silent apart from a mahogany-cased clock ticking gently on the mantelpiece. Mrs Khan sat opposite her husband, fiddling nervously with her bead necklace and looking anxiously, over the top of her reading glasses, at the door. She had heard Barbara coming downstairs and was anticipating the drama that was about to unfold, with a kind of sickening dread.

Barbara had mentally prepared herself for this moment often enough. She had lain in bed rehearsing her words and her gestures, even her voice intonations. She had paced the streets on her way to and from college trying to anticipate what her father might say and how she might react. In need of moral support, she had lectured Jason not to be late, but there was still no sign of him and she couldn't loiter in the hall indefinitely. She took another deep breath and went quietly but resolutely into the room where she stood, with her hands clasped together in front of her, trying to look assured but demure, looking first at her father and then her mother.

"Right," she announced. "That's me packed and ready. Jason will be calling round for me in a minute."

Mrs Khan smiled warmly, got up, went over to her daughter and made something of a show of lovingly embracing her.

"Have a wonderful holiday, dear. You've worked so hard at your studies and you deserve it!"

"Thanks Mum. You know, I'm sooooo excited about going to all these famous places you hear about and read about; Venice, Rome, Florence, Paris."

Mrs Khan took a step back and looked proudly at her daughter.

"You're very lucky, Barbara." She turned towards her husband. "Isn't she very lucky?"

Mr Khan grunted from behind his newspaper. Barbara took yet another deep breath and moved slowly towards him.

"Aren't you going to wish me a good holiday, then, Dad?"

Mr Khan peered over the top of his paper. His deep brown eyes, so often calm and reassuring, today looked uneasy, almost scared.

"You know perfectly well what I think of this holiday."

"Oh Dad! Come on! I've worked hard all year. I sooooo need a holiday. And this is a great opportunity to practice my language skills. It'll be really cool if I can improve my French and Italian. It'll open up so many opportunities for me."

"It's not that. You know perfectly well it's not that. You're doing well with your studies and that pleases me. It's this going off on holiday with your boyfriend…"

"Meaning?"

Barbara's determination to stay calm and be positive was already flagging in the face of her father's obvious hostility. Deep down, she knew he was going to be difficult – she had told herself as much hundreds of times – but it still didn't stop her getting annoyed. And the more she showed her annoyance, the more intransigent her father was likely to become.

"I don't need to spell it out, do I?" he continued from somewhere behind his newspaper. "I'd hoped we'd brought you up to respect this family's traditional values; to save yourself for your husband; to…"

"Dad, I've told you! We're going to be in the close company of a whole coach load of complete strangers most of the time. What do you think we'll be getting up to?"

"And at night?"

That was one of the many questions that she had been expecting. In a carefully rehearsed move, she rummaged in her shoulder bag and produced a crumpled piece of paper, which she thrust over the top of his newspaper and into his face.

"I've told you that too. We've got separate rooms. Look! Look! This is the holiday booking confirmation form."

She pointed to a section of the form.

"You see – there – two single rooms!"

Her father went quiet for a moment, struggling to find the right words to say. Barbara used the opportunity to kneel down beside him and kiss him affectionately on the cheek. Though still angry at what she saw as his unreasonably entrenched attitudes, she tried to talk softly and soothingly into his ear, still hoping that they could part friends today.

"This hasn't got anything to do with fact that Jason isn't – you know? After all, I'm British and so is he!"

Mr Khan fidgeted uneasily. Carefully, almost obsessively, he folded up his newspaper, placed it neatly beside his cup and saucer on the table and looked pleadingly at his daughter. She was growing up. She was becoming independent and free-spirited. There was another man in her life, a rival for her affections, someone who might ultimately take her away from him. He was finding it all emotionally difficult.

"No, no," he pleaded, his voice wavering. "I just don't like the idea of a daughter of mine going off on holiday alone with…"

"I lo… I like Jason a lot," Barbara interrupted. "But he's just a friend; a good friend. He'll be a good travelling companion. I know he'll look after me. I know he respects me."

At that point, the doorbell rang, to the collective relief, it seemed, of all three occupants of the room. Mrs Khan, who was nearest to the door, was first to react.

"I'll go," she said swiftly and hurried from the room. Barbara, who was still kneeling beside her father, spoke to him again.

"That'll be Jason. Try and be nice to him, Dad."

After a brief exchange of doorstep pleasantries with Mrs Khan, Jason came slowly and diffidently into the room. He was a tall, thin, young man with spiky, pale brown, almost ginger hair and pallid skin, which contrasted sharply with Barbara's dusky complexion. He seemed always to wear a T-shirt, jeans and trainers irrespective of the occasion and climatic conditions, and today was no exception. He had a certain youthful gaucheness and was clearly ill at ease as he entered the room.

"Hello, Barbara. Hello, Mr Khan," he ventured tentatively.

Barbara got to her feet and rushed excitedly towards him, just resisting the temptation to kiss him.

"Jason, Jason. Tell my dad. He's worried about me going on holiday with you. He thinks you're going to take advantage of me; that you might have your evil way with me."

Jason exchanged subtle glances with Barbara and surreptitiously crossed his fingers behind his back as he went into his prepared routine.

"Mr Khan, I respect your daughter far too much for that. And I respect you and Mrs Khan. I'll look after her properly, I promise. And we do have single rooms, you know."

"Yes, I've shown him the confirmation form," added Barbara.

Mr Khan barely acknowledged Jason's presence. He picked up his newspaper and started to unfold it. Mrs Khan tutted at this uncharacteristic show of ill manners but, as a strained silence had fallen on the room, she decided to bring matters to a rapid conclusion.

"Go on, off you go, you two. Enjoy yourselves and don't forget to practice your languages, Barbara."

"I've been practicing already," Barbara enthused. "Do you want to hear some Italian? *Si vende degli antifecondativi?*"

In truth, she wasn't quite sure why she chose the Italian for "Do you sell contraceptives?" as the sample phrase to use. Maybe it was a phrase that she had subconsciously memorised as one she might just need to use when they were in Venice or Florence or Rome. Maybe she just wanted to enjoy some small final act of defiance although she was pretty sure that neither of her parents spoke a word of Italian so the risk was minimal. Almost immediately, however, she regretted her impulsive choice of phrase. She became gripped with panic and paused nervously in case either of her parents asked her for a translation. Fortunately, they didn't. Instead, Mrs Khan beamed and started to applaud.

"Very good!" she said as she escorted them from the room. "Don't worry about him. I'll work on him," she whispered and then added, more loudly, "don't forget to send us a postcard or two, and don't forget my Belgian chocolates."

She leant forward, kissed her daughter softly on the cheek and then whispered in her ear "I think chocolates will be more use to me at my age than contraceptives!"

Barbara instantly pulled away and stared in alarm at her mother. But her mother just smiled, her eyes twinkling with mischief. One day she would have to tell Barbara about Lucia and her English husband, who used to live next door to them for a while before Barbara was born. She learned a lot of interesting Italian phrases from Lucia. Seeing her mother smiling wickedly, and greatly relieved, Barbara laughed and flung herself into her mother's arms.

"No Mum, I won't forget your chocolates. Bye, Dad!" she shouted, but there was no response. She kissed her mother affectionately, picked up her suitcase and, hand-in-hand with Jason, she left.

* * *

Joyce Armitage was a short, solid woman with a round, amiable face beneath short, permed grey hair. She had been married to Frank for over forty years so well knew what agonies to expect when the time came to lock up and leave. The tactic she favoured most was to make herself as inconspicuous as possible, retreating to the sanctuary of the bathroom or spare bedroom, on some pretext, until Frank had finished his locking-up rituals.

As usual, he had checked that all the taps were turned off – three times. He had checked that all electrical appliances had been turned off and unplugged – three times. He had checked that all the windows were closed and locked – three times. He had carefully adjusted the position of each set of curtains – three times. He had checked that all the gas taps on the cooker were turned off – three times – and he had checked that all the lights were off – three times. All of this laboured ritual was normal, if highly tiresome, but on this particular occasion, he seemed to have become strangely obsessed with the handle of the French window that led from the lounge out onto the small balcony of their flat. He had spent some time fiddling with it while leaning his tall, angular frame heavily against the door.

Curious to discover why Frank had taken even longer than usual to do his rounds of their compact flat, Joyce had emerged quietly and timidly from the spare bedroom and poked her head around the door of the lounge. She watched him, silently for a while, but, eventually, even she grew impatient and could restrain herself no more.

"What are you fiddling about at now?"

Frank hadn't noticed that Joyce had been watching him. He jumped slightly. He turned to face her. His brow was even more furrowed than usual.

"Eh… oh… No, I wasn't fiddling. I was just going onto the balcony to give the plants a final watering and I noticed the door handle felt a bit loose."

"Well, nobody's going to be using it while we're away."

"Ah, no, but we don't want to risk a burglar breaking in; the lock might be dodgy. I think I'd better go out onto the balcony to be sure. You'd better lock the door from the inside so that I can check that it's safe from the outside and that nobody's going to break in."

Joyce had learned to cope, most of the time, with Frank's compulsive habits. Unlike her spouse, she was usually patient, easy-going and unassuming – she had to be – but occasionally she still got frustrated with his obsessions, which, it seemed to her, had worsened as he got older and, now that he was retired, often felt oppressively intrusive. It was no wonder, she frequently mused, that her hair had turned grey at an early age, in contrast to her husband who had retained most of his dark, almost black hair, apart from a gentle greying at the temples.

"Oh, for God's sake!" she muttered in frustration, hands on hips.

Frank looked reprovingly at her, his pale blue eyes somehow pleading for greater tolerance.

"Please, Joyce, don't be difficult. You know I'll worry otherwise."

Frank would worry whatever, of course. He was one of life's worriers, but Joyce knew better than to argue. Blessed with a sharp intelligence and sound judgement, she usually knew when it was right to acquiesce, which was most of the time, and when it was right to stand her ground.

"Alright then, but be quick."

Frank opened the door and stepped onto the balcony. A blast of unseasonably cool, damp air caused him to stop momentarily and he shivered. Joyce closed the door behind him, turned the key, and locked it from the inside. Frank fiddled for some moments with the handle, leaning heavily against the door several times, but eventually satisfied himself that it held firm and was secure. He shouted to Joyce through the glass.

"That seems OK. You can open it up."

Joyce nodded with relief, but her relief turned quickly to dismay as she went to unlock the door only to find that the key had jammed and would not turn in either direction. After vigorously jiggling the key, but without success, she tried hitting it with her sturdy fist, but it still wouldn't budge.

"Come on, hurry up!" Frank called from outside.

"I'm trying, but the lock's stuck. The key's jammed!"

Joyce knew that she would be blamed for this. She had lost count of the times over the years that she had gently suggested that perhaps they should purchase a new double-glazed balcony door with up-to-date security locks, in the same way that she had occasionally enquired, in vain, about the possibility of a new fitted kitchen or speculated whether a refurbished bathroom suite would be a good idea; all to no avail, of course. Frank's parsimony had its place, but when something old and unreliable went wrong, she knew that it would be her fault.

"You stupid…" began Frank predictably.

"It's not my fault," she replied, standing her ground. "I was only doing what you asked me to do."

"Let me try from this side." Frank's notoriously fragile patience was wearing thin.

They both tried fiddling with the handle from either side of the door but the lock remained resolutely jammed.

"Well this is bloody brilliant!" Frank yelled.

Joyce glanced towards the heavens, seeking some kind of divine intervention. None came, but at least the brief pause helped her to calm down.

"I could try oiling the lock," she suggested.

"Worth a try I suppose," Frank conceded grudgingly. "There's a can on the shelf in the broom cupboard."

Joyce disappeared briefly and returned clutching a battered and rusty can of oil. Using the nozzle, she tried to ease some oil into the keyhole, but, after a couple of minutes, with the key still jammed fast and a steady trickle of surplus oil running down the door, she had to admit defeat.

"This isn't going to work. What shall I do now?" she asked lamely, while mopping up the misdirected flow of oil.

"Just leave well alone, while I think!"

Frank looked around him on the sparsely equipped balcony, hoping to find an answer to the problem, but two wooden folding chairs, a window box containing some lovingly cultivated annuals, several plant pots and an almost empty watering can didn't suggest an immediate solution. Then he noticed some of Joyce's old knitting needles that he had pushed into the soil and tied to some of the plants in the window box as makeshift stakes. Without hesitation, or indeed much thought, he pulled one of the thinner knitting needles out of the soil and thrust it into the keyhole, hoping to push the recalcitrant key out. But the needle stuck fast and as Frank tried to pull it out by wiggling it, the end broke off, leaving behind a jagged stub in the keyhole. Frank threw the broken needle angrily to the ground. He leant over the balcony rail and looked down at the ground below, but it seemed a dangerously long way down from two floors up. His brow furrowed even more than usual.

"I could try breaking the glass so that you could stand on one of the chairs and climb in," Joyce offered in desperation. She knew that it was hardly the perfect solution and anticipated Frank's scathing reply.

"That would be a big help. Then we'd have a broken window to get fixed before we could leave. No, no. You'll just have to call the fire brigade to get me down."

"Are you serious?"

"Well can you think of something better? Phone them and explain, but for God's sake hurry up or we'll miss the bloody coach."

* * *

The kitchen of the Cockrells' house displayed all the trappings of a comfortable lifestyle – an extensive range of modern fitted units, built in hob, concealed lighting, dishwasher, washing machine, fridge, freezer, well-stocked wine rack, state-of-the-art gadgetry and a sense of light and spaciousness that not even the incongruous presence of a traditional, solid pine dining table and six solid pine chairs in the middle of the room could dispel.

Julia was sitting at the table, her bony elbows resting on it and her chin resting in her gaunt, cupped hands, as she stared out of the window into the well-stocked and well-maintained back garden with its heavily decked patio, manicured lawn, ornamental pond, trellis fencing and summerhouse. Her blonde hair, streaked liberally with grey, tumbled freely over her long, thin face. She was so engrossed in her thoughts that she appeared not to notice the repetitive, rhythmic pounding of loud music on the ceiling above her, nor Trevor entering the room engaged, as he often was, in a conversation on his mobile phone.

"What do you mean resign? She can't resign just like that… She'll have to work her notice… Oh, sod it! Well, you'll just have to do your best to cover for her. Get hold of a temp from the agency or something… Yes, yes, I know. Oh, and you'll need to get that dodgy fire exit door fixed before the fire officer closes us down. See who you can get, but it'll have to be done in the next few days… What about Geoff Leggatt? No, I know… He's not brilliant, but it's not a difficult job and he is cheap. Anyway, it kind of keeps it in the family, if you know what I mean. See if you can get him to come in one evening next week, after the delegates have gone home… You've got my mobile number. Give me a call or send me a text if you get stuck!"

He rang off and, clearly annoyed, tossed his phone onto the table, where it skidded to a halt next to Julia's elbow. He ran his hand backwards and forwards over his short-cropped, dark brown hair and paced up and down the room. He often ran his hand backwards and forwards over his hair and paced up and down when he was stressed. He often got stressed. As he paced, he addressed the kitchen in general and Julia in particular.

"Bloody hell! Would you believe it? That's just what we need! Emma's resigned. She's got another job, closer to her parents. Her mother's quite ill and they want her to start this job straight away, so we'll have to let her go. Just when we're getting really busy!"

Julia continued to stare into space apparently oblivious to Trevor's rant.

"Do you think Mark will be alright on his own?" she asked, initiating her own separate conversation.

"You haven't been listening, have you?"

"Mmmm? Oh, sorry darling!"

"Emma's resigned."

"Oh dear! Is she the one with the long dark hair and big boobs? I always thought you rather fancied her."

Trevor pulled up a chair and sat down next to Julia.

"Me? No, no. I've never even noticed the size of her..." he pleaded, rather less than convincingly. "Anyway, she was bloody good at her job and she's going to be difficult to replace."

"Mmmmm. I'm a bit worried about Mark."

It was clear to Trevor that he was not going to elicit much sympathy for his plight from Julia. Instead, he sighed and raised a hand towards the still-thumping ceiling.

"Does he sound upset or ill?"

"I know, I know, but I've not left him on his own before. And then there's the cat..."

"Sorry, darling, but he is seventeen you know – Mark, that is, not the cat, obviously! He's got your mobile number. He's got my mobile number. He's got our full holiday itinerary. And his father only lives around the corner."

He looked across at Julia who was still staring dreamily into the distance. There was a look of vulnerability about her that he loved. He edged closer to her and placed a reassuring hand on her knee.

Neither of them noticed that the ceiling had stopped vibrating.

"Look, this is the first opportunity we've had to be on our own for any length of time since we got married. Let's try and enjoy ourselves, eh? I am sure he'll be fine."

He was about to place his arm protectively around Julia's narrow shoulders when the door opened and Mark shambled into the room. The young man nearly always managed, somehow, to give the impression of either having just got out of bed or of being just about to go to bed, though his irregular time-keeping meant that it was often hard to tell which. On entering the room, he headed straight to one of the many fitted cupboards and took out a large, patterned cereal bowl. From another cupboard, he produced a packet of breakfast cereal, from which he carelessly emptied a large quantity into the bowl, spilling some of the contents onto the laminate wooden flooring. He then went to the fridge, trampling on some of the spilt cereal in the process, opened the fridge door, took out a large carton of milk, took a swig from the carton and then poured some milk over the cereal in the bowl. He then took a spoon from one of the many fitted drawers, picked up the bowl, went over to the table, pulled out a chair, dragging it noisily across the floor, sat down opposite Julia and Trevor, without acknowledging them, and began to eat, noisily and eagerly.

Although discomfited by Mark's unexpected arrival, Trevor made a brave attempt at amiability.

"Ah, Mark. I was just telling your mother. You'll be fine looking after the house and Rosie?"

Mark had just filled his mouth with food but, unfortunately, that did not stop him replying. Trevor turned away as Mark began to answer, hoping that his freshly laundered cotton shirt would remain unsullied by the imminent onslaught.

"What? Oh, yeah, cool, no probs. You two go off and enjoy yourselves," he replied spraying food liberally about as he spoke.

He gave Trevor a knowing wink, then, without warning, Julia reached across the table and grabbed his hand, which happened to be holding a spoonful of cereal. The sudden act of clutching his hand jerked it forward, causing most of the cereal to topple from the spoon onto the table and over Trevor's mobile phone. Mark extricated his hand from his mother's grasp, scooped up most of the spilt and soggy cereal in his fingers and put it back in the bowl. Trevor grabbed his phone and turned away again.

"Are you sure you'll be OK?" Julia asked Mark anxiously.

"Stay cool, Ma!"

He pointed to one of the many fitted cupboards, which had been spattered with an assortment of adhesive "post-it" notes in a variety of garish colours, with various notes scrawled on them.

"I can read. You've left me instructions, you've left me phone numbers, you've left me money, you've left me food. You've left Rosie food. I've got phone numbers for the doctor, the hospital, the vet, the fire brigade, the police, Interpol, the United Nations! Dad's around the corner. We'll be OK. Come on, unwind! Here let me give you a hand with your luggage."

He put his spoon down, wiped his sticky hand on his shirt, stood up and left the room, grabbing a banana from the fruit bowl as he went. Trevor watched him go as he fastidiously wiped his phone with a tissue.

"One thing, I don't think he's going to starve!"

He got up, closed the fridge door and grabbed Julia's hand, firmly. She got up, a little reluctantly, and they followed Mark out of the room.

★ ★ ★

No matter how hard they tried, and despite always vowing to do better next time, Valerie and Brian Wood always found themselves in a last-minute panic to pack. In their small bedroom, in their small semi-detached house, there was chaos. On the bed, two well-travelled and rather scruffy suitcases, together with a large rucksack, were open, there were piles of clothes everywhere and Brian and Valerie were hurtling around the room, occasionally bumping into each other, opening drawers, cupboards and wardrobes and, apparently randomly, throwing a miscellany of items onto the bed.

Brian bore certain similarities to his suitcase, being well-travelled and rather scruffy. He was a gentle, pleasant and caring man but he was the sort of man who would manage to look scruffy in the world's best and most precisely tailored suit. Small and ungainly, with a mop of unruly thick brown hair and heavily rimmed glasses, he contrasted sharply with his tall, graceful, well-groomed and svelte wife.

When she was younger, and before she met Brian, Valerie had earned extra money by modelling part-time in the evenings – though she had never quite brought herself to tell Brian exactly what kind of modelling she had done – and she had always maintained a certain glamorous and graceful poise since those early days. By now, of course, she knew that Brian was probably never going to be the rich and famous musician she hoped he would be when she married him. He scraped a living of sorts, playing with a couple of local ensembles and doing some session work, but there was something missing. Maybe he lacked the necessary charisma, the ambition and possibly even the talent to make the big-time. Maybe he just didn't enjoy performing enough to excel at it. But, although Valerie's zeal may have been diminished by the passage of time, she couldn't quite bring herself to give up. In her humdrum existence, she needed her ambitions, however unattainable they may be.

Brian stood for a moment, hands on hips, and surveyed the scene of mounting chaos around him.

"It beats me why we always end up packing at the last minute."

"Well it would help if you remembered to put your clothes in the basket for washing a bit earlier."

"Yes, yes. So you keep saying."

He picked up some neatly ironed and folded garments from the bed, screwed them up and stuffed them into a corner of his suitcase. Valerie winced.

"That reminds me. I need to pack the travelling iron."

As she left the bedroom, Brian called after her.

"Better take the kettle as well. You know how you like your cup of tea. And don't forget the plug adaptor."

After several minutes rummaging around in the spare bedroom, opening and closing drawers and banging cupboard doors shut, Valerie returned clutching the kettle, iron and adaptor. They all looked well-travelled and rather scruffy. Valerie studied the kettle thoughtfully.

"Are you sure this kettle's alright?" she enquired. "It didn't work properly last time."

Brian was dismissive.

"Yes, yes. I checked them both, they're fine."

A further flurry of frenetic, disorganised activity saw the remaining items, including the kettle and iron, stuffed into suitcases. Brian closed his case, leaned heavily on the lid and zipped it up quickly, as though worried that some of the contents might suddenly escape. He stood back triumphantly.

"Right, I think that's it," he said, casually stuffing some more items into his rucksack.

"Don't forget the padlocks."

"Yes, yes!"

Resuming his frenzied endeavours, Brian hunted around for the errant padlocks while Valerie calmly and neatly completed her packing. She paused briefly, picked up her best powder blue swimsuit and studied it thoughtfully. The holiday brochure had not explicitly made mention of any of the hotels having a swimming pool and maybe there wouldn't be time anyway, but... She looked again at her suitcase, neatly folded her swimsuit and placed it carefully beneath a couple of dresses before closing it.

"Don't tell me, you've lost the padlocks," she complained, after Brian had been gone for a while.

"No, no. Here they are!"

He had returned, holding up two battered-looking padlocks, which he had found at the back of a drawer. He passed one to Valerie and they secured and locked their cases. Brian glanced at his watch.

"Right, it's time we were going!"

There was one final flurry of activity before Brian zipped up his large rucksack and flung it carelessly over his shoulder, scuffing it against the wall as he did so. Then, they grabbed their respective suitcases and both tried to squeeze through the bedroom door at the same time, before Valerie gave way, allowing Brian to stumble out first, making another scuff mark on the wall with his suitcase as he went. Behind them, on the bed, lay piles of discarded and apparently unwanted clothing.

★ ★ ★

With Peter safely ensconced in the bathroom, whistling tunelessly to himself in the shower, Gail Edwards took the opportunity to complete the last of the essential domestic tasks before they set off. She removed some crockery from the dishwasher and put it away in the cupboard, she emptied the contents of a couple of waste paper baskets into the dustbin by the back door and was just about to give her houseplants a final watering when she heard the doorbell ring. She cursed quietly and opened the door with her green plastic watering can still in her hand. She had short dark hair, brown eyes that sparkled and an almost permanent smile, which momentarily faded when she saw who was standing on the doorstep. The one person she didn't really want to see right now was her garrulous and inquisitive next-door neighbour, Carol. She was a large, jolly woman with long, straight dark hair and permanently alert eyes.

"Oh hello, Carol," she said, trying, unconvincingly, to appear pleased to see her.

"Hello, Gail. I just popped round to wish you and Peter a good holiday and to deliver Fred."

"Fred?" Gail looked mystified until Carol produced from behind her back a dog-eared teddy bear, about a foot long, with a royal blue ribbon tied securely around his neck. Suddenly she remembered that, in a moment of weakness, she had allowed Carol to persuade her to take the bear with her on holiday. Her smile froze.

"You remember Fred from the nursery school?" Carol continued. "You'd said you'd take him on holiday with you and take lots of photos of him as he travels around Europe. You know, for the notice board!"

"Oh, oh, yes of course, of course. Thank you!"

She suppressed an inner groan, took reluctant delivery of the bear and stood on the doorstep, with her smile still frozen, waiting for Carol to say something more. She didn't normally have to wait long, but, strangely, on this occasion, a long, uncomfortable silence followed. This was unlike Carol, Gail thought. Was she expecting to be invited in for a chat? Was she hoping to see Peter who, Gail suspected, she rather fancied? She had often joked about it with Peter who, while secretly flattered, found the whole notion quite absurd. She thought of mentioning that Peter was in the shower but wondered whether Carol might regard that as more of an invitation than a deterrent. In any event, Gail had no time or desire for further small talk with her neighbour this morning.

"Well, I'd better get back to…"

"How's Peter?" Carol interrupted, looking over Gail's shoulder into the neat interior of the house. Gail was not quite sure how to reply.

"He's… he's… OK. He's busy getting ready at the moment."

"I expect he's ready for a holiday isn't he? What with losing his mother suddenly like that. It must have been very upsetting."

"Yes, it was a big shock for him, of course. He *is* very stressed out and pretty tired as well, what with having to stand in for the deputy head for those few weeks in the run up to the *Ofsted* inspection. He's had to work very hard *and* he thinks he's going down with a cold. You know what men are like!"

There was another uncomfortable pause as the women eyed each other uncertainly from either side of the threshold. This time, it was Carol who broke the silence.

"Yes. Well, look after Fred for me. And give my love to Peter. I hope you both have a wonderful holiday. And don't forget to take lots of photos."

Gail visibly brightened at this unexpectedly early opportunity to bring the discussion to a close.

"Thanks, Carol. Oh and perhaps you could just keep an eye on the place while we're away."

"Of course; it's what neighbours are for. You can rely on me."

Although Carol was not Gail's ideal neighbour, she was the kind who could certainly be relied upon to keep a very close eye on their house while they were away.

"Yes, I'm quite sure I can," said Gail cheerily and with a hint of sarcasm that she hoped was lost on Carol. "We'll send you a postcard. Bye!"

She closed the door firmly, placed Fred carefully on the doormat, ready to be gathered up when they left, sighed and returned to her watering.

★ ★ ★

A shaft of weak daylight penetrated a small gap in the otherwise closed curtains and dimly illuminated the interior of a drab and functional bed-sit. From somewhere beyond the partly open casement window, there was the faint sound of birdsong and, from just behind the curtains, came the incessant buzzing of an angry insect.

Beneath the duvet, Miranda Bellamy began to stir slowly; she yawned, stretched and turned over. As she did so, she squinted sleepily between the strands of her long, dark, dishevelled hair at her alarm clock. Suddenly, she swore, sat bolt upright, picked up the alarm clock, examined it carefully and shook it. She reached for her watch, which she kept on her bedside table, and studied it through the gloom. She swore again.

"Oh, shit! Bloody alarm! I'm going to be late!"

With a mixture of anger and frustration, she hurled the clock across the room, where it ricocheted from a large battered cupboard and landed with a clatter somewhere in the shadows. She hurriedly got out of bed and, without pulling back the curtains or switching on the light, ran, naked, towards the bathroom door. In the gloom, she trod on her discarded alarm clock, partly lost her balance and thudded into the side of the now even more battered cupboard. She swore loudly, picked up the clock, hurled it across the room in a different direction, limped painfully into the bathroom and started running a bath.

★ ★ ★

Still imprisoned on his own balcony, Frank Armitage was growing steadily more restless. His tall, lean frame, a little more stooped these days, was beginning to double up and he was clutching his groin, with a pained expression on his face, while hopping anxiously from one foot to the other. In desperation, he shouted to Joyce through the window.

"How much longer are they going to be?"

"I don't know. They said they'd get someone here as soon as they could."

"Oh, it's no use. I don't think I can hang on any longer."

It was a cool, damp morning and the pressure on his notoriously weak bladder was becoming unbearable. He reached down for his watering can, positioned it in the darkest and least visible recess of the small balcony, checked to see that, as far as he could tell, no-one was looking, undid his flies and relieved himself into the can for what seemed like an ecstatic eternity.

★ ★ ★

The relief that Barbara Khan was experiencing was also ecstatic, but in a different way. After dreading it for weeks, she had survived her family farewell, difficult though it had been. Her father had at least stopped short of "forbidding" her to go on holiday and, for the next two weeks she was free. Not entirely free of course – she would soon discover that, on an organised coach tour, much of what she did and when she did it would be orchestrated with almost military precision – but, within those constraints, she would be at liberty to do as she pleased and free to say what she wanted to say. She was exultant.

Jason's friend Tom had dropped them close to the town centre and they only had a short walk through part of the pedestrianised shopping mall to the pick-up point where the feeder coach would collect them. As they hauled their suitcases on wheels behind them, Barbara's excitement was obvious. Despite the weight of her suitcase, she was almost skipping along the wide walkway.

"I can't believe it," she panted. "We've done it. We're actually going on holiday together."

She paused briefly to catch her breath.

"Hey, that was a brilliant idea, Jace, changing the details on the confirmation form."

Jason smiled smugly.

"Yeah. It's amazing what you can do with a good quality scanner and the right software."

"Two single rooms! That's soooo funny! Do you think my parents suspected anything?"

Jason suddenly stopped. He didn't answer and seemed strangely preoccupied. Barbara looked anxiously across at him.

"Jace, are you okay?"

Jason had stopped outside a sex shop selling toys, lingerie and other products "of an adult nature" and he was staring intently at the panoply of intimate items on display in the window. Enticed by the melange of feather boas, thongs, basques and mock leopard skin underwear, his pale complexion began to turn a more healthy pink. He winked at Barbara.

"Do you fancy getting some supplies in for the holiday?"

Barbara smiled mischievously but then started to look around furtively. Her excitement, her inquisitiveness and her growing sense of bravado were all drawing her inside the shop, but she did not want to risk being seen by anyone she knew. After all, it was Saturday morning and some of her friends might be out and about. If word got back to her father, she would be in desperate trouble when she returned home. Satisfying herself that the coast was clear, she giggled.

"Hey, shall we?"

"Yeah, come on. We've got a bit of time before the coach arrives. We don't want to have nothing to do at night, on our own, in all these different hotel rooms, in all these romantic cities, do we?"

"Jason Rogers, what can you mean?"

Lugging their suitcases through the shop doorway, they made their way inside, giggling.

★ ★ ★

The tour operator "*Conn Tours*" was a long-established company, which specialised in what it called "budget-priced escorted tours" by coach to various parts of Europe. Nearly all of the tours made use of the ferry services operating out of Dover and the company offered its "clients" two different ways of getting there. They could make their way to a "*convenient local pick-up point*," often some considerable distance from where they lived, where a small, rickety feeder coach, devoid of any suspension, and a driver with no apparent knowledge of the route, no satellite navigation, no road maps and no obvious sense of direction, would collect them and meander their way to Dover via a myriad of further pick-up points, wrong turnings, traffic jams, a possible further change of vehicle and any number of motorway service stations. Alternatively, clients could make their own way to Dover, by car, and take advantage of the "*specially negotiated and competitive parking arrangements*" at the port.

Trevor and Julia had chosen to make the relatively short journey from their Surrey home by car. Trevor hated delays and waiting around, but he also hated being late for anything so, given that the main routes into Dover could get very congested on summer weekends, he had allowed a generous amount of time to make the journey. They made unexpectedly good progress around the M25 and into Kent, however, and it looked as though they would arrive at Dover docks with a great deal of time to spare. Their departure had been a fraught affair, with Julia bidding a tearful farewell to Mark and Rosie, and, as they continued their journey, Trevor tried hard to engender a more relaxed mood.

"Ah, at last; it's good to get away," he mused.

"Mmmm."

"You still worried about Mark?"

"Mmmmm. You still worried about work?"

"A bit."

"Don't worry!" they cried together. This simultaneous and spontaneous outburst caused them both to dissolve into laughter and, in that instant, their mood changed. Suddenly, it seemed, they were on holiday, relaxed and happy.

Back home, on the other hand, Mark was at a bit of a loose end. The house felt big and empty now and, in truth, he was not nearly as confident about looking after himself, the house, and the cat as he had pretended earlier. He felt in need of reassurance and decided to go and see his father.

Geoff Leggatt was not, by nature, an early riser and he was in the middle of preparing his breakfast when Mark tried to ring the doorbell of his small, shabby terraced house. The bell didn't work. Geoff had been meaning to fix it for some time but hadn't got round to it, so Mark rattled the letter box. Geoff was not temperamentally suited to the kind of solitary existence that had been forced upon him since Julia left to move in with Trevor, and so was delighted to see his son. Unlike Trevor, he greeted him with genuine affability.

"Hello, Mark. What a nice surprise! Come in. I was just cooking myself some breakfast. Do you fancy some?"

"Yeah, I'm starving." It had, after all, been over an hour since Mark had eaten his last breakfast.

Geoff led the way into a small, basic kitchen. He had been planning to install some new units for some time but hadn't got round to it. He opened a small fridge that seemed to hum alarmingly loudly and replenished his frying pan with a fresh supply of bacon, eggs and sausages. Mark sat on a wobbly kitchen stool and watched him as he continued preparing his gastronomic feast. Mark sniffed the air. It was clear that Geoff's latest attempt to give up smoking had been unsuccessful, again.

"So have you seen the lovebirds off on their holiday?" Geoff enquired.

"Yeah, they're on their way."

"So, you've got the place to yourself now then?"

"S'pose so. Me, the cat, and several hundred 'post-it' notes."

Mark went thoughtful as Geoff took the plateful of breakfast, originally intended for himself, and, sweeping aside a few empty beer cans and the remains of yesterday's take-away, cleared a space on the small breakfast bar, and placed it in front of his son.

"I wish you and Mum were still together," Mark said, wistfully.

"Don't you like Trevor then?"

"Oh, he's alright I suppose. Mum seems happy enough. The house is nice. But he's always working at that bloody Conference Centre of his. Even when he's at home, he's working half the time – hammering away at his laptop or calling someone from his mobile – and… and we never go out anywhere or do anything, you know, as a family. The house seems very empty sometimes. Anyway, he's not my dad, you are!"

"You mean he doesn't lend you money like I do? How much do you want this time?" He reached nervously for his wallet.

"Oh, no. I'm OK for money. Mum and Trevor left me plenty. It's just, I miss you sometimes." Mark was finding it hard to say what he wanted to say. It all seemed too sentimental and soppy.

"If it's any consolation, I miss your mother too."

Mark looked up at his father. Though badly weathered by life, misfortune, alcohol and tobacco, he still had the swarthy good looks and natural charm that had once made him so attractive to Julia.

"Can't you get back together then?" Mark enquired.

"It's hardly that simple, is it? For a start, she's married to Trevor now. And we've kind of grown apart."

"And I don't suppose that business with Auntie Pat helped?"

"Er, no! I must admit, finding me in bed with her sister didn't go down too well with your mother for some reason."

Geoff served up his own meal and sat down on another wobbly kitchen stool, next to Mark. He had been meaning to fix the stools, like the doorbell, for ages but when he came home each evening, having spent the day repairing things for other people, he could never raise the energy or enthusiasm. He gazed in awe at the food rapidly disappearing from Mark's plate.

"Leave what you don't want, won't you?"

"Yeah, cool! I think she's still fond of you, though, y'know?"

"Not fond enough, I don't think. No, we've got to face facts. I was stupid. Your mother wasn't to blame, but it's all over. I mean, look around you; she wouldn't want to come back here, not after what she's used to now."

A depressing silence descended on the pair as they continued to eat.

"Is there anything I can do?" Mark asked, having cleared his plate.

"Apart from the washing-up, you mean?"

Geoff had been reflecting on their conversation while he was eating. Difficult though it would be, the idea of trying to win Julia back was an attractive one, if only to give Trevor something to think about, and maybe, just maybe, there was a way to do it.

"I tell you something that might work…" he said, pointing his fork at Mark.

★ ★ ★

Brian and Valerie had also opted to take their own car to Dover. Over the years, Valerie had never particularly warmed to the long, uncomfortable and often bumpy journeys by feeder coach, with the occasional snatched refreshment break at service stations of indifferent or irregular quality, while the rigid discipline of being in a particular place at a particular time, in order to catch the coach, had, in the past, proved to be especially challenging for Brian. Besides, he liked driving his car. It was not a new car, nearly nine years old now, nor was it noted for its comfort, but he had an unreciprocated fondness for all things mechanical and took great pride in servicing, maintaining and repairing the vehicle himself. Unfortunately, his unbounded enthusiasm greatly exceeded his technical competence and it was therefore no great surprise to Valerie when the car broke down after they had only travelled a few miles.

She stood forlornly on the pavement of a nondescript, dull suburban road, sheltering beneath a small red umbrella and securely cocooned in an elegant fawn raincoat, as the rain fell steadily. She was observing Brian's ample and very damp bottom protruding from beneath the bonnet. He had been working away for some minutes now and although the only feature that she could discern, his damp bottom, was entirely expressionless, Valerie sensed that, as usual, he was making no progress. Every year, she nagged him to join one of the major national motoring organisations like the AA or RAC, and every year, he took the suggestion as a slur on his mechanical talents and stubbornly refused to do so. So here she was, standing on the kerb, watching the rain falling unremittingly and splattering her newly cleaned black patent leather shoes. Her brittle patience snapped.

"I thought you were going to service the damn thing!" she grouched.

"I did service it. But obviously not very well!"

"I know the feeling!"

Brian emerged from beneath the bonnet, clutching a spanner. "And what is that supposed to mean?"

As he stood beside the car, Valerie was appalled by what she saw. His pale green shirt, that she had so lovingly ironed yesterday, was badly crumpled and covered in grease and oil stains. His hair was matted with a combination of rainwater and engine oil and a large, rapidly expanding damp patch covered most of the rear of his trousers.

"Look at the state you're in. Look at your shirt!" she shrieked.

"What did you expect?" replied Brian tartly. Valerie in one of her more caustic moods was not one of life's great pleasures and he could certainly have done without her sartorial observations just then. Her critique, however, like the rain, showed no signs of abating.

"We can't turn up with you looking like that. Everyone will stare at you. You'll have to change. And I bet you haven't packed enough shirts for the fortnight!"

Brian looked at his watch through the spattered lenses of his glasses, while trying hard to suppress a heavy sigh.

"There's no time for that now. I'll change when we get to Dover, if there's time."

Valerie was right, of course. She usually was. Despite having tinkered enthusiastically with the engine for some time, Brian was still no nearer to having located the source of the problem. He did not, of course, want to admit yet another technical failure to his unforgiving wife so, in desperation, he walked around the car, trying to look nonchalant, reached in through the driver's door and turned on the ignition. To his obvious astonishment, the engine purred sweetly into life. Brian punched the air in triumph and closed the bonnet as Valerie ran from the pavement, lowered her umbrella and got into the car. Brian sped off exultantly, if a little carelessly, splashing through a puddle and drenching an unfortunate passing pedestrian in the process.

★ ★ ★

As a result of her malfunctioning alarm clock, Miranda was running seriously behind her own carefully practiced schedule and was desperate to make up some time. While her bath had been running, she had prepared a basic breakfast, comprising a bowl of muesli and a mug of coffee and she was now sitting in the bath with her bowl in one hand and a spoon in the other. Her mug of coffee was perched precariously on the rim of the bath and, straddling the bath above her stomach, was a white plastic soap rack on which she had propped a clipboard to which some papers were attached. By sliding her feet up the bath towards her and raising her knees out of the water, she found that her thighs could just support the clipboard in a semi-vertical position while she attempted to read the notes.

The buzzing insect of hitherto uncertain origin, which had earlier helped to rouse her from her prolonged slumbers, turned out to be a persistent wasp. Attracted by some fragrant component of the muesli, or the strong aroma of caffeine, or the pungency of Miranda's bath salts, it had flown into the bathroom and was buzzing purposefully around the bowl, the mug of coffee, the bath and Miranda's face. After trying briefly to ignore it, Miranda swatted at it limply with her spoon, but without success. As it continued to buzz around her, now more frantically than before, she swatted at it again, this time much more vigorously – too vigorously as it turned out. Her energetic, if clumsy, swatting motion caused her bottom to slide from under her and she lost her balance. Her bowl of muesli toppled into the bath and, as her feet shot up into the air, her knees parted and the clipboard also fell into the water. Clutching frantically at the side of the bath to try and regain her balance, Miranda dislodged the mug of coffee, causing it join the other objects now immersed in the increasingly murky depths of the bath water.

Cursing loudly and at some length, Miranda reached into the water to retrieve her clipboard and papers. Inevitably, they were now little more than a soggy mess, dripping with water and covered in an unattractive amalgam of wet muesli and diluted coffee. The same amalgam had also attached itself randomly to various parts of her unclad anatomy. As she leapt from the bath, still swearing, and grabbed her towel, the wasp continued to buzz menacingly.

As the day wore on, the various feeder coaches began to converge on Dover from a variety of directions. In a complex operation, which required a harmonious combination of sympathetic traffic conditions, efficient drivers and scrupulously prompt "clients", the plan was for all of the coaches to arrive at Dover at more or less the same time. This would enable the transfer of passengers and their luggage onto the waiting rank of touring coaches to take place in one smooth, effortless burst of co-ordinated activity. That, at least, was the theory. So, if a feeder coach had been blessed with unusually light traffic and efficient time-keeping – something of a rarity – its passengers were likely to be rewarded with a generous stop at a service station for re-fuelling, some gentle exercise and a comfort break. If, however, the coach was running late, as was often the case, a five-minute comfort stop was as much as could be hoped for.

In their usual efficient way, Peter and Gail had organised a taxi to take them to their local pick-up point and their feeder coach had arrived encouragingly early. They made relatively unhindered progress in light traffic and, as a result, they were granted the luxury of an extended motorway service station break.

Peter was a pragmatist. Accepting the inevitable consequences of the passage of time, he had long since given up trying to cover his spreading bald patch with thinning strands of hair combed over his scalp from somewhere near his left ear and, instead, had cut his hair short and augmented his facial features with a small well-trimmed beard. Normally easy going and affable, he seemed unusually grumpy today, perhaps because of his cold, and he was in the middle of an animated conversation with Gail, as they alighted.

"You're not serious are you? We've got to take pictures of this damn bear everywhere we stop?" he asked incredulously.

"Not exactly everywhere, Peter, but I'd promised Carol that we'd take a good number and you know what's she's like."

"Only too well!"

"She still fancies you by the way! She was looking for you this morning."

"Then tell her I've left the country permanently. Tell her I can't face any more schools inspectors!"

Gail was inwardly annoyed with herself for allowing Carol to persuade her to take the bear on holiday, but she was determined not to let it spoil anything, particularly as Peter was especially in need of a good holiday.

"Anyway, this bear caper – it's in a good cause and it might turn out to be a bit of fun," she suggested with her usual easy smile. "A different slant for some your photos."

There was, of course, nothing that Peter could do about it and there was, on reflection, no point in belabouring the point. It was, after all, only likely to be a minor inconvenience and, like Gail, he would have to make the best of things.

"I always knew there was someone else in your life. Alright, let's get it over with. Go and stand over there. Does the bear have a name by the way?"

"Fred!"

"Oh, I see. Fred Bear. Very good!"

Gail had carried Fred off the coach and now she posed with him, self-consciously, alongside the coach, and with the entrance to the service station in the background, as Peter lined up his camera. Behind them, Dave and Susan, who had joined the same coach, but at an earlier pick-up point, walked purposefully past with a predictable objective in mind.

"Come on, we've got time for a bite."

"Honestly, after that breakfast you packed away?"

"Certainly! Grab something to eat when you can. That's my motto."

"I've noticed!"

Suppressing his instinct to question the necessity of taking a picture of a small bear propped up on a litter bin, against the background of a utilitarian motorway service station on a damp and gloomy day, Peter took the obligatory picture as quickly as he could, smiled self-consciously at a couple of inquisitive passers by, and suggested to Gail that they might want to grab a coffee as he felt in urgent need of a caffeine stimulus. They followed Dave and Susan inside.

Sitting in a discreet and distant corner of the large self-service restaurant, having arrived a little earlier on another coach, Barbara and Jason were drinking coffee, eating a pastry, and giggling while they stealthily examined the contents of the bags, which they had previously purchased from the sex shop. They were destined, it seemed, to spend much of their holiday giggling.

★ ★ ★

Two purposeful firemen had secured a ladder to the balcony rail. One of them remained at the bottom while his colleague climbed up onto the balcony. He was now trying to help Frank onto the ladder.

"Right, sir," he said, pointing to his colleague below. "If you can go down with Bob, I'll follow along behind."

Frank stood, gingerly, on one of the wooden chairs and, supported by the fireman, carefully eased one foot over the balcony rail, onto the ladder. Gripping hard on the rail, he then did the same with his other foot.

"Thanks very much. We're going on holiday today and I was worried we were going to miss our connection."

As Frank began his slow, methodical descent, the fireman looked around the balcony and tested the door handle and lock. He looked at the plants in the window box, well shielded from the steady rain by the overhanging floor of the balcony above.

"Don't worry sir. No damage done. I'm sure your flat will be quite secure until you get back. Mind you, nobody'll be able to get out here to water your plants while you're away and they're looking a bit dry already. I'd better do it for you now."

He reached down for the watering can. Only too aware of its contents, Frank wanted to stop him, of course, but as he balanced precariously on the ladder, with his mind focused on the impending descent and aware that he was probably being watched, covertly, by countless neighbours from behind countless net curtains, he couldn't bring himself to.

"No, no!!" he began, clinging desperately to the ladder, and then thought better of it. "Er, no, no idea that was part of the service."

"No trouble sir," the fireman replied as he liberally sprinkled the contents of the watering can over Frank's lovingly cultivated flowers. Joyce had been quietly watching the unfolding drama from inside the flat. She smiled contentedly to herself.

* * *

Tony Willis was a muscular man of average height, with straight dark hair and what had once been a sharp, thin face. These days, his nose was rather flat, as a result of a boxing injury sustained in his youth, and his features more rounded by too many dietary lapses. He was wearing the regulation company uniform of dark trousers and maroon shirt with the company logo prominently emblazoned in gold on the breast pocket.

He stood back briefly to admire the exterior of his coach, through a pair of rimless spectacles. He was not a great fan of the company's garish red and gold livery but he was proud of the near perfect condition of the bodywork. During the summer season, there was a bit of an unofficial contest between the fleet coach drivers for the best looked-after coach and Tony was usually the one to beat. No question, he thought to himself, that the coach looked good, even in the drizzle. The bodywork sparkled and the internal upholstery was immaculate. The engine, of course, was well maintained – it had to be – but it was just a shame, he reflected, that the company had not lavished the same attention on some of the irritating little mechanical problems that he had previously reported. The CD player still wasn't working properly, the front passenger door's mechanism was unreliable, sometimes needing a well-aimed kick to open or close it, the lock on the toilet door was stiff and some of the recliner buttons and levers on the seats were a bit stubborn and unpredictable. Fortunately, they were not used very often.

He had just pulled off the motorway and stopped for a short break before completing his journey to Dover and had used the opportunity to make a quick call to his wife on his mobile phone. He had been on the road for four weeks now, with only the odd day off and without a real break of any length.

"Yes, love, I'm fine," he said cheerfully into the phone. "Yes, that's right. I've just got this tour to do, then I'll be home for a week. How are the kids?"

He paused to listen to the reply.

"Tell Ben and Emily, Daddy misses them very much and he'll see them in a couple of weeks."

He paused again.

"Yeah, it's one of those breakneck tours round Europe – eight countries in 14 days. Up at the crack of dawn, clocking up the miles on the motorway, a different hotel every night. Loading luggage on, taking it off again… No, I've got Miranda Bellamy with me on this one. No, I don't know her that well, but we've worked together before and she seems very well organised, very efficient…"

★ ★ ★

Miranda had washed the waterlogged muesli and soapy coffee from the affected parts of her skin, given the bath a cursory clean, ushered the wasp out of the window with the aid of a couple of well-aimed swats from her damp clipboard and had finally got dressed, in her official uniform of dark trousers, maroon blouse and jacket. She was on the phone, waiting impatiently while it kept ringing.

"Come on, come on," she muttered to herself, drumming her fingers agitatedly on the arm of the chair. Eventually, the phone was answered.

"Good morning, Conn Tours," said Karen in a distant and detached voice. She hated being in head office on a Saturday. There were always problems with traffic jams, coaches breaking down, drivers not turning up, and passengers getting delayed or being taken ill. She had already had one hospitalisation to deal with this morning.

"Hi, Karen, it's me, Miranda!"

"Hi, Miranda." Karen sighed; she knew this was going to be another problem. Not that Miranda was any worse than some of the other Tour Directors but when one of them phoned in on a Saturday, it was always a problem.

"Karen, listen. You've got to help me. I'm due to meet up with the European Express party at Dover soon and I've dropped all my papers in the bath. The ink's run and I can't read most of them. My list of passengers, the coach seating plan, details of the hotels, the itinerary, they're all ruined…"

"Oh dear." Karen did her best to sound sympathetic while trying to stop herself from laughing at Miranda's misfortune.

"You couldn't fax or e-mail another set to the Dover office for me to pick up when I arrive, could you?"

"Love to Miranda, love, but we've closed our Dover office for the time being. You know what it's like with all these cut-backs at the moment."

"Oh, shit!"

"I can e-mail you the details to your home, if you like," Karen offered.

"But my e-mail link is so unreliable at the moment; it could take forever and my printer's nearly out of ink! I've been meaning to buy some more, but being away from home so much…"

Karen sighed again, more heavily this time. She didn't know how else she could help. She was stuck in the office, Miranda didn't have a fax machine and she couldn't think of anyone else who would have the necessary information. Sandra and Jill would be at the interchange to assist, but all they had were the lists of passengers and coach destinations.

"Sorry, love, but it's the best I can do," was all she could say. "You're staying at the Hotel Palourde near Bruges tonight, so I could get a set of papers to the hotel for you if that's any help and Tony should have a list of the passengers, tour itinerary and hotels."

Miranda was very sensitive about status. She would strenuously deny it if asked, but, at the start of the tour, she was always keen to make sure that everybody, including the driver, was aware that she was in charge. Tony could give the impression of being a bit withdrawn, almost surly sometimes, but he was one of the better and more co-operative drivers and she got on well with him; even so, she was the Tour Director and it wouldn't be right that Tony had more information than she did.

"Oh, bugger! I need the passenger list and seating plan for Dover really. Well, I suppose I've got no choice. You'd better e-mail them to me and we'll have to hope for the best!"

"I'll send the details straight away, and just in case, I'll send a set to the hotel as well. Oh, and by the way, a Mrs Armitage has just phoned. Some garbled message about a jammed balcony door, the fire brigade and a watering can. Anyway, they missed their pick-up so they're making their own way to Dover. Let's hope they're not too late."

"Just what I need, a couple of idiots delaying us before we've even started. Mind you, the way things are going, they might just be there before I am."

★ ★ ★

The ferry port at Dover, sandwiched between the white cliffs and the sea, is not generally reckoned to be a thing of beauty and, as the first small convoy of feeder coaches arrived, with drizzle continuing to fall unabated from a grey and depressing sky, it bore a sombre appearance.

Among the first to arrive was the coach containing, among others, Gail, Peter, Dave and Susan. The combination of an early start, residual tiredness, the beginnings of a cold, and a turgid journey on drab motorways in depressing weather had sent Peter into a sound sleep, from which he had to be roused with some vigorous prodding by Gail. Dave and Susan, meanwhile, had disembarked and wandered into the nearby reception and waiting area, where they were greeted by small areas of airport-style seating, some toilets, a "bureau de change", a couple of car-hire kiosks and a small coffee bar. There was nothing here to excite Dave's limited imagination, but a carpeted area leading off to one side offered the tantalising possibility of hidden treasures.

"I'm parched. I wonder if there's a bar somewhere!" Dave speculated.

"Don't start already. We should be trying to find out where and when our coach leaves."

"It's OK, we've got plenty of time. I'm just having the one."

"Hang on a minute; don't you think we should find out a bit more about what's happening first?"

Years of active participation in her husband's self-indulgent lifestyle had left Susan with what is often diplomatically referred to as a "fuller figure". She made some attempt to disguise the fact by wearing loose and flowing clothes and she kept her light brown, wavy hair quite long, in an attempt to hide the chubbiness of her face. But when Dave was heading briskly for a café, restaurant, pub or bar – as he often was – she could not hide the fact that she had some difficulty keeping up with him. As she tried to chase after her accelerating husband, she passed Julia and Trevor who were sitting, reflectively, on a couple of seats, surrounded by their newly purchased, matching, mint green luggage. They had already been at Dover for nearly two hours and had been struggling to fill the time. Trevor had purchased a copy of the Times and had spent a while grappling with the cryptic crossword. He had a nimble mind and often succeeded, but today he seemed to lack both the mental agility and level of concentration that was required, so he threw it down a little petulantly, and sat quietly, deep in thought. The spontaneous excitement and eager anticipation that they had briefly experienced on the car journey had long since evaporated, and the prolonged period of reflection had only served to engender more worry and anxiety. Julia was carefully examining her mobile phone.

"I wonder if I've got enough units on my phone," she mused.

"Mmm? Oh, they'll have phones at the hotels if we get stuck. Anyway, you don't need to worry. I'm sure Mark will be fine. He's got your number and the hotel details if he needs to contact you."

Another feeder coach pulled up outside and Barbara and Jason got off and bounced animatedly into the waiting area.

"Isn't this exciting?" Barbara asked, yet again. Jason looked around at the interior of the waiting area and at the disconsolate-looking people who were quietly gathering there.

"I've seen more exciting places! They're a bit old, aren't they, most of these people? Looks a bit like an undertaker's waiting room."

"It doesn't matter, does it? As long as there's not too much of a smell of mothballs and liniment when we're on the coach. Look on the bright side. Think of all those places we'll be visiting. Think of all the things we'll be doing."

"Yeah," Jason smirked. "We'll be getting up to some things that most of these old buggers won't be doing."

"Well more often, at least, I hope!" Barbara giggled.

★ ★ ★

After their initial mechanical failure, Brian and Valerie had surprisingly managed to arrive at Dover without further significant mishap. They had, of course, taken a couple of wrong turnings en route and it took Brian a while to find the designated parking area, but, eventually, he succeeded and he and Valerie started to unload their luggage from the boot. He had informed Valerie, with what he hoped was a suitable air of authority, that a bit of damp must have got into the engine earlier but neither he nor Valerie was very convinced and Valerie's mood had not greatly improved. She studied Brian carefully as he closed the boot.

"Look at the state of that shirt, Brian! You can't possibly start your holiday looking like that, you really can't."

"So you said. But what was I supposed to do? I had to fix the car."

"You'll just have to get a clean shirt out of your suitcase and we'll try and rinse that one through when we get to the hotel tonight."

"Yes, yes, OK."

With a familiar air of resignation, he dropped his suitcase onto the ground, reached into his trouser pocket and withdrew a bunch of keys. After a close examination of the dozen or so keys, he selected one, crouched down and tried to unlock the padlock on his case. He failed. He selected another key and tried again, but the padlock still wouldn't budge. After flipping, with increasing desperation, through the rest of the keys, which were very obviously not the right ones, he turned hesitantly to Valerie.

"Val. Have you got the keys to our padlocks?"

In an instant, Valerie's mood changed from resigned irritation to outraged incandescence.

"Oh, for God's sake don't tell me you've left the keys behind!"

"Well, I don't seem to have them. I was hoping you might…"

"And you didn't think to check that you had the keys before we left?"

"I thought they were on my key ring and we were in a bit of a hurry."

"God! Some holiday this is going to be!"

★ ★ ★

The interchange at Dover docks is often viewed as a necessary evil by many who choose to travel around Europe by coach. For passengers, it can sometimes be frustrating, protracted and chaotic, while, for those entrusted with the responsibility for ensuring that everything goes smoothly, it is a complex and challenging task, having to match arriving passengers with their luggage and successfully transfer both onto the correct touring coach.

The job of ensuring that the operation went smoothly fell to a small group of "*Conn Tours*" representatives who were each given a smart uniform and responsibility for their own clipboard, together with some general information about who was making their own way to Dover, who was going on which coach, and which bay each coach was leaving from. In the past, "*Conn Tours*" employed a generous number of such representatives, but these days, it was usually just two – Sandra and Jill. When things were going according to plan, which wasn't often, they were usually very visible, sporting wide, fixed, cosmetic smiles, carrying their clipboards with pride and willingly offering information to anyone who asked. On those occasions, however, when there were delays, or late alterations to the schedules, they quickly disappeared from view, like some fleeting mirage.

Detailed, specific information about each tour – coach seating plans, itineraries, timings, and hotel details – were provided to individual Tour Directors, who were expected to be on hand as the feeder coaches started to arrive, to welcome the new arrivals on board their coach and to ensure that their luggage was correctly loaded.

Tony had, as usual, arrived promptly at Dover and had parked his coach, carefully and proudly, in the bay allocated to his tour, but he could find no trace of Miranda. This was most unusual as Miranda was one of the more organised Tour Directors, being something of a stickler for punctuality and order. He hunted around, but enquiries of the brace of elusive clipboard carriers elicited little concrete information, except that there had been a brief message from head office that she was on her way but might be slightly delayed.

Tony cursed. Any delay at this stage might mean them having to cross the Channel on a later ferry than planned and this in turn would mean a later than scheduled arrival at their overnight hotel. As he sat sullenly aboard his coach, looking anxiously at his watch and observing each of the other six tour coaches beginning to load up, some members of his party were beginning to grow restless. They had ascertained, from either Jill or Sandra, that Tony's coach was the right one for them – the "European Express" holiday – but were growing restive at the lack of any further information or any obvious sign of action, particularly as some of the other coaches were starting to move away. Some of the more impatient members of the group began to edge along the side of the coach, in steady rain, towards the open coach door and it was Dave, well lubricated from his recent successful trip to the bar, who spoke first.

"Excuse me, is this the European Express coach, only there doesn't seem to be anything very "express" about it at the moment?"

Tony looked anxiously around but there was still no sign of Miranda.

"Yes, that's right, but you'll…"

"Any chance of getting on the coach, then? It's tipping it down out here."

Tony was an efficient and experienced driver, but life on the open road had not prepared him to be an effective communicator. That was, after all, the role of the Tour Director.

"Have any of you seen Miranda, the Tour Director?" he asked optimistically.

Dave continued in his capacity as self-appointed mouthpiece for the group.

"There's no bloody sign of anyone. We were just told to wait here by some woman strutting about with a clipboard and she's buggered off now!"

Tony got up from his seat, moved over to the open door, leant out and peered along the side of the coach. There were a lot of damp and unhappy-looking people milling about. He was keen not to exceed his authority, whatever that was, but equally did not want to get off on the wrong foot with his group, particularly as he needed his meagre salary to be well augmented by generous gratuities at the end of the holiday. He had another look round in the vain hope that he would catch sight of Miranda, but he was out of luck.

He stepped outside and moved quickly along the line of people, counting them as he went. He knew from his own paperwork that a total of 40 "clients" were expected and his rapid calculations suggested that 38 of the group had assembled and were now beginning to surround him, rather menacingly, he thought.

"Are all your suitcases here?" he asked the group in general, pointing to a ragged assembly of damp suitcases which had been abandoned near to the closed luggage hold. There were various nods and shouts of "yes".

"Yes, they're all here and they're getting bloody wet!" Dave affirmed confidently without any supporting evidence to back up his strident claim.

"Look, I don't have a list of the coach seating plan, so when the Tour Director gets here, you'll probably have to change seats, and it is your responsibility to make sure your cases are loaded, but if you want to get on while I start to load them......"

His words were lost in the ensuing stampede as 38 people headed towards the coach doors, each one determined to be first on board. Leaving them to organise themselves, Tony began to load the luggage into the hold, checking the label on each suitcase against his list of passengers. When most people had clambered aboard and the melee was beginning to subside, Brian and Valerie slipped quietly off the coach and approached Tony. Urged on by Valerie, Brian spoke.

"Excuse me, could we have a word?"

Tony looked up as he continued to load the suitcases and tick them off against the names on his increasingly damp list. The sight of Brian in his oil-stained and bedraggled clothes did nothing to improve Tony's fragile mood. He didn't much care for damp clients sitting on his pristine upholstery at the best of times, but anyone who might leave grease or oil stains behind was a complete anathema.

"Yes." Tony's response was distant and edgy.

"You see, we've locked our suitcases and we've just discovered that we don't have the keys to the padlocks and…"

Tony's brow furrowed. He was battling to load the cases in the rain, he was getting very wet, his potential passengers were growing increasingly impatient, there was no sign of Miranda, they stood a real chance of missing their booked ferry and now a couple of idiots, one of whom was covered in oil, were asking for help to open their suitcases. He chose his words carefully, though his tone of voice betrayed his true feelings.

"As you can see I'm a bit busy and things are a bit chaotic just at the moment. I'll see what I can do if I have time but you might have to wait until later on."

Brian was about to say something more when Miranda suddenly appeared, out of breath and with heavily flushed cheeks. She was dressed in her smart Tour Director's uniform, although, to the trained eye, it was clear that her make-up had not been applied with its customary precision. On a damp, grey afternoon, a pair of dark glasses protruded incongruously from her breast pocket. She was pulling her suitcase with one hand and brandishing her still damp clipboard in the other. A voluminous black canvas bag was draped over her shoulder.

"Where the hell have you been?" Tony asked with a mixture of anger and relief, as the last of the remaining touring coaches began to pull away and head towards the ferry.

"It's a long story but my alarm didn't go off and then I had to wait for another set of papers to be e-mailed to me. I'll explain later. How are we for time?"

"A bit pushed; no-one's in the right seat and I think I may be a couple short." He glanced at his list. " Name of Armitage, I think."

Miranda glanced at her list.

"Yes, that's right, Mr and Mrs Armitage. We had a message."

Almost immediately, she heard somebody calling and looked around to see Frank and Joyce rushing towards them, as best they could, carrying their heavy suitcases. As Frank struggled for breath, a red-faced Joyce managed to gasp a few words.

"Mr and Mrs Armitage. Sorry we're late; we phoned your emergency number to explain."

"We got a message of sorts," Miranda replied rather stiffly. Tony meanwhile glanced at his watch again.

"We're going to have to leave in a minute. You'd better hop on and find a couple of seats. I'll get your cases loaded with the others."

As they climbed breathlessly aboard, Frank turned to Joyce.

"Did you hear how much he charged me? It would've been cheaper to buy the damned taxi!"

Inside the coach, only traces of the earlier chaos were visible. After some jostling, one or two minor collisions and a handful of polite apologies, most of the passengers had settled into their chosen seats, although a small handful were still obstructing the aisle as they loaded their hand luggage and waterproofs onto the overhead racks. There was much animated conversation, some clearly reflecting the normal high levels of excitement and anticipation, prevalent at the start of any holiday, but there were also a few disconcerting rumbles of discontent with some still complaining at the lack of information and organisation and others expressing concern that their coach remained stubbornly static while all the other coaches had set off towards the ferry.

Miranda bustled briskly aboard, quickly counted the passengers and, satisfied that they were all on board, gave a thumbs-up to Tony who started the engine and accelerated away. Recovering her composure after her troubled start to the day, Miranda switched into her well-rehearsed, well-groomed and professional role as Tour Director. She was now firmly in charge. She turned on the microphone by her seat at the front and began to speak, her voice sounding confident and controlled.

"Good afternoon, ladies and gentlemen and welcome to "Conn Tours" and to the European Express holiday. My name's

Miranda and I'm your Tour Director for this holiday. I'm sorry for the slight delay in getting away. This was due to an administrative problem with your seat numbers, which I have now sorted out. Right now, we're in a bit of a hurry to make the next ferry, so that we can get you to your hotel in reasonable time this evening. So, we'll sort out your proper seat numbers as you get back onto the coach when the ferry arrives in Calais. Also, I'll tell you more about the tour and the itinerary, then. We will be arriving at our hotel in Belgium fairly late this evening, so I'd advise you to get something to eat and drink while we are on the ferry. Shame about the weather but I hope you enjoy the crossing and I know you're going to enjoy the holiday."

Trevor and Julia, being more nimble and a decade or two younger than many of their fellow travellers, had managed to secure the front seats in the coach, immediately behind Miranda. This gave Trevor a good vantage point from which to discreetly study her sleek, dark hair and shapely contours, as she made her first announcements. He turned to Julia who seemed less restless now they were irrevocably on their way, and clutched her hand affectionately.

"She's right, you know. I think we are really going to enjoy this holiday!"

★ ★ ★

CHAPTER 2

Arrivals

It was still raining, though the occasional heavy, soaking downpours, which had been a characteristic feature of the morning, had cleared, to be replaced by a steady, fine, cool drizzle. As a result, the open passenger decks of the Apollo Line cross-channel ferry were damp, draughty and uninviting, with wet seats and a keen breeze whipping across them. It was a Saturday afternoon in the middle of summer and the ferry was crowded. With the upper, open decks off limits to all but the foolhardy few and those desperate for a cigarette, every "below decks" amenity was straining under the pressure of intensive use. There were queues for the bars, restaurant, toilets and the checkouts in the duty-free shop.

Spurred on by Miranda's advice – not that he needed any – Dave was determined to make the restaurant his first objective. Unfortunately, there was a considerable number of coaches on the ferry and, as his coach was the last to board, a couple of hundred other passengers with the same idea were ahead of him. Shuffling slowly up the crowded, narrow staircase from the back of the car deck where the coach was parked, Dave and Susan did their best to make headway but neither was built for speed, nor squeezing nimbly into small gaps and, when they did finally locate the self-service restaurant, a substantial and slow-moving queue had already formed ahead of them. For Dave, there was little in life more frustrating than being able to see his food and to smell his food, but to have to queue patiently before he could take possession of it. He spent his time constructively, however, complaining to Susan about lack of staff in the restaurant, how the queue could have been organised better, how only the British queue anyway and how, unless the queue moved a lot quicker, they were likely to arrive in Calais before they were served.

Others had different priorities. Frank, a man with less patience even than Dave, had eschewed the restaurant queue for the time being. Badly stressed by the morning's events, still suffering from the shock of the taxi fare and expecting the ferry to roll on the swell, his appetite had, for the moment, deserted him. Encouraged by Joyce, he had purchased his first camcorder with part of his retirement lump sum and was hoping to return home with a highly polished visual record of their holiday. Unfortunately, Frank was no technophile and, for someone who occasionally had difficulty operating an electric toaster, this was likely to be an optimistic aspiration. Nevertheless, he had decided to test his new camcorder, together with his technical competence, by taking some footage from the deck of the ferry as it left Dover.

Joyce had been desperate to find Frank another hobby when he retired – even he couldn't play bowls all the time and she couldn't bear the prospect of him hanging around the flat with nothing much to do, playing his radio loudly, fiddling with things, constantly tidying things away and checking up on what she was doing all the time – but she had to admit that a camcorder might turn out to be too mechanically challenging for him and his notoriously frail patience. He had studied the manuals that came with it, of course, though he rarely made it past the first two or three pages of technical explanation before he dozed off, and he had practiced in their flat, a little sheepishly, Joyce thought, and without sharing the results with her, but this was the first time it was to be used with serious intent – it was a momentous occasion.

The day had gone badly so far and Joyce was fearing the worst. She could not raise much enthusiasm for being dragged onto a wet and windy top deck, especially as she had been to the hairdressers only two days earlier, but she wrapped a scarf securely round her head and grudgingly acquiesced in the forlorn hope that this might mark the triumphal launch of a successful and time-consuming new hobby.

As the ferry began to move slowly, almost reluctantly, away

from its berth and out towards the rough, open sea, Frank seemed confident enough, outwardly at least. Placing his feet wide apart, so as to brace himself against the buffeting wind, he pointed the camcorder towards the receding white cliffs and pressed a button with great authority, but when he started to mutter to himself and fiddle inexpertly with a few more buttons, Joyce's hopes began to fade.

"Are you sure you know how to work that thing?" she asked.

"Yes, of course. One of the buttons is a bit stiff, that's all," Frank replied defensively.

"Well, do you think you could hurry up then? It's freezing up here on deck."

"I'm doing the best I can, but I don't want to rush things and then mess them up."

While Joyce tried to recall the last time Frank had rushed anything, she noticed Peter, who was taking a picture of Gail holding up Fred, with the white cliffs in the background. Thinking she recognised Peter as one of the travelling companions on the coach that she had literally bumped into, she gave him a shy smile, which he reciprocated. She also recognised Barbara and Jason up on deck and still finding something to giggle about; they were very different in age and attitude to most of the rest of the coach party and were keen not to miss a second of their departure from England. Up until the moment that the ferry began to move towards open water, Barbara had half expected her father to materialise from somewhere and try to abduct her back to the family home, so she was determined not to miss the sight of the white cliffs disappearing slowly into the gloomy distance, even if it meant getting wet and even if the cliffs had a distinctly grey hue on this miserable afternoon. It was an important symbolic confirmation that, for the next two weeks, she was free.

Julia and Trevor had made for the bar, where they planned to grab a snack and sip gently at a couple of fortifying drinks in the hope that this would relax them and engender a more mellow holiday mood. But the bar area was crowded and the stresses of travelling made it difficult to relax. They managed to find a couple of free seats in a particularly noisy and cramped part of the bar and Trevor resumed his crossword but his progress remained frustratingly limited. With his hopes of a conventional and intellectually satisfying solution fading, he inserted random letters in all of the still blank squares, looked triumphant and placed it with a flourish on the small bar table in front of him. Julia burst out laughing; it was an encouraging sign.

In the crowded ferry shop, Brian and Valerie had decided – or rather Valerie had decided – that Brian could not wear his oil-stained shirt for a moment longer, and was going to have to buy a new one. The choice on offer was limited and not really suited to Brian's naturally baggy style but, eventually, he found a polo-style shirt, in green and grey hoops, which he thought might be acceptable. He held it up and asked Valerie what she thought. Valerie well knew that whatever Brian bought, he would look scruffy in it and the horizontal hoops would exaggerate the rotundity of his physique but, as long as it was in roughly his size and not too ostentatious, it would do.

"It's not much of a shirt, Brian," she observed disparagingly, "but it looks as though it's the best you're going to get in here and you need to get out of that thing you're wearing as quickly as possible."

"Yes, yes. I suppose so. I'd better get it then."

Having queued for some time to purchase his new shirt, and moaned for some time at its cost, Brian took it, still in its bag, into the nearest toilet. Looking around furtively, he went over to a washbasin and removed his watch, which he placed on the fitted surface alongside. He then took off his oil-stained and creased shirt, which he tossed onto the same surface, and washed his hands, arms and face thoroughly, removing most residual traces of engine oil and grease. He dried himself off as best he could using an ineffectual hot air blower and some toilet paper which he garnered from a vacant cubicle, took his new shirt out of its bag, put in on, admired himself in the mirror above the washbasin, took the shirt off again to remove the price label which he had just noticed and put it back on, tucking it into his trousers. He then swept his old, discarded shirt into the empty bag and, in doing so, accidentally swept his watch onto the floor. He didn't notice. He then flushed the paper that he had used down the toilet and, without a backward glance, he left, treading on his watch as he went.

The ferry continued its laboured journey to Calais across the grey and choppy Channel. Dave and Susan eventually got served in the restaurant. Sensing that this might be his last "British" meal for two weeks, Dave didn't venture beyond the serving area displaying the pies and chips, demolishing his meal in a fraction of the time they had spent queuing for it. Susan also made rapid, though tidier, progress through her chicken salad.

Frank had failed to make much progress, rapid or otherwise, with his camcorder, the white cliffs had disappeared into the low cloud long before he was ready and Joyce made it very clear that she had spent long enough on deck, "standing around like a lemon." They needed to eat, so they made their way to the restaurant before it closed, for a hastily, though only partly, consumed plate of fish and chips.

As the ferry finally eased itself into the docks area at Calais, the usual announcement was made, in French and English, asking all passengers to rejoin their vehicles. Many members of the tour party – perhaps not used to travelling on a ferry, maybe disconcerted by the jostling crowds and anxious not be late – had been queuing for an unnecessarily long time at the top of the stairs leading down to the car decks and, once the doors were opened, they shuffled slowly down the crowded staircases to rejoin the coach, where they found Miranda, by now a model of smooth efficiency, waiting by the door with her ubiquitous clipboard in hand and a welcoming smile on her face.

This was the first real opportunity Miranda had had to meet members of the party individually, to assess their general level of physical fitness, to identify any possible difficulties that lay ahead and to look for potential troublemakers. Dave and Susan had not rushed to return to the coach and found themselves standing impatiently in a queue again, just in front of Frank and Joyce. Eventually, it was their turn to be greeted.

Miranda smiled. "Hello. Could I have your name please?"

"Dave," said Dave unhelpfully, playfully fluttering his eyelids.

"Fuller. Mr and Mrs Fuller," added Susan, more sensibly.

Miranda looked down her list while mentally earmarking Dave as a potential nuisance.

"Let me see; Mr and Mrs Fuller, seats 5 and 6."

She looked up and saw Frank and Joyce. Her smile froze a little.

"Ah, Mr and Mrs Armitage; you're in seats 3 and 4, at the front behind the driver."

Barbara and Jason were next in the queue. Miranda went through the same routine.

"And what is your name?"

"Er, Rogers."

"That's Mr and Mrs Rogers, is it?" asked Miranda, consulting her clipboard.

"No, actually, it's Mr Rogers and Miss Khan," said Barbara defiantly, sensing Miranda's slight frostiness.

"Oh, I see," Miranda said rather stiffly. "You're in seats 7 and 8."

The coach had a traditional lay-out with pairs of front-facing seats in rows on either side of a central aisle. Towards the centre, the serried rows were punctuated, on one side, by a drinks-making machine, behind which was the second exit door and, off the steps leading down to it, a small toilet. Next to the driver, a small pull-down seat was provided for the Tour Director.

Conn Tours' policy was to allocate the seats on the coach, starting at the front, according to the date of booking. As Joyce had booked this holiday almost as soon as they had returned from Eastbourne last summer, she and Frank were at the front, with Peter and Gail, habitual early bookers because of the need to travel during the school holidays in August, across the aisle. Behind them, in the second row, were Jason and Barbara, and across the aisle, Dave and Susan. Julia and Trevor were in the third row, immediately behind Dave and Susan. On the opposite side of the aisle, behind Barbara and Jason, were two vacant seats.

Frank was slightly deaf, a long-standing affliction he had

inherited from his mother, although, over the years, Joyce had become convinced that his deafness was conveniently selective, particularly when he was required, or expected, to spend money. A genuine symptom of his affliction, however, was his tendency to speak more loudly than most. If previous form was anything to go by, some of his observations, intended only for Joyce's ears, were bound to be overheard by those sitting close by, including Tony and Miranda in front and Barbara and Jason behind. Equally inevitably, many of these comments were certain to be embarrassing, insensitive or provocative. He had barely sat down, for example, when, being a tall man, he started to complain about the relative lack of legroom in the front seats and how they should design their coaches better.

The remainder of the tour party comprised primarily middle-aged or elderly couples although there was a party of four women travelling together and an emasculated looking son, called Nigel, travelling with his elderly and cantankerous looking mother. It being the school holidays, there were also two families with young teenage children, and, immediately behind Julia and Trevor, there were two smartly-dressed elderly ladies. They were clearly long-term friends who regarded the coach tour as more of a social event than a sightseeing holiday. Whenever they were travelling, they were destined to keep up a virtually continuous and increasingly irritating dialogue covering a wide range of trivial topics.

Brian and Valerie were the last to arrive. Brian had turned the wrong way out of the toilet and took some time to find his way back to the shop where Valerie was still browsing eagerly among the cosmetics. In trying to return to the coach, they also took a wrong exit from the stairs and ended up on a different car deck.

"Sorry we're late, we got a bit lost."

"Yes, well, never mind – you must be Mr and Mrs Wood? Seats 11 and 12."

Miranda noted the manufacturer's label dangling from the back of Brian's new shirt, something neither he nor Valerie had appeared to notice, and mentally identified him as one to watch. Brian's question confirmed her initial diagnosis.

"I don't suppose there is any chance that we can get at our cases is there? You see…"

"Not at the moment, I'm afraid; as you can see, we're just about to drive off. Is it urgent?"

"It's just that…"

He was cut short by Tony shouting that they were being waved off the ferry and they had to scramble aboard into the two vacant seats behind Barbara and Jason. Miranda kicked the door closed and they moved off for the start of their adventure.

★ ★ ★

There was an air of expectation as the coach left the ferry port, but the first close-up views of France through the industrial and commercial outskirts of Calais are not noted for their panoramic beauty and even the sight of a pleasant sandy beach, surrounded by dunes, was rather ruined by the continuing rain and the brooding presence of an unsightly chemical works behind it. As the coach gathered speed and joined the motorway, Miranda decided to begin her formal introduction and she reached for the microphone. She was well used to doing this and, although she spoke in pleasant, articulate tones, her tone of voice somehow lacked sparkle and her well-rehearsed routine was devoid of any kind of improvisation or spontaneity.

"Welcome to France," she began, as though reading from a script, "and the start of what I am sure will be an enjoyable holiday. Before we go any further, I'd like to introduce my colleague on this tour, our driver, Tony. This is a very exciting day for Tony, because he's never driven a coach on the continent before!"

When Miranda was being trained by the company for her role as a Tour Director, it had been impressed upon her that a joke or two was a good way of helping to break the ice with each new set of "clients". She was even given some tried and tested examples that she could use. Miranda, however, was not a natural joke-teller – she had no inherent sense of humour or timing – and her first attempted quip elicited no more than a startled silence from most of the coach party. Frank's brow furrowed more deeply.

"Only joking!" she explained. "Tony is actually very experienced, he knows all the routes we'll be taking and we are all in very safe hands."

Without interrupting her commentary, Miranda glanced across at Tony and gave him a brief, knowing smile. Without taking his eyes from the road, he reciprocated with a smile and a wink.

"We are both going to do everything we can," she continued, "to make your holiday as enjoyable as possible. Now, first, just a quick reminder that, as we have crossed the Channel, we have to advance our watches one hour, so the time is now 7.15 European time."

This announcement provoked a minor flurry of activity, as those who had not already done so began to advance their watches one hour. In Frank's case, the activity was accompanied by a loud commentary about the pointlessness of France being on a different time from Britain. In Brian's case, it brought the sudden and unwelcome realisation that he had lost his watch.

"Oh, hell! I must have left my watch on the ferry. Now I come to think of it, I remember taking it off when I went to change my shirt, but I don't remember putting it back on."

Valerie's mood had not improved.

"I don't believe this. We've only been on holiday for a few hours and, so far, you've locked our cases and forgotten to bring the keys, covered a perfectly good shirt in oil and left your watch behind."

"Don't fret so, love. We'll get into the cases when we get to our hotel. The shirt will wash and the watch was only a cheap one."

"My mother bought you that for your birthday!"

"And…?"

"Alright, it was cheap but that's no reason to lose it. What's my mother going to say when she sees you're not wearing it?"

"Best not invite her round for a while then!"

Miranda, meanwhile, was continuing with her well-rehearsed introductory talk.

"This evening we're going to be heading over the border into Belgium and straight to our hotel which is near Bruges. It should take about an hour and a half or so, so it will give me a good opportunity to tell you a bit more about our holiday."

Dave was aghast. "An hour and a half?" he complained to Susan, "I'm parched already!"

He reached down, unzipped his travel bag, which he had conveniently placed on the floor between his feet, removed a can of beer and opened it.

"Firstly," Miranda continued, "one or two bits of information about our coach. We do have a toilet on board towards the back by the rear exit. We will be making regular comfort stops and, for obvious reasons, we'd prefer that you only use it in an emergency."

Joyce patted Frank gently on his thigh, and whispered reassuringly "they'll be making regular comfort stops so you'll be alright." Frank, however, wasn't so sure. Because they had left it late to buy their meal on the ferry and, because he never rushed his food, he had not found time to visit the toilet before they had to return to the coach and the contents of the bottle of mineral water that he had imbibed with his meal, seemed to be working its way through his system with alarming rapidity. He fidgeted uncomfortably in his seat, glanced out of the window at the rain and reflected on how soon the first emergency might occur. Susan watched Dave take the first long, satisfying swig from his can and she too wondered just how soon an emergency might occur. Miranda, meanwhile, was in full flow.

"Above your heads, there are some controls that will adjust the air vents if you are getting too hot or too cold. Also, your seats do recline a little, if at any stage you want to have a bit of a rest. If you press the lever or button next to your arm rest, you'll find the seat reclines gently."

Peter had woken up early that morning with a sore throat, a headache, aching limbs and a general feeling of lethargy. A long, tiring journey coupled with too much time spent standing in the rain taking pictures of a sodden teddy bear had done nothing to help and he felt in need of some sleep. He tried to persuade his seat to recline, following Miranda's instructions, but he had to press the lever hard several times before, reluctantly it seemed, the seat angled back slightly. Gail, however, could not get her seat to recline at all, despite several increasingly energetic attempts. She exchanged glances with Peter and shrugged.

"It doesn't look as though we'll be getting much sleep on the coach, does it?"

"The other thing I need to say about the coach," Miranda continued, "is that we are going to be spending a lot of time together on it and Tony needs to keep it clean and in good working order. We'll be stopping regularly for refreshment breaks so we would ask you not to eat your meals on the coach. There is also a drinks machine on board. We've got tea, coffee, soup, hot chocolate and mineral water available and, in a little while, I'll be coming along the coach to see if anyone wants a drink. I would add though that we do not permit alcohol to be consumed on the coach."

At that precise moment, Dave was taking another hearty swig from his can of beer. On hearing Miranda's grievously unwelcome news, he pulled a face, sank lower in his seat and took another swig. Susan was unimpressed.

"For God's sake, Dave!"

"Well, what am I supposed to do? I've opened it now!"

Having completed her necessary public announcements about the coach and its facilities, Miranda paused only briefly before launching into a prepared introduction to the tour itinerary.

"Now, as you probably realise, we are going to be seeing a lot of very exciting and interesting places on this tour, but we are going to be covering a lot of miles, so we'll be starting each day pretty early. I'll give you the details later, but most days we will be leaving our hotel at around 8.00 or 8.15."

Peter exchanged more glances with Gail and they shrugged again.

"It doesn't look like we'll be sleeping much in the hotel either!"

The coach windows were beginning to steam up as the steady rain continued, the evening light was starting to fade and the flat landscape of Northern France continued to hold few visual delights. But, somehow, Jason and Barbara were still finding something to giggle about and the news of the early morning starts prompted a suggestive leer from Jason.

"Looks like lots of early nights then, eh?"

Barbara giggled.

Meanwhile, Miranda was into her stride and continuing apace.

"Hopefully, you've all been sent a copy of the tour itinerary and I'll go through it with you in more detail when we are travelling tomorrow but, just to remind you that, in the morning, we'll be visiting the beautiful city of Bruges, where you'll have some free time to wander around and have some lunch before we depart. In the afternoon, we'll set off for Amsterdam, stopping briefly en route at Kinderdijk to have a look at the biggest collection of working windmills in Holland. We'll arrive at our hotel in time for our evening meal and then, if you want to, you can join us for our optional excursion to the famous Red Light District with a local guide to show you around. I'll give you the details tomorrow."

News of the optional tour of the Red Light District, only obliquely referred to in the holiday brochure as "Amsterdam by Night", generated some momentary animation among an increasingly weary group of tourists. Dave had been slumped low in his seat, still holding his near-empty can, trying to look as inconspicuous as possible, when Susan nudged him hard in the ribs.

"Are you ready for it, big boy?" she enquired playfully.

Dave looked uncomfortable, puffed out his cheeks and then took another large gulp of beer. Susan thought she could detect a few beads of sweat breaking out on his forehead. Jason and Barbara, meanwhile, continued to giggle, prompting Frank to turn round and stare at them rather severely.

Miranda's commentary continued remorselessly in the background.

"The following day, we'll be spending the morning in Amsterdam, where we will visit a diamond factory and where you can also take an optional boat trip around some of the beautiful city canals. Then, in the afternoon, we'll be heading into northern Germany for our overnight stay. The next morning, we'll have a cruise on part of the Rhine, past the famous Lorelei rock and then, in the afternoon, visit the beautiful old walled town of Rothenburg..."

Unusually, Frank had played no part in making the arrangements for this particular holiday. Joyce had been so frustrated when they had returned, cold and miserable, from their last traditional British seaside holiday that she had booked this one at the first opportunity, when he had been out playing bowls, and had not told him anything about it until the balance of the holiday payment was due and the deadline to apply for new passports was fast approaching. It was the kind of thing she only did extremely rarely and, until now, she had managed to keep much of the detail from him. She knew that it was a highly risky strategy and that, if anything went wrong, she would be blamed but, she figured, it was at least worth a try in order to do something different. Frank, of course, had not been pleased when Joyce informed him of her little deceit – he had been looking forward to returning, once again, to the Bandstand Hotel in Eastbourne and didn't like Joyce keeping secrets from him – but after his initial outraged explosion, followed by a period of grumpy reflection, he had allowed himself, perhaps reluctantly, to be persuaded by Joyce that maybe it was time to do something different and, yes, maybe he would enjoy himself, particularly as he had a new camcorder to use. That was until he heard the details of the itinerary coming from Miranda.

"Bloody hell," he protested loudly, "you didn't tell me we were going to be getting up at dawn and dashing about all over the place like maniacs!"

"Stop moaning. I thought it would be something different – we don't have to do it again if we don't like it. But at least it makes a change from another holiday in Eastbourne!"

"Oh and what's wrong with Eastbourne?"

"There's nothing much wrong with it as such. It's a perfectly pleasant resort though we do seem to be a bit unlucky with the wind and the rain. Then there's the smell of vapour rub in the hotel; and the fact that we've been there every year for at least the last ten. Honestly, we've seen just about every visiting brass band that there's ever been and heard every piece of music in their repertoires, at some time or another we've sat on every seat on the entire length of the prom, the manager of that little café around the corner from the hotel knows what you're going to order before you've even sat down and we've seen Beachy Head lighthouse more often than the coastguards."

"I'm sorry you feel like that, love. I wish you'd said earlier though, because I've booked us a long weekend at the Bandstand Hotel in September. There's a good band on…"

"You've done what?"

"I know, I should have told you but, then again, I don't remember being told about this holiday."

"Huh!" Joyce folded her arms and stared angrily out of the window.

Julia, meanwhile, was peering broodily out of her window at what she could still see of the featureless northern French countryside, half-listening to Miranda's commentary and half-overhearing the conversation of the two elderly ladies in the seats behind her, who were apparently discussing the protocols of invitations.

"Do you think they forgot to invite me," one was saying. "Or did they do it deliberately?"

"Oh, I should think it was an accident," the other replied.

"Only I don't want to turn up if they don't want me to be there."

"Why don't you phone them up and ask them?"

"Oh, I couldn't do that; it would be too embarrassing!"

"OK, I'll phone them then."

"Oh, no, you couldn't do that; they'd know I've been talking to you!"

Julia glanced round, hoping that if she looked displeased, they might shut up for a while. They didn't, so she leant across and spoke quietly to Trevor.

"Geoff and I had a cruise up the Rhine a few years ago," she observed casually. "Mark came with us."

"Did you enjoy it?" Trevor asked, hoping for a negative answer.

"Well, Geoff got drunk, tried chatting up the bar-maid and threw up in the toilet. A bit like most week-ends at home really except the bar-maid was German."

Trevor laughed. "I promise you it will be different this time."

"I'm sure it will!"

For everyone on board, it had been a long, occasionally fraught, and desperately tiring day. Many had left home very early in the morning, in order pick up their feeder coach and, as they travelled on at a steady, unremitting speed, with dusk rapidly descending, a kind of soporific torpor broke out. Except, of course, for the two elderly ladies who continued to debate the etiquette of invitations, and for Barbara and Jason, whose youthful exuberance continued unabated.

"Bonjour monsieur," said Barbara suddenly to Jason.

"Bonjour mademoiselle," replied Jason, slightly taken aback.

"Isn't this sooo exciting, Jace? We're actually in France on holiday together – on our own!"

"Yes it is. Mind you we're not exactly on our own, like, are we?"

He glanced behind him, down the aisle, at the rows of grey upholstered heads resting on the grey upholstered seats, before continuing in a whisper.

"It's a pity there aren't more other people of our age here. It's a bit like being surrounded by friends of my parents. It feels like they're watching us all the time."

"Yes. Still the travel agent did warn us there'd be quite a lot of older people on the tour. And we don't have to stay with them. Whenever we stop somewhere, we can go off and do our own thing. And we'll be doing plenty of things that many of these old codgers won't manage!"

"Yeah. I'm looking forward to it," he agreed with a certain lascivious glee.

He gave Barbara a playful tickle in the ribs which prompted her to shriek, which, in turn, prompted Frank to look round and stare severely at them again. Anxious to avoid falling out with her fellow travellers, however old and cantankerous they may prove to be, and aware that many of them might be apprehensive about the behaviour of "young people", Barbara immediately apologised before accidentally kicking the back of Frank's seat, causing him to turn round and stare again.

As the coach crossed from France into Belgium and an increasing number of heads began to slump forward with eyes closed, Miranda made a timely foray down the coach to ask if anyone wanted a drink. Dave had secreted his now empty beer can in his travel bag and politely declined Miranda's offer. Brian and Valerie, however, felt in need of some fortification after a difficult day and, after a minute or so, Miranda returned holding two drinks.

"There we are; one tea and one chocolate."

Miranda reached across to hand the drinks to Brian and Valerie and, in doing so, thrust her tightly trousered bottom almost into Trevor's face across the aisle. He viewed it intently. Valerie, meanwhile, could not resist another dig at her hapless spouse.

"For God's sake, don't spill that drink down your shirt, Brian."

"Yes, yes. I won't!"

Miranda's tactic of offering drinks after most of her "clients" had fallen asleep was a deliberate one as it kept her deployed on an activity that she loathed for the minimum amount of time. Nevertheless, the sight and sound of Miranda preparing and distributing some drinks proved too much for Frank's recalcitrant bladder and, although they were probably less than half an hour away from their overnight hotel, he had no choice but to make a dash for the on-board toilet.

The first indication that all was not well came when Joyce felt a tap on her shoulder. She looked round to see Nigel, the downtrodden son of the harridan. They occupied the seats closest to the toilet and he had been instructed by his mother to go and inform Joyce that, judging by the sounds of knocking and shouting coming from within the toilet cubicle, her husband had somehow managed to lock himself in. Joyce feigned a show of agitated concern and asked Nigel if he could go back and reassure her closeted husband that she was arranging for some immediate help. Nigel nodded dutifully – he was used to doing so – and returned back down the coach. Joyce, meanwhile, smiled broadly and relaxed contentedly in her seat for several minutes before reluctantly informing Miranda of Frank's predicament. Miranda was not very gifted technically, nor was she at her best when required to improvise. She marched rapidly down the coach, carried out a brief, rather terse conversation with Frank through the cubicle door, tried to turn the handle of the miscreant door a couple of times without success and returned to report the problem to Tony.

The journey had been going well, in spite of the weather, and Tony had been looking forward to a prompt arrival at the hotel, so he was far from delighted at Miranda's news. But he had no choice. He turned off the motorway, found a safe roadside location in which to stop, retrieved his trusty and well-used box of tools from an overhead locker and set about securing Frank's release. Using a large, formidable-looking screwdriver, which he inserted into the crack behind the door, he was able to get enough leverage to prise the door open, inevitably breaking the lock in the process.

The delay had been only relatively minor, fifteen minutes or so, but, coming towards the end of a long journey, it was a frustration to all on board, not least to Tony who now had the problem of a broken lock to contend with and to Frank who stomped back to his seat, complaining loudly about the indignity he had just suffered and the inexcusable malfunction of such a simple mechanism as a lavatory door lock.

Miranda, for her part, resumed her seat and her commentary as though nothing untoward had happened.

"After we leave the hotel in the morning, I'll give you details of the optional excursions that are available to you. So that I can arrange them all for you, you will need to mark on the forms which I'll hand out, which ones you want to go on…"

As the coach got to within a mile or two of its destination, darkness had descended outside and fatigue had descended inside.

Most of the passengers, even Barbara, Jason and the two elderly ladies, had fallen asleep.

★ ★ ★

It was slightly later in the evening than planned, and no longer raining, when the coach finally arrived at the Hotel Palourde, set in an industrial suburb of Bruges. Like many of the hotels favoured by the tour company, it had clearly been selected more for its convenient access to the main arterial motorways, its capacity to receive coach parties and its reasonable cost, than for any outstanding architectural features or scenic location. In the dimly lit, semi-darkness of the car park, it appeared to be of modern, unimaginative and unsophisticated design rising to three floors. The external walls were uniformly grey, with the exception of a small blue and white canopy above the entrance doors, and the windows were identical, small and square. Inside the hotel, every corridor and every room looked exactly the same and the rooms themselves had clearly been equipped to accommodate the overnight traveller in adequate comfort rather than the long-stay visitor in luxurious splendour.

Once Tony had manoeuvred the coach into a convenient parking spot, Miranda hopped nimbly off the coach, clutching her clip-board and, watched intently by Trevor from within the coach, made her way under the canopy and into the hotel while Tony opened the luggage hold and began to decant suitcases onto the damp tarmac.

After a short delay, but one in which the coach occupants, now awake and anxious to get to their rooms, began to fidget restlessly, Miranda returned with some fresh papers attached to her clipboard. She reached for the microphone and began to issue the mandatory instructions.

"OK. We'll be leaving the hotel at 8 o'clock sharp in the morning. Breakfast will be at 7.15 in the ground floor dining room, and when you go down to breakfast, please make sure you have left your cases outside your room so that we have got time to load them onto the coach for you. Your room keys are waiting at reception, so I'll just give you your room numbers and then you can leave the coach and collect your key. It looks as though most of you are going to be on the first floor."

She started to read from one of her new sheets of paper.

"Mr and Mrs Armitage; room 101," she began. Frank snorted.

"I might have guessed. It just had to be didn't it? Well, that's just about the perfect end to a perfect day!"

Unfazed, Miranda continued through her list.

"Mr and Mrs Cockrell; room 106. Mr and Mrs Edwards; room 102. Mr and Mrs Fuller; room 104. Mr Rogers and … Miss Khan; room 103. Mr and Mrs Wood; room 105…"

For all Dave's faults, Susan found much comfort in the predictability of his behaviour. He was less concerned about locating room 104 than about whether there was a bar, how long it stayed open and where it was located. As they waited impatiently, in yet another queue, to collect their key at the utilitarian reception desk, he looked around and almost punched the air with delight as he spotted a small but well-populated and attractive bar area.

As Miranda continued to read from her list and, as more and more people descended stiffly down the steps, and walked, with varying degrees of ease, across the car park and into the hotel, Brian and Valerie remained on the coach. When all of the other passengers had left, they approached Miranda. This time, it was Valerie's turn to ask the question.

"Excuse me. Did Tony mention the problem with our suitcases? You know, they're locked and we've forgotten the keys. Will you…"

Like everyone else on the coach, Miranda had experienced a wearisome, occasionally frustrating and chaotic day and she was rather hoping that she had seen the last of her "clients" until the morning. Besides, she had other plans for later in the evening. She tried hard to smile, as she had been trained to do, but it lacked any semblance of warmth or spontaneity.

"No, no, he didn't mention it but when your cases have been delivered to your room, er, let me see, room 105 isn't it? I'll pop along and try and sort something out."

"Thank you very much."

"It might be a little while though before I can get to you."

While Dave was intent on a close inspection of the bar and the opportunity to sample the full range of Belgian beers on offer, Jason and Barbara seemed in a particular hurry to get to their room. Eschewing the growing and slow-moving queue for the lift, they sprinted up the stairs, taking them two at a time, and dashed eagerly along the first floor corridor. Barbara inserted the key in the door, with Jason attached to her waist, and rushed into the room. They switched on the light and looked excitedly around. Suddenly their euphoria turned to disappointment.

Their room was furnished adequately, if unspectacularly, with modern built in drawer-units and wardrobe space, a chair, several lamps, a mirror and a large television. The walls were inoffensively plain and pale, hung with a couple of mass-produced abstract prints which, together with pale yellow curtains and a mustard carpet, provided the only real colour. A door led into a bathroom with a modern shower cubicle, toilet and washbasin. But there was one major problem!

"Oh, no. Jace, it's single beds!"

"Oh, sod it!"

Jason dropped his rucksack in the middle of the floor – a regular habit – and went over to inspect the beds. He bent down and looked underneath and then pushed tentatively at the foot of one. At the head, there was what appeared to be a small free-standing bedside unit between the two beds. Jason studied the situation thoughtfully for a moment before concocting an action plan.

"Mind you, I don't think it would be too difficult to move them together. Shall we try?"

"I think we should!" Barbara enthused.

"Right! Come on then, give me a hand!"

★ ★ ★

In the adjacent, identical room, Peter and Gail carried out a detailed inspection of their facilities. They were not especially concerned about the presence of single beds – a good night's sleep was uppermost in their thoughts – but, after a thorough search of the wardrobe and drawer units, it seemed that they too had a problem.

"Only one pillow each, I'm afraid," Gail observed ruefully.

Throughout the day, apart from the odd tetchy moment, Peter had done his best to remain philosophical and phlegmatic, despite the dreary weather, the long journey, the unexpected presence of their extra, ursine travelling companion, and his own delicate health, but it was becoming an increasing struggle to remain upbeat as his considerable reserves of patience began, finally, to run out. He sniffed and looked dejectedly at Gail.

"It doesn't look as though I'm going to sleep very well, especially with this cold coming on," he whimpered.

Gail smiled at him in her usual reassuring way.

"Stop worrying about how well you're going to sleep. I expect you'll go out like a light, like you usually do."

"Sorry, love. Quite right!"

Suddenly, their conversation was interrupted by an unexplained series of bumps, thuds, squeaks and muffled scraping noises that seemed to be coming from the next room. They listened intently for a minute or two before Peter posed the obvious question.

"What's that noise?"

"Don't know. Sounds like somebody moving furniture about."

"I'd better get my ear plugs out, then."

★ ★ ★

Inside room 106, Trevor and Julia threw their bags onto the nearer of the beds and looked around disappointedly at the insipid furnishings and decor. On hotel visits, Trevor was always keen to collect new and original ideas on how best to furbish the residential units at his conference centre but, on this occasion, he was unrewarded. Trying to make light of the situation, Trevor smiled, went over to Julia and lightly embraced her.

"At last, we're on our own," he whispered soothingly into her ear.

Julia, however, was continuing to scour the room with that anxious look that always gave Trevor a sense of foreboding. But her face brightened encouragingly when she spotted what she was looking for.

"Yes. Ah, there's a telephone. Good. I'll just give Mark a quick call."

"But you only saw him a few hours ago!"

"I know and I'm sorry, but I'll relax more knowing he's alright. And you want me to be relaxed don't you?"

It had been a day of vacillating moods and, although Trevor was visibly irked by Julia's continued fretting about Mark, he reckoned that it had to be in his best interests to display as much forbearance as he could muster.

"Alright, but try and make it quick," he said, trying to sound tolerant but with an unmistakeable hint of petulance in his voice. He started to unpack his travel bag while Julia sat on one of the beds, picked up the phone, which was positioned on one of the bedside units, followed the printed instructions on how to obtain an outside line and dialled Mark's number.

Mark had felt restless and a bit lonely since his mother and Trevor had left. It was one of those Saturdays when all his mates seemed to be busy, so he had invited his father round to spend the evening with him; he knew he would bring plenty of beer. Mark had been expecting his mother to call so he was quick to answer the phone when it rang.

"Mark? Mark? It's Mummy!"

"Oh hi, Mum." Mark tried to sound surprised.

"Just thought I'd phone to let you know we've arrived at our hotel."

"That's cool!"

"So, is everything alright with you?"

"Yeah, no probs!"

Across the capacious lounge, Geoff was sitting comfortably in a capacious armchair with a capacious glass of beer in his hand. As Mark continued to talk on the phone, he quietly cleared his throat and started to speak in a loud falsetto voice.

"Mark, darling, how much longer are you going to be on the phone?" he trilled.

His action had the desired effect. Julia was immediately intrigued.

"Mark, who's that I can hear?" she asked with an obvious hint of curiosity. Mark was trying hard not to laugh.

"No-one, Mum!" he spluttered

"When are you coming upstairs?" Geoff continued in resonant falsetto.

"Mark, who is that? What is she saying?" Julia asked with increasing agitation.

"It's just something on the telly," Mark replied, deliberately trying to sound unconvincing. "Hang on, I'll turn it off!"

He turned towards Geoff and put his finger over his mouth. Geoff nodded, beamed smugly, drank from his glass and fell silent.

"Is that better?" Mark asked, innocently.

"Yes, that's better. How's Rosie?"

"She's fine. She's eaten all her tea and has gone to sleep on your bed."

"Ah, that's nice!"

Trevor had finished unpacking his bag. He went over to the bed where Julia was sitting, sat down beside her and gently massaged the nape of her neck. He knew what effect it would have.

"Listen Mark, I'd better ring off now. We're phoning from the hotel and I don't know how much they charge."

"No probs, Ma. Stay cool! Don't keep Trev waiting!!"

"Cheeky! Night, Mark, I'll be in touch!"

Julia put the phone down and closed her eyes in obvious pleasure as Trevor continued to massage her neck, gradually extending the range of his dextrous fingers to her shoulders and upper back. Sensing that his gentle massage was having the desired effect, his hand strayed slightly further down her back and he gently undid her bra.

"I'm sure he had a girl with him," Julia suddenly announced, without opening her eyes, or apparently realising what Trevor had just done.

"Really! How do you know?"

"I heard a female voice in the background. Mark tried to kid on it was coming from the television but I know when he's lying. Anyway, I heard her call his name!"

"It could all be quite innocent," observed Trevor as he slowly began to unbutton her blouse.

"I bet it was that little slut Gemma from number 29!"

Trevor froze mid-button. A new, distracting train of thought had been triggered by her last remark. He stood up, ran his hand over his hair and began pacing the floor.

"That reminds me. I wonder how Mike's got on trying to find a temporary replacement for Emma."

For much of the day, Julia had been tense and anxious and an increasingly exasperated Trevor had been forced to use every weapon in his romantic armoury to try and engender in her a more relaxed and contended mood. Now, when he had finally succeeded, it was his turn to be tense and anxious and it was Julia's turn to be exasperated.

"He's got your number hasn't he?"

"Yes."

"Well, he hasn't phoned or texted so I'm sure everything is alright."

"Mmm. Still, I think I'd better phone just to make sure."

"Aaaah!"

Julia fell backwards on the bed in frustration and thumped her fists on the duvet.

★ ★ ★

Brian and Valerie were sitting quietly in their room, Brian on one of the beds and Valerie in the one niggardly armchair that had been provided. They often sat quietly in their room. Valerie had examined Brian's discarded oily shirt with distinct reluctance and had left it to soak for a while in the washbasin. Brian had made a half-hearted attempt at unpacking his rucksack, but there was little more that they could do now until they could get into their suitcases. Their conversation, such as it was, had run out some time ago and they were both sitting, staring blankly ahead in an atmosphere of deepening gloom. Valerie glanced impatiently at her watch and tutted loudly. Brian tried to do the same until he remembered that he had lost his watch. In desperation, he put the television on and, using the remote control, tried to find a French or Belgian channel that looked interesting. He was not having much luck when, eventually, they heard a loud and impatient-sounding knock at the door. Valerie, who was nearer, got up and let Miranda in. She bustled briskly into the room carrying what looked like a small metal saw, and a file.

"I've borrowed these tools from Tony. Your cases are just outside here. If we can bring them in, I can try and cut through the locks for you."

Brian put the remote control down on the bed, got up, went out into the corridor and brought in the cases, which he lifted, one onto each bed. There were certain aspects of the role of a Tour Director that Miranda thoroughly enjoyed. She liked the feeling of power that went with the job and she enjoyed being in control of a well-behaved and good-natured group. She relished the, albeit infrequent, positive feedback that she got from clients who were enjoying themselves and, on the rare occasions that she could find the time and opportunity, she still enjoyed sightseeing. But she was a slave to detailed planning and organisation, and she was not at her best when things were going wrong or when, under pressure, she was required to act spontaneously, using her initiative and judgement, or work hard to rectify a particularly tricky situation, a failing that she had already amply demonstrated when Frank had locked himself in the toilet earlier.

As she began to saw away at the padlocks, it became obvious that this particular task was one for which she lacked the necessary enthusiasm, muscle power and skill. After little more than a perfunctory attempt, several exaggerated grunts and a few excessively pained facial expressions, she threw down the saw and thoughtfully examined her carefully manicured and highly polished nails.

"It's no good. I'll have to go and get Tony. Won't be long!"

She bustled out as quickly as she came in, leaving Brian and Valerie to resume their silent vigil.

★ ★ ★

Back in room 103, Jason and Barbara had succeeded in pushing the two beds together and they had hastily unpacked their overnight essentials, including a small alarm clock, which Barbara had scrupulously set for 6.30.

"There, that should do for the morning. Now, what else will I need tonight?" she asked, trying to effect an air of innocence. "Ah, I remember!"

In a state of rising excitement, they began to unpack the items that they had purchased from the sex shop earlier in the day. Barbara produced some very skimpy and sexy lacy black and red underwear, which she teasingly held up in front of her. In the subdued lighting of the hotel bedroom, her deep brown eyes seemed especially sultry and seductive. Her dark hair, which she had kept tied back for most of the day, now flowed freely and alluringly over her shoulders.

"Well, what do you think, Jace?" she pouted.

Jason began to advance towards her with more than usual colour in his cheeks and an unmistakeably lecherous look in his eyes. Barbara held out an arm and gently pushed him away.

"Steady, tiger, or I may have to use these!"

She produced, from her bag, a pair of handcuffs with red fur trimmings, which, with her right hand, she brandished in Jason's face.

"Oh, you wouldn't do that, would you?" Jason simpered.

Barbara's left hand, meanwhile, travelled slowly and gently down the front of Jason's jeans. Her exploratory probings confirmed that it was not just the general level of excitement that was rising.

"Just try me, tiger," she pouted again. "My, you're a big boy aren't you?"

"As big as this?" asked Jason as he produced a large, phallic-shaped, pink-coloured vibrator from behind his back.

Barbara's eyes grew wider and her mouth fell open.

"Oh, you are very a naughty boy," she purred. "I might have to punish you later."

While Jason continued to hold the vibrator in front of him, she began stroking it provocatively between her thumb and forefinger.

"Turn it on then!"

Jason switched it on but nothing happened. He looked carefully at it, shook it vigorously and switched it on again. Still nothing happened.

"You did remember to get the batteries for it?" asked Barbara.

"Oh, shit. No. Bugger. Now what?"

"Hang on a minute. I wonder…"

Barbara had been looking quickly around the room and her excited eyes alighted on the small alarm clock that she had recently set. She went over to it, prised the back off and removed the batteries. She took the vibrator from Jason, opened the battery compartment and dropped the batteries in. She switched it on and the vibrator hummed suggestively into life.

"You are brilliant!" trumpeted Jason.

"I know. Try me!"

Unable to contain their rising passions any longer, they lunged at each other and began to fumble energetically, if not particularly skilfully, at buttons, zips and any other fastening devices that got in the way of their ultimate goal. As they frantically undressed each other, they scattered discarded items of clothing around the room.

★ ★ ★

Valerie and Brian's temporary attempts to embrace the Trappist philosophy and, at the same time, savour the manifold delights of Belgian television on a Saturday night, were interrupted by another knock at the door. This time it was Brian who answered it, to find Tony standing outside, looking displeased and carrying his toolbox. He too entered briskly.

"Miranda tells me you've still got a problem with your suitcases." He sounded irritated.

"I'm afraid so."

"OK, let's have a look."

He strode purposefully over to one of the beds, threw his room key onto it, opened his toolbox, took out a small metal saw and began to saw away powerfully at one of the suitcase padlocks.

★ ★ ★

Dave and Susan had wasted little time in familiarising themselves with the hotel bar, situated close to the reception area, but discreetly partitioned from it, and liberally furnished with subdued lighting, mock leather sofas, easy chairs and small, glass topped tables. They had already substantially improved their knowledge of the local beers when Frank and Joyce strolled in, ostensibly for a nightcap but, in reality, to drown their sorrows and soothe their tempers.

It was Saturday night, the hotel was pretty full and the bar area itself was crowded. Having finally ordered their drinks from the obviously harassed bar staff, which Frank did by speaking loudly and slowly in his own form of pidgin English, they looked around for somewhere to sit. The only seats they could find were a pair of easy chairs positioned at either end of the mock leather sofa that was creakingly accommodating the full weight of Dave and Susan. With several beers inside him, Dave was at his convivial best and keen to befriend his fellow coach travellers. He beckoned enthusiastically to Frank and Joyce.

"Come over and join us!" Dave called cheerily across the bar to Frank. Introductions began immediately.

"I'm Dave, this is Susan."

"Hello, I'm Joyce."

"And I'm Frank."

Grateful for an opportunity to talk to someone other than Dave and not noted for her reticence, Susan was the first to venture into the area of polite conversation, studiously ignoring any references to toilets and locks.

"So, are you enjoying yourselves?"

"Well, it's been a pig of a day, frankly, but I must say, we are looking forward to the holiday," Frank replied, earnestly but inaccurately. "To be honest, we often don't get further than Eastbourne on holiday but I managed to persuade Joyce to have a change this year."

Joyce had just started to drink from her glass of sweet sherry when Frank spoke. She spluttered. Although he was often obsessive and more than occasionally irascible in private, Frank greatly enjoyed the company of others – much more so than his own – and he usually oozed with avuncular bonhomie on social occasions. It's what made him popular at the bowls club and, in his younger days, at the cricket club. Ignoring Joyce's spluttering, he continued.

"I mean, once we finally got served, I was quite surprised how easy it was to order a drink back there, not knowing much of the language."

"Dave's never had a problem ordering a drink, have you Dave?" replied Susan.

"Never!" confirmed Dave. "Mind you, I've had a problem paying for it sometimes, though!" he chuckled.

Having finally stopped choking on her drink and, like Susan, grateful for the chance to talk to someone other than her husband, Joyce joined the conversation. She turned to Susan.

"This is our first coach tour abroad. I mean, we've been on coach tours before, but they've always been in the UK and nearly always bowls tours. Do you do these kinds of tours very often?"

"No, not often. We sometimes go to Spain or Majorca, or even Greece, but we thought we might like to see a bit more of Europe for a change."

"You mean you did!" Dave interrupted.

"The trouble with Dave is that he misses his English food after a while." Susan sounded apologetic, as though excusing a naughty boy for a minor transgression.

Dave nodded emphatically and began to look wistful.

"Aye," he confirmed, "after about five minutes, actually. Come to think of it, I could murder a bacon butty right now!"

"I know what you mean," Frank agreed. "Some nice traditional English food with a good strong cup of tea is what I need. Do you know, we've been on the road all day and I have to keep reminding myself what country we're in. I think I probably missed one when I was in the toilet earlier. If we keep up this pace every day, I'm going to be too knackered to do anything."

"Oh, I'm sure we are all going to enjoy ourselves," said Joyce, as heartily as she could, but with little real conviction.

"Probably," agreed Frank reluctantly, "but I think there are going to be times when I'm going to feel a bit like a sheep at a sheep-dog trials – always being herded somewhere. I love to just wander off somewhere for a while… go at my own pace… go where the fancy takes me, or sit quietly and watch the world go by. And I am going to miss the sea, the smell of the ozone, the sound of the seagulls…"

Dave was still looking wistful.

"Aye, fish and chips out of the paper… and jellied eels… and ice cream on the prom…"

Susan gave Dave one of her famed and feared looks. "Here we go; back to food again!"

"Don't forget the wind and the rain…" added Joyce.

"Yes, and a pint or two while you wait for it to clear up," Frank replied rubbing his hands together gleefully.

"Too right! Just as long as we don't have to spend too much time on the coach, in the company of the fair Miranda, getting parched."

"I saw you admiring her bottom earlier," Susan teased. Dave looked uneasy and decided to change the subject. He cleared the final dregs from his glass and slammed it firmly on table.

"Ahem, would anyone like another drink?"

★ ★ ★

In Brian and Valerie's room, Tony had been working away strenuously at the offending padlocks for some time and beads of perspiration were starting to appear on his increasingly furrowed brow. But he found sawing through the padlocks easier than cutting through the oppressive atmosphere in the room and, sticking resolutely to his task, he eventually succeeded.

"There we are," he gasped. "I've had to saw through both of your padlocks, I'm afraid, but at least you can open your suitcases now."

"Thank you ever so much. We're very grateful."

Brian unzipped his suitcase and folded the lid over onto the bed as his clumsily packed clothes exploded out of their confinement and spilled onto the duvet. Tony, meanwhile, had produced some string from his toolbox, from which he cut two generous lengths and handed them to Valerie. Unlike Miranda, who seemed to regard Brian and Valerie as a bit of a nuisance, and having got over the initial irritation of having his short evening disturbed, Tony seemed genuinely concerned about their plight and apologetic that he had found it necessary to break their padlocks.

"I don't have any spare padlocks I'm afraid, so you won't be able to lock your cases but, if you tie a piece of string round them before you leave them outside in the morning, they'll be fine. Maybe you can pick up some more padlocks on your travels."

Valerie and Brian thanked him profusely and he picked up his toolbox and left.

★ ★ ★

Julia had stopped thumping the duvet now and she was lying on the bed, motionless, face-up, eyes closed, with the top two buttons of her blouse, and her bra, tantalisingly undone. Trevor, meanwhile, was pacing up and down the room, still talking on his mobile phone.

"Yeah, yeah, OK mate… Yeah, you'd better make sure you get the advert out first thing on Monday… Yeah, well done! Give me a call if you have a problem. Oh, by the way, have you got someone to sort out the fire escape yet?… Yeah, Geoff will do. Cheers, Mike."

Trevor put the phone down, smiled with relief, turned and spoke to Julia. She was breathing deeply and regularly and Trevor watched for a second as her exposed cleavage moved rhythmically up and down. He sat down quietly beside her, reached into her open blouse and placed his hand gently on her partly exposed breasts.

"Well, they've got through the day OK. Mike seems to think he can get some extra help in from Monday, and Geoff's booked to do the fire escape door on Thursday, so they should get by. Julia! Julia!"

Wearied by the emotional turmoil of the day, Julia had fallen deeply asleep where she lay. For Trevor, it meant a change of plan.

"Oh, great!" he muttered as he tiptoed quietly into the bathroom and turned the shower on.

★ ★ ★

In the hotel bar, the beer and the spirits were flowing freely and the Armitages and Fullers were developing a surprising kind of rapport. It was probably alcohol-induced because they were not particularly alike. Frank was, by nature, an obsessive worrier whereas Dave usually had a carefree, happy-go-lucky approach to life. Susan was loud and earthy while Joyce was more staid and timid. But they had sufficient in common – an inherent mistrust of foreigners, a dislike of authority and a strong belief in fairness and justice – as well as belonging to, more or less, the same generation, with all its inherent attitudes and prejudices.

Throughout most of his working life, Frank had occupied minor clerical positions in public service industries, where certain traditional standards of appearance were required, and he had not yet learnt how to dress casually in retirement or on holiday. He still wore a white shirt, carefully ironed grey trousers, polished black shoes and a jacket or blazer. His one concession to retirement and informality had been occasionally to discard his tie. Dave, on the other hand, had no such inhibitions. As a builder by trade, he was used to dressing casually and made few concessions to the niceties of social etiquette or fashion. He was wearing a short-sleeved check shirt, with the top two buttons undone, exposing a hirsute chest. His dark blue denim trousers, straining slightly at the waist, had a baggy, shapeless appearance.

Having listened intently to Frank's narrative on how he

managed to get locked in the toilet on the coach, he folded his arms across his chest as Frank regaled them, with some embellishment, with a thorough and somewhat repetitive account of his morning encounter with the firemen.

"Anyway, the fireman picked up the can and started watering our plants. God knows what they will look like when we get back."

"Like Sweet Peas I expect!" Dave chortled. "Or bog plants."

Frank then downed the remainder of his beer, prompting Joyce to return him to practicalities with a gentle admonishment.

"Talking of which," she said "you've had enough beer for one night. You know what that'll make you do in the night!"

Frank laughed.

"Yes, you're right. Better go, before I have to, if you see what I mean! Good night."

As Frank stood up, Joyce, her tongue loosened by rather more sherry than she was accustomed to, turned mischievously towards Dave and Susan.

"Honestly, he's still a 'twice a night' man but not in the way he once was."

"Oooh, give me a glimpse of flannelette and whalebone and I'll soon show you!"

"Stop fantasising and get upstairs!"

Frank and Joyce said their farewells and left. Dave, meanwhile, began to study his half-empty glass. Susan could tell what he was thinking. It wasn't difficult.

"Yes, and you'd better not have too much more either. Don't forget it's an early start in the morning."

"Yes, I suppose you're right." Another wistful look spread across his rubicund face.

★ ★ ★

Brian had finally finished unpacking what he thought he might need overnight, most of which, with an absence of forethought, he had buried at the bottom of his suitcase, and had stuffed some clothes and toiletries into a drawer.

"Well, I reckon that's all I'm going to need for the morning.

The rest can stay in my suitcase," he declared, with an air of satisfaction.

He threw a few rejected items back into his suitcase and, with a triumphant flourish, he lifted up the lid, closed the case and manhandled it onto the floor, while he looked around for a convenient corner to store it in overnight. As he placed the suitcase on the floor, he noticed Tony's room key, still lying on the bed where he had left it.

"Hello. Somebody's left their room key here."

Valerie was still sorting out her clothes for the morning and was taking her time folding each item neatly before placing it tidily into a drawer or draping it carefully on a hanger. She stopped what she was doing and inspected the key that Brian handed her.

"Well, Tony was the last one here. Anyway, it's got the room number on it, look '150', so it should be easy enough to find. You'd better go and return it while I check on the state of your shirt, but I expect it's ruined."

"Yes, yes. I'd better go and return it then."

"Take care, don't get lost. Don't lose anything. Don't break anything."

"Yes, yes. Point taken!"

Brian took the key from Valerie and turned towards the door. He was about to leave when he heard Valerie clear her throat in the false, affected kind of way she used to attract his attention. He turned round to see her holding up the key to their room with a supercilious expression on her face.

"You might need this when you come back!"

Brian nodded sheepishly, collected the key and left. As he stepped out into the long, dimly lit, magnolia painted corridor, he was faced with rows of identical featureless doors, stretching away into the distance both to his left and right. His unreliable sense of direction had deserted him and he could not seem to decide in which direction to go. As he dithered, he recognised Dave and Susan walking slightly erratically down the corridor, returning to their room, Dave having been finally prised off the mock leather sofa and escorted by Susan from the bar. Dave had a ruddy glow and a vacant smile on his face. Concluding that the smile was a sign of friendship, rather than inebriation, Brian decided to share his dilemma with them.

"Excuse me. I wonder if you could help. We think our driver has lost his key."

"He'll have trouble starting the coach in the morning, then," Dave chuckled a little tipsily.

"What? Oh! No. His room key."

Brian held up his own room key and read it. "You don't happen to know where room 106 is?"

As Dave stood swaying slightly, his smile faded and a look of puzzlement took over his otherwise vacant face.

"Yes, it's right behind you. You've just come out of it."

"What? Oh! No. Sorry, wrong key. I mean room 150."

In his state of mild intoxication, Dave was struggling to comprehend what Brian was talking about. He liked a bit of fun, but he was beginning to wonder whether Brian was – accidentally or deliberately – just wasting his time, or, worse, simply winding him up. In exasperation, he pointed to the directional signs on the wall.

"No, but if you follow the signs on the wall. You see, rooms 141-160 are in that direction and…"

Brian was far from stupid. Although he could be naïve at times, he was an intelligent man and normally had no problem interpreting numbers and following directional signs – like complicated music scores, they were an everyday part of his working life. But when he was stressed, as he was now, parts of his brain seemed to shut down. He looked blank.

"Oh, never mind." Dave continued. "Follow me. You go in Sue. I'll be back in a minute."

"OK, but don't be long – and no slinking off back to the bar."

"As if I would!"

Dave studied the signs on the wall again, taking longer than usual to get them into focus, and for his brain to process the information, but, eventually, he lurched off down the corridor with Brian in pursuit. As they reached room 150, Dave heard something that stopped him in his tracks. He held up his hand to stop Brian's lumbering advance, pressed his index finger to his lips as a sign to Brian to keep quiet, cupped his ear to the door and listened intently for a moment or two. A lecherous smile spread across his face. He grabbed hold of Brian around the shoulders and pulled him over to the door.

"Here we are," he said innocently. "I think there's somebody in there but it sounds as though they might be busy, if you know what I mean. I'd try knocking gently on the door, if I were you."

Innocently, Brian failed to grasp the significance of Dave's remark, but he nodded dutifully and tapped very gently on the door, with a single knuckle. He stood and waited patiently for a few moments but there was no response from inside the room.

"I don't think anybody's coming."

Dave started to chuckle again. "I wouldn't be too sure of that if I were you! Tell you what, why don't we just leave the key in the door?"

"If you're sure it will be OK."

"Course it'll be OK. Have you got any other suggestions?"

"Er, no. No, not really."

Brian approached the keyhole timorously and started to insert the key.

"Here let me help you," offered Dave, through a barely suppressed fit of mirth.

While giving the impression of trying to help Brian, Dave's juvenile sense of mischief, exacerbated by his mild intoxication, had taken over. As Brian was lamely pushing the key into the lock, Dave improvised a theatrical trip and crashed heavily into the door, deliberately turning the handle at the same time. The door flew open, as he planned, and Brian, who was still inserting the key into the lock, half stumbled into the room.

By clinging uncertainly onto the door frame, Dave stopped himself from stumbling into the room in Brian's blundering wake and he hung back in the semi darkness of the corridor, while Brian, squinting in the contrasting bright light of the room, tried to take in what he was seeing. Lying on the bed were Tony and Miranda, both naked, and in robust sexual union. Tony was lying on his back, while Miranda was kneeling on her haunches astride him. She was rocking rhythmically backwards and forwards while Tony's muscular hands were tightly gripping her firm, ample breasts. As Brian staggered, blinking and uncomprehending, into the room, Miranda looked round, saw him and instinctively screamed. Anxious to avoid drawing further attention to their compromising predicament, Tony tried to place a hand over her mouth.

★ ★ ★

Having abandoned their search for extra pillows, Gail and Peter had retired to bed early, but, bothered by his cold, the strangeness of the bed, and the assorted muffled, alien noises that characterise large hotels at night, Peter was only sleeping fitfully when there was the sudden sound of a distant scream. He awoke with a start and sat bolt upright. As he tried to recover his scrambled senses, he became aware, vaguely at first, of a strange continuous humming noise, which sounded as though it was coming from the adjoining room. His first confused thought was that it might be someone using an electric toothbrush, but the moans and sighs of pleasure that accompanied the noise, soon convinced him otherwise. Nobody could enjoy cleaning their teeth that much or for so long! His listened for a moment or two, looked across forlornly at Gail who was sleeping soundly, coughed quietly, had a drink of water, fluffed up his single pillow, put his ear plugs in and tried to settle down. From the next room, the sighs and moans were gathering momentum before reaching an excited, noisy and prolonged crescendo.

★ ★ ★

CHAPTER 3

Up and About

The hotel breakfast room was functional and square shaped, approached through a short corridor at the rear of the ground floor. Around the sides of the largely featureless room were serried rows of chairs and tables set for breakfast and, in the centre, on a group of carefully arranged tables, trolleys and stands covered with white cloths, was an ample array of cereals, meats, cheeses and preserves, hard-boiled eggs, croissants, bread, bread rolls, yoghurts, fruit, fruit juice and hot drinks.

For many, the previous day had been wearisome and, for some, the night, spent in unfamiliar surroundings on unfamiliar beds, had been an uncomfortable and restless one. A 7.15 breakfast, therefore, found many members of the party in a subdued and somnolent mood. Individuals were trickling slowly into the breakfast room and there were a few mumbled greetings, but the general atmosphere was restrained and muted. In a far corner of the room, Miranda sat quietly, on her own, at a small table, a cup of coffee and croissant in front of her, barely acknowledging anyone, but carefully observing each of her "clients" as they arrived.

The two elderly ladies had been the first to arrive for breakfast by some margin. They hadn't really been listening the previous evening when Miranda announced the timings, but had a vague feeling that the coach was due to leave at 7.15 so they arrived at 6.30, well before the breakfast room was open to the public, and passed the time sitting in the reception area comparing supermarket prices. Frank and Joyce had arrived promptly at 7.15. Frank's delicate digestion favoured a leisurely breakfast – if he bolted his food, he might regret it later, as indeed might some of his fellow travellers – but, having chosen a table to sit at, he was most dismayed to be informed by Joyce that there was no menu to choose from and no waiter service. This was certainly a far cry from the Bandstand Hotel, Eastbourne.

Nigel and his mother arrived soon after Frank and Joyce. After a cursory and, judging by her facial expression, not entirely satisfactory examination of the fare on offer, Nigel's mother plonked herself down regally at a vacant table and imperiously directed her put upon son to join the growing queue and select the requisite delicacies for her breakfast.

Dave was one of the few who had enjoyed a good night's sleep, thanks in part to his generous alcoholic intake the previous evening, and he and Susan were, inevitably, also among the first to arrive. Displaying no morning after-effects, Dave was enthusiastically piling his plate high. Watching his antics with no great surprise, but no great pleasure either, Susan was moved to comment.

"I thought you didn't like continental breakfast?"

"I don't," whispered Dave conspiratorially as he tried to balance a hard-boiled egg onto his overflowing plate, "but it's the only thing on offer and some of this might come in handy for lunch later."

He put his plate down, looked around furtively, surreptitiously wrapped two bread rolls, some ham and a hard boiled egg in a couple of paper serviettes and slid them discreetly into his travel bag, while Susan looked on disapprovingly. Over the many years she had known him, she had always been impressed by Dave's resourcefulness when it came to ensuring that his stomach was full. Years ago, she recalled, when work was scarce and money was in short supply, he had even been known to put on his suit, wander down to the crematorium, attach himself to the largest and most well-heeled looking party of mourners, vaguely claim to be an old friend of the deceased and inveigle an invitation to the post-funeral family gathering where there would be plenty of free food on offer. Once there, he would devour as much as he could, as quickly as he could, before making his excuses and leaving before suspicions were aroused.

By now, Brian and Valerie had wandered vaguely into the

breakfast room, selected their provender and strolled over to an empty table. Miranda had been watching them carefully and, as soon as they sat down, she sidled shiftily over and sat down opposite them.

"Good morning. Em, I'm sorry to trouble you. It's about last night…" she began, in little more than a whisper.

Brian had, of course, wasted no time in conveying the news of his unscheduled and unwelcome entry into Tony's room to Valerie, whose mood had been greatly lightened by the anecdote. She had agreed with Brian that they might just be able to turn that encounter to their advantage if they needed to do so for any reason. For the moment, however, Brian, who was anxious to start his breakfast, feigned innocence.

"Yes, Val and I were very grateful to you and Tony for what you did," he paused briefly, observing, with some pleasure, the look of confused embarrassment on Miranda's face, "to help get our suitcases unlocked. Many thanks."

"What? Oh. No, no, not that," she gulped. "I mean later, in Tony's room. You see, the thing is, well… we're not really supposed to do that kind of thing… the company doesn't approve and of course Tony wouldn't want his wife… I mean… when in Rome. Not that we were, of course… Anyway, the thing is, er, it would be much easier if… you know… you hadn't seen us, last night… you know… we wouldn't want everyone knowing what we'd been up to. I mean, I hope I can rely on your discretion… and, er, if, in return, there is anything we can do to help with your holiday, well, do let me know…"

Brian smiled knowingly at Miranda who looked flustered and ill at ease.

"Thanks. We'll bear your offer in mind. And don't worry; your secret is safe with us. I was only returning Tony's key after all – I don't remember seeing anything untoward!"

"That's great. I knew you'd understand. Well, I must let you get on with your breakfast."

Visibly relieved and, as a result, much more composed, Miranda got up and returned, with greater assurance, to her table, her croissant and her lukewarm coffee. Brian glanced across to a nearby table where Dave was looking at him over his mountain of food and smiling. Dave winked knowingly at him and gave him a "thumbs up" sign.

★ ★ ★

Outside, the previous day's rain had cleared away and a cool watery sun was beginning to penetrate the early morning mist. Tony had risen early, unexpectedly bumped into the two elderly ladies, grabbed a quick breakfast before the rest of the tour party arrived and had been at work for some time. He had effected a temporary repair to the lock on the toilet door, though it really needed replacing and he doubted that it would stand up to the rigours of a two-week tour; he had also prepared the coach – checking the engine and tyres, cleaning the windscreens, removing any residual litter from inside and generally tidying up – before the day's journey began. He was now in the process of loading up the suitcases, which had been collected by the hotel porters from outside each room. He was consulting a piece of paper and looking rather distracted, however, as Miranda, sporting her sun glasses in the pale morning sunlight, bustled up to him.

"Tony, I've managed to have a quiet word with Mr and Mrs Wood about last night. They seem quite understanding. I don't think we'll have any serious problems if we look after them."

"Good, we'd better not. If a word of this gets out..."

"Look, don't start having a go at me. It wasn't me who left his key behind! Anyway, I don't see why you had to take your key with you in the first place, with me already ensconced in your room."

"Force of habit, I suppose. Anyway, I wouldn't have needed to have gone to their room, if you'd managed to get their suitcases open!"

"You didn't have to leave your key behind though, did you?"

"Yes, yes alright; point taken," replied Tony rather peevishly. "Anyway, I've got another problem right now – I don't have any cases for room 103. Rogers and Khan. You'd better pop up and find out what's happened."

"Oh, shit! I didn't see them at breakfast either, come to think of it."

★ ★ ★

Inside room 103, the pale yellow curtains remained securely drawn closed, and a silent, semi darkness prevailed. There was no sign of movement. Strewn around the murky interior of the room was the evidence of the previous night's revelry. Barbara's newly acquired, scanty underwear, which she had never actually got a chance to wear, lay discarded on the floor, together with a jumbled assortment of cast off clothing. A pair of handcuffs was lying at the foot of the bed and an abandoned vibrator rested motionless and exhausted on Jason's bedside unit. In the beds, which were still pushed together, were the indistinct outlines of two motionless shapes. Jason and Barbara lay blissfully asleep beneath a pair of crumpled duvets.

At first, the persistent knocking at the door failed to rouse either of them, but, as it became louder and more frantic, Jason began to stir, slowly at first, but then, as he began to recover his senses, extremely rapidly. He leapt, naked, out of bed, grabbed a lumpy pillow to protect his modesty and ran over to answer the door. Miranda stood outside in the corridor. She scrutinised him thoroughly up and down and then tried to look beyond him into the gloomy interior of the room.

"Er, sorry to disturb you, but you ought to know that the coach leaves in fifteen minutes and we haven't got your suitcases yet."

As realisation dawned, Jason turned even whiter than usual, his pallid, scrawny frame starkly illuminated by the lights in the corridor.

"Oh my God! We must have overslept. Look we'll get ready as quickly as we can and we'll bring our cases down when we come."

Instinctively, he held up a hand as a gesture of apology and the pillow slipped from his grasp, allowing Miranda the opportunity to admire his callow nakedness in all its spot-lit morning glory. Transfixed by the sight of his manly delights, she became momentarily distracted.

"Alright, but don't be, er, don't be too... long! Er... you'd better not hang around... Er, I mean, you'd better get up. Er, I mean, hurry up. I'll leave you to it."

Miranda finally averted her gaze and, pink and flustered, fled quickly down the corridor.

"We'll be down straight away," Jason shouted after her.

Covered in embarrassment, but nothing else, Jason bent down, retrieved his pillow, covered himself up again and closed the door. Barbara had woken on overhearing the commotion and had leapt out of bed, grabbed the alarm clock and examined it.

"Oh no! We forgot to put the batteries back in the clock last night!"

"Never mind about that now. There's nothing else for it. We'll have to gather our things together, get ready as quickly as we can and get down to the coach."

"What about breakfast?"

"No time, I'm afraid. We'll have to grab something when we stop."

"Have I got time for a shower?"

"Only if we share!"

"Cheeky!"

Jason playfully pinched Barbara's naked bottom before switching on the light and launching a frenetic rush to tidy up the room and pack their cases. They both scrambled around, gathering handfuls of clothing and assorted belongings that were strewn around, and stuffed them carelessly into their respective suitcases before Jason realised that he hadn't left out any clothes for the day and had to unpack again. Barbara, meanwhile, was frantically searching the room for something.

"Have you seen my bra?" she shouted.

Jason fumbled around in his suitcase and his pale cheeks flushed a little as he held it aloft. Barbara snatched it from him.

"My mother warned me about people like you," she teased.

"Lucky you didn't take any notice then," he shouted as they disappeared hastily into the bathroom.

★ ★ ★

Amid the early morning bleariness, there was a keen sense of expectation as the passengers boarded the coach for the real start of their holiday and an early opportunity to do some proper sightseeing. Behind her sunglasses, however, Miranda was more careworn as she came aboard and reached for the microphone. For her, this was just the start of another working day; one that had already been a little fraught.

"Good morning," she announced with no great enthusiasm, eliciting a response, albeit muted, from only the more animated members of the party.

"Did you have a good night?"

"Some of us had a better night than others!" Dave whispered quietly to Susan.

"I'm afraid there's been a bit of a mix up over timings this morning," Miranda continued, as diplomatically as she could, "and, as a result, two of our party got up rather late. But they are on their way so we should be away shortly. While we are waiting, let me just tell you about today's itinerary. When we leave…"

Miranda hesitated at this point because Peter, who was sitting immediately behind her, had sneezed, loudly and without warning, and was now blowing his nose with resonant gusto.

Frank was not at his best in the early morning, especially without a full English breakfast inside, and at a time when he would normally have still been in bed. Feeling irritable, he took advantage of Miranda's hesitation to make one of his characteristically sarcastic observations to Joyce.

"Yes, *when* we leave…"

"When we leave," Miranda resumed, "we'll have just a short drive into Bruges where you will have the whole morning available…"

"Or what's left of it…" Frank interjected again, more loudly this time, prompting Joyce to whisper sternly, "Stop it Frank!"

"…to explore this beautiful city. And then, after lunch, we'll be leaving Bruges for our afternoon drive to Amsterdam…"

As Miranda continued to fill time as best she could, Jason and Barbara came dashing out of the hotel, carrying their suitcases, rushed, half-stumbling across to the coach where Tony was waiting impatiently to load them, and scrambled aboard. Jason's shirt had a familiar, crumpled look and his face was unshaven and stubbly. Barbara's hair was wet and dishevelled and she was still brushing it as she clambered aboard. This was an inauspicious start to their first coach tour and they were anxious not to upset their fellow travellers.

"Sooooo sorry, everyone. Overslept, I'm afraid," Barbara apologised quickly and with obvious embarrassment.

As they sat down breathlessly in their seats, Dave leaned across the aisle. Jason expected him to remonstrate with them for their tardy arrival and was taken aback when Dave smiled benevolently.

"Have you had any breakfast?" he enquired.

Jason was even more taken aback by Dave's question. "Er, no," he replied, finally, as he settled into his seat and put his seat belt on. "We didn't have time."

"Thought not. Do you want some?"

Looking stealthy, a talent at which he excelled, Dave reached casually into his travel bag and produced a paper serviette containing what looked liked two slightly battered, hard and flaking bread rolls. Jason looked at Barbara who shook her head emphatically while continuing to brush her hair.

"Er, nnnno thanks. I'm sure we can get something in Bruges. But thanks for the offer."

"OK. Your loss," Dave replied cheerfully, replacing the food parcel in his bag.

The coach was just about to pull away when Barbara suddenly yelled "hang on a minute!" She had discovered the hotel door key still in her pocket and, as Miranda rather truculently kicked the malfunctioning coach door open, Barbara dashed back into the hotel. Frank harrumphed loudly.

★ ★ ★

After a short and straightforward journey, Tony parked the coach on the southern outskirts of Bruges, close to the railway station and, as Miranda was quick to point out, only a short walk across the road, over the bridge, past Minnewater and into the centre of the city. After alighting from the coach, the party quickly dispersed, each individual keen to explore the delights of Bruges in his or her own way.

Unsurprisingly, after their chaotic start to the day, Jason and Barbara rushed into the city centre, rapidly located a boulangerie and disappeared inside to purchase a belated and very welcome breakfast.

Frank and Joyce proceeded at a more leisurely pace, taking in the early morning sights and sounds as the city slowly awoke from its slumbers – the sound of horses hooves echoing on the still damp cobbles, a shutter blind close by being rolled back, church bells striking solemnly, boats on the canals being quietly prepared for another day of energetic activity, ferrying countless tourists from countless countries up and down the medieval waterways. Eventually, they made their way into the still relatively deserted Markt square, the hub of the old city, where Frank busied himself trying to film the gabled buildings and the colourful street cafes that lined the perimeter of the square, and the horses and carriages being assembled, in military fashion, in the middle. As Frank was leaning back, jerkily filming the top of the belfry which towered majestically over them, dominating the skyline, Joyce, who had been quietly absorbing the sights of the city and inhaling the fresh early morning air with undisguised pleasure, made an unwelcome observation.

"I'd bet there'd be some nice views from the top."

Frank straightened up rather creakily, switched off his camcorder, looked up at the belfry tower with some dismay and turned round in a state of agitation.

"You're not serious are you?"

"Deadly serious. What's the point of coming to these places if you don't see the sights? Come on!"

It was now abundantly clear that Joyce was revelling in every new experience – good or bad – that the holiday had to offer and she set off apace, with Frank trailing unwillingly in her energetic wake, muttering to himself and forlornly hoping that there might be a lift to the top.

There was no lift, of course, but they battled resolutely up all 366 steps, mostly spiral and narrow, occasionally fighting against the tide of the early morning visitors coming down, with Joyce leading the way. Once at the top, Frank stood virtually motionless for several minutes trying to recover his breath while Joyce, ever more keen to shed the vestiges of her acquiescent domestic existence, enjoyed the unexpected quiet by taking in the spectacular views of Bruges spread out below, the grandeur of the medieval squares and the traditional red roofed merchants' houses lining the sides of the shimmering, meandering canals. In due course, Frank felt sufficiently recovered to try and film the views but, predictably, he could not seem to get his camcorder to work properly. As usual, when faced with apparent technical malfunction, he swore and randomly pressed a few buttons, but to no good effect.

"What the hell is the matter with the bloody thing?" he exploded.

"You mean we've climbed all the way up here and now you can't get the camera to work?"

Frank grunted, said something under his breath and studied the camcorder intently. As he did so, he was accidentally pushed from behind by one of a number of tourists ascending to the cramped viewing platforms and jostling to get the best vantage points. He turned around angrily to confront the guilty party, whoever he or she might be.

"Oi, oi, watch what you're doing!" he remonstrated to no-one in particular.

His outburst produced not the merest glimmer of apology from anyone standing within close proximity, but, on studying his camcorder again, he discovered that it was now recording.

"Ah, wait a minute. It seems to be working OK now."

"That wasn't a case of operator error was it?" asked Joyce innocently.

"Certainly not. It's these bloody foreign cameras!"

* * *

Brian and Valerie had also arrived in the Markt square but,

possessing neither map nor guide book – another of Brian's oversights – they had taken a convoluted, circuitous route to reach the square, taking in a good many of the less impressive side streets, some of which they were pretty sure they had seen more than once. A great deal of time had elapsed since they first arrived in Bruges and, from a quick glance at a rack of attractive and varied postcards outside a small shop, it was obvious that, during their random meanderings, they had managed to miss most of the main sights. With the time available now limited, it seemed increasingly unlikely that they would stumble across many of the sights without some help. So, despite the extravagant cost, they decided to hire one of the many horse drawn open carriages lined up and waiting for business.

Spurred on by the driver, the horse set off at a surprisingly brisk trot across the cobbles, while Brian rummaged in his battered rucksack for his battered camera. He finally found it, near the bottom, just as the carriage turned a corner and swept alongside one of the many picturesque canals. Determined to make amends for his previous lapses by capturing the scene, Brian held the camera to his eye, but the carriage was rocking and he couldn't seem to quite get the exact view he wanted so he leant forward unsteadily in his seat, just as the carriage veered sharply around another corner. Caught unawares by the sudden change of direction, Brian was jolted backwards into his seat and the camera flew from his grasp and fell with an unpleasant sounding clatter onto the cobbles below.

It took a little while for Brian to explain to the driver what had happened and for the driver to bring the briskly trotting horse to a halt. When Brian was finally able to run back and retrieve his camera, he found it sufficiently cracked, dented and scuffed to fear the worst. Gingerly, he picked it up, inspected it thoughtfully and shook it. He then tried to take a picture with it, but it refused to respond.

"It looks like it's broken, love," he confessed to Valerie who had, by this time, finally caught up with him after making precarious progress in her high-heeled shoes on the uneven cobbles.

Valerie had been wearing the kind of condescendingly patient expression she reserved for those occasions when she was doing her very best to make allowances for Brian's innate clumsiness, but the news that the camera was probably broken, coming less than twenty-four hours after the incidents with the shirt, the watch and the luggage, proved to be well beyond her limited tolerance level and she unleashed another volley of vitriol at her accident-prone spouse.

"I might have known! Do you know, when I woke up this morning, I thought that maybe, just maybe, yesterday was nothing more than a bad dream and that today would be fine. But it's not getting any better is it? God knows what damage you'll do in a fortnight. Why didn't you have the cord around your wrist or, preferably, around your neck – very tightly?"

"I'm sorry, love, I was in a hurry to take the photograph. I didn't think. By the way, what's the time?"

Valerie glanced at her watch.

"The time's getting on and we'll need to get some lunch soon!"

"Look, there's not much time now, but when we get back on the coach, I'll try and fix the camera and if I can't, then we'll try and buy a new one…"

" …and a new watch!!"

"Yes, yes. And a new watch when we get to Amsterdam."

"A lucky charm or two wouldn't go amiss either."

★ ★ ★

Armed with a well-thumbed pocket guidebook, Peter and Gail had been ambling, hand-in-hand, around the city with far more calm purpose than Brian and Valerie. Peter had prepared well, in his usual thorough way, and knew what he wanted to see during their brief visit. They had strolled along the length of Minnewater, enjoyed the tranquillity of the Beguinage convent, paused to admire the pictures being offered for sale in a small square, visited the Memling museum in its medieval setting, looked inside a couple of churches – one of Peter's favourite pastimes –

and admired the spectacular interior of the Basilica of the Holy Blood. Their schedule had been quite hectic and by the time they had reached the Dijver, alongside one of the most photographed waterways in Bruges, fatigue had begun to overwhelm Peter. He spotted a low stone bench, stopped briefly and then walked over to it.

"Do you mind if we sit down for a few minutes?" he asked, wearily.

Gail smiled indulgently and tried to hide her natural concern. This lethargy was most unlike him. Normally on sightseeing trips, particularly those steeped in history, she struggled to keep up with his boundless energy.

"No, of course not. Are you alright?"

Gail knew that Peter was far from well. The sparkle had gone from his eyes and his normal brisk and purposeful walk had been reduced to a laboured stroll. She sounded concerned as they sat down.

"Yeah, it's just that this cold's taken a bit of a hold of me today. You know, not much energy – my legs feel heavy."

She pecked his cheek affectionately.

"I'm so sorry, love. You've been really looking forward to this holiday, especially after all your hard work and, you know, your mum and so on."

"Yeah, still nothing I can do about it. I just hope Fred doesn't catch my cold!"

He smiled, albeit a little weakly, waved at Nigel, across the street, who was trudging dutifully behind his mother as they visited yet another shop selling lace nicknacks, and gave the enigmatic bear, who was sitting in Gail's lap, a friendly pat on the head. Gail, relieved that Peter's sense of humour had not entirely deserted him, feigned mock outrage.

"Oh, I see and what about me?"

"Oops, sorry! We'd better make sure he doesn't catch anything from you either," Peter chuckled. Gail took a playful swipe at Peter's arm.

"You're well enough to be rude then!"

Peter tried to laugh, but the effort made him cough, so he

just smiled gently. While he had been sitting on the bench, he had been watching, with interest, the tourist boats cruising up and down the canal. A thought occurred to him.

"Come on, let's see if we can get on one of those boats down there – see the rest of Bruges the lazy way. We should just have time."

Peter stood up and walked slowly towards the jetty where the boats were loading up with tourists. Gail followed, uncomplainingly, in his wake, still trying to smile and holding on tightly to Fred.

★ ★ ★

Frank and Joyce had returned safely to "terra firma" from the top of the belfry. The climb down had given Frank the opportunity to complain loudly, and at considerable length, about the mechanical failings of his camcorder, the rudeness of foreigners, the difficulty in getting back down the narrow spiral staircase when everyone else seemed to be going up, and the improbability of finding something remotely edible for lunch. Fortunately, most of his diatribe was drowned out by the sound of the bells in the tower striking the hour with unbridled clamour, forcing Frank to cover his ears and complain loudly, but unheard, about the cacophony.

As they wandered away from the Markt square, broadly retracing their steps of earlier in the day, Joyce noticed that Frank seemed to be walking uncomfortably. His stride pattern was shorter than usual and he appeared abnormally hunched. Maybe, she mused, he hadn't quite recovered from climbing up and then down the steps in the belfry. Maybe his feet were uncomfortable on the cobbles. Maybe his continental breakfast, to which he was not accustomed, had disagreed with him in some way.

"Are you alright, love?" she enquired. "It doesn't look as though climbing all those stairs did you much good."

"No, it's not that. I really need to do a pee and it's getting pretty urgent. Good God, aren't there any toilets in this place?"

"We'll have to ask somebody. Hang on, I'll get my phrase book out."

Joyce normally carried a voluminous bag with her whenever she and Frank were away from home for more than a couple of hours. Its contents varied, depending upon circumstances and season, but today it included a purse, a small collapsible umbrella, some sun cream, a brush and comb, an old camera, a basic pack of cosmetics, spare reading glasses, a box of plasters, a packet of tissues, some insect repellent, bite cream, headache pills, medication to stop constipation, medication to stop diarrhoea, some sweets, a needle and cotton, a bottle opener, a notepad and pen, a book to read and, somewhere, a phrase book. Joyce plunged a hand deep into her bag and rummaged around. Frank, meanwhile, was hopping up and down as though the cobbles were on fire.

"For God's sake hurry up," he pleaded in desperation, through clenched teeth, as Joyce, having eventually located her phrasebook, started to flick randomly through it. Unable to wait any longer, Frank called "where are the toilets?" very slowly, at the next person he saw, a smartly dressed young man striding briskly along in the opposite direction.

Though somewhat startled at being shouted at in this way by a slightly deranged stranger, the man seemed to be local, knowledgeable and a fluent English speaker. He directed Frank back the way he had just come, to the Markt square where he would find a toilet located behind the bell tower. Frank looked slightly disappointed and disbelieving – he didn't really trust foreigners, he couldn't recall seeing toilets behind the bell tower and, in any event, he was hoping that lavatorial salvation might be closer to hand – but he had no choice other than to retrace his painful steps in the direction that he was given, as quickly as he could, with Joyce trailing along in his wake. En route, they passed one of a plethora of souvenir shops, which, amongst other things, sold a prominently advertised range of local beers. Through the window, they caught sight of Dave eagerly replenishing his supplies of local brew. Dave happened to look up, saw Frank out in the street and playfully raised a bottle of beer to his lips. Somehow, this innocently intended gesture seemed to exacerbate Frank's predicament and, with one hand placed firmly on his crotch and his eyeballs beginning to bulge, he started to rush down the street with even more urgency than before. By now, Joyce, whose legs were much shorter and sturdier than Frank's, was lagging some distance behind.

Eventually, Frank arrived at the bell tower and, to his surprise, he found the public toilets exactly where he was told they would be. By now in considerable discomfort, he rushed inside while Joyce caught up. A couple of moments later, he emerged, hopping about, in what appeared to be acute pain. Breathlessly, Joyce rushed over to him.

"Quick, I need some small change. There's a woman with a bloody plate in there," he grunted through clenched teeth.

"How much?"

"Oh, I don't know. Just give me some of those small brown coins."

Joyce began rummaging in her bag again.

"For God's sake, hurry up!" Frank pleaded, now virtually bent double with concentration and pain.

Under pressure, Joyce easily got flustered and Frank's persistent cajoling didn't much help. She continued to rummage. Eventually, running out of both patience and continence, Frank plunged his hand into his pocket, produced a ten Euro note, shouted "this'll have to do!" and dashed back into the toilets with one hand already unzipping his flies.

★ ★ ★

Brian and Valerie's visit to Bruges, which they had been especially looking forward to, had been a disaster. They had missed most of the sights, paid more money than they could afford for the aborted carriage ride, and now had a broken camera to add to their growing list of casualties. There was a glacial tension between them as they returned to the coach.

For Frank, the visit had been physically demanding, culturally baffling and more than a little uncomfortable for a while, but for

Joyce, notwithstanding her husband's curious antics and barrage of complaints, it had been a revelation. Belatedly, she was beginning to realise that there was a world full of new experiences out there waiting to be discovered – it stretched far beyond the local shops, south coast seaside resorts and any number of drab municipal bowling greens – and she was determined to do her best to discover it and to savour it, with or, if necessary, without Frank.

Peter and Gail would doubtless have enjoyed themselves more if Peter had been feeling better, but the boat trip had been both relaxing and informative and Peter seemed brighter as they returned at a staid pace to the coach.

For the rest of the party, apart from Nigel, it had been a pretty successful visit; the sun had shone, and they had seen Bruges at its sparkling best. It had oozed medieval charm, the beautifully ornate buildings looked radiant in the fresh morning sun, the swans glided effortlessly along the tranquil canals and the souvenir shops, selling a wide range of lace, chocolate and beer, had come up to expectations. Trevor and Julia had enjoyed a relaxing perambulation around the city and Julia was proudly carrying a large box of Belgian chocolates in a bag, which Trevor had purchased in a therapeutic, though not entirely altruistic, attempt to rekindle the romantic atmosphere they had briefly enjoyed the previous evening. Barbara had also remembered to purchase some chocolates for her mother while she and Jason had explored every inch of central Bruges at breakneck speed and with a degree of youthful energy that their travelling companions could only marvel at. They had even found time to purchase a couple of local confections for lunch, which they were consuming at an unhealthy speed as they waited to board the coach.

Dave and Susan had also arrived back to board the coach in good spirits. Dave was carrying a bag full of assorted Belgian beers and looking especially pleased with himself. He looked across at Barbara and Jason, who were still eating, with his usual mischievous sparkle.

"Making up for lost time, are we?"

"Yeah, we seem to have got an appetite from somewhere!"

Barbara giggled. Somehow, when she giggled, she exuded a kind of innocent flirtatiousness. Without apparently being aware of it, her behaviour and mannerisms could be coquettish. Dave gulped hard.

For Miranda, this was one of the critical moments of the tour. She was pretty sure that she was going to have problems with a few members of the party – that was not unusual in a group of forty – and she could only hope that Brian and Valerie would preserve the promised diplomatic silence over the previous evening's little incident, that Frank's complaints would amount to nothing more than hot air and that Dave's adolescent humour would not get him, or anyone else, into trouble. But, for the moment at least, it was a huge relief to find that every member of the party had got back to the coach on time. Whatever other difficulties she may experience with this group, it did look as though they were going to be good timekeepers and that was a vitally important virtue on a high-speed tour such as this. As the coach pulled away, she reached for the microphone in a more relaxed and upbeat frame of mind.

"Did you all enjoy Bruges?"

There were a few self-conscious cries of "yes" from inside the coach and a good many nods of agreement, except, of course, from Frank.

"All that water and no bloody toilets," he whispered loudly to Joyce.

"We've got quite a drive ahead of us now," Miranda continued. "We'll be heading east across Belgium, around Antwerp and then north through Holland to Amsterdam. We expect it to take us about four and a half hours, but we will have a break en route to look at the windmills of Kinderdijk."

Brian rather wished that Miranda hadn't used the word "break". He was frowning as he carefully scrutinised his battered camera. As he gently shook it, he could hear an ominous rattle. He tried to take a picture through the coach window but the camera failed to respond. He sighed heavily as he prepared himself for Valerie's wrath.

"No, that's definitely broken."

Calmer than she had been earlier, Valerie also sighed heavily. Annoyed though she was, there seemed little point in berating her husband again. After all, he hadn't broken the camera deliberately and anyway there was nothing that could be done about it now. They needed to put their run of bad luck behind them and look forward.

"We'll have to try and buy another one when we are in Amsterdam," she suggested, more benignly than Brian was expecting.

"Yes, yes. We can ask Miranda about that later."

★ ★ ★

Inside the coach, the initial exhilaration following the stimulating visit to Bruges had largely given way to a mixture of tedium and post-lunch fatigue as the scenery outside took on a repetitive and lacklustre appearance. As the coach kept largely to the network of fast, direct motorways, much of the scenery was flat, residential, urban and industrial.

Miranda tried to while away some time by describing, in precise but unexciting detail, the selection of optional excursions available to the tour party – there were evening tours of Amsterdam, Rome and Paris, a canal boat trip in Amsterdam, a gondola ride in Venice, a guided tour of Rome, a lake trip at Lucerne, a trip up a Swiss mountain and a visit to Versailles – but she somehow contrived to make them sound more exhausting than exciting.

Feeling tired, Dave yawned and stretched. He whispered to Susan.

"Well, if we're going to be on here for a while yet, I'm going to sample one of these beers. Let's hope it's not as flat as this countryside or as dull as Miranda's commentary!"

He began to reach inside his travel bag, which, as always, he had placed conveniently on the floor by his feet, and located one of the bottles of beer that he had purchased in Bruges. Susan, meanwhile, was quick to express her displeasure.

"Dave, you're not supposed to drink beer on the coach. Remember what she said yesterday!"

"She won't notice if I'm careful. I'm not going to be waving it around, if you'll pardon the expression."

"No, but I expect she'll be coming round to offer us drinks soon."

"Maybe, but I'll see her coming and I'll have plenty of time to hide the bottle in the bag."

Looking guilty, he leant forward, sunk low in his seat and quietly removed the bottle top.

In the seat in front, Peter was feeling off colour. After their invigorating boat trip, he had felt better for a while, but he had now suffered something of a relapse. He had a sore throat and the rigours of the morning's excursion, coupled with the monotony of the journey and Miranda's droning monologue, induced in him an overwhelming sense of weariness. He sneezed again.

"Not feeling any better?" Gail enquired sympathetically.

"Not really."

"You heard what Miranda said. We've got a long drive ahead of us. Why don't you try and grab a bit of sleep? You'll probably feel better for that."

"Perhaps you're right. But make sure you wake me up if we come to anything interesting, though."

He rested his head on the headrest and closed his eyes but he could not seem to get comfortable; he was too upright. After fidgeting for a while, he decided, without much optimism, to try and recline the seat. He fiddled with the lever on the side of his seat but nothing happened. He fiddled with it again, more vigorously this time, but still nothing happened. Then, with a rare flash of irritation, a sure sign that he was not feeling well, he thumped the lever as hard as he could and, without warning, the back of his seat jolted sharply backwards.

Behind him, Dave was still leaning forward, enjoying an illicit gulp or two of beer. As he slowly savoured the taste, made all the more satisfying by the surreptitious nature of the activity, he closed his eyes, momentarily, in pleasure and was caught totally unawares as the back of Peter's seat suddenly lurched rapidly towards him and hit him solidly in the face. He jumped in surprise and the shiny glass bottle slipped from his grasp, fell to the floor and shattered spectacularly, creating a sticky, frothy puddle on the floor.

Dave leapt to his feet. His normal healthy ruddy glow was turning into a more violent, blotchy redness. He wasn't sure whether to feel angry – a perfectly good drink of beer had been ruined and that, in his eyes, was a heinous crime – or to feel guilty, like a naughty schoolboy caught red-handed breaking the rules, and as Miranda rose sternly from her seat and bore down on him, with a thunderous look on her face, he was determined, like any naughty schoolboy, to deflect the blame onto others. His target was Peter.

"What the… What the hell do you think you're doing?" he yelled at Peter.

It was not in Peter's normally sanguine nature to shout back. Besides, he was feeling too fragile and embarrassed. Instead, he became meekly apologetic.

"Look, I'm very sorry. This lever on my seat must have jammed."

By now, Miranda had arrived, bristling with indignation, and was inspecting the broken glass and the expanding pool of frothy beer beneath the seat. Her cheeks flushed, she thrust her bosom out, tried to make herself look as imposing as possible and lectured Dave in the severest of matronly tones.

"Good God! I thought I reminded you yesterday not to drink beer and such like on the coach. Look at the mess you've made."

Dave had never taken too kindly to being reprimanded by anyone, except possibly Susan. He didn't care much for figures of authority, or people like Miranda, who came across as ludicrously pompous and self-important, or what he regarded as unnecessary and bureaucratic rules. Resentment was welling up inside him. He was about to open his mouth and say something highly derogatory when Susan intervened.

"Dave! Don't you dare!"

Still standing, Dave stared angrily at Miranda for what seemed like an eternity, his red blotchy face growing ever more vivid and his fists slowly clenching, before he gradually began to gain control of his emotions and subsided back into his seat.

In his weakened state, Peter was still feeling guilty about the incident and he tried to intercede with Miranda.

"I think it was partly…"

Miranda, however, was not in a mood to listen. She was still simmering.

"It's no good," she raged. "We'll have to stop the coach while we clear up this mess before it all goes sticky and before the broken glass does some damage!"

She turned and bustled off to the front of the coach, where she spoke briefly to Tony.

"Can you stop somewhere? There's beer and broken glass all over the floor."

Tony nodded as she spoke into the microphone.

"Ladies and gentlemen; I'm very sorry, but as you probably realise, there's been a bit of an er… accident. We've got a broken bottle here near the front and I'm afraid we're going to have to stop for just a few minutes while we clear up the mess."

The news, unwelcome though it was, was treated with typical British phlegm by most of those on board – the incident had, after all, added some colour to an otherwise lacklustre journey – although Frank of course couldn't resist a loud theatrical "tut".

After only a few minutes, Tony found a service station to pull into and, without displaying much obvious emotion, he busied himself, with bucket and mop, clearing up the mess that Dave's spillage had made. He would be purposeful and thorough; he always was. Most of the passengers took the opportunity of the enforced break to get out of the coach and stretch their legs – some lit a cigarette, some stood silently watching the traffic trundling remorselessly by, others stood in small groups discussing the incident or merely passing the time of day. Frank, with a pocketful of small change at the ready, disappeared into the service station in search of a toilet.

Peter had found a small, low wall, behind which was the filling station, and was sitting on it, holding his head in his hands and looking troubled. Gail was sitting next to him, still trying to smile and talking gently to him. Miranda, meanwhile, was continuing to berate Dave.

"This is all your fault. You knew you weren't supposed to drink beer on the coach."

Dave was still struggling with his emotions. He was desperately trying to control his innate instinct for petulance or, worse still, violence, and was still intent on deflecting the responsibility for the incident onto Peter. He nodded in his direction.

"Well, I didn't know that idiot over there was going to come hurtling backwards towards me."

"That's hardly the point is it? I made it very clear yesterday that you weren't supposed…"

Suddenly, Dave held up his hand as though to acknowledge his guilt. His anger started to subside. He wasn't achieving anything, he realised, by trying to offload the blame onto somebody else. Nobody was fooled and it wasn't really fair on Peter. It was time for a different approach. He lowered his voice to a whisper and moved closer to Miranda, still with his hand raised. Instinctively, Miranda started to back away.

"Yes, yes fair enough, I suppose. I shouldn't have done it, I apologise and I won't do it again," agreed Dave, almost choking on the words. "But if I were you, I'd try to be a bit more understanding, if you know what I mean. You see, it wasn't just Brian over there who saw what you and Tony got up to last night…"

He winked knowingly at Miranda, who turned a vivid pink as she became suddenly flustered again.

"I don't know what you mean!" she protested unconvincingly.

"Let's put it this way. It wasn't Horlicks I saw you enjoying with Tony last night, was it, although it might have been something hot and steaming, if you get my meaning?"

Miranda's face turned bright red. She was no longer bristling with self-righteous indignation. Her tone, so authoritarian only moments ago, was now anxious and hesitant.

"Ah, er…er," she stuttered. "Well, I mean, if you promise not to drink any more beer on the coach, er, I'm sure we can overlook it this time. Of course, we wouldn't want to tell anyone else about last night, would we?"

Dave tapped the side of his nose with his index finger and winked again at Miranda.

"You can rely on me…"

Gail, meanwhile, had left Peter sitting quietly on the wall, feeling sorry for himself, and walked deliberately over to where Dave, Susan and Miranda were standing. Dave stopped in mid-sentence and eyed Gail suspiciously. Gail smiled at him reassuringly. It was something she was good at. Years of working as a doctor's receptionist had prepared her well in the art of smiling reassuringly.

"I'm sorry to interrupt," Gail began. "I've just been talking to my husband. He's feeling a bit off colour and he's quite upset at what's just happened."

"And so he should be," added Dave rather pompously.

"And I think it would do him a lot of good," Gail continued, "to relax and get a bit of sleep but we don't need the front seats to do that. As we now know, neither of the recliner levers or buttons at the front is working properly anyway and none of us wants a repeat of what's just happened, do we?"

"Too right!"

"So we were wondering if you, er…" At this point, Gail realised that she was not sure of Dave's name. Dave sensed her discomfort.

"Gilbert," he chirped.

"Ah, Gilbert, yes, thank you; …and your wife would like to change places with us…"

"My name's Susan and, by the way, my husband's name is actually Dave," Susan interjected apologetically.

Gail had refrained from mentioning the restricted leg room in the front seats but as Dave and Susan were rather shorter in stature than she and Peter, she didn't think it would be much of a problem for them. And for Dave, there were some obvious advantages to being in the front seat. There was no chance, of course, that he could partake of any more prohibited liquor, but he figured that Miranda and Susan would be watching him so closely wherever he sat that it wouldn't really make much difference. On the other hand, if they sat at the front, they could look out of the front window, not that the scenery was anything special at the moment but it could improve, it would be easier to have a chat with their newly discovered companions, Frank and Joyce, across the aisle and, above all, it could provide him with an opportunity to seek retribution by being able to embarrass and provoke Miranda from close quarters. He smiled graciously at Gail.

"How nice and what a generous offer, er…"

"Oh, er, Gail."

"Then we accept your offer, Gail. I can be that much closer to my favourite tour guide! She'll be able to keep a closer eye on me!"

By now, Tony had signalled that the broken bottle and its contents had been cleared up and people began to climb back on board. With much feigned coughing and a surfeit of gesticulation, Dave and Susan made something of a contrived show of taking their seats at the front, with Peter and Gail now sitting behind them. As usual, Frank was not slow to comment.

"Hello, has teacher put you in the front row to keep an eye on you?"

Dave's fertile, if juvenile, imagination was already relishing the unexpected opportunities for mischief that being in the front seat might afford.

"Yes, I've been a naughty boy apparently. You never know, I might get a good spanking later!"

He winked at Frank and stared at the back of Miranda's head hoping for a reaction but, for the time being at least, there was no response.

Behind Dave, Peter turned round in his seat and spoke, a little diffidently, to Trevor and Julia.

"Excuse me. Sorry to bother you. Would you mind if I reclined my seat a bit? I don't want to cause a problem, or another accident."

Trevor had been surprised, of course, to see Peter and Gail sit down immediately in front of them but he had no quarrel with what was a polite and reasonable enquiry.

"No, no. Not at all," he said, waving his arm dismissively.

With some trepidation, Peter reached for the lever beside his seat, applied gentle pressure and the seat reclined slowly and smoothly, just as it was intended to do. Peter smiled with relief and settled back to rest as their journey continued through the flat Dutch hinterland.

★ ★ ★

The windmills of Kinderdijk are a favourite destination for some European coach operators. They offer a convenient stopping point on the way north to Amsterdam, there are toilet and refreshment facilities and, particularly in the height of summer when their sales turn, the nineteen windmills, lining both banks of the canal, are an impressive sight. They are also free.

As members of the coach party disembarked, there was a certain predictability about their behaviour. Dave and Susan headed, at some speed, towards the café, while Frank, despite his recent comfort break, found himself being propelled by Joyce into the public toilet. Barbara and Jason set off along the canal-side path, hand in hand, at a brisk pace. Peter and Gail, accompanied of course by Fred, ambled along more sedately.

Brian and Valerie were especially captivated by the sight of the ancient windmills, lit by bright, clear sunlight, with their sales serenely turning, as they stood like gentle sentinels along the tranquil reed-lined canal. Sadly, they had no working camera to record the scene and were volubly reflecting on their ill fortune when Peter and Gail strolled past. Peter stopped.

"Look, I hope you don't think we're eavesdropping, but we couldn't help overhearing. We always bring a spare camera with us on holiday, just in case we lose one or it breaks." He paused momentarily, realising that he was sounding a bit smug at Valerie and Brian's expense, but there was no response, so he continued.

"So, if it helps, we can dig it out of our suitcase at the hotel this evening and you are welcome to borrow it until you can find yourself a new one."

Valerie smiled, unusually warmly, and tilted her head flirtatiously to one side.

"That's very kind of you," she gushed. "But, hopefully we can pick one up in Amsterdam tomorrow. But thanks anyway."

"OK, but if you change your mind…"

Smiling, Gail led him gently away. When they were out of earshot, she spoke quietly to him.

"Don't think you can avoid taking pictures of Fred by giving our cameras away," she chided good-naturedly. "And don't think I didn't notice how she looked at you!"

Peter smiled. Gail's vivid imagination now had both Carol, their next-door neighbour and Valerie, a complete stranger, fancying him. "Well, don't forget I'm competing with Fred for your affections now," he teased as Gail administered a playful thump.

Brian and Valerie, meanwhile, decided to stop at the small souvenir shop on their way back to the coach, so that they could at least purchase a couple of postcards as some kind of photographic memento of their visit.

★ ★ ★

For the second consecutive occasion, every member of the touring party arrived back at the coach at the appointed time. This augured well for the rest of the tour. Miranda, wearing her ubiquitous sunglasses, greeted most of them warmly enough, although she directed a more forced and frosty smile at Dave, Susan, Brian and Valerie.

Once back on the road, the coach travelled smoothly and uneventfully north, in heavy but free-flowing traffic – lighter on a Sunday than during the rest of the week – on its way to Amsterdam. For many of the passengers, this soporific leg of the journey afforded them an opportunity to doze, fitfully in most cases, although Peter slipped into a deeper sleep. The two elderly ladies launched into a lengthy discussion about the merits of wheelie bins and the problems of fortnightly rubbish collections, Barbara and Jason found something to giggle about, while others gazed out of the window at nothing in particular, or read a book or a magazine. Miranda busied herself plying her clients with refreshments – Dave sensibly refused – until they began to get close to their overnight hotel. Then she returned to her seat and went into her well-rehearsed microphonic routine.

"We'll shortly be arriving at our hotel. This evening, dinner will be at 6.30. For those of you joining us on the optional excursion to Amsterdam's Red Light District, we will be leaving at 8 o'clock. Tomorrow morning, breakfast will be at 7.45 and we will leave the hotel at 8.30. Please make sure your luggage is outside your room when you go down to breakfast at 7.45."

The words "Red Light District" had set Barbara and Jason off into another paroxysm of giggling and the rest of Miranda's announcement was lost on Frank. He turned and stared at them with a look of mock disapproval.

"Hey, no hanky-panky in the Red Light District! You two need to get a good night's sleep so you're not late again tomorrow morning. And don't forget to set your alarm!"

Jason stopped giggling long enough to reply briefly, "Don't worry. I'm expecting to be up quite early," before collapsing into giggles again.

★ ★ ★

The Matjes Hotel, at the end of a narrow, meandering lane in an attractive, traditional Dutch village by the edge of the water, was part of the "Graag Gedaan" chain of hotels. It was a modern building, largely lacking in genuine character, although a small architectural concession made to local building styles had resulted in the entrance lobby having a high gabled roof, and there were mock red and white painted shutters, nailed to the walls, either side of the wood-framed windows along the symmetrical front of the building. The hotel was run efficiently enough and the rooms were clean and well-decorated, though with few characteristics that would distinguish them from the rooms in any other "Graag Gedaan" hotel, or similar middle-range city hotels in other parts of the country.

Tony had to kick the front door of the coach to open it and, as the passengers began to disembark, Miranda was dutifully positioned to help them off. Valerie stopped to have a word with her.

"Er, excuse me."

"Yes," replied Miranda, reacting a little stiffly before remembering, with a cold shudder, the reason why she had to be pleasant to Valerie and Brian, at which point her tone became more conciliatory.

"Yes, Mrs Wood."

"Sorry to bother you again. We just wanted to ask if we will have enough time to buy a new camera and watch in Amsterdam tomorrow, what with all the organised activities and everything?"

"Yes, of course, if you want to – you'll probably have a couple of hours or so of free time."

"And we'll need some more money, I'm afraid, so will the hotel here be able to cash a travellers' cheque?"

Miranda's tone became a little more brusque.

"Should be no problem, but you'll have to ask at reception, I'm afraid."

"Oh, OK. Thanks."

★ ★ ★

After an ample but unspectacular meal, consumed in an ample but unspectacular dining room, which included heavily salted pea soup followed by heavily salted chicken cutlets, those members of the party who had signed up for the optional excursion to Amsterdam's Red Light District assembled outside the hotel entrance, on a clear, twilight evening. Nigel watched them assemble, a little ruefully, from the hotel lounge, where his mother had positioned herself, with a large cup of coffee, in order to get a good view of the many comings and goings.

Feeling uncomfortably guilty about participating in the evening's activity, Frank glanced around the dimly-lit car park to see who else was coming on the excursion. Barbara and Jason were there of course, clinging closely to each other in a way that Frank found faintly distasteful. Surprisingly, the two elderly ladies were there, although they had been chatting when Miranda had been explaining the purpose of the evening and thought they were going into Amsterdam for some late night shopping. They were to experience window-shopping of a very different kind. Equally surprisingly, Frank could see no sign of Dave and Susan.

The group of 20 or so was introduced to the guide for the evening, a tall, bespectacled, academic-looking young man called Jacob, who seemed far too earnest and innocent to be undertaking such a task. As the evening wore on, however, it became increasingly clear that, somehow, he had managed to acquire an exhaustive knowledge of his subject, which he conveyed in a pleasantly relaxed and non-salacious manner.

The coach journey from the hotel took about half an hour before Tony pulled up close to Amsterdam's famous central station and the tour on foot began. Jacob led the group confidently through a confusing maze of side streets and alongside narrow canals, where the lights of the city shimmered and reflected in the water, until he reached the heart of the Red Light District, where ladies of a bewildering variety of nationality, age and size flaunted themselves at the brightly lit windows of the tall, narrow buildings that lined the canals, while the cosmopolitan passers-by went about their business, whatever that was. From time to time, Jacob would stop, gather his group around him and point out a sight of particular interest, like an old church or the convent located at the heart of the district, or a museum of erotica, or to explain the "specialities" on offer in that particular part of the district.

Barbara and Jason, energetically following Jacob's every step and hanging on his every word, found the whole experience both enthralling and enlightening and were animatedly pointing at, and occasionally commenting upon, the plethora of exotic sights arrayed before them. Frank, by contrast, had been strangely subdued for much of the tour. For all his faults, he had remained scrupulously faithful to Joyce throughout their long, conventional marriage, and he felt distinctly uncomfortable in this hedonistic and Bohemian environment. He was far from home and very much out of his element. At length, he turned to Joyce and spoke.

"Well, this is certainly something you don't see in Eastbourne!"

"I should hope not," Joyce replied, trying to sound prudish in a way that Frank would expect and disguising just how much she was enjoying yet another new experience. "The most exciting thing you've ever done in Eastbourne is legging it when you see the deckchair attendant coming."

After some vacillation, Peter and Gail had decided to go on the trip, despite Peter's indisposition, both figuring that an outing like this would do him more good than sitting around in the hotel feeling sorry for himself. On several occasions, as they took in the spectacle, they found themselves standing next to Brian and Valerie, a more than coincidental circumstance that Gail thought Valerie might be orchestrating. Brian spent much of his time staring wide-eyed and open-mouthed, prompting Valerie to suggest that it might be a good idea if, once in a while, he blinked. Like Joyce, she had tried to sound suitably disapproving, not wanting to reveal to Brian how exhilarated, almost liberated, she felt in this vibrant kind of environment.

Deliberately moving slightly apart from the crowd and steering Peter well away from Valerie, Gail smiled her easy smile and squeezed his hand.

"So, has all of this made you feel any better?" she enquired, quietly.

"Do you know I'm not sure that it has? To tell you the truth, I am a bit worried about all those scantily clad young ladies sitting behind draughty windows with only the pale glow of a red light to keep them warm. They might catch cold as well!"

Gail had always enjoyed Peter's sense of the absurd. Laughing, she joined him in his fantasy world.

"You'd think they could afford to buy some curtains and some warm blankets if nothing else! Do you think we should have brought Fred?"

"Oh, no; I think it might have shocked him! Mind you, a picture of him with this lot in the background would have livened up Carol's nursery school wall no end!"

* * *

Trevor and Julia had decided not to go to the Red Light District. Julia had been particularly sensitive about dalliances and deviations of a sexual nature ever since Geoff began to go astray and she had been primly disinterested in the excursion from the first moment it was announced. Trevor, meanwhile, still fostered hopes of a quiet romantic evening, followed by an early night.

They had a leisurely drink in the bar, partly to quench the thirst that they had developed over dinner, and then, in mellow and tranquil mood, returned to their room. Julia sat on the bed looking wistful. It was a look – one of innocent vulnerability – that Trevor couldn't resist and, whenever she looked wistful, as she often did, his instinct was always to comfort her. So he sat down beside her and placed his arm protectively around her thin shoulders, feeling a tense rigidity in her that did not augur well. He tried to look into her hazel eyes but she kept staring thoughtfully into the middle distance. His plan for a romantic seduction was in need of some rekindling.

"Well, this is nice isn't it?" he ventured. "Alone together in a hotel bedroom in one of the great romantic capital cities of the world."

He paused while he waited for a reply but Julia seemed not to hear a word he said. He tried again.

"The whole evening ahead of us. Just you and me."

He paused again and playfully patted the bed, but there was still no reaction from Julia. He tried again.

"Nice comfortable bed. A little bit of alcohol inside us – not too much, of course. Very relaxing, this, isn't it?"

Throughout all of Trevor's unsubtle but persistent wooing, Julia had continued to stare, unblinking, into the middle distance apparently oblivious to his presence. Now, at last, she responded.

"I think I'd feel more relaxed if I knew everything was alright at home."

Trevor's careful plans for a romantic evening were unravelling. Now, he was angry. Exasperated, he stood up, ran his hand over his hair and paced up and down.

"Oh, for God's sake not again," he exploded. "Right… right. You phone home if you must but make it quick. I'm going to take a shower."

Julia went to say something but Trevor had already stormed into the bathroom and slammed the door behind him. After a momentary hesitation, and with a heavy sigh, she picked up the phone and dialled home. She waited for what seemed like an eternity before Mark answered, although he was, of course, expecting the call and was well prepared.

"Hello, Mark, it's me," Julia began.

"Oh, hi, Mum!"

"I just thought I'd telephone to see how you were."

"Mum, I'm cool and you know you don't need to keep phoning me."

"No, no, I know. But I worry about you."

"No need to, Mum. I'm fine and before you ask, I'm eating well and everything in the house is fine."

"And how's Rosie?"

"Ah, well, I am sure she's OK, but tell me, Mum, do cats get hay fever?"

"I don't think so. Why?"

"Well, it's just that she's been sneezing a lot today and her eyes are watery."

"Omigod, she's got cat flu!" Julia screamed down the phone. Her vocal explosion brought Trevor running, naked, from the bathroom.

"What the hell is wrong?" Trevor demanded.

Julia looked anxiously up at him before speaking again to Mark.

"Hang, on a minute, Mark." She placed her hand over the receiver and spoke agitatedly to Trevor. "Trevor, it sounds as though Rosie's got cat flu!"

"Hasn't she been vaccinated?"

"Yes. but……"

Still angry, Trevor snatched the phone out of Julia's hand and bellowed into it.

"Hello, Mark, Trevor here. Look, first thing in the morning, if she's no better, take her to the vet. Don't worry about the bill; I'll pay it when we get back. Just do it!"

Trevor slammed the phone down and, suddenly feeling enervated, slumped onto the bed. After a few moments strained silence, he got up, still naked, and began to pace up and down the room. Though still simmering with rage, he knew he needed to collect his thoughts before he said something that would only make matters worse. He was all too aware of Julia's fiery temper and he could sense that she too was simmering. He was right. Aggrieved and distressed by what she perceived to be Trevor's insensitive attitude, she would have thrown something hard at him if only there was something other than a pillow to hand. Instead, she sniffed a couple of times and turned to face Trevor. She was shaking with emotion.

"You didn't have to do that, you know. Slam down the phone like that. I hadn't finished talking to Mark. Anyway, it's not his fault; he's only looking after things."

Trevor had continued to pace the room, deep in thought. He raised a hand in defensive acknowledgement.

"Yes, yes I know and I'm sorry. I'm sure he'll cope. It's just that I so wanted us to have a nice romantic evening."

"Well you can forget that. I doubt I'll sleep tonight for worrying about Rosie."

"Oh good!" Trevor replied with more than a hint of sarcasm in his voice. "In that case, I think I'll go back down to the bar for half an hour."

He opened the door and had stepped angrily into the corridor before the realisation that he was still naked dawned. It was at that moment that Miranda happened to be walking along the corridor towards her room. She had taken the evening off, leaving the coach party in the hands of Tony and Jacob and was looking forward to a quiet hour or two in her room catching up on her paperwork and reading a few more pages of the novel that she had brought with her. Suddenly confronted by a totally naked

Trevor rushing out into the corridor, her first instinct was to scream but there seemed to be something very fragile and vulnerable about Trevor standing there, embarrassed, not knowing quite what to say or where to put his hands.

"Is everything OK?" she heard herself saying, somewhat absurdly.

"Y-y-y yes thanks," Trevor stuttered before rushing back into his room and slamming the door.

Standing alone in the middle of the now deserted corridor, Miranda found herself staring at the door that had just slammed shut, half-hoping that Trevor might emerge again. But he didn't, of course, so Miranda just smiled and retreated quietly to her room.

Mark, meanwhile, had put the phone down and was smiling complacently. The plan seemed to be working. He looked across at Rosie who was sitting quietly and contentedly, if a little drowsily, on the chair next to him and stroked her affectionately.

"Promise you won't tell anyone I lied about you and that you haven't been sneezing!" he said, smugly.

* * *

Dave and Susan had also decided not to go the Red Light District. For all Dave's "alpha male" bravado and priapic behaviour, his performance in the bedroom had been virtually non-existent for some time. Years of over-indulgence, especially where alcohol was concerned, a diminishing libido and the onset of middle age had badly affected his sexual performance. Susan was surprisingly tolerant of his bedroom failings; perhaps, secretly relieved. Never over-blessed with finesse, Dave's sexual prowess, even in his prime, owed more to enthusiasm than skill and Susan felt no great sense of deprivation when impotence set in. Indeed, if the uncomfortable truth be told – and Susan herself was too ashamed to admit it – she was far more attracted to the likes of Miranda and Barbara than to Dave or any of the other assorted specimens of manhood that assembled on the coach each day. All in all, then, neither felt that a visit to the Red

Light district would be a good idea. While it was unlikely to rekindle Dave's passion – if anything, it was more likely to be a sad reminder of pleasures past – there was a real risk that the sight of so much nubile and available female flesh might kindle, in Susan, the kind of passion that she would, on the whole, prefer to keep suppressed.

Instead, they put on their coats and went for a brief walk. They found a pleasant, wide path that ran out of the village and along the side of the lake, but with the light beginning to fade and groups of aggressive midges hovering menacingly, they returned hastily to the hotel and adjourned to the bar. The bar area had been decorated and furnished in an attempt to create some synthetic local character. There were solid wooden tables, benches and stools in cosy alcoves with sepia prints and photographs hanging from the light panelled walls.

Dave and Susan found a vacant table in a small alcove, from which Dave was able to indulge rigorously in his current favourite pastime, sampling the extensive range of Dutch beers on offer. He had been in the bar for some while, working his way through the plentiful choice of local brews with customary enthusiasm, and was showing clear signs of inebriation when Frank and Joyce arrived back from their evening expedition. Frank had no trouble spotting Dave at the bar, leaning on it heavily for support, while loudly ordering more drinks.

"Ah, I thought I might find you in here…"

"Well, as I'm not allowed to drink on the coach," Dave slurred across the bar, "I thought I'd better pack a few away this evening. So what are you having?"

"A beer and a sweet sherry if that's alright. Our throats have been dry ever since dinner."

Frank and Joyce sat down beside Susan on a couple of rickety, uncomfortable wooden stools.

"So does the Red Light District hold no appeal for you two?" Joyce ventured.

Susan exchanged a brief, nervous glance with Dave who was still at the bar.

"Not with the wife here!" he replied, before turning to the

barman to order the drinks for Frank and Joyce.

"Wrong answer, Dave!" Susan called back to him. Dave took a couple of slightly unsteady steps towards their table while he waited for the drinks to be poured. He was gesturing wildly with his hands.

"What I meant to say of course is who needs to go to the Red Light District when you have a wife as beautiful, as sexy, as…"

"Alright, don't overdo it." Susan turned to Frank and Joyce. "Did you two enjoy the tour?"

Frank looked faintly embarrassed.

"It was quite revealing, if you get my drift, but, all in all, it was a bit disappointing really. No sign of the famed red flannelette or whalebone anywhere."

Dave paid for the drinks, brought them unsteadily across to the table and sat down heavily on the wooden bench, next to Susan.

"Never mind; maybe a drink or two will make you feel better!"

"Ironic, isn't it?" Joyce interjected, now beginning to feel more relaxed in Dave and Susan's brash company. "Just about the first time that Frank has got his camcorder to work properly and our guide advised us that we shouldn't do any filming. Apparently if he filmed any of the girls at the windows, there was a chance that Frank and his camcorder could both have ended up in the canal."

"Never mind!" Frank observed, with misplaced confidence. "I've the got the hang of it now. There'll be no more mistakes from now on."

★ ★ ★

In Peter and Gail's room, Peter had slumped wearily onto the bed and closed his eyes. Although he had rallied, briefly, a couple of times during the day, his cold had taken more of a hold now, as it often did in the evening, and he was starting to feel the effects of a busy schedule. A look of concern spread across Gail's normally serene face. She leaned over Peter and gently stroked his forehead.

"How are you feeling now?"

Peter shook his head and pulled a face.

"Oh, you know. Not too great, I'm afraid. I'm sorry I've not been firing on all cylinders. We both needed this holiday and I don't want to spoil it."

"Don't worry about it. You didn't do it deliberately. Let's just concentrate on getting you better soon so you can enjoy the rest of the holiday. I took the precaution of bringing some cold remedies from home. They're the ones that Doctor Penfold normally recommends. Why don't you take something now and with a bit of luck you'll have a better night and feel OK in the morning?"

"Mmm. I'll try. Unfortunately, I think we're next door to the Brummie Bonkers again. Heaven only knows what they'll get up to after what they've seen this evening. They were bad enough before."

"Well whatever they do, let's hope they do it quietly. In any case, they're bound to run out of steam sooner or later."

★ ★ ★

Peter was right to be concerned. On returning with indecent haste to their room, Jason and Barbara had planned to act out a fantasy based on what they had witnessed earlier. Wearing only a skimpy black, sequined bra and matching thong, purchased from the sex shop, Barbara had perched seductively on an upholstered round stool in front of the dressing table, with her sleek, dark hair trailing alluringly over her shoulders and the dressing table lamp providing subtle back lighting. She crossed her legs slowly, thrust her bosom out as provocatively as she could and tried her best to pout siren-like at Jason. He was sitting on the bed, enraptured by Barbara's enticing performance, and holding a handful of Euro notes. He held up some of the notes and shouted "thirty Euros" across the room. Trying hard to suppress her desire to laugh at the preposterousness of the situation, Barbara did her best to appear disdainful.

"Thirty Euros? I wouldn't even shake your hand for thirty Euros, let alone anything else."

"Forty Euros!"

"Do me a favour. What do you take me for?"

"Not forty Euros, obviously. How about fifty?"

"Well, I might be able to do something for fifty!"

Jason was now in a state of high excitement, as was only too evident from the growing bulge in his trousers. He stood up and shouted "sixty" across the room. Barbara was silent for a moment or two while Jason hopped expectantly from one foot to the other.

"Sixty and some chocolates!"

"It's a deal!"

"C'mon, let's see the colour of your money!"

Jason hastily counted out sixty Euros and laid the notes on the bed.

"Now let's see the quality of the goods!" he shouted impatiently.

Slowly and sinuously, Barbara removed her bra, paraded over to the bed, as seductively as she could, leapt onto Jason, pushing him backwards onto the bed and scattering the Euros onto the floor, and began to unzip his trousers.

★ ★ ★

In the hotel bar, Frank carefully finished his single drink, making sure that he had completely drained his glass, and placed it firmly and neatly on the solid wooden table in front of him. It was his turn to buy the drinks. He looked at his watch.

"Well, we're going to have to love you and leave you now, I'm afraid; another bloody early start in the morning!"

Across the table, Susan also checked her watch.

"Yes, I think I'm going to turn in as well," she said, before downing the last of her vodka and tonic and placing her glass even more firmly, but far less neatly, on the table.

She rose ceremoniously from the bench, picked up their room key from the table, bade goodnight to Frank and Joyce and began to walk off. When she was halfway to the lift, she turned around to see Dave still sitting down, smiling vacantly at nothing in particular and rocking slightly from side to side.

"So are you coming, Dave?" she called, although her hectoring tone rather implied that it was more of an order than a question. Dave looked vaguely in Susan's direction, trying, but failing, to get her into clear focus.

"Hang on, I haven't finished yet."

"Well, come up when you're ready but don't be too long. You've had more than enough to drink already and that stuff's strong."

"I'll be alright, don't nag. I'll be up in a minute."

He waved a friendly arm in the general direction of Frank and Joyce who were standing, waiting for the lift, and started to drink from his half-full glass.

★ ★ ★

In their room, Brian and Valerie had embarked upon another of their increasingly frequent and lengthy silences, neither party knowing quite what to say, each sitting demurely on their own bed. For a while, Valerie reflected to herself, she had rather enjoyed the Red Light District. There was an edge to the place, a raw excitement that she missed, a kind of tense, uncertain relationship between the girls and the punters that she empathised with. Indeed, she had been quite aroused, for a time, by some of the sights she had witnessed, but that was before the constantly milling crowds, the incessant noise and the glaringly bright lights began to make her head ache. Eventually she kicked off her elegant, but not especially comfortable shoes, stood up and strolled across the room towards the window. She stared out at the unremitting blackness of the lake.

"Well, that trip was certainly an eye-opener!"

"It certainly was," Brian responded emphatically before slipping back into thoughtful silence. Eventually, he spoke again.

"Do you know what I fancy after all that?"

Maybe if he had posed that question an hour or so ago,

Valerie reflected, he might have been surprised at her response, but now her feet were throbbing almost as much as her head. She turned sharply towards Brian.

"You can forget that!"

"No, no – I fancy a good old fashioned British cup of tea."

Valerie's mood lightened.

"Well, we did bring our kettle – shall we have a brew up?"

"Excellent idea!"

With fresh surge of energy, they strode briskly across to their respective suitcases, which were leaning against the wall by the door, lifted them onto their respective beds and started to rummage. When Valerie rummaged, she delved gently into the contents of her suitcase, using nothing much more than her carefully manicured fingertips, and felt around, cautiously and tentatively. When Brian rummaged, he grabbed each item and tossed it onto the floor until he found the one he was looking for. After a few moments of dainty and superficial rummaging, Valerie produced the plug adaptor from her suitcase and held it aloft triumphantly. Almost immediately, Brian produced the kettle from his now virtually empty suitcase and held that aloft. They both laughed as the tribulations of the day, for the moment at least, became a distant memory.

Having found the kettle, their next task was to locate a socket. They searched their room thoroughly; it didn't take them long. They looked behind the beds and beneath the dressing table but to no avail. At one point, Brian tried to unplug the television but it seemed somehow to be locked into place.

"There must be a bloody socket somewhere," he said in frustration. "How the hell do they vacuum the room?"

"There's not one that I can see!" Valerie confirmed, with a heavy sigh, her earlier glacial attitude now somewhat thawed by the prospect of a cup of tea.

In desperation, Brian wandered into the bathroom. Almost immediately, there was a cry of triumph.

"Aha, found one!"

"Well done. I'll be right there."

Valerie gathered up the kettle and adaptor and headed purposefully towards the bathroom.

* * *

The hotel bar had emptied rapidly during the last few minutes and Dave found himself almost alone. He looked around, rather morosely, tried, with some difficulty, to study his watch and, slowly and reluctantly, drained his glass.

After a few moments of almost comatose inactivity, he rose unsteadily to his feet, swayed slightly, tried to walk, felt a little dizzy and had to lean heavily on the table for support. While trying to recover his balance and clear his muzzy head, he noticed his waterproof, zip-up jacket, which he had worn when he and Susan had gone outside for their brief walk, lying on the floor beneath the bench that he had been sitting on. Cautiously removing one hand from the table, he tried to reach his jacket, but it was too far away. Still clinging onto the edge of the table firmly with one hand, he stretched out a leg and just managed to drag the jacket towards him with his foot, but he still needed to bend down to retrieve it. An easy enough manoeuvre most of the time, it proved to be surprisingly challenging to Dave in his present condition and, as he carefully bent down, his dizziness returned and he fell heavily to the floor, striking his cheekbone on the edge of the bench as he fell.

The bar steward had been watching Dave's performance, from a safe distance, with a mixture of anxiety and amusement. The hotel management adopted a fairly tolerant attitude towards guests who over-imbibed as long as they could pay for their drinks and didn't get abusive or violent, so he had not felt it necessary to intervene. But as soon as Dave fell, he had no choice but to rush to his aid. Dave, meanwhile, had hauled himself slowly and precariously upright, clutching his jacket in one hand and the edge of the table in the other. After rubbing his cheekbone thoughtfully, he affably assured the steward that he was fine, that he didn't need any help and that he was sorry for his momentary and inexplicable loss of balance.

While the steward made his way back to the bar, Dave decided that, as he had gone to all the trouble of retrieving his jacket from the floor, he ought at least to put it on. So he steadied himself by leaning his sturdy frame against the table, held his jacket aloft in his left hand, quickly released his right hand from the table and tried to force it rapidly into the armhole. After two or three increasingly shambolic attempts, he finally succeeded in putting his right arm into the left sleeve. Deciding, at this juncture, to abandon the project, he withdrew his arm, draped his jacket uncertainly over his shoulder and, with a cheery wave in the general direction of the bar steward, meandered off vaguely towards the lift.

It took him a minute or two to locate the lift, and a further minute or two to press the button with sufficient force to summon it. When the lift finally arrived, he stepped clumsily inside, but, as the door closed firmly behind him, he was gripped by a sudden panic. Susan had gone off with the key and, in his befuddled state, he couldn't remember his room number, or, for that matter, the floor his room was on. There was only one course of action he could take – he would have to ask the receptionist for assistance. He stared blankly at the impressive panel of buttons inside the lift and, after a few moments deliberation, selected one, more or less at random, and pressed it in the hope that it would open the door. It didn't. Instead, the lift climbed smoothly and without interruption straight to the top floor.

Several minutes elapsed, with the lift unexpectedly stopping at several different floors – some more than once. At each stop, Dave got out of the lift, looked around him with gathering confusion and stumbled back inside before he finally re-emerged from the lift on the ground floor and, looking still more befuddled, weaved his way over to the Reception Desk. The receptionist, a serious-looking, bespectacled young lady, eyed him with a mixture of curiosity and ill-concealed disdain as he leaned heavily against the desk, burped loudly and leered at her. He went to speak but suddenly found that he was having the greatest difficulty articulating even the simplest of words.

"Ah, I wonder if you can… er… if you can… you know. The thing is… the thing is… the missus has gone off with the er…

wotsit for the door and er... I can't, you know, er... remember what room I'm in..."

"Ah, I see," the receptionist replied calmly, reaching beneath the desk and producing a printed list. "You're with the Conn Tours coach party?"

"Am I? Ah, er... yes, I think I am. Tonn Cours, yes that's right. How did you, er... know?"

"I was here when you arrived. What is your name?"

"Ah, er... Dave! Or is it Gilbert?"

"No, no, sir. Your last name."

"Ah, er... let me think... ah, yes, Fuller!"

The receptionist looked down the list, turning her head slightly away in order to avoid inhaling the toxic fumes from Dave's breath.

"Mr and Mrs Fuller. You are in Room 229, second floor."

"Room 992. Thank you mery vuch."

Dave took a couple of unsteady steps and then turned and went back to the desk.

"I don't suppose you could er... wotsit... er write it down for me, could you?"

"Certainly, sir." The receptionist produced a compliments slip, wrote the room number on it and handed it to Dave who stuffed it casually, and not very securely, into the pocket of his casual and not very secure trousers.

Eventually, and following another unexpected trip to the top floor, Dave arrived on the second floor. The lift opened into a slight alcove with no direct view of the corridor. Slightly disorientated by this, Dave staggered uncertainly out of the lift, tripping forward as he did so. The piece of paper with his room number on detached itself from his pocket and floated gracefully to the floor. As he stooped to pick it up, his jacket, which had been draped insecurely over one shoulder, also dropped to the ground. Feeling very dizzy again, he bent down to retrieve both items, lost his tenuous balance and dropped onto all fours in the alcove.

As he struggled to regain his balance and clear his head, he heard a door creak open a little way along the corridor. Thinking it might be Susan and anxious not to draw attention to himself in his present predicament, he peered furtively around the edge of the alcove and saw Miranda creeping stealthily out into the corridor. She looked nervously in both directions and, seeing nobody around, scuttled to the adjoining room and knocked on the door. After a moment or two, the door opened a fraction and, with another furtive look around, she dashed inside.

Watching the little scenario unnoticed, Dave smiled knowingly to himself. Using the wall for essential support, he slowly picked himself up and began to walk erratically down the corridor in what he hoped was the direction of his room.

Valerie, meanwhile, had filled the kettle from the washbasin tap, attached the adaptor to the plug and inserted the adaptor into the socket. She switched on the kettle. Immediately there was a flash, a loud bang and all the lights went out.

The corridor was plunged into sudden and total darkness. Dave stood motionless – or as near to motionless as he could manage in his inebriated state – for a moment. Leaning against the wall for support, he heard a muffled scream coming from a nearby room. He waited for a moment or two, but as the lights showed no immediate sign of coming back on, he decided to stumble his way towards his room. Unfortunately, in the sudden blackness, and with less than total control of his senses, he had become disorientated again, and there was a loud thump followed by a groan, as he walked into the opposite wall, followed by another thump and another groan as he fell heavily to the floor.

★ ★ ★

In a nearby room, in total darkness, two bodies were moving about under the duvet.

"Oooh, what are you doing?" a muffled female voice asked.

"Trying to find my torch," a male voice replied.

"Well you won't find it down there… mind you there is something here…"

"No, no, not that… Oh, I don't know though!"

★ ★ ★

126

CHAPTER 4

Misbehaving

It was a glorious, fresh, clear morning as the sun's early rays glinted on the tranquil, seemingly endless waters of the lake. For the fortunate ones whose rooms overlooked the water, it was a spectacular and exhilarating start to the day. Less spectacular and exhilarating was the hotel breakfast, although the food was wholesome and plentiful enough, even if it didn't quite reach gourmet standards.

In order to reach the breakfast room, situated at the back of the hotel, with large windows looking out over the lake, guests had to file their way past the reception desk. The more keenly observant amongst them – not that there were many at such an early hour – would have noticed Miranda, already sporting her trademark sunglasses on her head, in animated discussion with the morning receptionist, a plump, fair-haired woman with sharp features and piercing blue eyes.

For obvious reasons, Brian and Valerie wanted to keep a particularly low profile this morning and did their best to sidle past the reception desk unnoticed. But Brian wasn't designed for stealthy, streamlined sidling and, as he clattered into an empty chair, Miranda turned round, spotted them and stepped neatly in front of them. Her stance – legs apart and arms folded – was confrontational and her mood assertive.

"Ah, Mr and Mrs Wood; just a moment, if I may! The receptionist here tells me that they have traced the source of last night's blackout to your room. She thinks it was probably a faulty appliance, like a hairdryer perhaps, or a razor possibly, or a kettle, maybe?"

Though often deeply critical in private of her husband's frequent hapless escapades, Valerie was normally fiercely loyal in public and leapt immediately to his defence. "I really don't know…" she began, before Brian, affronted by Miranda's accusation, interrupted.

"There's nothing wrong with our kettle. We've used it plenty of times before. If you ask me, there's something wrong with the electrics in this…"

Miranda was in no mood for any prevarication.

"May I draw your attention," she interjected, "to paragraph 25 on page 73 of your holiday brochure which specifically states that you should not use electrical appliances like kettles…"

"Well, like I say, we've used our kettle plenty of times before and we've never had a problem."

An uncomfortable and prolonged silence followed, with Miranda and Brian eye-balling each other, rather like two punch-shy boxers circling each other, probing for a weakness. As Valerie closed ranks with her husband, it was Miranda who broke the impasse. She narrowed her eyes and almost spat the words at Brian.

"You know, you are beginning to try my patience."

Another intransigent silence followed before Brian, never very good at confrontation, decided on a change of tactics. He lowered his voice into what he hoped was a calm, conciliatory tone.

"Then, I'm very sorry and I hope we don't try your patience any more but, of course, we don't want your little secret getting out, do we?"

Miranda's assertive pose suddenly collapsed. She took a step or two backwards, unfolded her arms, removed her sunglasses from her head and began to fiddle nervously with them.

"Alright, alright. Just, just… try and be a bit more careful in future."

"We'll be model holiday-makers from now on, I promise!" Valerie assured her calmly, as she pulled Brian away and ushered him into the breakfast room.

★ ★ ★

A good night's sleep had apparently done little to ease the

underlying matrimonial tensions between Trevor and Julia. As they approached the breakfast buffet in a predatory kind of way, Trevor was doing his best to sound understanding and reassuring.

"You know you really must try to stop fretting. I'm sure everything is alright."

Julia smiled wistfully as she pounced on an unsuspecting carton of yoghurt, throttling it in a vice-like grip and placing it, lifeless, onto her plate.

"I know, Trev, but it isn't that easy I'm afraid. I'm trying very hard, you know, but I do worry so about Mark."

"But if he gets into difficulties…"

"What?"

"Er, not that he will, of course, but he does have neighbours and his father close by."

"Oh, yes, I'm sure his father will be a big help. He's had seventeen years to help Mark and he hasn't managed it yet!"

Trevor reached for a bread roll and placed it carefully on the edge of his well-filled plate. He was used to being conciliatory and he was normally pretty good at it – it was a basic requirement of his job – but it was clear that what he assumed were comforting words were not having the desired effect on Julia. He tried again.

"Well, Mark can use a phone – he's proved that, these last two nights – so I am sure everything is fine. Do try and relax."

"That's easy enough for you to say…"

Julia wore a look of melancholy as she poured herself a coffee and they wandered off in search of a vacant table, still deep in discussion.

Behind them, Barbara and Jason had arrived, looking clean, smart, relaxed and a good deal fresher than much of the breakfast, around which several flies were beginning to hover, purposefully. They made a beeline for the well-stocked tables, set out alongside one wall, displaying the multifarious delights of the breakfast buffet, and started to pile their plates high. Behind them, Frank and Joyce arrived – later than usual because Frank had taken a long time to check that both his suitcase and the door to their room were securely locked – and exchanged greetings with them.

Perhaps distracted by the choice of food in front of him, or the fly which had perched on the rim of his glass of fruit juice, and still displaying some of the symptoms of youthful gaucherie, Jason's greeting was less than effusive. Frank seized upon it.

"Hello, you sound a bit tired this morning." He ignored Joyce's sharp nudge and continued. "I suppose you were up late after your trip to Amsterdam! Still at least you won't be late for the coach this morning!"

Free from the stifling attitudinal shackles of her father, and increasingly relishing the freedom that the holiday was bringing, Barbara was quietly savouring the prospect of gently trying to shock some of the apparently more staid and elderly couples that, it seemed, over-populated the tour. From what little she knew, Frank and Joyce seemed ideal candidates.

"No, we sooooo couldn't afford to be late again," Barbara replied cheerfully. "Not after yesterday, so Jason and I were up and at it early this morning." She giggled.

"Very probably," Frank spluttered as he surveyed the buffet selection. He was about to make another ill-chosen remark, when he was distracted by the sight of Susan and Dave slowly entering the room.

Dave had lost his normal ruddy complexion and his characteristic joie de vivre. His face was ashen, he had a small cut on his nose, an angry looking weal on his cheekbone and a colourful bruise above one of his half closed eyes. He seemed to be finding the sun painfully glaring as it streamed into the room through the large windows and held up his hand to shield his eyes. His approach to the buffet area was strangely hesitant – not normal for Dave at any time, but certainly not when food was to be had. Frank, of course, could not resist a comment and, as usual, it was made loudly and with the minimum of sensitivity.

"Good God, what a sight! What happened to you last night?"

Dave winced as Frank's voice came booming across the room at him. To save him further pain, Susan replied on his behalf.

"I beat him up again."

"Does teacher know you've been drinking and got into a fight again?" Frank continued to boom.

Dave held his head in pain and winced again.

"Ssssh. Not so loud for Christ's sake!" he pleaded.

As he approached the buffet tables, he tried to focus on the plates of bread, croissants, preserves, meats, cheeses and eggs spread on the tables in front of him, but the plates seemed to be spinning and a strong feeling of queasiness overcame him. Somehow, he seemed only to notice the fat on the slices of ham, the grease on the croissants and a fly settling on a slice of cheese. He gulped hard and looked away.

"I think I'll just have some coffee this morning," he observed weakly.

"Bloody hell – no breakfast?" exclaimed Susan. "You must be poorly."

"Don't shout. Please don't shout!"

Peter and Gail had now joined the buffet scrum. Peter's eyes were tinged with red, as was the end of his nose, he looked unusually pale and he had a persistent cough. Susan surveyed him critically.

"….and you don't seem much better!"

Peter did his best to smile reassuringly. "I'm fine, it's just a bit of a cold," he croaked weakly. "I'll be better with some food inside me!"

Peter began to fill his plate. Dave watched him, gulped again and turned rapidly away. His hand was shaking as he tried to hold the cup of coffee he had just poured before he shambled away to a distant table.

Meanwhile, Trevor and Julia had located a vacant table, set for four, sat down and were continuing their animated conversation. Trevor was still trying, and largely failing, to be soothing, accommodating and reasonable. For the most part, he had an equable temperament, but, for the moment at least, he didn't seem to be making any progress and was becoming increasingly frustrated.

"Darling, I know it's difficult, but I'm sure lots of others here have left sons or daughters looking after their house and they don't seem worried."

"I'm not sure you understand, do you?"

131

"I'm trying to. Believe me, I'm trying to."

"I mean, for a while, my whole world had fallen apart. It's not easy, you know, coming home and finding your husband in bed with your sister."

"No, I suppose not."

"I lost my husband, I lost my sister…"

"You lost your no claims bonus!"

"You're not taking this seriously, are you?"

"I am, believe me, I am! It's just I'm not sure that ramming your sister's car was altogether a good idea."

"It was parked on our drive while she was upstairs parked on my husband! What did you expect me to do – give it a wax and polish?"

For all her gentle wistfulness, a quality that Trevor loved, he well knew that Julia possessed a vicious temper when sufficiently roused. For the three years that he had known her, he had always tried, therefore, to be a paragon of reasonableness, even if, occasionally, it meant giving in to her. Usually, he found that appeasement worked, but not today, for some reason.

"This holiday wasn't such a good idea, was it?"

Julia reached across the table and grasped Trevor's hand firmly – with much the same tenacity that she had grasped the unfortunate yoghurt a little earlier – as he was about to eat a spoonful of cereal. Although slightly built, she had a grip of iron and, under extreme pressure, the spoon turned in Trevor's hand and a large dollop of soggy cereal fell onto the table. Apparently not noticing what had happened, and without releasing her grip, Julia pressed Trevor's hand down onto the table and directly into the morass of spilt cereal.

"It was a wonderful idea, Trevor," she enthused, still gripping his hand tightly. "So thoughtful, as always – but as I'm trying to explain, Mark and Rosie meant so much to me when everything else was falling apart that I'm kind of missing them now."

"I see," Trevor replied unconvincingly, while trying to extricate his hand from Julia's vice-like grip and wipe the cereal from it with his serviette. After Mark had suffered the same fate on the morning they left, he was learning that it wasn't necessarily a good idea to sit opposite Julia in earnest discussion, when trying, at the same time, to consume a bowl of cereal.

"But I really will try not to worry so much, I promise!" Julia assured him.

Following their unwelcome encounter with Miranda, Brian and Valerie were a little distracted and had taken an unusually long time selecting the ingredients of their respective breakfasts. Looking around for somewhere to sit, Valerie saw two empty chairs at Julia and Trevor's table and two empty chairs opposite Nigel and his mother. She headed, unhesitatingly, for Trevor and Julia's table and they sat themselves down. But, before they had found time for the normal exchange of bland pleasantries, Julia fired a direct question at Valerie.

"I bet you're not worried about anything are you? I bet you're relaxed and enjoying yourselves?"

Valerie was visibly taken aback at this uncomfortably direct and etiquette-breaking approach from Julia and it took her a second or two to consider how she should react. It felt very much as though she and Brian were intruding on some kind of intense, private conversation and she was anxious to avoid saying anything that might cause offence or inflame passions that were already running high.

"I'm not so sure," she replied at last, through a fixed and nervous smile. "We don't seem to be having much luck with anything so far, losing things, breaking things! It's costing us a fortune and Miranda is none too pleased with us."

Suddenly, without warning, Brian thumped the table, causing it to wobble alarmingly, and the crockery to rattle. Julia, Trevor and Valerie all jumped in synchronised alarm.

"That reminds me," he declared forcibly. "I was going to cash some travellers' cheques at reception. I must do that now before we leave, otherwise I won't be able to buy a new watch and camera. Please excuse me." He gulped down a mouthful of coffee, wiped away a small residual trickle from his chin, leaped to his feet and rushed off, leaving Julia, Trevor and Valerie gaping open-mouth at his rapidly departing figure.

★ ★ ★

The receptionist was talking on the phone and half turned away from Brian when he arrived. He had to wait with increasing impatience for a minute or two before she finished her conversation, replaced the telephone and looked directly at Brian with her piercing eyes.

"Oh, er, um, excuse me," Brian stuttered. "Would you be able to cash this travellers' cheque for me?"

"May I have your passport, sir?"

Brian was nonplussed by the receptionist's question.

"I beg your pardon?"

"I need your passport, sir," the receptionist observed with a curious, harsh-sounding mid-Atlantic accent.

Brian found using plastic credit or debit cards on holiday a bit of a liability. On previous excursions, he had lost one and had another chewed up by a malignant cash machine in a small French town. So, he usually made sure that he had enough money with him when he and Valerie travelled abroad, but he always brought some travellers' cheques with him as a precaution. He wasn't used to cashing them, however, but these were unusual and costly circumstances, and, with his mind still reflecting on the earlier discussion with Miranda, he jumped to the wrong conclusion.

"Now look," he protested. "It was an accident with the kettle. You don't have to confiscate my passport, surely?"

The receptionist looked momentarily puzzled while, at the same time, piercing him with her icy blue eyes.

"No sir. I need your passport number before I can cash your cheque. It's standard practice with travellers' cheques."

"Oh, I see. I didn't realise. I'm s..s..sorry."

Greatly relieved and not a little embarrassed by his outburst, Brian reached into the back pocket of his ill-fitting trousers, then into the other back pocket, then into both hip pockets before reality dawned.

"Oh, bloody hell, I think I've packed it in my suitcase. Don't go away!" This time, it was the receptionist's turn to gape open-mouth as Brian receded rapidly into the distance.

★ ★ ★

Outside, the sun was slowly rising in a clear, blue sky, although it was still early morning and the elaborate gabled roof of the hotel entrance was casting a deep, chill shadow over most of the forecourt. As usual, Tony had breakfasted early so that he would have ample time to prepare the coach, to his own exacting standard, for the day's journey, and to load the passengers' luggage. Despite the cool breeze, he had eschewed extra layers of clothing, wearing just a plain short-sleeved cotton shirt, with the company logo prominently emblazoned across the breast pocket, and light perspiration, from the efforts of hauling the luggage on board, was glowing on his forehead. Miranda had temporarily discarded her sunglasses in the deep shade of the car park and was wearing a sturdy dark blue jacket over a crisp, official company blouse. Nevertheless, she was still shivering in the cool, breezy air, as she began to greet the first of the passengers with her well-rehearsed routine. There were still several minutes to go before the scheduled time of departure but some early arrivals, including the two elderly ladies, were already gathering by the coach. Quietly, Tony ushered Miranda away from the group before speaking.

"Did you find out who turned the lights out on us just when things were starting to get interesting last night?"

Miranda looked around furtively, checking that she could not be overheard. She put her sunglasses back on – a habit she seemed to have developed when she wanted to be secretive.

"Yes, we're pretty sure it was our old friends, Mr and Mrs Wood again. Talk about lightning striking twice! Seems like they plugged in a faulty kettle or some such."

"And have you spoken to them?"

"Of course I have."

"And?"

"It's a bit tricky really, isn't it? Mr Wood was quick to remind me that it was he who caught us at it the other night. "Our little secret," he called it. They might be a pain, Tony, but I think we should try and keep them happy, within reason, otherwise they could spill the beans and make life awkward for us both…"

She looked round to see Brian hurrying purposefully towards

her, apparently in a state of some agitation, his un-tucked shirt and un-brushed hair both flapping, in unison, in the breeze. She took a deep breath.

"Look out! Here we go again!" she mumbled before greeting Brian as effusively as she felt able.

"Ah, Mr Wood. I was just telling Tony…"

"I'm very sorry about this," Brian interrupted, breathing heavily, "but do you think I could have my suitcase back for a moment. I've put my passport in it and they need it at reception so that they can cash my cheque."

Tony exchanged glances with Miranda. He could sense her eyebrows were raised, even behind her sunglasses. He made a big point of looking at his watch.

"Look, we really need to be setting off in a minute."

Brian looked across at Miranda and winked knowingly.

"Please?"

Miranda exchanged further glances with Tony.

"Oh alright, Tony will get it for you but please be quick…"

Looking suddenly sullen, Tony went over to the luggage hold, unlocked it and began rummaging inside for Brian's suitcase – fortunately it was easy to find, being of a strangely nondescript shape and tied up with string. As Tony leaned inside the hold, Miranda stood and admired the cloth of his thin trousers tightening over his firm, muscular buttocks. As her thoughts strayed, she noticed Dave ambling slowly past her, looking bruised, grey and unwell. Enjoying Dave's obvious discomfiture, she greeted him with a particularly hearty "good morning". Dave winced again.

"If you say so; only, you will try not to shout into the microphone today, won't you?"

* * *

On board the coach, most of the passengers had quickly settled into their seats. A few were still placing items in the overhead racks and one or two remained outside finishing their essential, post-breakfast cigarettes. Trevor and Julia were still deep in soul-searching conversation. Behind them, the two elderly ladies had begun a conversation, which would continue for some time, about what colour one of them should paint her front room and which D-I-Y shop might have the best and cheapest range of stock. After yesterday's unexpected tour of the seamier and steamier side of Amsterdam's nightlife, they concluded, with great emphasis, that no shade of red should be employed in the re-decoration.

In front of Trevor and Julia, Peter blew his nose with some force and, in front of Peter, Dave fixed his stare resolutely on the front window while groaning quietly to himself. Susan ignored him. She had often had cause to remind Dave of the pointlessness and expense of alcoholic over-indulgence and had little sympathy for him when he failed to heed her "advice". Across the aisle, behind Barbara and Jason, the seats normally occupied by Valerie and Brian were conspicuously empty. Outside the coach, Brian had opened his suitcase, ransacked the contents for his passport and dashed back into the hotel, leaving Valerie to pick up the various items of clothing and travelling ephemera that he had strewn about, re-pack his suitcase more neatly and tie the string around it.

Miranda climbed aboard, removed her sunglasses, reached for the microphone, looked directly at Dave and, with the hint of a supercilious smirk, began to talk into it, conspicuously more loudly than usual.

"Good morning! We are sorry for the slight delay this morning…"

Despite a good night's sleep, an ample breakfast and the reassurance of a recently emptied bladder, Frank's demeanour remained disappointingly but predictably sour. His brow was still deeply furrowed.

"Not again! What is it this time?" he protested loudly. Miranda pretended not to have heard him and continued.

"We are just sorting out a little luggage problem and then we'll be on our way to Amsterdam. A short journey this morning – 30 minutes or so. When we arrive, we'll take you first to a diamond factory, where you can see diamonds being cut and learn a little about the process and then, from there, there is an optional one-hour boat trip around some of the canals of the city. For those of you who do not want to come on the boat trip, there will be plenty of free time this morning…"

Growing increasingly irked at what was, so far, only a minimal delay, Frank interrupted again.

"We are not going to have any free time if we don't leave soon!"

Before Miranda could continue, Brian and Valerie scrambled aboard with Brian clutching his passport and a small wad of Euro notes. They nodded apologetically to those around as they settled into their seats. Tony loaded their suitcases, climbed aboard, kicked the door shut and the coach pulled away.

The lakeside setting of the hotel was picturesque enough – a pleasant change from the usual suburban or commercial location – but the one major disadvantage was that the only access to and from it was a narrow winding lane with an assortment of villagers' houses, a couple of shops and some farm buildings dotted along both sides. The coach had only travelled a short distance when it rounded a bend and encountered a small group of workmen who were industriously repairing the road ahead. A large hole had been drilled and various bits of substantial machinery, including a mechanical digger, a heavy roller, a crane and a couple of vans were positioned in such a way that it was just possible for a car to pass between the road works and the buildings that lined the side of the road, but definitely not a coach.

Tony had no choice but to pull over to the side of the road and stop. Miranda put her sunglasses on, kicked the door open, alighted swiftly from the coach and, trying to look forceful, strode briskly towards the workmen. There followed an animated discussion with much arm waving and gesticulating, and an apparent show of petulance from Miranda as she stood, defiantly, with her hands on her hips.

Sensing that Miranda's limited negotiation skills had failed to achieve any kind of positive outcome, Tony got off the coach and went over to join her. Some further gesturing and arm waving took place before Tony – himself not noted for his negotiation skills – and Miranda headed disconsolately back to the coach.

Aboard the coach, there was some restiveness. Some occupants fidgeted uneasily, others muttered to each other – loudly and continuously in Frank's case – and others – with the exception of Brian – glanced with increasing frustration at their watches. Outside, the sun continued to rise invitingly in a cloudless sky.

Once back on board, Miranda made the unwelcome announcement.

"Unfortunately, as you can see, there are men digging up the road in front of us and we can't get past. They tell us they're going to be here for at least another two or three hours and they cannot, or will not, move to let us past."

"Oh, for God's sake," Frank interrupted loudly. "Is there nothing you can do to win them over?" Miranda ignored him.

"They tell us that there is another route out of the village, back the way we came, just around the bend, but it's not really a road – more of a dirt track. It's bumpy and narrow and tends to get flooded, but they tell us it should be just wide enough for the coach to go down and as it's our only hope, let's keep our fingers crossed and wish Tony luck! We'll have to reverse a little way and turn."

The track proved to be interminably long, sinuously winding and every bit as bumpy as the workmen had indicated. Although Tony drove with his usual skill and care, trying to avoid getting his bodywork scratched, splashed or covered in mud, the occupants of the coach were getting badly bounced around. For Dave, in his fragile, badly hung-over condition, the roller-coaster ride was proving to be especially tortuous. He had turned a distinct shade of pale green when he emitted a particularly loud and sorrowful groan.

"Are you alright?" Susan asked somewhat unnecessarily and without evincing much sympathy.

"I think I'm going to be sick," Dave replied through clenched teeth.

"Well you'd better make a dash for the toilet, then."

Dave rose unsteadily from his seat, swayed a little and started to retch. As the coach went over another fierce bump, he lurched forward and vomited spectacularly. Sitting immediately in front of him and still reflecting on her recent altercation with the road menders, the unsuspecting Miranda bore the brunt of the deluge, much of which covered her freshly washed hair and her shoulders and cascaded down her neck and back. She screamed.

It took Tony several minutes to find somewhere to stop. He had to get to the end of the track, navigate through the outskirts of the village and onto the main road where he was able to find a roadside service station. While Miranda dashed inside carrying a roll of paper towels, which she had retrieved from an overhead locker, and her suitcase, which Tony had retrieved from the luggage hold, Tony busied himself with bucket and mop, cleaning up that part of the mess that had somehow missed Miranda.

Most of the passengers took the opportunity of the unplanned stop to get off the coach and many stood around in small groups debating the incident, bemoaning the delays or speculating on what might happen next. Dave propped himself up uneasily against a lamppost, looking pale and breathing heavily. Susan stood morosely next to him, with her arms folded, feeling deeply embarrassed and still showing no obvious sign of sympathy for her husband's predicament.

"I warned you last night about the strength of some of these foreign beers, didn't I? I said they were stronger than you're used to, didn't I?"

"Yes, yes, you did. And are you happy now?"

Before Susan could answer, Frank marched up, with his brow still deeply furrowed, looking flushed and angry. Never a patient man, his simmering fury had been growing with every fresh delay and was about to boil over. With his eyes bulging and the vein in the middle of his high forehead throbbing, he accosted Dave.

"For God's sake, can't we get through a single journey without you making a mess of some kind and delaying us all?"

Seeing Frank towering menacingly over Dave, who somehow was contriving to look small and frail, Susan abandoned all hostilities against her husband and leapt to his defence. She moved towards Frank, still with her arms folded. Though nowhere near as tall as Frank, she was a sturdy woman and was not easily intimidated.

"Leave him alone, he's not well."

"Not well? Not well? I hardly think that was medicine he was drinking by the gallon last night!"

Dave knew from occasionally bitter personal experience that, if roused sufficiently, Susan was more than capable of holding her own, but the last thing he wanted right now was an unseemly argument breaking out on the pavement. He moved unsteadily away from the lamppost.

"Look, I didn't know we were going to have such a bumpy ride," he protested. But Frank's rage was not ameliorated.

"Oh and I suppose somebody forced you to get pissed last night."

Dave had had enough. He was feeling rough. Frank was behaving boorishly to him, and worse, to Susan. He knew he had no real excuses to offer for his behaviour, he couldn't even blame anyone else, but he hated being told off, so he resorted to plain, old-fashioned abuse.

"Oh shut your gob!"

"What did you say?" retorted Frank.

"I said, "Shut your gob!""

"Don't you talk to me like that!"

Frank raised his hands and clenched his fists, as though he was going to strike Dave. Dave immediately tried to push Frank away and they began to jostle each other. Peter had been standing close by. Though the air in the vicinity of the petrol station and the busy main road was not exactly fresh, he had been trying hard to inhale it in great gulps in a vain attempt to ease his nasal congestion. But as the jostling broke out, he went instinctively into his practised playground routine, immediately rushing between the combatants with a cry of "Come on, come on, break it up!" Dave and Frank each took a step backwards and glared warily at each other, while Peter continued to stand uneasily between them. Eventually, Dave smiled weakly at Peter.

"You saved Frank from a good hammering there, Pete. You

know, on reflection, I think it might be a good idea if you go back to your seats at the front, don't you? I don't want to be sitting any closer to Miranda or Frank than I have to, at the moment."

"In theory, possibly," Peter replied, "but in view of recent events, I'm not sure I want you sitting behind me!"

Dave held his head again.

"Don't shout, don't shout! Why is everybody shouting?"

Frank had backed off a little and was busy dusting himself down after his imaginary brawl with Dave, while Joyce was trying to drag him away to a safer distance. But he was still angry so, from that safe distance, he shouted back at Dave.

"We wouldn't be shouting if it wasn't for you. God knows what the lovely Miranda will say and do when she's finally cleaned herself up."

Dave winked at Frank and held out a conciliatory hand towards him. He didn't often bear grudges and wanted to make peace. After a tentative handshake, he tried to place an arm around Frank's shoulder but couldn't quite reach so, with a shaky hand across Frank's back, he started to guide him gently away from the rest of the group.

"You know, Frank," he whispered, "I think you'll find she won't be quite as upset with me as you might think. Shall I let you into a little secret about Miranda and Tony?"

★ ★ ★

After the passengers had spent a seemingly interminable period waiting around and growing ever more frustrated, Miranda finally emerged from inside the service station. She had changed her clothes. Instead of the smart trousers with heavy jacket and blouse she had sported earlier, she was now wearing a pale yellow t-shirt and faded blue jeans. She was carrying what looked to be her discarded and badly soiled clothes, with obvious disgust, at arms length, in a plastic bag and she was dragging her suitcase behind her. Her hair was soaking wet and straggly. Her ubiquitous sunglasses concealed the redness in her eyes but could not disguise the faint traces of tearstains and smudged mascara on her cheeks.

Rather imperiously, she handed her suitcase and the plastic bag to Tony, tore off another paper towel from the now much depleted roll and was trying to dry her hair with it as she made a beeline for Dave who was still standing, a little shakily, next to Frank.

"I suppose you're satisfied now are you? Are you? Well, I've just about had it with you!" she ranted.

Dave flinched again as Miranda's strident tones reverberated around his sore head.

"Don't forget..." he began to reply as Miranda paused for breath, but before he could get another word out, she resumed her finger-wagging onslaught.

"Look, I don't care what you might have seen, or what you might be threatening to do – any more trouble of any kind from you and you are off the tour. Do I make myself clear?"

Dave glared defiantly at her and opened his mouth as if to say something but Susan, fearing the consequences of what Dave might say in this highly volatile situation, gave him one of her notorious withering looks and called "Leave it, Dave," with such vehemence that Dave flinched, turned and moved slowly and meekly away.

Satisfied that she had dealt effectively and unequivocally with Dave and that her authority remained unquestioned and unchallenged, Miranda turned to everyone who was standing around.

"OK, everybody back on the coach, we've got a lot of time to make up."

As the passengers re-assembled on the coach and, after a further, largely amicable, debate with Dave and Susan, Peter and Gail resumed their original seats at the front. As Peter sat down, he sneezed loudly. Miranda, who was about to sit down, jumped and looked around with wide-eyed alarm.

Behind Peter and Gail, Susan was remonstrating with the hapless Dave.

"I suppose you're happy now are you? Have you any idea how much you've embarrassed me? Have you any idea how much you've annoyed everybody else on this coach? Honestly, if you don't behave yourself, you'll get us both thrown off!"

"Yes, yes, don't you start – I get the message."

"And don't you dare go boozing in the bar this evening!"

"I've no doubt you'll make sure I don't."

As the coach belatedly resumed its eventful and protracted journey, Miranda reached for her clipboard, studied the official programme for the morning and glanced at her watch with more than a little consternation. It was palpably obvious that, following their various hiatuses and delays, some major changes to the itinerary would have to be put in place. Miranda's anger at the morning's events was still raging within her, to the extent that she was finding it difficult to concentrate on the schedule and the adjustments that were needed, but, after studying her papers for a time, making a few rapidly scribbled notes, and conferring with Tony, she finally managed to concoct some kind of revised plan. She was not at her best in a crisis and so much time had been lost that her plan was no more than a poor, quickly assembled compromise. She knew, of course, that it was unlikely to win universal approbation and, fearing an adverse reaction from the group, and an almost certain high volume intervention from Frank, she reached for the microphone with some trepidation. Her voice seemed to carry less authority than usual.

"In view of the..er… several delays this morning, we're going to have to change our schedule slightly. Our boat time has been pre-booked and we can't change that, so when we finally arrive in Amsterdam, for those of you who have booked this option, we are going to have to go straight there. Then, when the boat trip ends, after an hour or so, we'll go on to the diamond factory…"

She had got no further when the inevitable happened. Frank was still infuriated by the morning's events. Never a patient man, he was notoriously intolerant of what he saw as incompetence or selfishness in others, failings that he was often guilty of himself, of course. Now Miranda was threatening to derail his trip to Amsterdam. He leapt angrily to his feet.

"Hang on a minute. It wasn't our fault we've lost all this time this morning. Maybe some of us don't want go on the boat and, if time is limited, maybe some of us might not want to go to the diamond factory…"

Yet again, Joyce was greatly discomfited by Frank's intemperate behaviour and desperately anxious to avoid yet another "scene" developing. More in hope than expectation, she tried, in her own quiet way, to ameliorate the situation.

"Some of us might," she whispered to Frank. "Anyway don't knock it; they'll have toilets there."

Frank, however, was in his rabble-rousing element and he continued unabashed and unabated, seemingly oblivious to Joyce's discouragement. Since the end of his active trade union days, he had quite missed the opportunity to address an audience and he was making up for it now. He was in full, unstoppable flow.

"Some of us might want to use our increasingly limited time to do a bit of sightseeing in Amsterdam..."

A few anonymous cheers coming from somewhere near the back of the coach convinced Frank that he had a receptive audience and spurred him on to greater invective.

"After all, how many of us are going to buy a diamond?"

"Not you, obviously!" muttered Joyce ruefully.

"I need time to buy a watch and a camera," added Brian, somewhat inconsequentially.

"There you are, you see..." said Frank, pointing to Brian as though he had just made a profoundly telling point, and warming still further to his task.

"Well, I thought I might buy a diamond," added Trevor diffidently. Julia squeezed his arm, looked wistfully at him and simpered, "Oh Trevor."

Miranda was flushed and flustered. Although she had fully anticipated some kind of adverse reaction to her proposals, she had not expected a full-scale public debate to break out. Normally her authority and her decisions went unchallenged. Normally she could instruct an entire coach party to go and jump in the river and they'd do it, but this one, orchestrated by Frank, was very different. Faced with this unprecedented insurgence, she didn't know how to react. Sensing her predicament, Tony leaned across and spoke quietly to her.

"You'd better try and let them do what they want, within

reason, otherwise we could have a riot and we're in enough trouble as it is."

Miranda could feel the beads of perspiration breaking out on her forehead and her throat growing ever more dry. She swallowed hard and conceded the point with as much ill grace as she could muster.

"Alright, alright, this is what we'll do. This is what we'll do. We'll go straight to the where the boat is. Those of you who are going on the boat ride can get off there. Then those of you who want to go to the diamond factory can stay on the coach…"

But, this did nothing to stifle the debate, which continued to rage around her. This time it was Barbara, increasingly confident, who stood up.

"But we want to do the boat trip *and* the diamond factory…"

There were more anonymous cheers from the back of the coach.

"Alright, alright, alright," Miranda conceded, holding her arms up as though about to surrender. "Hands up, those of you who are coming on the boat trip." She paused while a considerable number of hands were raised. "OK, now who wants to come to the diamond factory?" She paused again while fewer hands were raised. "OK, thank you. Now only keep your hands up if you *don't* want to come on the boat trip but *do* want to come to the diamond factory."

Every hand went down. Miranda breathed an audible sigh of relief.

"Right, this is what we'll do. When we arrive at the boat, those of you who want to go off and do sightseeing or shopping or whatever you want to do are free to do so. I'll give you directions into the city centre and tell you where you go to pick up the coach later. For those going on the boat trip, we'll collect you at 11.30 and then those who want to go to the diamond factory can come with us. Those who want to go off into the city can do so. We'll pick everybody up at 1.30."

Frank, who was still on his feet and not at all placated by Miranda's muddled attempts at re-organising the morning's events, interrupted again.

"What a bloody shambles! You could at least make it 2 o'clock and give us a bit more time." There was more vocal encouragement from the back of the coach.

Miranda was in an impossible situation. She knew it and Frank knew it. If she refused to extend the deadline until 2 o'clock, there was no knowing how Frank and his growing band of loyal disciples might react. He was obviously relishing his position as self-appointed guerrilla leader and milking it for all it was worth; in addition, there were one or two of his cronies who knew far too much about her dalliances with Tony and might "go public" if she dug her heels in. She suspected that Frank was perfectly capable of orchestrating some kind of organised protest or resistance, but, on the other hand, if she gave in to his demands, her position of authority would be weakened, a precedent would be set and she would be vulnerable to further demands for concessions, in one form or another. Faced with this dilemma, Miranda did what she usually did when put under pressure and used "the rules" as her excuse.

"I'm sorry, but our schedule says we've got to leave by 1.30...

"Bugger the schedule!!" shouted Frank, growing ever more militant. "What time did your precious schedule say we were going to be arriving in Amsterdam? A lot earlier than we will do, I bet!"

While Miranda struggled to reply, Dave stood up – no easy task for him, feeling as he did. He swayed a little uncertainly, causing Peter to duck, waved a hand vaguely in the direction of Miranda and spoke, more quietly and solemnly than was his custom.

"I'd be really grateful if people could stop shouting! Look, it was partly my fault we are so late. I'm sure Miranda won't mind if we get back at 2.00!"

He tried to smile, as charmingly as he could under difficult circumstances, at Miranda but she was stubbornly determined not to give any ground, especially to Dave, who she saw as one of the main perpetrators of her problems.

"But Tony has got to have a bit of an afternoon break, otherwise he'll be breaking the law, and we've got quite a long run to our hotel and if we arrive late…"

Reluctant to shout over the hubbub that seemed to be enveloping him, Dave clapped his hands together a couple of times, although the noise they made was barely less tolerable to his sensitive ears than the shouting he was trying to avoid. He did, however, get everybody's attention.

"Look, look," he pleaded. "Just phone the hotel and tell them we might be a bit late. I'm sure they'll understand. You can blame me – everybody else is. But I really don't want to be the cause of these good folk not enjoying themselves."

In desperation, Miranda looked across at Tony who had been trying to concentrate on navigating the coach around congested urban streets and into the centre of Amsterdam with the furore of public debate going on around him. "Better do it," he whispered with an air of resignation, "and pray there are no hold-ups on the roads this afternoon."

Miranda sighed heavily again – she had run out of allies and options.

"Alright, alright, you win. But this is *only* because of the exceptional circumstances this morning and you must be back sharp at two!"

★ ★ ★

Frank was feeling pleased with himself, his little victory over "management" bringing back fond memories of his trade union days. With a good deal of preening self-importance, he led the way onto the boat and sat at the front, with a satisfied smile. As the boat began to cruise serenely along the canals, he took out his camcorder, held it ostentatiously to his eye and began to film. After a moment or two, Joyce, who was sitting dutifully and deferentially beside the hero of the hour, while suppressing the urge to throttle the living daylights out of him, reached across, as discreetly as she could, and removed the cap from the lens. Frank looked around sheepishly and smiled awkwardly at Joyce.

A cosmopolitan and energetic city like Amsterdam has much to offer the tourist, irrespective of age, background and interests, though Frank found its youthful vibrancy an unnerving contrast to the more genteel ambience of Eastbourne. For some, like Trevor and Julia, there was ample opportunity to kiss and make up and stroll quietly, hand-in-hand, soaking up the tranquil elegance of some of the grand canals like Prinsengracht, Keisersgracht and Herengracht. For the erudite, there was the opportunity to visit some of the many art galleries and museums. For the less erudite, like Dave and Susan, there was a plethora of small cafes, with tables and chairs placed temptingly on the water's edge, to choose from, though Dave was less than impressed when Susan restricted his liquid intake to one small cup of bitter coffee.

For the younger, more energetic and adventurous tourists, there were plenty of lively choices, but for Barbara and Jason, there was an obvious priority – a return to the Red Light District which they could explore more intently and more anonymously now they had more time and less company. A museum of the erotic and a sex shop were early recipients of a visit as they proceeded around the area, with wide-eyed wonderment.

For Peter and Gail, there was time to do some sedate sightseeing in the glorious late morning sunshine, to visit a museum or two and to take more pictures of Fred. Peter's pace remained lethargic, however, and his stamina was unusually suspect.

For Valerie and Brian, the most pressing priorities in this hectic, frenetic and occasionally confusing city were to purchase a new camera and watch. After wandering aimlessly around for a while, not quite sure which direction to go in, they stumbled upon a small store, just off the Dam, where some reasonably priced watches were displayed. Scrutinised carefully by Valerie, Brian made his selection, from the cheaper end of the range, paid for it and placed it ceremoniously on his wrist. Shortly afterwards, they stumbled across another shop, aimed mainly at the tourist trade, which offered a small selection of basic cameras. Despite his self-proclaimed but unsubstantiated technical prowess, Brian was, in truth, more comfortable with a basic, easy-to-operate camera and Valerie was more comfortable knowing that Brian had only a basic, easy-to-operate camera. So, some more Euros changed hands and Brian emerged from the shop proudly holding his new camera.

"For God's sake keep it around your neck this time," Valerie instructed stiffly. On closer inspection, however, it was clear that the small cord attached to the small camera was only big enough to go around Brian's wrist so he made a point of placing it securely around his wrist and thrusting his hand deep into the darkest recesses of his trouser pocket. They then strolled off without any great degree of purpose, direction or urgency.

Before long, as is inevitable in Amsterdam, they arrived at an attractive waterfront where tall pastel coloured, gabled merchants' houses towered over a neat line of houseboats, casting their calm reflections in the gently flowing waters, presenting Brian with an irresistible opportunity to test his new camera. Having satisfied himself that he could operate it – a task that took several minutes – he crossed the road to the water's edge, checked the direction of the sun, carefully pointed his camera at the view and successfully took his first picture, capturing the vista across the shimmering water to the elegant houses beyond, as Valerie looked on from the other side of the road. Satisfied with his first attempt, Brian turned back in her direction, holding his camera up in celebration, looked right instead of left, and took one pace into the road.

While searching doggedly for a new watch and camera, Brian had been strangely oblivious to the huge number of cyclists in the city and the speed at which they travel. Now, as he took one pace into the road, looking right, three cyclists bore down fast on him, from his left. Seeing the fast-approaching peril, Valerie shouted a warning and pointed towards the onrushing cyclists. Looking quickly to his left, and finally sensing the danger he was in, Brian instinctively took a step backwards. Fortunately, his surprisingly swift action averted a painful collision with the cyclists, who sped rapidly past him. Unfortunately, his step backwards was a large and inelegant one. With all the grace of a penguin on ice, he caught his heel on a loose paving slab, lost his footing, stumbled and fell backwards over a small railing, plummeting out of sight and into the canal behind him, landing neatly between two houseboats. There was a loud splash as Valerie rushed over, shouting for help.

★ ★ ★

Although Miranda had been forced, with the utmost reluctance, to concede the later than planned departure time, she realised, after she had calmed down, that she could put the extra time to good use by visiting a local launderette and trying to clean the clothes that Dave had so spectacularly soiled earlier on. She could, of course, only begin the search for a launderette after the visit to the diamond factory – which she had endured on countless occasions and which always seemed to take an insufferably long time – had ended, and it took a while to find one and to understand how to operate its slow and inefficient machinery. Whereas the time had passed so slowly at the diamond factory, it was now racing by and, as two o'clock rapidly approached, it was evident, to her chagrin, that she herself was in danger of being late. The renegotiated deadline had given her and Tony little room for manoeuvre and it would be quite unthinkable for her to be the one who failed to arrive on time. Glancing anxiously at her watch, she was forced to abort the final spin cycle, stuff the still wet clothing into a bag and race, at full speed, back to where the coach was waiting, outside the big hotel opposite the station. As she rushed back towards the coach, trying to look as anonymous and inconspicuous as possible, she overtook a steady stream of people she recognised, making their way back.

It wasn't long before she passed Barbara and Jason, who were almost jogging back with unbounded energy, still giggling and carrying one or two purchases, which they seemed anxious to keep hidden from sight, in an anonymous plain bag. Further on, Trevor and Julia were returning at a brisk but more controlled pace, radiantly hand-in-hand, without an apparent care in the world. A little nearer the coach, she overtook Peter and Gail, trudging wearily back, and Dave and Susan, looking unusually subdued. Further down the road, the two elderly ladies, clutching "C&A" carrier bags, were returning at a stately pace, as was Nigel, clutching his mother's arm in one hand and her shopping in the other. Right by the coach, Frank and Joyce had just arrived, with Frank complaining loudly, for some unknown reason, about the manners of young people.

Gasping for breath after her hectic dash, Miranda hurled her still damp bag of laundry into the luggage hold and checked her watch. Ignoring Frank's deliberately loud and sarcastic remark about some people "cutting it fine, even with an extra half-hour," she counted those who had already returned, together with those who she could see approaching the coach and concluded that only Brian and Valerie were unaccounted for. Still breathless, she checked her watch again and looked anxiously down the road. There, in the distance, she saw, to her immense relief, the unmistakeable silhouettes of Brian and Valerie, making their way steadily towards the coach. At first glance, all seemed to be well, but as they got closer, it was clear that something was wrong.

On a gloriously dry and sunny day, Brian was soaking wet. His hair was matted and clinging damply to his scalp. His glasses were smeared and perched lopsidedly on his nose. His clothes, not exactly smart at the best of times, were muddy and bedraggled. There was a steady stream of water dripping from his shirt and trickling down the outside of his trousers. His badly scuffed shoes squelched as he walked, leaving a trail of wet footprints behind him. His camera, dripping water, was still hanging forlornly, and somewhat pointlessly, from his wrist. Valerie was walking alongside, but slightly apart from, her waterlogged husband, still looking incongruously elegant in her matching mint blouse and shoes with cream trousers, but with a look of stunned incredulity on her face.

For a while, as they loomed closer, Miranda stared open mouthed, but as they finally reached the coach, she felt compelled to comment.

"Oh no, I don't believe it!"

"I'm afraid Brian fell in the canal and…" Valerie began apologetically before Miranda interrupted.

"Oh, for God's sake!"

"We were wondering," Valerie continued. "Would it be

possible to get our suitcases out of the hold so that my husband can find some dry clothes?"

For those who had returned to the coach grumpy or tired – Frank, Dave and Peter amongst them – Brian's sodden arrival was proving to be a great tonic and there was much suppressed merriment at his expense.

For Miranda, however, it was no laughing matter. She looked impatiently and pointedly at her watch. Still not fully recovered from her dash back to the coach, her cheeks and neck were flushed and she was breathing heavily. Trevor, who was standing nearby, was watching her intently. Yet again, Brian was presenting her with an awkward dilemma. She didn't really want a further delay but didn't much care for the idea of a disgruntled Brian boarding the coach in his current saturated state.

"We're already running very late," she observed acidly.

"I know, I know," replied Valerie. "But he can't really travel on the coach like this, can he? After all, you had to change *your* clothes earlier and…." Valerie stopped, realising that perhaps it was better not to pursue that particular topic.

Miranda looked across at Tony who had been observing Brian with evident distaste. He had already had to clean the inside of the coach once today and clearly did not relish Brian further sullying his immaculately maintained interiors with the contents of an Amsterdam canal. With no more than a surly grunt, he alighted from the coach and made his way to the luggage hold.

"We don't have much choice then do we?" Miranda concluded ungraciously. As she was studying Tony's firm muscles, while he opened the hold and reached inside for the now familiar shapeless suitcase with string tied around it, she happened to glance up and noticed Trevor staring at her in apparent fascination. She turned towards him.

"Yes, can I help you?"

Trevor looked away quickly in his embarrassment. "Er, n..no, it's OK thanks," he stuttered.

For some reason, the still recent image of Trevor standing naked and vulnerable in the middle of the hotel corridor flashed briefly into Miranda's mind. Her already flushed cheeks turned an even brighter pink.

★ ★ ★

The coach had been travelling for a few minutes, negotiating the nondescript city suburbs, when Brian clattered clumsily out of the toilet, loosening the lock that Tony had only repaired the day before, carrying his wet clothes in a crumpled bundle. His hair was still matted and damp, his glasses still spattered and lopsided and his clothes still creased and ill fitting but, at least, they were, for the time being, clean and dry. As he made his way back to his seat, he heard someone shout "Well done, Brian!" and a smattering of applause broke out. Unsure quite where the accolade had come from and whether it was sarcastic or genuine, Brian ignored it, returned to his seat, threw his wet and discarded clothes into the overhead rack and handed the still damp camera to Valerie.

Valerie took the camera and tossed it peevishly into her bag.

"You know, I think it might be an idea if I look after any more cameras that we buy!"

"Yes, yes," Brian agreed. He looked intently at his watch, removed it from his wrist, held it to his ear, shook it vigorously and handed it, sheepishly, to Valerie.

"And the watch…"

Valerie tossed the watch into her bag.

"And I think I'd better keep an eye on the time from now on!" she said with such force that Brian, who was well used to her strident comments, cowered momentarily in his seat.

"Yes, yes…"

★ ★ ★

As the afternoon passed, the coach made unremittingly steady progress out of the Netherlands and into Germany following the autobahn in a south-easterly direction, past Cologne and towards Koblenz. After a couple of hours on the road, it pulled into an impeccably smart looking autobahn service area for a brief comfort break. As usual, Miranda reminded everybody of the need to return to the coach promptly but, on this occasion, she seemed to do so with particular emphasis.

Frank was anxious to be first out of the coach so that he could visit the toilets before a queue built up – any waiting around in a queue might prove to be both uncomfortable and irritating for him. Joyce was also hoping that he wouldn't be long, but for a very different reason. She had spent the last couple of hours on the coach mulling things over and had reached what for her was a momentous decision. Fighting against her ingrained, almost life-long, instinct to go along with Frank because it was usually the easiest and least stressful thing to do, she had decided that there were things she needed to say to him.

During the day, she had grown increasingly concerned about the exhibition that Frank had been making of himself. After all, she reflected, she had come on holiday to relax, not to get stressed and embarrassed every time Frank opened his mouth, for fear of what he was going to say or who he might upset. Over the years, Joyce had tolerated most vagaries of Frank's moods, his obduracy, his impatience, his intolerance, his temper, with a degree of resignation. After all, it hadn't seemed to matter much when Frank was working or when it was just the two of them in the privacy of their own home. Not now though! Although they were only a couple of days into their holiday, the world – or at least a small part of it – was belatedly opening up to Joyce. After forty years of a mundane, sanitised, almost reclusive domestic existence, she was beginning to see new opportunities and enjoy new experiences. She found herself envying the energy and youthful curiosity of Barbara, the irreverent earthiness of Dave and Susan, the unassuming charm of Peter and Gail. But Frank had seemingly been doing his best to spoil it for her with his obsessive routines, his constant curmudgeonly behaviour and his rabble-rousing antics and she had decided that enough was enough.

As she waited nervously for Frank to emerge from the toilet, she was briefly distracted by Susan and Dave, who passed her, heading purposefully towards the attractive looking café area.

"Come on, let's go and get ourselves a coffee," Susan enthused. Dave sounded less keen.

"Strewth, not another cup of coffee. What are you trying to do – keep me awake this afternoon?"

"I'm trying to cure your hangover and stop you making another exhibition of yourself, that's what I'm trying to do."

"And you're not the only one," Joyce pondered to herself as Frank emerged safely from the automatic toilets, a look of sublime relief on his face. They went into the café, bought their cups of coffee and pastries and sat down; Joyce took a deep breath and, uncharacteristic though it was, went onto the offensive.

"So, come on love, what's bugging you?"

"What do you mean?" Frank was visibly startled by Joyce's unusually direct question.

"Well, I haven't been married to you for all these years without knowing that you can start an argument in an empty room if you're in that sort of mood, but I had hoped that you'd lighten up a bit on this holiday. However, so far today you've nearly come to blows with Dave, you've led a small mutiny, you have been very unpleasant to Miranda on several occasions, particularly when she was doing her best to sort out the revised timings this morning and you spent most of our time in Amsterdam moaning about something or other. So, what's bugging you?"

Frank was crestfallen. He hadn't realised how much his boorish behaviour was upsetting Joyce. A look of deep hurt spread across his face.

"I don't know really, love," he responded meekly. "I'm just not sure I'm cut out for this kind of holiday. You know me; I like to be able to take my time, do what I want to do, when I want to do it and I don't like to be ordered about!"

"Don't I know it!"

"And having to spend so much time on the coach with people I'd normally cross the road to avoid. I mean, Dave can be quite amusing when he's had a drink or two but he doesn't know when to stop, as was only too apparent this morning, and he has the mentality of a rebellious teenager. Talking of which, those two giggly kids sitting behind us seem quite convinced they've just invented sex. And then there's Brian. I ask you. How can anyone be so accident-prone?"

"You mean like locking yourself out on the balcony of your own flat?"

"Alright, alright, point taken."

Joyce found herself becoming unexpectedly emotional. Feelings that she had kept bottled up for years suddenly poured out of her.

"You know, if you hadn't messed up your career by falling out with so many people – people who mattered – maybe we wouldn't have had to spend our retirement in a pokey little flat. Maybe we'd have had a nice house and garden. Maybe we'd have a few more friends that we could socialise with. Maybe we could afford better holidays."

"I see! It's all coming out now, isn't it?"

Joyce wiped away a tear. She hadn't meant to cry, or to say some of things she had just said. She had been determined to be tough and to keep going when Frank got difficult as he surely would. But now, she was crying.

"I'm sorry, love. I didn't really mean it," she blubbered. "Take no notice. It's just that I was so looking forward to this holiday; something a bit different after all these years; a break from our routines. Something a bit more adventurous and…"

"And I'm spoiling it for you?"

She nodded. "Well you're certainly not helping!"

Frank had been stunned and upset by Joyce's outburst. For all his faults, he loved her dearly and hated to think that he had made her cry. Although he could not bring himself to admit it – he never could – he knew that there was much truth in what she had been saying. He reached out, placed a reassuring hand on each of her shoulders and looked fondly into her watery eyes.

"Look, it's early days yet. I expect I'll get the hang of this touring lark and I promise I'll try to behave myself better. How's that?"

Joyce wanted to say more – she felt suddenly emancipated and there was so much she wanted to say – but she wasn't sure that she could control her emotions and they needed to be back on the coach.

"Alright. Come on, drink up and be merry!" She sniffed, forced a smile, drained her cup and got up, leaving most of her pastry, uneaten, on the plate. Frank followed her, for once not knowing what to say.

★ ★ ★

Resuming its long journey, the coach travelled on along the drab, unchanging but efficiently fast autobahns of western Germany before, at last, it reached Koblenz, the overnight destination. As the coach approached the hotel, Miranda reached for the microphone and, a little sniffily, addressed the coach-bound entourage.

"In view of our, er, later than planned departure from Amsterdam, I'm afraid we are only going to have about twenty minutes after we arrive at the hotel before dinner this evening. We will of course arrange for your cases to be delivered to your rooms as normal, but if you want, you can take your cases with you so that you can freshen up and change before dinner."

Valerie looked Brian up and down critically.

"Mmm, I think that might be an idea, Brian."

"Yes, yes."

As the passengers prepared to disembark after their long haul, Dave, with a substantial amount of caffeine in his blood, was wide-awake. He glanced across at Susan. She was sound asleep.

★ ★ ★

The Hotel Wappenschild, like many others on the itinerary, had been selected more for its convenient location, its reasonable prices and its ability and willingness to cater for coach parties than for any particular culinary, scenic or architectural merits. It was a modern, four-storey, cream-coloured building comprising two wings, built at right angles, with the main entrance at the inside corner of the junction. Its location, on the edge of a business park, close to the autobahn, was uninspired and its rooms, though functional, had a tired, characterless feel. The plain magnolia coloured walls of each room had assorted scuff marks, chips and scratches, as did much of the mass-produced, dark brown furniture. The beds were hard and the views out of the small windows across the autobahn or outskirts of a business park were depressing. The only concession to colour was the presence of a dark maroon carpet in each room, together with matching curtains.

Julia, however, was, as usual, not paying too much attention to the fatigued décor or the industrial views as she and Trevor entered their room on the third floor. She looked round quickly, ignoring the stained carpet, chipped furniture and grubby walls, and checked her watch.

"Ah, good; there's the phone. I've just got time to phone Mark before dinner."

Trevor was weary after the long journey. He sighed heavily and flopped onto the bed, expecting the mattress to give slightly under his weight. It didn't.

"Really, you do surprise me!" he said, rubbing the small of his back thoughtfully.

"I've been worried about poor little Rosie all day."

She picked up the phone, dialled home and waited. Trevor, meanwhile, decided to amble slowly and more stiffly than usual into the bathroom to freshen up.

Mark had been expected the phone call and he wasted little time in answering it.

"Hello, Mark?"

"Oh hi, Mum!" He tried to sound surprised.

"Hi darling, I'm so sorry to disturb you again but I just had to phone to find out how Rosie is?"

"Ah, right! Now I don't want you blaming Dad for what happened!"

"Oh my God. What's happened? What's happened?"

"Well, he took Rosie to the vet this morning, like you asked. She had an injection and that was, like, OK, apart from the bill.

Better break it to Trev gently. And he brought her back OK but... well, she must have got a bit, like, spooked at the vets and, when we let her out of her box, she just flipped, shot out through an open window and, like, we haven't seen her since!"

"Oh my God, no. Is anyone looking for her?"

"Yeah, Dad's out there somewhere ... I haven't seen him for an hour or two either. And we've got some of the neighbours helping."

"How could you, I mean, how could he?"

"Stay cool Mum, it's nobody's fault. I'm sure she'll come back when she's, like, hungry."

"Right, that's it, we're coming home!!"

Trevor had, of course, been covertly listening to the conversation from behind the bathroom door. Julia's last comment had galvanised him into rapid action and, much less stiffly now, he dashed from the bathroom, rushed over to the phone and, for the second consecutive evening, snatched it from Julia. He shouted down the phone.

"Listen, Mark, take no notice. Tell me what's happened?"

"Like I was saying to Mum, Rosie disappeared after we brought her back from the vet and..."

"Go out and help search for the bloody cat. We'll phone you in the morning to find out what's happened."

He slammed the phone down and ran his hand over his hair, while he paced up and down on the already threadbare dark maroon carpet. Julia, meanwhile, burst into tears.

Back home, Mark put the receiver down and chuckled nervously. He looked across to where his father was sitting comfortably, laughing quietly, with a can of beer in his hand and Rosie curled up asleep on his lap. He smiled benevolently at Mark.

"Mark you're a star. What acting! You were absolutely brilliant!"

A look of concern spread across Mark's face.

"Yeah, right. Don't you think we're being a bit rotten though?"

"It's what you wanted, isn't it?"

"Yeah, I suppose. It's what we both wanted in a way, but we're really buggering up their holiday. I'll bet there'll be a blazing row this evening! You know what Mum can be like!"

"Tell me about it!"

★ ★ ★

The evening meal at the Hotel Wappenschild turned out to be a buffet affair. The capacious dining room was dimly lit – probably to conceal the quality of both the décor and the food – and, at one end, three immaculately uniformed waiters stood stiffly to attention behind a pile of gleaming plates and a series of tureens and hotplates. Each guest was handed a tray and then filed past the line of waiters who placed small portions of bland-looking, unappetising food onto plates and into bowls before handing them to the guests. The first course was a kind of watery, highly salted vegetable soup and the main course consisted of a couple of slices of some form of fatty meat loaf with a small quantity of anaemic-looking boiled potatoes and a spoonful of cold vegetables. The third course appeared to be a watery crème caramel.

Dave's appetite had slowly returned after a day of Spartan rations and a generous infusion of caffeine and he was now ravenously hungry. So, when it came to his turn to be served, he pulled a face, stood rigidly to attention and held out his plate for more. He got no response from the waiter.

"Is this all I get, pal?"

The waiter shrugged and began to serve the next person in the queue. In frustration, Dave turned to Susan.

"Bloody hell! You wouldn't give this to your dog would you?"

Susan laughed.

"Be careful what you say, Dave, that could be somebody's dog on your plate!"

"Funny you should say that. I thought I recognised the fur on this meat!"

★ ★ ★

Ordinarily, twenty minutes might just have given Frank enough time to freshen up, after the inevitable visit to the toilet, the fastidious washing of hands, the extensive combing of hair to ensure that every strand was in its correct place, the straightening of the tie and the excessive brushing of the jacket, but any spare time had been eaten away by the advance of technology. Instead of the traditional door-key, they had been handed a plastic "swipe card" to insert in a slot on the door. Muttering loudly, Frank had several failed attempts to open the door before reluctantly handing the card to Joyce, who opened it first time.

So, after carefully ensuring that all the taps in their bathroom were turned off – three times – and after checking that their room door was locked properly – a longer than usual ritual because of the new card technology – Frank and Joyce made their way downstairs to discover that they were among the last to arrive for dinner. When they had finally been served, with Frank moaning loudly about the slowness of the queue and how there would be no food left by the time their turn came round, there were not many empty seats left. Casting vainly around in the dimly lit room, they noticed two spare seats next to Nigel and his mother. Then they noticed two more opposite Barbara and Jason. Their exuberant youthfulness did not make them the dining companions of choice, hence the two empty seats, and Frank was a bit reluctant to share a table with them – they would inevitably start to giggle or obfuscate on some aspect of youth culture about which he was bound to know nothing, or make the kind of sexual innuendos that he didn't understand or much approve of at the dinner table and in mixed company – but there seemed to be little choice and the only visible alternative was worse.

"Remember our discussion! Be nice to them," Joyce observed quietly but firmly to Frank as they made their way across the dining room, clutching their sparsely filled trays. Frank nodded and smiled, but in a way that left her unconvinced.

"Do you mind if we join you?" Frank began, politely enough.

Barbara looked up fleetingly from her food and saw Frank towering over her, smiling, but managing to look somehow quite sinister in the shadowy light. She was no more enthralled at the prospect of Frank sitting with them than Frank was. He was bound to talk about bowls, or holidays in Eastbourne, or the "problems with young people today" or talk graphically about his ailments as, in her experience, people of his age were inclined to do. But they didn't have a lot of choice about their dining companions and, to be fair, Frank had been polite, so she would return his politeness.

"Of course not!" She tried to sound convincing.

Scared of what Frank might say if there was any kind of lull in conversation, Joyce was uncharacteristically forward and launched straight in.

"So how are you enjoying the holiday so far?"

"Oh, it's great!" Jason enthused, with his mouth half full of food. "We've not been on holiday together before and haven't really been abroad much either."

"Yeah," Barbara agreed, animatedly. "And we've done sooooo many interesting things already."

"And that's just in the hotels!" added Frank in one of his loud whispers, as he noisily embarked on his lukewarm soup, consuming it rapidly, apart from the odd spot or two that somehow managed to splash onto his tie.

Anxious to avoid any more of his provocative remarks, Joyce kicked him in the shin, under the table, with considerable and surprising force, and Frank winced. Joyce had obviously meant what she said earlier, so, in order to avoid severe bruising and multiple contusions, he decided to keep quiet a while and took a tentative mouthful of the main course.

"God, what is this muck?" he exploded.

Joyce gave him another reminder in the shins – after all they had discussed earlier, he was starting to embarrass her again. She leaned across to Jason apologetically.

"You'll have to excuse him. He doesn't much like foreign food."

"Well, I certainly prefer food that I can eat," he retorted. "The bloody vegetables are stone cold and this meat – whatever it is – tastes like rubber. I'm sorry but I'm going to have a word about this."

With a sense of rising dread, Joyce snapped at Frank.

"Frank, remember what you promised!"

"Yes love, I know, but we've paid good money for this muck and I don't like to be conned."

Frank was firmly set on his course of action. He stood up, angrily flung his serviette onto the table, straightened his soup-stained tie, stuck his jaw out and marched off importantly in the direction of Miranda and Tony who were dining on their own in a particularly dimly lit, secluded corner of the room, where they hoped not to be disturbed. Joyce bit her lip and buried her head in her hands. She felt tears welling up again, praying that Frank was not about to make another scene. For a moment, she wasn't sure whether she should chase after him and remonstrate with him, or run and hide, or dive under the table, but all of those options, she mused, would only draw unwanted attention to herself. On reflection, she felt it would be better to continue to converse with Barbara and Jason and pretend that nothing untoward was happening. She dabbed each eye gently with her serviette, leaned conspiratorially across the table and forced a weak smile.

"I'm so sorry about Frank. We don't usually get much further than Eastbourne for our holidays, I'm afraid. Same hotel every year, same food, same routines, same boring old fart of a husband! I just felt I wanted a change this year but I'm not sure I've done the right thing. We're too set in our ways, you see…"

At that moment, her train of thought was interrupted by the sound of raised voices coming from a neighbouring table. Trevor and Julia, sitting at a small table laid for two, were arguing again.

"Look it's only a cat," Trevor pleaded. "She'll be fine. She'll come back when she's ready."

"Only a cat? Only a cat?" Julia shouted. "A bloody cat, I think you called her earlier! How can you be so insensitive? You really haven't got a clue how much that cat means to me have you? I'm sorry, but if they haven't found her by the morning, we're going to have to go home!"

"What do you mean by that? I don't understand."

"What is it about the phrase "we're going to have to go

home" that you don't understand? I should have thought it was obvious. I don't know how you can expect me to enjoy myself out here knowing that Rosie's gone missing. And Mark will be distraught. He'll get no help from his father who will, of course, be useless as usual. And when he does finally show up, you can bet your life he will have been at the pub all evening! No, I'm sorry, we're just going to have to go home!"

Trevor had used just about every tactic he could think of to make a success of this holiday. He had tried, at various times, to be romantic, understanding, tolerant, patient, rational, forceful, angry, but it seemed there was nothing he could do or say in the face of Julia's rising temper. For the moment, he just felt weary and exasperated.

"Oh I see," he fumed, running a hand over his hair. "*We're* going to have to go home, are we? No, no. You can go if you must – I can't stop you – but I've paid for this holiday, I need a break and I don't see why…"

"Oh, so that's your attitude is it? Well I'm glad I found out now…"

Trevor was very well aware of Julia's capacity for violent temper tantrums when she was sufficiently roused – the damage to her sister's car was evidence of that – but he was still unprepared for what happened next. Quivering with rage and no longer in control of her actions, Julia reached forward, grabbed Trevor's plate of food, tipped it into his lap, stood up with such force that her chair fell backwards, clattering loudly onto the floor, and stormed off.

Trevor stood up and frantically tried to retrieve what food he could from his lap using a combination of his serviette, his cutlery, and his fingers. He looked up briefly to see where Julia had gone and found almost everyone in the room staring at him. An uncomfortable, tense silence had descended. It was broken by Dave, shouting across to Trevor from several tables away.

"Look on the bright side, Trev. At least you don't have to eat it now!"

While Julia's tantrum was the centre of attention, Frank had marched across to Miranda and Tony's table and was berating them about the quality of the food.

"I mean, this really isn't edible."

"I can understand your frustration," Miranda replied with strained, well-rehearsed, disingenuous politeness. For her, the day could not end soon enough.

"Oh can you?" Frank bellowed. "Well tell me what you are going to do about it, then?" He jabbed his finger several times on the table for effect.

"Well, er, um. I shall report your concerns to the hotel manager, but they're not going to prepare another meal for you all…"

"Don't forget that we've paid good money for this holiday and we expect…"

"And I will of course report your complaint to the company, but…"

"Yes, well see that you do, because…"

He was interrupted by Julia rushing up in tears.

"I'm sorry to trouble you," she sniffed. "But I think I'm going to have to go home in the morning and…"

All through his life, Frank had made a habit of interrupting other people, usually without apology or excuse, but it was a very different matter when someone else tried to do the same to him, even when he was being boring, pedantic and repetitive, which he often was. He stared with momentary incredulity at Julia before rounding on her, waving his arms about extravagantly as he did so.

"Hang on a minute; I hadn't finished talking to Miranda here."

Julia was not in a mood to be cowed. Although several inches shorter than Frank, she moved aggressively towards him.

"Can't you wait a minute, this is an emergency?"

"No I can't. I was here first. Please, let me finish, I'll only be a moment."

"Bloody men, you're all the same!"

With Frank's earlier scuffle with Dave still disturbingly fresh in his mind and fearing that the confrontation was about to get out of hand, Tony got to his feet and tried to manoeuvre himself between Frank and Julia. Frank was still hopping around and waving his arms about theatrically. Fearing that he might accidentally get caught by a flailing limb, Tony held up an arm to protect himself as he squeezed between Frank and Julia and, in doing so, inadvertently caught Frank a glancing blow on his shoulder.

"Don't you start hitting me!" Frank immediately shouted at Tony.

"I wasn't hitting you," Tony protested. "I was just trying to…"

Still raging and now forced to stand back while Frank and Tony faced up to each other, Julia exploded again.

"Bloody men!" she shrieked for the second time and, without warning, she pushed the table over towards Miranda causing plates, cutlery, food and glasses to crash spectacularly and noisily to the floor.

For the second time that day, Miranda found herself covered in something unpleasant. She shouted across to Tony.

"Get her out of the bloody way!"

Tony moved to grab Julia's arm but, with surprising strength for one so slightly built, she pushed his hand away and it caught Frank another blow, this time to the chest.

"You're bloody hitting me again," Frank shouted. He tried to aim a retaliatory swipe at Tony but, reviving the boxing routines of his youth, Tony took a nimble step back. Caught off balance by Tony's deft manoeuvre, Frank's swinging arm made contact with nothing more than thin air and he lost his footing. He slipped on the gooey morass of vegetables and crème caramel covering the floor and fell over the fallen table, crashing heavily amongst the debris.

By this time, several diners, led by Peter, and followed by a couple of the waiters, more animated than they had been all evening, had rushed over. They separated the combatants, helped Frank to his feet, escorted him and Julia away and began to clear up the mess.

★ ★ ★

Later that evening, Tony and Miranda were walking wearily along a hotel corridor with predictably care-worn expressions. Miranda's clothes were once again heavily soiled.

"Did you manage to get everything sorted out downstairs?" she asked.

"Just about, I think. Understandably, the hotel staff weren't too thrilled. I've told them we'll let head office know in the morning and they can sort out any damage claim direct. Let's face it, though, it is a crap hotel. I don't know why they keep sending us here. You can't argue with our friend Mr Armitage on that point."

"No, that's true, I suppose, although he didn't have to go to those lengths to make his point. And has he calmed down now?"

"Just about, I think. His missus gave him a damn good ticking off and led him away. I didn't think she was capable of laying into him the way she did. And have you managed to sort Mrs Cockrell out?"

"Kind of. I had to take her into the lounge and sit and listen to her ranting on for a while about men and their lack of sensitivity. She's calmed down a bit, fortunately, but she's still pretty upset and is quite determined to go home tomorrow with or without her husband. If she still feels the same in the morning, I've told her I'll try and contact the airport and get her on a flight back. She can get a taxi from the hotel."

"And Mr Cockrell?"

"They've obviously had a mega row but he seems quite subdued and stunned by it all at the moment – almost as though he's in a state of shock. I don't think he quite knows why his wife flipped, but he seems quite determined that he's staying on. Of course, things might be different in the morning."

"And tonight?"

"The manager was surprisingly cooperative, all things considered. I think he realised that if they spent the night together, Mrs Cockrell could have trashed the room by the morning, so they've found her a spare room and she's moving into that for the night. Honestly, I don't know what we're going to tell head office."

"I think the official story should be that Mrs Cockrell lost control, as a result of which, it was agreed that she should go home. But we need to be careful what we say about Mr Armitage, in view of everything that's happened. And I think he knows about us, too, from something he hinted at earlier. I suggest that the official line is that he was only trying to help but unfortunately, he lost his footing. What do you think?"

There was a pause. Tony was expecting Miranda to reply but when, at length, she spoke, it was more of an outpouring of emotion than a response to his question.

"Honestly, I do not believe this lot. Have you ever known a tour like this for accidents, damage, disruptive behaviour? So far today, I've been puked on, argued with, shouted at, abused and had my dinner thrown all over me. I've had to apologise to the managers in both hotels, and it's only the third day. I tell you I'm not sure I'm going to be able to cope with them for another ten days. I'm going to lose my temper with some of them before long."

"Well see that you don't. We don't want any of them spilling the beans, if you know what I mean."

"I know, but I'm getting so stressed, Tony!"

By now, they had reached the door to Tony's room. They stopped outside, awkwardly, not knowing quite what to do. It was Tony who solved the dilemma.

"Of course, I know of a great cure for stress! And look at the mess your clothes are in. You really need to get them off!"

He put his card in the lock, briskly opened the door and whisked Miranda, spluttering, inside.

* * *

The explosive events in the dining room had made a big impression on the coach party. Dave made a typically flippant observation about how cabaret time had not been mentioned in the holiday brochure, but most members of the group seemed strangely subdued, almost frightened, as though anxious not to disturb the delicate equilibrium that had, for the moment, descended.

In Brian and Valerie's room, Valerie was pulling Brian's damp and stained clothes from a plastic bag. She studied them with a familiar air of displeasure but was unexpectedly sanguine as she spoke to Brian.

"You know, at this rate, you're going to run out of clothes before the end of the holiday. I think I'd better try and rinse these through in the basin tonight and we'll leave them to dry overnight…" She paused, distracted by a passing thought.

"Yes, yes. Thank you, love!" Brian replied quickly. "I'm very sorry! I think I'd better not leave the coach from now on!"

★ ★ ★

The embargo, which Susan had imposed on Dave's drinking, together with Frank's rapid and ignominious departure, under escort, from the dining room, meant that Dave and Susan had retired unusually early – and soberly – to their room after a brief and disappointingly lacklustre post-prandial constitutional. Susan had seized the unexpected opportunity to enjoy a long relaxing soak in a hot bath, leaving Dave at a loose end, sitting on the bed, reading a two-day old newspaper that he had picked up on the way to Dover.

"God, I'm parched!" he announced quietly to himself, as he came across a beer advert, while turning the pages of the newspaper. He looked at his watch. "I bet the bar's still open!" He looked around furtively. "I wonder!"

He got up from the bed, went over to the bathroom door and half-opened it. He was confronted by a warm, suffocating blanket of steam, which he tried unsuccessfully to peer through.

"You alright in there?"

From somewhere within the vaporous confines of the bathroom, he heard Susan reply.

"Fine thanks!"

"Shall I hop in and join you? I could scrub your back for you." He knew what the answer would be.

"You'll do no such thing, Dave Fuller. I just want to have a good long soak, thank you very much. It's been a stressful day, one way and another."

"OK then, I get the hint, but you'll regret turning down the offer!"

"I don't think so, somehow!"

Dave closed the bathroom door, grabbed the remote control from the bedside unit and switched the television on. After a couple of minutes of random channel hopping, he found a German language channel which was broadcasting a hearty, raucous, but completely unintelligible game show. He turned the volume up a little, quietly removed his shirt, rummaged in his suitcase and produced another one of his Hawaiian shirts, this time in shades of violet and green, which he proudly put on. He then sidled over to the bathroom door, listened intently to the sound of Susan unhurriedly continuing her soak, tiptoed over to the door of their room and began to open it gently.

Outside, in the corridor, Julia had emerged, red-eyed and distressed, from the room that, up till now, she had shared with Trevor, and was dragging a heavy suitcase behind her. With her head resolutely down, staring impassively at the worn maroon carpet, she trudged slowly and miserably along the corridor and was just passing Dave and Susan's room when Dave backed quietly and stealthily into the corridor, while still looking back anxiously into the room. Not noticing where he was going, he didn't see or hear Julia behind him and backed into her, tripping and falling backwards over her suitcase. As he fell, his hands reached out and he instinctively grabbed hold of the nearest object, which, in this instance, happened to be Julia herself. She screamed as he accidentally pulled her down on top of him ripping her dress and half pulling it off in the process.

A little further down the corridor, Tony's door slowly opened and Miranda crept surreptitiously out, while still adjusting the top buttons on her blouse. Immediately, she saw Dave and Julia writhing in a heap on the floor and started to walk over towards them. Then she suddenly stopped, appeared to change her mind and crept quickly and silently away to her own room, before disappearing swiftly inside and closing the door firmly behind her.

Susan, meanwhile, thought she had heard a scream coming

from outside the door. She couldn't be sure because of the noise coming from the television, so she called to Dave, but had got no answer. Suspecting that Dave had fallen asleep in front of the television – a favourite pastime of his – but with a degree of nervousness, she rose regally from the bath, wrapped her still-dripping, ample frame, as best she could, in the small scratchy bath towel provided, went into the bedroom and looked around in vain for Dave. Finding no trace of him, she rushed across to the door and opened it to find Julia, with her dress badly torn, slapping Dave hard around the face.

"What the hell...?" she shrieked.

★ ★ ★

CHAPTER 5

Alarums and Excursions

Julia did not sleep well. By the morning, she was no longer angry. Instead, she felt overwhelmed by a deep sense of melancholy and desperate languor. After a restless night alone with her thoughts, she had risen early and taken a lukewarm shower. Feeling slightly more refreshed, she had wandered back into the bedroom, still drying herself as best she could on a threadbare towel, and sat miserably on the bed. After a few moments of quiet reflection, she got up, went over to the window, drew back the curtains and stared impassively at the early morning sun, just rising above a couple of shuttered warehouses and the first of the rush hour commuter traffic speeding purposefully along the autobahn. She sighed heavily, went over to the bed, reached for the phone and started dialling. She continued to dry herself as she waited impatiently for the phone to be answered. Eventually she heard a sleepy and distant voice.

"Hello, Mark?... What do you mean, what time do I think it is?"

Julia looked at her watch, which she had discarded on the bed beside her.

"It's nearly seven o'clock." She paused. "Oh, no! I'd forgotten we were an hour ahead! I'm sorry, but I had to phone to find out if you got Rosie back..."

★ ★ ★

Brian and Valerie had slept surprisingly well, under the circumstances, but, when they finally awoke, it was more with trepidation than anticipation. After the misfortunes and dramas of the previous day, neither of them was particularly keen to get the new one underway. Eventually, Valerie dragged herself reluctantly out of bed, her ankle-length sheer blue nightdress serenely uncrumpled, and went over to the cold radiator from which Brian's bespattered and decidedly crumpled clothes had been hanging overnight. A quick examination was all that was needed.

"Your clothes aren't very dry yet, I'm afraid. I'll have to put them back in this bag and hope that we can dry them out tonight."

From somewhere beneath the duvet she heard a muffled "Yes, yes!"

* * *

Julia had finished her phone call. She sighed thoughtfully, wearily applied the dryer to her tousled hair, slowly got dressed and was starting to pack, or at least to throw the few things that she had previously unpacked in the general direction of her open suitcase, when she heard a knock at the door. She walked reluctantly over to the door and cautiously opened it a crack. She could see Trevor standing outside. He had not shaved this morning, his eyes were bloodshot and heavy and his face seemed more lined and careworn than usual. In the unflattering light of the corridor, he seemed much older.

"Hello," he ventured tremulously.

"Oh, it's you!" responded Julia, somewhat obviously.

"May I come in?"

Julia hesitated for a moment and looked around as though searching for some reason why he couldn't come in, but eventually she opened the door, turned her back on him and resumed her packing. Trevor entered nervously. He clasped his hands firmly in front of him. He had been rehearsing what he was going to say for some hours and wanted to get it right. He tried standing still but, after a few seconds, started to pace the floor.

"I...I just came to apologise for last night. I've been lying awake all night fretting. It was very selfish of me – I realise that now – it's just that I'd forgotten, you know, how important your cat is to you. You and she… and Mark… well you've been through a lot together and…" His voice tailed off as his emotions began to take over and he gestured limply with his hand.

Julia busied herself under the pretence of packing, moving around the small room, opening drawers that were obviously empty while resolutely ensuring that she made no eye contact with Trevor and appearing oblivious to what he was stumbling to say or to the emotional battle that was obviously raging within him.

"I phoned home again this morning…" she suddenly announced.

Trevor glanced at his watch. She seemed calm enough, on the surface at least, but the fact that she had already phoned home and was packing did not bode well.

"What? Already?"

"Yes, I know. Mark wasn't too pleased!"

"I bet he wasn't. And have they found Rosie?"

"Yes, yes. She's back home now."

"Whew, what a relief! So you won't need to go home now, then?"

There was a long uncomfortable silence as Julia hesitated for a moment or two, then resumed her packing. Trevor continued to pace the room.

"Oh no, there's something else, isn't there?" he asked desperately.

Suddenly, Julia stopped what she was doing. For the first time, she turned and looked straight at Trevor. There was a sadness, an anxiety in her eyes that gave Trevor no cause for optimism.

"It's Geoff, you see. He fell out of a tree trying to retrieve Rosie and he's broken his ankle!"

Trevor heard himself laugh out loud. He couldn't help it. It was good news, of course, that Rosie was safe, but, somehow, it was even more gratifying that Geoff had hurt himself.

"I need to be with him, Trev!" Her voice had a weak, apologetic tone. For a moment Trevor thought that she was having a joke at his expense but that wasn't really her style and there was an earnest intensity about her that she couldn't disguise. He started to pace the room again.

"You're joking! It's only his ankle. He'll mend. He's quite good at putting his feet up and resting, as I recall. After a few weeks... Hang on a minute though; he was supposed to be fixing the fire escape at the centre. Damn. I'll have to phone Mike later!"

Julia smiled her wistful smile, went up to Trevor and kissed him gently on his stubbly cheek. Her sleep-starved night had afforded her ample opportunity to think. Maybe she wasn't thinking straight – she knew that – but she had reached a momentous decision. It was almost certainly the wrong decision, she knew that too, but, somehow, after all that had happened, she couldn't contemplate any other. She spoke quietly as she fiddled nervously with the top button of the check shirt he was wearing.

"Trevor... you're a lovely man... and I expect I'll come to regret my decision, but I miss Mark so much and I miss Rosie and, well, yes, I miss Geoff too, in a funny way. I feel a long way from home and right now I just want to be with them all."

Trevor backed away and ran his hand over his hair.

"I see." He didn't of course, but for the moment at least, he couldn't think of anything else to say.

"Anyway," Julia continued, more confidently now, "after the exhibition I made of myself last night, and after being molested by that oaf Dave, I think it would be better all round if I went home."

This was the first that Trevor knew of Dave's ham-fisted encounter with her and he felt he needed to know more.

"What the hell did Dave do?"

"Oh, I'm pretty sure it was an accident, but it didn't feel like it at the time. He wasn't looking where he was going, we collided in the corridor when I was moving to this room, he tripped over my suitcase and we kind of ended up in a heap on the floor. My dress got a bit torn. I don't think his wife was too impressed when she came out and found me slapping his face, but she did try to reassure me by saying that Dave would only ever assault a woman if she was carrying a tray of drinks!"

Trevor started pacing up and down the room again. Then, suddenly he whirled round, went over to Julia and placed a hand gently on each of her shoulders.

"What can I do to persuade you to change your mind?"

"Nothing, but why don't you come back with me? I'm sure we could work things out. And you need to sort things out at work, especially now Geoff's hurt himself."

Trevor glanced out of the window. The sun had risen slightly further above the warehouses. Traffic continued to roar along the autobahn, its volume steadily increasing. Down below in the hotel car park, Miranda was standing by the coach talking to Tony. Her dark hair shimmered in the morning sunlight. Her freshly laundered blouse was buttoned tightly across her firm bosom. She smiled at something Tony was saying. It was a radiant, relaxed smile.

As he continued to stare out of the window, he began to have a series of disconnected, random thoughts about Mark back home. He thought of him sitting at the table chomping his way remorselessly and loudly through a seemingly endless supply of food, while he and Julia were trying to have some kind of meaningful conversation. He thought of him coming home at three o'clock in the morning, slamming the front door, crashing up the stairs and stumbling noisily into the bathroom, from which a variety of distinctly unpleasant sounds would then emanate. He reflected on those all too rare occasions when he was able to chill out, listening to a Mozart CD, only to be nearly deafened by the cacophony of rhythmic, thumping sounds coming from Mark's room overhead. He shuddered slightly. He then thought of Rosie walking purposefully across his lap, with her needle sharp claws exposed. He thought of her leaping heavily onto the bed and miaowing, just when he and Julia were sharing a moment of intimacy. He thought of the occasional dead bird or rodent that Rosie would leave triumphantly in the middle of the kitchen floor. Finally, he thought of Geoff sitting at home with his ankle in plaster, a beer in his hand and a smug grin on his face, being pandered to by Julia. He shuddered again. He had made his decision. It was almost certainly the wrong decision, he knew that, but, somehow, after all that had happened, he couldn't contemplate any other.

"No, no, no. I don't think I will," he replied, as he continued to look out of the window. "Frankly, I need a break from work and I don't think there'll be much room for me just at the moment in your cosy little family reunion. Besides I need time to think… you know?"

"So you're staying then?"

Trevor nodded and sat down on the bed, staring as though transfixed at the carpet beneath his feet. Julia sighed again. She was sighing a lot this morning.

"Oh well, I'd best be on my way, then. I'll pop down and tell Miranda – she'll be pleased at least – and then if I can book a flight, I'll get the receptionist to order me a taxi to the airport. I'll give you a call when I get home."

She sat down beside Trevor and kissed him lightly on the cheek.

"And you'd better come downstairs with me, otherwise you'll miss breakfast."

Trevor nodded and got up slowly.

"The condemned man ate a hearty breakfast, eh? Are you joining me?"

"No, I don't think I will. I'm not very hungry and I don't think I could face them all after the exhibition I made of myself last night. I certainly don't want to see anything more of that moron Dave or that pompous idiot, Frank!"

★ ★ ★

The early morning sun shining through the windows made the dining room seem brighter and bigger than it had in the subdued artificial light of the previous evening. Breakfast was, as usual, a buffet affair but the stiff, solemn, uniformed waiters of the previous evening were no longer in evidence and the atmosphere seemed a little more convivial. There was, nevertheless, an unmistakeable tension in the air following the previous evening's incident, of which little visible evidence remained apart from some slight stains on the floor tiles.

After the previous night's entanglement with Julia, Dave was sporting more cuts and bruises, this time over his other eye and on his left cheek. He bustled busily around the buffet tables, plundering various breakfast offerings while trying to conceal his newly acquired facial injuries from his fellow travellers. It was his inevitable misfortune, however, to bump into Frank. Frank had spent a difficult evening being soundly lectured by an emotional Joyce on how an Englishman abroad should behave and how he was spoiling the holiday for her. The lecture had been repeated, in an abbreviated form, this morning and he had come down to breakfast suitably chastened and with every intention of being a model of decorum. But it is difficult to change the habits of a lifetime overnight and, as soon as he caught sight of Dave's down-turned battered face, he could not resist a comment.

"Bloody hell, you didn't get bladdered again, did you?"

Dave opened his mouth to reply but before he could say anything, Susan was replying on his behalf.

"No he didn't. But I caught him trying to sneak off to the bar *and* wrestling with that, that, that trollop Julia on the floor. So I hit him!"

Dave looked sheepish. He had been lectured by Susan with much the same vehemence that Frank had suffered at the hands of Joyce; nevertheless, with no hangover to endure, he was determined to enjoy his breakfast this morning and was piling his plate high. Frank watched him with a mixture of grudging admiration and consternation as he balanced a bread roll on top of two others already jammed onto his plate.

"Oi, oi, leave some for those of us coming behind!"

Dave looked up at Frank in mock apology and feigned to tug at his forelock.

"Oooh, sorry! For God's sake, please don't make another scene in the dining room. And please, don't hit me as well! I've got enough cuts and bruises already."

"Don't you start! I've had Joyce going on at me most of the night and again this morning!"

"It's no more than you deserve," added Joyce firmly while guiding Frank to a distant empty table. As he sat down, Frank sensed the imminence of another lecture.

★ ★ ★

Outside, it was another clear, mostly sunny morning, although there was rather more cloud in the sky than on the previous couple of days and a fresh, blustery breeze gave the air a chilly feel. Miranda was, as usual, standing by the entrance to the coach, freshly laundered and with her clipboard in hand, smiling mechanically from behind her sunglasses as each member of the party boarded. Breakfast had been punctual and surprisingly incident-free. Everybody – well, almost everybody – had been on their best behaviour and she was hopeful that, this morning, they would actually manage to get away on time. Most of the party, not anxious to overstay their strained welcome at the Hotel Wappenschild, were already on board, or gathered by the coach, at least five minutes before they were due to depart. The exception, of course, was Julia who was standing, alone and downcast, beneath the canopy of the hotel entrance, with her suitcase beside her, shivering slightly in the cool morning air and peering anxiously down the road in the direction from which she imagined her taxi would arrive.

Trevor, meanwhile, had decided that he was not feeling well this morning. Maybe he had caught Peter's cold or maybe it was the effects of a sleepless night and his emotional traumas, but he felt listless and lethargic. He stood slightly apart from everyone else assembled beside the coach, wishing he had worn a jumper over his pale check shirt on this cool morning, and looking ruefully across at Julia, still perhaps hoping that she would change her mind or that at least she would acknowledge him with a smile or a wave, but she continued to look fixedly down the road. After a moment or two, he turned away, smiled weakly at Miranda and boarded the coach.

Trevor desperately wanted to sneak unobserved into his seat and he even climbed aboard via the rear door so that he could approach his seat without running the gauntlet past Frank and Dave who were bound to offer some unsolicited wisecrack or insensitive comment. He really didn't want to have to explain why he was suddenly on his own, or catch anybody's eye so, having quietly slid into his seat, he began to stare steadfastly out of the window at nothing in particular. It wasn't long, however, before Dave looked round and asked the inevitable question.

"'Ello, Trev. Has she walked out on you then?"

Blunt, unsubtle, indelicate and direct, Dave's question was the one that Trevor had been fearing, but half expecting. He should have told Dave to mind his own business – he knew that – but, for some reason, he couldn't bring himself to do so. He should have made his answer more convincing; he knew that too.

"Er…no..no. She's had to go home; bit of a family crisis."

"So she's not walked out on you then?"

"Oh, no, we're fine! Really!"

"So is that why she moved into her own room last night, then?"

If Trevor wasn't prepared to tell Dave to mind his own business, Susan certainly was. She favoured him with the special look that she reserved for those occasions – increasing in number, it seemed – when Dave had gone simply too far.

"Dave, leave it. It's got nothing to do with you!"

"She's right," Trevor agreed. "It's got nothing to do with you, except of course that I don't imagine Julia greatly appreciated being mauled by you last night. But alright, yes, if you must know, we had a bit of a disagreement and she's going home."

That should have been the end of the conversation of course but, for some reason, Dave seemed abnormally oblivious to the warning signs coming from Susan.

"Oh, dear, oh dear. Women eh? You see, my wife, she won't leave me. God knows I've tried, but she just stays and beats me up instead."

He pointed to his collection of head wounds while Susan glared fiercely at him.

"For God's sake leave him alone! You've got no right to have a go at Trevor, particularly after your behaviour last night!" she shouted at Dave before turning to Trevor. "I am so sorry about him. Try to take no notice."

In the front seats, Joyce noticed Frank, alerted by the commotion, turn round. She sensed that he was itching to join in the conversation, especially as public debate on the coach was now becoming something of a regular occurrence. But after the events of the last couple of days, and based on her experience of over forty years of marriage, Joyce was sure that anything Frank said was unlikely to offer solace to Trevor at this difficult time. She wasn't prepared to take the risk.

"I might be walking out on my old man soon if he doesn't behave himself better," she observed loudly for the benefit of nobody in particular.

Though a little disconcerted by Joyce's increasing assertiveness, Frank was determined to have his say. He turned on her.

"You were the one who wanted to come on this damned awful tour!" He turned round in his seat and looked across at Trevor. "God knows why you want to carry on, Trevor, you've got the perfect excuse to leave!"

In the front seats on the other side of the aisle, Peter and Gail had taken no part in the public debate – it wasn't their style – but had begun talking animatedly to each other, with the occasional subtle glance in Trevor's direction. Their conversation was curtailed, however, by Miranda's first announcement of the day.

"Good morning ladies and gentlemen." She didn't wait for a response. "We have another fairly short run this morning to Boppard on the banks of the Rhine, where we will join the boat for our cruise, which will take us past a number of picturesque villages, castles and, of course, the famous Lorelei rocks. Then we will visit the delightful ancient walled town of Rothenburg, where you'll have time for lunch and some sightseeing before we continue our journey to our overnight hotel near Innsbruck."

When Miranda paused, Peter resumed his conversation with Gail before leaving his seat, walking tentatively down the coach, holding on carefully to the backs of the seats, as it swung round a sharp bend out of the hotel car park, and sitting down with greater force than he had intended, next to Trevor.

"May I?" he asked Trevor somewhat superfluously.

After Dave and Frank's unsubtle and unhelpful contributions, Trevor had been hoping for the opportunity to gather his thoughts quietly for a while, perhaps enjoy a short doze, and he did not receive Peter's unexpected arrival very graciously.

"I hope you haven't come to gloat, or to have fun at my expense like certain other people on this coach!"

"Oh, no, no. It's just that, well, we couldn't help overhearing what's happened…"

"You and the rest of the coach, I shouldn't wonder."

"Quite. Anyway, I've just come to say that if you want a bit of company… Somebody to talk to… you know… Gail and I… we'd be happy for you to join us, maybe over a meal or for a drink. Not that we are trying to impose or anything, but sometimes… you know…we've been through quite a lot ourselves recently and we know how important it can be to have someone to talk to. That's all I wanted to say…"

Peter had had no time to rehearse what he was going to say and he felt that he had rather made a mess of things. Resisting the temptation to dash back to his seat and bury his head in his hands to cover his embarrassment, he sat quietly, waiting for a response. But Trevor didn't respond – not immediately anyway. He just sat and stared out of the window, apparently oblivious to Peter's presence, while the two elderly ladies behind, apparently oblivious to everything that was going on around them, began a long and rambling dialogue about the increasingly complex and outlandish storylines in a couple of television soap operas. After waiting for what felt like a couple of minutes, Peter coughed and got up to leave, concluding that his intervention had not been welcome. But as he stood up, Trevor suddenly turned round, reached out and grabbed his arm, pulling him back into the seat.

"You know, that's really nice of you and I'm sorry if I was a bit rude. I might like to take you up on your offer at some stage. On the other hand, I hope you won't be offended if I just stay by myself and kind of reflect quietly on things for a while."

"Quite understood. We'll leave the offer with you… No offence either way." Peter smiled with relief and scurried back to his seat.

★ ★ ★

As Miranda had promised, it was a relatively short trip south from Koblenz to Boppard and a rare prompt departure from the hotel, coupled with a trouble-free journey, meant that the coach party was allowed the unexpected privilege of some early morning free time in Boppard to explore its medieval market square, its pavement cafes and its souvenir shops, before assembling on the quay to board the boat. Although no-one had said so, in so many words, the wording in the holiday brochure and Miranda's carefully phrased announcements had given the distinct impression that the coach party was about to board a specially chartered boat. There was some disappointment, therefore, when it became evident that the boat was in fact a standard commercial passenger boat that plied up and down the Rhine, making scheduled stops en route for passengers to get on or off, and that it was already quite full when it finally made its stop at Boppard.

Miranda had asked the coach party to assemble together, beneath a lamppost on the quay, so that she could ceremoniously and methodically issue each person with a ticket. As a result of this time-consuming exercise, they found themselves towards the back of the throng, jostling with each other to get aboard the already crowded boat.

Dave's muscular build, and years of practice, could often enable him to elbow his way to the front of a queue, but he was not so effective in tight spaces and, on this occasion, he found himself in serious competition with Brian who, with surprisingly strong forearms, was advancing himself quickly through the crowd. As Brian was about to clamber on board, Dave turned towards Valerie who had been following serenely in Brian's chaotic wake.

"For God's sake don't let Brian go anywhere near the edge of the boat. There's a lot of water down there."

From somewhere nearby, they heard Frank's tremulous voice rising above the multi-lingual babble. He was not enjoying the experience. He hated crowds and abhorred the foreign tendency to jostle and shove rather than to queue in an orderly, dignified and civilised fashion.

"I wish you hadn't mentioned water," he wailed. "I hope there isn't a queue for the toilet."

"I hope there isn't a queue for the bar!" Dave shouted over his shoulder, as he was swept along in the crowd. Susan, meanwhile, had crept round on Dave's blind side and playfully tugged at his shirt collar.

"You can forget that idea. It's far too early in the morning and we're going straight up on deck."

For all Dave's muscle power, he found himself caught in something of a logjam and was soon overtaken by the slim but athletic figures of Jason and Barbara.

"And you two had better get up on deck too and soak up the sun," he called after them. "You look as though you could do with some fresh air!"

The boat had two decks. The lower deck was enclosed, with rigid wooden benches bolted to the floor and windows spattered with water and whatever other fluids had recently cascaded from the upper deck. Its main advantage on a hot day was that is was next to the bar and, of course, on a cold, rainy day, its occupants were well shielded from the elements. The upper deck, split in two by the central stairwell and access doors, was, by contrast, entirely open to the elements. The chairs, resembling cheap, plastic patio chairs, were not bolted to the deck and could be freely moved about. This invariably led to a great deal of furniture moving and jostling for position, as passengers tried to secure the best vantage points, while the boat slowly pulled out into the middle of the river.

On the upper deck, Jason and Barbara, fleet-footed and

determined, had been fortunate enough to locate a couple of empty chairs placed together, near the back and sheltered from the aggressive breeze, where they could enjoy a quiet cuddle, some restorative sunbathing, a bit of sightseeing and, of course, a good giggle. While Frank was paying his routine visit to the toilet, Joyce searched in vain for a couple of empty seats towards the bow. Nigel had managed to find one at the side for his mother, which she sat on with due pomp, but the only other free seats were in the centre of the deck, with a restricted view. Reluctantly, Joyce bagged two of them. Surprisingly undeterred by the less than satisfactory vantage point, Frank decided, on his return from the toilet, to stand and he swayed slightly from side to side in the breeze as he tried to film some of the passing scenery, over and, occasionally, between the heads of his fellow travellers. Gail, meanwhile, had somehow squeezed into a small gap by the rail where she posed with Fred while Peter took yet another picture of them, this time with a Rhine vineyard in the background. Under Valerie's eagle-eyed supervision, Brian watched them, a little reflectively, perched firmly on a chair well away from the edge and cursing the absence of a camera as yet another picturesque castle, high on a riverside cliff, drifted by.

On the less crowded lower deck, Trevor found a quiet corner away from the crowds, where he sat by himself, immune to what was going on around him, quietly watching the scenery as it drifted sedately past the window. The sun was shining through the window and Trevor was beginning to feel quite warm. Still feeling lethargic, and perhaps hypnotised by the boat's tranquil passage down the river, or perhaps still feeling the after-effects of his emotional trauma and sleepless night, he began to feel drowsy. After a while, he started to doze, lightly at first, but then he drifted into a deeper sleep.

After making lazy progress down the river, the boat slowed as it passed the famous Lorelei rock, a scratchy piece of music interrupted the scratchy, pre-recorded commentary on the scratchy public address system and Brian rued the loss of yet another photo opportunity. Frank, on the other hand, managed to film some decent fragments of the rock, between the heads of his fellow passengers, and when the lens was not being obscured by his index finger. Shortly afterwards, the boat made its scheduled stop at Oberwesel and the coach party, closely chaperoned by a watchful Miranda, disembarked and walked a few yards down the road to where Tony was waiting with the coach.

The ninety minute boat trip had been viewed in advance with some anxiety by Miranda. There were all kinds of opportunities for misadventures or misunderstandings, with the risk that somebody would disembark at the wrong stop but, seemingly, it had passed off without incident. Nobody had fallen in the water, there had been no fights or embarrassing incidents, everybody – or so she thought – had got off at Oberwesel as instructed, everybody had found their way to the coach and it had left on time. From her seat at the front, Miranda made a cursory check of the passengers on board and, smiling with relief, felt that this rare occurrence should not go unrecognised. She reached for the microphone.

"Well congratulations! You all made it back to the coach on time, nobody fell into the water and there were no mishaps of any kind."

She could not disguise the heavy hint of sarcasm in her voice, however, and it did not go unnoticed. But, for once, Frank kept his voice down as he whispered to Joyce.

"Sarcastic bitch! If she wants to behave like that..."

He turned and began to whisper conspiratorially to Jason and Barbara, but they were interrupted by Dave's alarm call.

"Where's Trevor?" he suddenly shouted in Miranda's direction.

Miranda turned round quickly. During her cursory check, she had noted the empty seat, next to the aisle, formerly occupied by Julia, but in her relief that everything had apparently gone well, and that Brian had returned safe and dry, she had assumed, without actually checking, that Trevor had boarded the coach. He had seemed sensible, intelligent and trustworthy – not the sort to disappear or get confused – but, nevertheless, she knew that she should have counted each individual and that she had made a fundamental and embarrassing error. She rose quickly from her seat and rushed to where Trevor should have been sitting, as though expecting him to materialise, magically, from somewhere. But there was no sign of him.

"Oh, shit!" she shouted. "Has anyone seen Trevor recently?" Her question was greeted with an ominous silence.

"Oh, shit, shit, shit!" She turned and raced back to the front of the coach, sat down, and leaned across towards Tony.

"Tony, Tony! Trevor's not on the coach. We might have left him behind at Oberwesel but, if he's not there, he must be still on the boat somewhere. You may have to drive onto to Bacharach and we'll see if we can intercept the boat when it stops there. Oh my God. He's very depressed at the moment – I hope he hasn't done something stupid!"

Though irritated at the necessity of another enforced detour, albeit quite minor, Tony tried to be reassuring. "He most probably forgot to get off. You know, mind on other things. I'm sure someone would have noticed if he'd tried to throw himself overboard."

They returned quickly to Oberwesel, but there was no sign of Trevor at the embarkation point so they decided to try and race the boat to Bacharach. Fortunately, the road from Oberwesel to Bacharach was reasonably direct and reasonably clear of traffic and the coach arrived well ahead of the gently cruising boat. While Tony found somewhere to park, Miranda waited anxiously on the quay, staring intently up river as the boat came slowly into view around a bend, gradually – very gradually – getting closer until, at last, it began to move alongside the small jetty. Peering through the crowds of people on deck, and to her immense relief, she thought she could identify Trevor. She could see him yawning and rubbing his hand over his hair. She thought she could recognise his check shirt and his favoured fawn chino trousers.

Confused, and not a little bewildered, Trevor looked agitatedly around. A party of boisterous young people, who boarded the boat at Oberwesel, had soon stirred him from his slumbers but, when he looked around and couldn't find any of his fellow passengers on board, he knew something was wrong. A brief chat with one of the crew confirmed his fears. Now his only chance was to disembark at Bacharach and hope that the coach was there to meet him. Fortunately, he caught sight of Miranda waving frantically at him from the quayside and, waving back, he hastened quickly from the boat. After the morning misadventure, he was so relieved to see Miranda waiting for him that he abandoned his normal reserve, embraced her warmly and kissed her ebulliently on the cheek. Locked momentarily and tightly in Trevor's arms, Miranda found herself again recalling the image of him standing naked and vulnerable in the middle of the hotel corridor. She lingered slightly longer in his grasp than she should, enjoying the memory of that encounter and his strong embrace.

Somehow, Trevor was now even more reluctant to join the coach than he had been at the start of the morning, but, as it turned out, Frank and Dave seemed unexpectedly sympathetic to his ordeal. After all, they agreed, it was mainly Miranda's abnormal complacency that had caused the problem. No doubt, she would be reminded of her lapse before too long.

★ ★ ★

As Frank made a point of studying his watch carefully, the coach left Bacharach and headed south-east through Germany, into Bavaria and along part of the "romantic road" towards Rothenburg for a lunch-time stop. Chastened by her uncharacteristic error in not noticing that Trevor was missing – after all, whatever her failings, she had always prided herself on her thoroughness and her attention to detail – and aware that she alone had been the cause of yet another delay, Miranda made only a reluctant and brief foray down the coach, offering teas, coffees and other refreshments, while the occupants busied themselves with their usual travelling pastimes – reading, listening to music through their personal stereo systems, chatting, looking out of the window and dozing. The two elderly ladies passed the time talking proudly and competitively about their respective grandchildren and how well they were doing at everything.

As the coach approached Rothenburg, Miranda returned to her seat in order to announce the arrangements and timings for their visit.

"We'll shortly be arriving at the magnificent medieval walled town of Rothenburg, where you can enjoy the many sights of this splendid town and get a bit of lunch. We'll be leaving there at 2.30."

Frank, who had been unexpectedly subdued since they left Bacharach, had been lying in wait. He was still simmering at Miranda's earlier sarcastic remarks and, making an exaggerated point of looking at his watch, he held three fingers above his head, straightened the tie that he still often insisted on wearing and, oozing with pompous self-importance, jumped to his feet.

"Is that all the time we are going to get?" he asked with a dramatic earnestness. "No, no, I'm sorry, but that's just not good enough. It doesn't really give us long enough to see the many sights as you put it, especially as we have had yet another delay this morning, through no fault of our own I might add, and we've got to get some lunch. And some of us aren't as nimble as we used to be, you know. No, no, I'm sorry but we've paid good money for this trip and we want to be able see the places we stop at properly without having to rush all the time. And at our time of life, we might not get another chance to see them."

Miranda remained seated and outwardly calm though she felt her stomach churning. Since Frank's little insurgence of the previous day and, in view of her earlier faux pas, she had been half-expecting another rebellion, but she was determined to avoid a repeat of the previous day's public debate and she knew she needed to be firm. She tried to sound resolute.

"I'm sorry, but we've got to leave at 2.30, otherwise we may not get to our overnight hotel in time…"

Unfortunately for Miranda, Frank was in his adrenaline-fuelled element. Apparently undeterred by the embarrassment of the previous evening's incident in the hotel dining room, seemingly oblivious to Joyce's remonstrations and boosted by Dave's confidential disclosure, over breakfast, of Miranda and Tony's nocturnal activities, he was enjoying himself more than at any other time so far on the holiday. Just managing to resist the temptation to call his fellow travellers "comrades" or "brothers," he continued.

"I'm sure our overnight hotel can adapt to slight delays. Anyway, if it's anything like the last one, we're not in too much of a hurry to get there."

This remark drew some laughter from the back of the coach. It was all the encouragement Frank needed; rightly or wrongly, he now sensed that he had the support of his fellow travellers and would use it to try and force another concession out of Miranda.

"You see, we've lost time on virtually every stop so far for one reason or another and today has been no exception, so it's about time we made up for some of it. So I suggest we leave at three."

In her fairly brief and chequered career as a Tour Director, Miranda had occasionally pondered on what might happen if all of her "clients" took it upon themselves not to turn up at the time they had been asked to. She couldn't very well leave without everyone, so it was largely a matter of relying on their cooperation and good will. But if, for some reason, their cooperation and good will ran out…

"I'm sorry, but we just can't…" she heard herself saying, limply.

Frank stepped into the aisle, moved a couple of steps down the coach and spread his hands out, in a gesture of appeal, towards his fellow passengers.

"What do you all think?"

Around the coach, there was a sea of nodding heads. "Three o'clock," Dave agreed vociferously. "Yes, that's more like it," someone shouted enthusiastically from the back of the coach. Miranda went to say something but stopped herself and looked across at Tony for help. He shrugged his shoulders as he started to manoeuvre the coach into the official coach park. There was nothing Miranda could do, of course, and she knew it.

"Alright, as the delay was partly my fault this morning, three o'clock it is, but don't anyone be even a minute late back and don't anyone get any fancy ideas that this is the way it's going to be from now on!"

Frank held a clenched fist aloft in a gesture of triumph and there was a smattering of applause as people prepared to get off. While he stood there, glowing with triumph, Joyce crept quietly off the coach to join the queue for the nearby toilets. Frank would have to wait his turn, even if it proved to be uncomfortable for him and his recalcitrant bladder.

★ ★ ★

Rothenburg ob der Tauber, to give it its full name, is generally described as being a charming walled town where, structurally, little has changed since the middle of the seventeenth century. The main streets, which radiate from the central Marktplatz are lined with old half-timbered gabled houses, and many of the original city walls and towers are still in place, nestling alongside gothic and medieval churches. Recognising its appeal for the modern-day tourist, the town authorities had not been slow to encourage the introduction of a wide range of souvenir shops, restaurants and cafes, while still preserving the medieval character of the place.

As they strolled gently from the coach park towards the town centre, Peter and Gail were suddenly joined by Trevor.

"Hello!" ventured Trevor tentatively. "I wonder… would you mind if I join you for a while… You know…? I don't want a repeat of what happened earlier. I think I need someone to keep an eye on me!"

Gail smiled radiantly at him.

"Not at all, we'd be delighted, wouldn't we Peter?"

Peter blew his nose loudly and nodded from behind his handkerchief.

Dave and Susan, meanwhile, had discovered a gabled, half-timbered branch of *McDonald's* in the heart of the town and had rushed joyously inside. For Brian and Valerie, the simple pleasures of a small bakery had satisfied their lunchtime appetites and they left the shop with their purchases in a bag, looking for somewhere suitable to sit and eat them. Frank and Joyce, meanwhile, began a thorough search for something akin to a genteel seaside tearoom, with gingham tablecloths, silver cake-stands, lace doilies and young waitresses wearing white aprons – they were out of luck.

★ ★ ★

Back at the coach, Tony and Miranda were trying to relax, enjoying the calm of an empty coach and eating a light baguette lunch that Tony had purchased earlier when Miranda was on the boat. Between bites, he spoke.

"That wasn't spontaneous, you know – what happened earlier. It was all too slick. I'm sure they'd planned that little rebellion."

"I know. It's a damned nuisance we left Trevor behind at Oberwesel; it rather played into their hands. It's that bloody Frank Armitage. I should have got rid of him after the incident in the dining room last night. I would have been justified."

"Mmm. Hindsight!"

Without warning, Miranda's face crumpled and suddenly she looked frightened and vulnerable. The aura of calm control that she tried to exude when her "clients" were around had deserted her. She burst into tears. Tony left his seat, went over to her and placed a strong, comforting arm around her.

"I don't know what I'm going to do now, Tony," she sobbed. "I've lost them – they're in control." Tony took a handkerchief from his pocket and gently started to dab Miranda's damp cheeks.

"Well, you've got two choices as I see it. You can either give up altogether and relinquish control to them, which means they'll do what they want when they want – God knows what that'll mean – or you'll have to take control back again. That means you make it clear that the time we leave is not negotiable and that we will start leaving people behind if they're late, even if that means everybody. I'm sure the company will back you up if you explain. Throw anyone off the tour if they misbehave. Be tough and don't back down!"

"Yes, I know, I know, but some of the ring leaders keep threatening to report us two for… you know. It's bad enough for me, but you've got a wife and kids back home."

"Mmm. Tricky, that. But we may have no choice. We may

have to call their bluff. Let's see how it goes for the rest of the day and decide this evening."

★ ★ ★

Unable to find any vacant, conveniently situated seats, Brian and Valerie were finally forced to settle uncomfortably on the steps between the arcaded columns at the front of the Rathaus in the Marktplatz. Valerie was dressed in a smart lilac, knee-length dress and was finding it hard to perch elegantly on the shallow stone steps. Brian, with his open necked shirt, baggy corduroy trousers, open-toed sandals, and a natural tendency to sprawl, was much more at ease. It was the height of the tourist season, the town was heavily congested with visitors and the steps were crowded with people of all ages eating pastries, rolls, baguettes, cakes, fruit and all kinds of snacks and sweet confectionary, as well as consuming any number of sugared drinks. As a result, the whole area had become a haven for wasps and a number buzzed loudly and persistently around Brian and Valerie as they ate. Valerie had never been comfortable in the presence of these seemingly hostile creatures, she still remembered being badly stung as a child, and the final vestiges of her calm, unruffled elegance vanished as she swatted wildly at any wasp that came within arms reach. This served only to make the wasps more persistent and aggressive and, as they continued to swarm noisily around her, she lashed out even more violently, accidentally striking her flailing arm, painfully, on one of the large, colonnaded stone pillars just behind where she was sitting. Clutching her sore arm, and wearing an exaggeratedly pained expression, she grabbed what was left of her lunch and ran off, in something of a panic, to the other side of the Marktplatz, where she was eventually joined, at a lugubrious pace, by a smirking Brian.

★ ★ ★

Frank and Joyce had eventually contented themselves – inasmuch as Frank was ever contented – with a pavement café and a couple of omelettes for lunch and, a short distance from the Rathaus, Frank had discovered some primitive public toilets which, despite his usual grouch, he was only too grateful to use. As he emerged, shaking his hands vigorously in an effort to dry them, the first person he saw was Barbara, wearing tight jeans, leaning forward, with her bottom stuck out, and pouting provocatively for Jason, who was taking a photograph. With a look of distaste, he retreated hastily back into the toilet, but the cocktail of nauseous smells that greeted him drove him back out again and he scampered hastily away with Joyce in gasping pursuit.

★ ★ ★

Having finally beaten off the persistent wasps long enough to complete their lunch, standing up in a shaded corner of the Marktplatz and well removed from the swarming colony, Brian and Valerie were strolling around the town, absorbing the plethora of impressive sights and sounds. Valerie's arm no longer felt sore, though she felt sure that an ugly looking bruise would erupt over the next or two, and her calm serenity had returned; even Brian appeared untroubled. There had been no disasters – nothing had been lost or damaged – and their luck, it seemed, was finally changing. As they gently turned a street corner, however, Brian heard a nearby clock chiming three times. With some unease, he looked up at the clock, high on a medieval tower, and confirmed that the hands on the face were pointing to three o'clock. He glanced at his wrist before remembering that he wasn't wearing a watch.

"What do you make the time?" Brian asked Valerie trying to make his enquiry sound as casual as possible.

Valerie studied the elegant gold-plated timepiece on her elegant wrist.

"Ten past two. We're okay for a little while yet."

Brian pointed nervously to the clock.

"Are you sure?"

Valerie nodded before looking up at the clock. It was an old clock and probably kept erratic time, she told herself, but by way of reassurance, she held her watch up to her ear. She could hear nothing. Looking worried, she studied the second hand to see if it was moving. It wasn't. Her calm serenity evaporated. With a look of rising panic, she shook it.

"Bloody thing has stopped," she cried. "Must have been when I caught my arm on the pillar back there!"

Before she had finished, Brian had already broken into a disjointed trot, straining every sinew, his short stubby legs pumping up and down furiously as he tried to inject some momentum into an unwilling and badly streamlined body.

"Jesus Christ, we're late again!!" he called over his shoulder.

They dashed off as rapidly as they could with Brian demonstrating all the silken running skills of a sumo wrestler and Valerie following uncertainly in his wake, trying, and failing, to run both swiftly and safely in a pair of high heeled shoes on the uneven cobbles of the old streets. They had run about fifty yards or so, when they realised they were heading in the wrong direction. They stopped, turned and galloped off in the general direction of the coach park.

Although the route back to the coach park, located just beyond the town wall, was not particularly difficult, it was quite a long and undulating trek and, with many of the narrow streets bearing a passing resemblance to each other, Brian and Valerie made several short but time-consuming detours before they finally arrived back at the coach, breathless and twenty minutes late.

Miranda was, of course, wearing her sunglasses, but this time, it was mainly in an attempt to hide the redness in her eyes. At first, she thought that everyone had had the good grace to return to the coach by the newly "negotiated" time, but she did not want to run the risk of leaving anyone behind again, so she checked very carefully; it didn't take her long to realise that Brian and Valerie were missing. By the time they lolloped into view, Miranda had abandoned any remaining semblance of calm professionalism. She was visibly shaking while trying to control a further flood of tears. As Brian and Valerie scrambled aboard she said nothing and looked away. Valerie, however, thought it politic to try and apologise.

"I'm so sorry we're late. My watch stopped and we lost track of time."

With her emotions in turmoil, Miranda still said nothing. She sat in her seat and looked, very deliberately, at the floor, breathing heavily, as the coach screeched away pitching Brian and Valerie heavily into their seats.

As the coach sped off in a southerly direction towards southern Bavaria and the Austrian border, Miranda spent some time trying desperately to regain control of her emotions. She took a few swigs of water from a plastic bottle, swallowed down a couple of pills which she had quietly removed from her bag, gulped several times, removed her sunglasses, dabbed her eyes, took a couple of deep breaths and turned, almost in desperation, towards Tony.

"What now?" she sniffed, remembering their recent conversation.

"No choice, I'm afraid," was Tony's curt reply. "It's a risk, but we've got to take it, otherwise it'll be anarchy!"

Miranda nodded. She took another couple of swigs of water and some more deep breaths before reaching for the microphone. She did her best to talk calmly but there was an unmistakeable tremor in her voice and, as she continued, it became louder and more shrill. Her words poured out in an unstructured and ill-considered torrent.

"Well, congratulations! Yet again, we've managed to leave late, even when we allowed you to have an extra half-hour and you all promised to be back promptly by three o'clock. God knows what time we'll get to our hotel now… We're going to hit the rush hour later on… I shall have to phone ahead and apologise… Perhaps I can remind you all at this point that company policy does not require us to wait for anyone who is late back. In future, we intend to leave on schedule and on time. Anyone who isn't back on time will have to make their own arrangements to catch up with us… There will be no exceptions and no negotiations. Is that clear?"

By the end, Miranda's outburst had become little more than an angry rant. It did, however, have the effect of silencing every member of the coach party, with no-one, not even Frank, or the two elderly ladies, daring to say anything.

Dave had greatly enjoyed his visit to Rothenburg, but he had consumed his lunch with undue haste and his digestive system was now protesting. In the strained silence, he accidentally let out a loud burp. There were a few nervous giggles but they were quickly suppressed, even those of Barbara and Jason, as the coach travelled silently on.

The lengthy afternoon journey was completed in an eerily tense quiet, broken only by the two elderly ladies having an earnest dialogue about their most recent visit to the new indoor shopping centre in their local town and lightened only by the briefest of comfort stops, with everyone hurrying back to the coach with at least five minutes to spare. Throughout the journey, Miranda remained firmly in her seat, head down, fiddling with forms and assorted sheets of papers, and scribbling some notes. She made only the tersest of announcements and conspicuously failed to offer refreshments to anyone.

As the coach got closer to the Austrian border, the landscape became more undulating and, eventually, the coach party was treated to its first sight, through the windows, of the majestic Alps with traces of snow still covering the highest peaks, white clouds scudding across the escarpments, the occasional distant waterfall, and increasingly pretty villages scattered along the verdant valleys. As the coach drove on through the mountains, spirits began to lift a little.

★ ★ ★

The Hotel Ritzerbach, on the outskirts of Innsbruck, was built in traditional Tyrolean chalet style with ornately carved and decorated wooden panels adorning the walls and a high gabled roof extending over individual balconies lavishly furnished with tubs and baskets of brightly coloured flowers. At first glance, it held the promise of better things than the Hotel Wappenschild and the passengers were surprisingly upbeat as they prepared to disembark. Before they could complete their escape, however,

Miranda made the inevitable announcement. Her mood had clearly not improved.

"Because of the er… further delays this afternoon, you'll just have time to check into your rooms and come straight back down to dinner. We'll get your cases unloaded and taken to your rooms while you are having dinner. And in the morning, breakfast is available from 7.15, when you will need to leave your suitcases outside your rooms. We intend to leave at 8 o'clock sharp! And I do mean sharp!"

With that, Miranda put her sunglasses on, tossed her dark hair petulantly and flounced off the coach, leaving the passengers feeling distinctly cowed. As they scrambled and jostled to get off the coach, Frank turned and shouted at Brian and Valerie.

"This is all your bloody fault, you know. All you had to do was get back to the coach on time…"

But before Frank had a chance to say any more, or a startled Brian and Valerie had the opportunity to respond, Joyce bellowed "Leave it, Frank!" in such an uncharacteristically strident and aggressive way that Frank became momentarily dumbstruck, allowing Joyce to drag him off the coach without uttering a further word.

★ ★ ★

The foyer of the Hotel Ritzerbach had ornate, oak panelled walls, liberally hung with fussy prints, faded pictures and sepia photographs, and an unobtrusive reception desk displaying a brass bell and a small stand of postcards. Unlike the previous hotels on the itinerary, it had the comfortable feel of a friendly, family home.

The intimate foyer was far too small for Tony to stack all of the suitcases in, so he started to decant them into a sparsely furnished lounge area, which led off from the foyer and adjoined the bar and dining room. Tony had just delivered two especially large and heavy suitcases to the lounge when, from the bar area, he heard a voice he recognised.

"Hi, Tony!"

He looked up, smiled broadly, laid the suitcases on the floor and walked briskly into the bar. Behind the bar was a fair-haired young woman with deep brown eyes, a healthy tan and a ready smile. She was wearing a traditional Tyrolean blouse and as Tony approached, she leant forward over the bar, displaying a formidable décolletage.

"Hello, Lisa," Tony effused, planting an affectionate kiss on her cheek. "What the hell are you doing here? How are you?"

"I'm fine, thanks. I'm working here now; for the time being anyway. Gosh, you look hot!"

Tony wiped some glistening beads of perspiration from his forehead.

"Do I? I'm not surprised. I don't know what some of 'em put in their suitcases but they weigh a ton."

"So how are you, you old bugger?"

"Oh, not too good, I'm afraid! I tell you, things are bloody awful. We are having a nightmare tour."

Lisa looked intrigued. "Tell me more!"

"Look, I'd better get on, we're running late! What time do you finish tonight?"

"Nine o'clock, after your lot have finished dinner, if you want to buy me a drink."

"It's a date! See you later!"

★ ★ ★

In keeping with the rest of the hotel, the dining room offered a pleasant, if slightly cosmetic, Tyrolean ambience, with ornamental shutters either side of the windows, carved wooden wall panels, ornaments of a sugary, sentimental nature festooned across most of the available surfaces, an over-abundance of lace trimmings and long solid wooden tables, seating up to twelve people, adorned with vases of fresh alpine flowers. Frank and Joyce, Dave and Susan, Barbara and Jason and Peter and Gail found themselves seated at the same table for dinner. This arrangement was mainly out of choice – those seated at the front of the coach had developed an uneasy camaraderie – although there was some apprehension about whether Frank would make another embarrassing scene this evening. Although on nodding terms, Peter and Gail formally introduced themselves to Barbara and Jason, from whom they had heard many an intriguing noise in many a neighbouring hotel room. Having consumed an appetizing starter of beef broth, the main course – the ubiquitous Wiener schnitzel – was placed in front of each of them by Lisa or one of two other attractive waitresses, each dressed in Tyrolean style. Frank looked suspiciously at his plate before stabbing the schnitzel with his fork as though trying to prevent it from escaping. Joyce, who was feeling so much more liberated and confident now and whose irritation with Frank was mounting so rapidly that she could tolerate no more of his jingoistic and curmudgeonly behaviour, snapped at him.

"It is dead, you know, Frank," she observed sarcastically. "It's not going to move about!"

"I'll take your word for it," Frank grumbled, while continuing to poke the schnitzel with obvious suspicion. "But what did it die of, that's what I want to know? I'm sorry, but somehow, I still feel safer with English food."

"Me too!" Dave chimed in enthusiastically. "A nice plate of curry, or a pizza. Or a pile of fried cholesterol on a plate, that's what I'm used to."

He looked playfully across the table at Barbara and Jason, who had shuffled their chairs as close to each other as they could, and were tucking into their food voraciously. Jason had cut his food into small pieces and was trying to eat it with just his fork in one hand while, beneath the table, his other hand was surreptitiously caressing the inside of Barbara's thigh.

"And I suppose you're still enjoying this are you?" Dave asked, somewhat obviously. Barbara looked up guiltily before fixing Dave with her limpid, deep brown eyes and playful smile. Susan looked across at Barbara, casually at first but then more intently, as though somehow transfixed by her aura of youthful innocence, coupled with a kind of unwitting flirtatiousness that exuded from her; a quality that, outside of the bedroom, Barbara was probably unaware that she possessed.

"Yeah, it's cool," Barbara enthused. "We were saying to Frank and Joyce last night, before, er… well, before we started dinner, that we've never been away on holiday together before."

"In fact, we've never really, like, been abroad before, unless you count a day's shopping trip to Calais," added Jason dramatically, before devouring another piece of schnitzel.

"Well no," Barbara agreed. "But I soooo want to travel. That's why I'm studying languages – French and Italian mainly."

"Yes, that's the thing," said Frank with unconvincing and not entirely spontaneous enthusiasm. He was trying to avoid any repeat of the events of the previous evening – or indeed even a reference to the previous evening – and was putting on a show of enforced conviviality. "Do this kind of thing when you're young. Especially now we're in Europe. One big happy band, eh? Trouble with us, I suppose, is that we've spent too many years not going outside England, not even to Calais."

"Even a trip onto our balcony at home can be a bit too much of an adventure sometimes," Joyce added enigmatically. Frank didn't seem to hear.

"I must admit, I do miss it though," he confided, wistfully. "I can't really take to being herded like cattle by some highly lacquered control-freak." Dave nodded his agreement.

"I think we'd noticed that! Mind you, I do agree. If Susan and Peter over there hadn't held me back the other day, I would have hit her by now."

Susan started at the mention of her name. Looking pink and flustered, she realised that she must have been staring at Barbara for some time now, so, before Barbara noticed, she looked away guiltily and began to stare at Dave instead.

"That's your answer to everything, isn't it?" she admonished.

At this point, Trevor made a belated appearance in the dining room. He had been sitting upstairs in his room for some time, studying the large, empty double bed and trying to decide whether to go down for dinner. He wasn't feeling particular hungry or particularly sociable but, in the end, he decided that sitting around moping in his room was only depressing him and maybe the company and the conversation around the dinner table might cheer him up. Just as long as he wasn't going to be sitting next to Dave or Frank, he thought to himself as he went downstairs. One of the waitresses intercepted him as he made his tentative way into the dining room and gestured to an empty seat next to Peter and on the same table as, and virtually opposite, Dave and Frank. He suppressed a groan. As he sat down, another waitress rushed up with a bowl of soup and placed it firmly in front of him.

"Hello, Trevor. How goes it?" asked Peter, rather nasally. Trevor took an unenthusiastic taste of his soup.

"Oh, not great, I'm afraid. I keep asking myself what I've done wrong."

"Ah, that's women for you," Dave philosophised. "You never know what you've done wrong until it's too late."

"Never mind, luv, it's always fun when you find out!" Susan added, while continuing to fix Dave with an intimidating stare.

Most of the guests had already made good progress through the main course when Brian and Valerie arrived, breathless and anxious. They looked around at the full dining room hoping to avoid having to sit with Frank. They were, however, immediately pounced on by one of the waitresses and were ushered to the two spare seats opposite Trevor and next to Frank. They groaned. Though elegantly attired as normal, Valerie seemed unusually distressed and was close to tears. Frank looked up from the task of chasing the remains of the schnitzel round his plate long enough to notice Brian and Valerie sitting down but not long enough to sense the mood they were in. As usual, he pitched in with all the tact and subtlety of a sledgehammer.

"Bloody hell. Not late again?"

Immediately, Valerie burst into tears. Brian tried to comfort her and offered her a crumpled, grey handkerchief from his crumpled, grey pocket, to help stem the tears. Valerie chose instead to dab her cheeks daintily on the lace serviette in front of her.

"I tell you, I can't stand much more of this," she sniffed. "We just seem to have one accident after another. We haven't got a camera or a watch that works, half of Brian's clothes are dirty or wet, we keep turning up late because of one thing or another. We feel we're letting you all down…"

She burst into tears again, more loudly this time, and there followed an awkward silence as everyone sitting around the table simultaneously began to inspect the lacy white tablecloth with an unusually keen interest. This was not what Trevor wanted – his hopes of a distracting and lively conversation had been thwarted. It was Dave who eventually broke the silence.

"Well, you've certainly taken the pressure off me today and I'm most grateful. Tell you what, why don't you stay close to us and we'll look after you. When we get to Venice, we'll share a gondola and keep an eye on you both."

"That's very kind…" Valerie began to reply through her tears, when Frank suddenly clasped his hand to his forehead, in a mannered way.

"Oh, my God! Venice! Water! You'd better put him on a lead or something, Valerie."

"You can borrow one of the one's Susan got for me, if you like!" Dave smirked before receiving a painful dig in the ribs and another menacing look from Susan.

The meal, tastier than most they had experienced during the holiday, proceeded uneventfully. Trevor, Valerie and Brian were all eased into the conversation, which grew increasingly banal and trivial as the diners all tried to avoid any subject that might cause offence or distress. As most of them neared the end of the apple strudel, Gail was watching Trevor pick reluctantly at his food with her usual intense but well-meaning concern.

"Come on Trevor, eat up. It'll do you good," she urged with an easy, almost maternal smile.

Trevor pushed his plate away. "No, I'm sorry but I'm just not very hungry. I think I'll go for a bit of a walk if you don't mind."

He got up and left the table. His dining companions watched in silence as he walked slowly away with a melancholic air.

Barbara, meanwhile, had been trying hard to sit still and remain composed, but she was finding it increasingly difficult to do so as Jason's continual caresses were becoming steadily more arousing. For her, therefore, Trevor's departure was timely. She pushed her empty dessert plate towards the middle of the table and suddenly stood up, causing Jason to recoil backwards in surprise.

"Yes, I think we'll be going too," her voice somehow sounding more sultry than usual.

"Eh, you two!" Dave smirked. "Don't wear yourselves out. Save your strength for the morning – it's another early start…"

Frank groaned at the prospect of another early start.

★ ★ ★

It had been a particularly challenging and stressful day and Tony was grateful for the opportunity to unwind in the bar for an hour or so. Like the rest of the hotel, the bar had a carefully manufactured, rustic charm. Small hand-crafted wooden tables and chairs, cosy nooks and dim lighting gave the room an intimate feel – so different from the large, impersonal, mass-produced facilities that had proliferated elsewhere on the tour. Tony had bought a large beer for himself and a glass of red wine for Lisa, which he took over to the table where she was sitting, still dressed in her Tyrolean uniform. He sat down with an almost audible sigh of relief and smiled across at Lisa with genuine warmth. She had always been one of his favourite travelling companions.

"So tell me," he began. "I'd heard you'd given up being a tour guide but I had no idea you'd settled here."

Lisa took a small sip of her wine and leaned forward, once again displaying a generous cleavage. She held her glass delicately by the stem, raised it in front of her generous cleavage, slowly dipped her forefinger into the wine, then placed it into her mouth and sucked gently. Tony could feel beads of perspiration forming again on his brow. She smiled back at Tony. "Oh, I'm not sure I've settled here but I was chatting with Franz, you know, the manager when I last came here with a tour party. I told him I was thinking of quitting and he offered me a job on the spot. He was looking for somebody who liked meeting people and could speak English. I'd just split up with my boyfriend and I fancied doing something different so I took it. It's been fun but I'll probably move on at the end of the summer, though. I don't much like the cold winters and I'm starting to miss my friends back home. Anyway, what about you? Still driving coaches I see."

"Yep, but I'm not sure for how much longer. We keep hearing rumours that the company is in a bit of financial trouble and the tour we are on at the moment is an absolute nightmare. I am afraid Miranda has completely lost …"

Before he could say any more, Miranda strode briskly into the bar. Her flowing dark hair had a lustrous sheen, she wore only a light and subtle touch of make-up and she sported a low-cut dress with a décolletage to match Lisa's. Fortunately, Tony saw her approach and he smiled weakly in her direction. As she caught sight of Lisa, her expression became one of overt suspicion. Realising that he had forgotten to tell Miranda about Lisa, Tony quickly jumped to his feet and pulled out a chair next to him for Miranda to sit on.

"Miranda, this is Lisa. You saw her briefly at dinner. Lisa, meet Miranda."

The two women smiled stiffly at each other before Miranda sat down facing Lisa across the table and leant forward towards her as though trying to intimidate her in some kind of battle of the bosoms. Tony did his best to look Miranda in the eyes – not an easy task – as he felt fresh beads of sweat beginning to form on his already damp forehead.

"Lisa used to be a tour guide, sorry, tour director, like you. I don't think you ever met 'cos I think Lisa left not long after you started. Anyway, apparently she works here now."

At this relatively reassuring news, Miranda began to relax a little. She breathed a massive sigh of relief, thus momentarily causing her bust to swell threateningly in Lisa's direction.

"Oh I see. Well, you made the right decision. You've no idea the problems we're having with this tour. I'm thinking of getting out of it myself…"

"Good idea!" Tony agreed.

"Meaning?"

"Er… definitely a good idea to be moving on; I mean, you don't want to get stuck in a rut, do you? Can I buy you a drink?"

★ ★ ★

Greatly aroused by Jason's gentle but persistent caresses, Barbara had grabbed him by the hand, which felt surprisingly clammy, and had led him upstairs, at indecent speed, to their room. Once inside, she quickly undressed him and pushed him onto the bed. It was her turn to be the dominant one – it usually was. While he lay there giggling, she pulled a pair of handcuffs from her luggage and used them to secure his left wrist to one of the ornamental, carved wooden bedposts. She then moved nimbly away from the bed and slinked seductively around the room, gradually divesting herself of all clothing. When she was completely and unashamedly naked, she leapt onto the bed, straddled her highly aroused partner and begun to "ride" him in an energetic and frenzied manner.

In the next room, Gail and Peter had returned from dinner at a more sedate pace and in a far less excited state. Peter tossed the large key with an even larger fob onto the wooden table at the foot of the bed and then stopped as he heard the by now unmistakeable sounds of the bed creaking rhythmically, and orgiastic sighs and moans coming from the next room.

"Oh, bloody hell," he exploded. "Not those two at it again… do they ever stop! Why do we always have to be in the room next to them?"

Gail smiled. Not the easy, gentle smile that came so readily to her in public. The smile she now sported was a more coquettish, more sensual one. She sidled up to Peter, stroked what remained of his hair, nibbled his ear and whispered.

"Well, of course, if your cold isn't *too* bad tonight, we… er… we could have a go at setting up in opposition."

"What?? Oh, I see! Now that's not a bad idea."

He started to unbutton his shirt, slowly and methodically, without the frenzied, impromptu gusto that characterised Barbara's performance on such occasions.

The beds in the Hotel Ritzerbach looked, superficially, like double beds, with one king-size duvet, but, in fact, they were single beds pushed together beneath a wall-mounted, carved headboard with an ornamental wooden bedpost on each side. Normally the two beds were secured together but, as Barbara and Jason's enthusiastic lovemaking became more vigorous, the beds began to slide slowly, almost imperceptibly, apart. Both participants were far too passionately aroused to notice what was happening until some particularly forceful pelvic thrusts from Barbara forced the beds wide apart so suddenly that Jason, still handcuffed to the ornamental bedpost, disappeared, with a loud thump, through the gap between them. With nothing beneath her for support, Barbara fell heavily on top of him, causing him to emit a loud shriek of pain.

"Oh shit. My shoulder... my bloody shoulder... Oh God!"

In that one moment, all the build-up of sexual frisson evaporated. Barbara lifted herself off him with the utmost care and looked anxiously at him.

"You OK, Jace?"

Jason screwed his ashen face up in pain.

"Does it bloody look as if I'm OK?"

Starting to shake, Barbara leant over him, her flowing dark hair gently brushing against his face and carefully touched his shoulder. This resulted in another shriek of pain.

"Don't touch it, don't bloody touch. Just get me some help... Oh God!"

In the adjoining room, Peter and Gail's passions were slowly starting to kindle. Having been married for nearly thirty years, they well knew what each other liked and were proceeding in a far more leisurely, comfortable and well-rehearsed way than their neighbours. Nevertheless, a number of garments had been removed and the pleasures of mutual caressing were heightening when they heard Jason's first cry of pain. It brought an immediate halt to their intimacy. They then heard Jason's second cry. Peter hastily replaced his discarded clothing and ran towards the door.

"Sounds as if he needs some help."

"Oh, thanks very much Peter. I could use some of your help in here as it happens."

"You could go if you like. You work in a doctor's surgery."

"Yes, but I'm only a receptionist, as you well know!"

"OK, I'll be back in a minute."

"Alright, but don't leave it too much longer. And don't go interrupting anything!"

As Peter left the room, Gail's smile evaporated. She thumped the bed in frustration and, as she did so, she caught sight of Fred peering inscrutably at her from the bedside unit.

"And what are you looking so damned smug for?" she demanded.

Fred continued to stare, impassive and unblinking, until Gail petulantly swung her arm out and swept him to the floor, where he lay, motionless, face down on the blue carpet.

Beginning to panic, Barbara had been trying desperately, but unsuccessfully, to raise the reception staff on the telephone when she heard a knock at the door. "Thank God!" she cried as she threw the phone down and raced towards the door. She was about to turn the handle when, belatedly, she remembered that she was still naked, so she grabbed the duvet from where it had fallen to the floor and was still trying to wrap it around herself as she opened the door.

Peter was standing there, a little self-consciously, looking both concerned and curious. He tried hard to make eye contact with Barbara as he spoke, but he found it hard to prevent his eyes from wandering to Barbara's obviously naked body as it spilled out of the carelessly wrapped duvet. Occasionally, he peered beyond her into the room. Noticing Barbara's look of wide-eyed panic, he hesitated before speaking.

"Er, is everything alright? You see, we are, er, next door and, er, we heard these screams coming from your room and…"

Barbara was clearly frightened and her lips were trembling. She released one hand from the duvet and pointed behind her into the room. The duvet began to slip further from her body. She tried to grab it back, but with only partial success.

"Its Jace," she cried. "He's… he's had a bit of an accident. The bed gave way and he…"

Hearing Jason's groans and sensing that this was a genuine emergency, Peter brushed past Barbara and into the room where he stood still for a moment as he surveyed the scene. Jason was lying, naked, on the floor between the two beds, which were splayed widely apart. He was still handcuffed to the bedpost and was writhing in pain.

Peter rushed over. "Bloody hell! Where does it hurt, son?"

"It's my sodding shoulder. It feels as though it's been yanked out of it's socket!!" Jason managed to reply through clenched teeth.

Peter bent down and was about to touch Jason's shoulder.

"Don't touch it. Christ, don't touch it!" he yelled.

Peter withdrew his hand but stared intently at the injured and misshapen shoulder for a few moments. He turned to Barbara who was hopping about agitatedly behind him.

"He needs proper medical treatment. I'll go and get some help. You wait here. And while you're waiting, you can get those handcuffs off him and cover him up. Try and get some trousers on him, at least!"

As he spoke, the duvet slipped again, exposing still more of Barbara's naked flesh.

"And you'd better cover yourself up too while you're about it."

★ ★ ★

Trevor's solitary promenade had not lasted very long. The streets surrounding the hotel were dark and uninviting. The breeze, which had persisted all day, had turned more blustery and chillier as night fell and some icy spots of drizzle were beginning to fall. Besides, the walk had been intended to help him get his muddled thoughts in order, to clear his head, to work out a course of action but, if anything, his thinking was now more confused and befuddled than it was before. He stood, for a moment, on a street corner watching the headlights of a passing car picking out spots of drizzle. There were two people in the car, a man and a woman, and they were laughing as they drove past. He was alone, far from home and very miserable. Turning his collar up, he decided to beat a hasty retreat back to the hotel. Before he went to bed, he would need to phone Mike about Geoff Leggatt's reported injury and sort out someone else to repair the fire escape door, so he didn't want to be too late getting back, but that could wait for a while. First, he headed straight for the welcoming lights of the bar, where he hoped a stiff drink or two might help to jettison his jumble of unwanted thoughts and act as a therapeutic nightcap.

On entering the bar, the first thing that he noticed was Miranda and Lisa facing each other across a table, talking animatedly and leaning so far forward that their combined embonpoint virtually obscured the table top from sight. As he stood by the bar, Trevor was so transfixed by this unexpected and welcome vision that it took the barman three attempts to attract his attention.

"What, oh, er, sorry. Can I have a whisky?" he finally stuttered while still gazing in awe at the vista before him. Hearing Trevor's voice, Miranda glanced across at him and half smiled. Embarrassed, he quickly looked away.

He was just about to pay for his drink when Peter rushed into the bar. The exertion of dashing down two flights of stairs had turned his face red and brought on another coughing attack. After wheezing and spluttering for what felt like several minutes, he had gathered his composure sufficiently to go over to where Miranda was sitting.

"I'm sorry to trouble you but can I have a word?" he gasped.

Miranda had been feeling more relaxed than at any other time during the day. After her initial apprehension, she was enjoying Lisa's company and comparing reminiscences of tours they had been on, people they had met and potential disasters they had survived. With a comforting drink in her hand, she was beginning to put the manifold tribulations of the day behind her. Peter's flustered arrival, then, was an unwelcome interruption and a reminder that her official duties never really ended. Not that Peter had been any trouble so far – quite the reverse – but his sudden rubicund, wheezing appearance was unlikely to be the herald of good news. Her "clients" usually only wanted to talk to her when they had a problem. She tried to suppress a sigh.

"Yes, of course," she replied unconvincingly.

Peter glanced with some anxiety at Lisa.

"Er, in private, if that's possible. You see, it's rather delicate."

Miranda frowned and replaced her glass firmly on the table.

"I suppose so!"

She got to her feet, straightened her dress and reluctantly followed Peter as he led the way through the door and into the adjoining, deserted, darkened lounge.

From their respective vantage points, Tony, Lisa and Trevor could not hear a word of the ensuing conversation, but they could just see enough of the animated gestures and facial expressions to conclude that something genuinely urgent or important was being discussed. Eventually, Miranda and Peter rejoined Tony and Lisa. Miranda was still frowning.

"I'm sorry. There's been a bit of an accident, apparently, upstairs," Miranda announced loudly. "It's Jason Rogers. It looks like he was being shagged bandy by Barbara, fell off the bed and injured himself."

Tony spluttered into his drink at the same moment that Trevor, still standing at the bar, spluttered into his. Peter, meanwhile, squirmed and looked at the floor in embarrassment. He had been hoping to deal with the matter in confidence and with the utmost sensitivity, but Miranda clearly favoured a less subtle approach.

"I'm just going up to his room to see for myself," Miranda continued. "But it sounds like it could be a bad injury. I may have to get him to hospital for X-rays and some treatment."

Tony was sniggering as he mopped up his spilt drink.

"What's he damaged?" he asked, while trying hard not to laugh out loud.

"His shoulder, actually. What did you think?" Miranda replied frostily. "I'm not sure this is very funny, you know, Tony. Anyway, I could be some time, so I'll see you in the morning."

Miranda bustled off importantly with Peter in gasping pursuit. Trevor followed them both, calling "Is there anything

I can do? I've done some first aid training!" He got no response.

Some time later – he wasn't quite sure how much later as he'd rather lost track of time while they were assessing the situation, trying to get Jason dressed and calm Barbara down – and having left Miranda summoning a taxi to take her, Jason and Barbara to the hospital in Innsbruck, Peter crept quietly back into his room. Gail was laying face up, naked and motionless on the bed. Her eyes were closed and there was a contented smile on her face. Undoing his shirt buttons, Peter headed straight for the bathroom, stopping, en route, to pick up Fred and replace him on the bedside unit. Once inside the bathroom, he began to talk to Gail through the open door.

"Sorry about the delay, love. It's as well I went to help, though. Poor old Jason was in a pretty bad way. From my limited first aid training, I'd say he'd dislocated his shoulder when he fell between the beds. Poor Barbara was in a total panic, as you might imagine. Anyway, they're on their way to hospital now. Honestly, talk about "coitus interruptus!" Still, at least they won't be doing anything to interrupt *us* for a while. Now then, where were we?"

He emerged from the bathroom having removed his shirt and sat next to Gail on the bed. She was clearly fast asleep. He squeezed her arm gently. She opened her eyes, blinked sleepily at him and sighed.

"You're a bit late, I'm afraid," she whispered before closing her eyes and drifting off back to sleep.

"Oh well! Better forget that idea then, Pete," he said to himself. Fred, meanwhile, was looking inscrutably at him from the bedside unit. "And you can stop looking like that," he muttered, before standing up and flinging Fred back onto the floor.

★ ★ ★

After a long, relaxing bath, and wearing only her sheer blue, ankle-length nightdress, Valerie had finally plucked up the courage to remove Brian's damp and crumpled clothes from the plastic bag that they had been travelling in all day. She studied them, at

213

arm's length, with palpable distaste, before she hurled them onto the bed. Tears were welling up again.

"Oh, Brian, look at the state of these clothes. You're never going to be able to wear them unless I give them a good iron."

Brian had been sprawled quietly in a chair, wearing only a creased t-shirt and baggy boxer shorts, trying to operate the television with a remote control device that was clearly not working. But, as Valerie spoke, he suddenly became animated. He jumped to his feet.

"No, no," he shouted, waving the remote control in Valerie's direction as though trying to turn her off. "You're not planning to use the iron after what happened with the kettle, are you?"

"It'll be alright, won't it? I mean, we've used the iron abroad before and never had a problem."

"No, no. But we've used the kettle before abroad and never had a problem, until the other night."

"Don't worry. I'll take full responsibility. We can't have you walking around looking like a tramp for the rest of the holiday, now can we?"

She removed the iron and adaptor from her suitcase and began to search the room for a socket. Brian returned to his chair, shut his eyes and placed his hands together in silent prayer. Valerie, meanwhile, found a spare socket next to the dressing table and plugged the iron in. To Brian's immense surprise and considerable relief, there was no loud bang and the lights stayed on.

"There you are, you see," said Valerie triumphantly. "I said it would be alright."

Brian opened his eyes fully and looked around in apparent disbelief.

"Yes, yes, you did," he admitted.

★ ★ ★

It was after midnight when Miranda finally returned to the hotel, by taxi, and trudged wearily through reception. The night porter, a small, balding, elderly man with a pale complexion, was on duty and had obviously been briefed about Jason's accident. He looked up as Miranda walked past, still wearing her sunglasses for some unknown reason.

"Everything OK?" he enquired with a heavy Germanic accent, whilst pointing to his shoulder. Miranda stopped, removed her sunglasses and turned to address the porter. She spoke slowly.

"I think so. I've left them at the hospital. As I thought, his shoulder was dislocated but they've put it back and they're patching him up. They'll bring him back here when they've finished. He shouldn't be too long. One thing though – that should put an end to their passionate antics for a while!"

Miranda smirked. The porter nodded and smiled, though it was the kind of uncertain smile which suggested that he hadn't fully understood all that Miranda had said. Miranda was about to walk on when he remembered the message he had for her.

"I have a message. Tony said goodnight and he'll see you in the morning."

Miranda nodded, smiled at him and went over to the lift.

★ ★ ★

Valerie had spent a long time doing the ironing. It was not a task that she enjoyed, particularly late at night, and especially when she was tired and emotionally fragile, but she was unceasing in her determination to smarten Brian up. Using a makeshift ironing board, comprising a towel spread over the surface of the dressing table, she finally finished ironing the last item – a shirt – which she folded neatly and held aloft with pride, before placing it carefully and precisely on the tidy pile of previously ironed clothes for Brian to choose from in the morning. She yawned, looked across at Brian, who was reaching under the bed to try and retrieve one of the batteries that he had removed from the remote control device, before dropping it on the floor, and went into the bathroom to prepare for bed.

Brian enjoyed a mechanical challenge and he had become greatly preoccupied with trying to fix the television remote control. He had removed both batteries, changed them over,

215

tried to warm them in the palm of his hand, changed them over again, warmed them on the towel Valerie was using to do the ironing, dropped one on the floor, changed them over again, pressed all the buttons several times and, finally, hunted around in vain for some spare batteries. Eventually and reluctantly, he was forced to abandon the malfunctioning gadget and went over to the television where he began adjusting the controls, and switching channels, manually. With Valerie in the bathroom and Brian devoting all his attention to getting the television to work, they failed to notice that the iron was still plugged in and resting on the towel, which was beginning to smoulder. Some smoke was also starting to rise ominously from the socket. Although Brian was vaguely aware that the room was filling with smoke, he assumed that it was steam coming from the bathroom and paid little attention until, suddenly, the fire alarm went off.

Miranda had been walking wearily back to her room, along the quiet, deserted, wood-panelled corridor, when the fire alarm went off. She jumped and stopped dead in her tracks while, all around her, doors started to open and the corridor began to fill with confused and anxious-looking people, some wearing their nightclothes. Through the growing hubbub, a little further down the corridor, Miranda caught sight of Tony's door opening and then watched open-mouthed as he and Lisa dashed out into the corridor. They had done their best to cover themselves up by quickly grabbing whatever they could from the room – Lisa seemed to be wearing Tony's jacket, a pair of pink briefs and very little else while Tony was busy zipping up his trousers – but the inference from their joint exit from Tony's room and their comparative state of undress was all too obvious. Almost instantaneously, the commotion stopped and everyone froze. Horror-struck, Tony and Lisa looked down the corridor and their gaze met Miranda's. There was a short hiatus, when nobody moved, and then, above the continuous din of the fire alarm, Miranda screamed.

★ ★ ★

Outside the hotel, a hospital vehicle drew up. Barbara got out from the passenger seat and, together with the uniformed driver, she helped Jason slowly and carefully out of the back. His left shoulder and upper arm were encased in a substantial sling and he winced as he stepped groggily out of the vehicle. They thanked the driver, watched as the vehicle pulled quickly away and then, in cool, steady drizzle, with Barbara doing her best to support her still shaky partner, they walked, slowly and unsteadily, around the side of the hotel towards the entrance.

Barbara had stopped panicking once the doctor had told her that they had managed to put Jason's shoulder back and that he should eventually make a full recovery, and she was in a more reflective frame of mind now.

"You know, I'm sure I read somewhere that beds in Austrian hotels are single mattresses in a double frame so it shouldn't have come apart," she observed, thoughtfully.

"Well, this one certainly wasn't."

"Mmm. How are you feeling now?"

"Oh, I'm OK, more or less. A bit wobbly, but I'm not in too much pain at the moment – I think the painkillers they gave me are starting to work. I thought the doctor was a bit nosey though, wanting to know how I'd dislocated it."

"Important that they know, I suppose, how the injury was done."

"Mmm. I'm sure it made their day. I'm sure they're all back there at the hospital, having a good laugh at my expense." He shivered in the cool, damp air. "Come on, let's get up to bed. I need to try and get some rest."

As they turned the corner of the hotel and made their way towards the entrance, they were confronted by a group of people who, on the dimly lit forecourt, they could just identify as being fellow members of their coach party. For some reason, a few of them seemed to be wearing their nightclothes and dressing gowns. They noticed Frank standing solemnly towards the back of the group, with what looked like striped pyjamas protruding from beneath his grey, daytime trousers. Nearer the front, they observed Dave, apparently still in his usual clothes, apart from the fact that he was wearing odd shoes and no socks. They were standing in a loosely grouped circle, watching intently as, in the middle, on the damp ground, Miranda and Lisa were wrestling with each other. Lisa was at something of a disadvantage as she was struggling – and largely failing – to preserve most of her modesty beneath Tony's torn jacket but, nevertheless, she had a good hold of Miranda's long hair and was using her sharp nails to good effect on any bare flesh she could find. While most of the group stood and watched, silently transfixed by the gladiatorial contest, Dave appeared to be encouraging the combatants with both word and gesture, almost as though he'd had a bet on the outcome. Peter and Trevor, meanwhile, were trying hard to pull the protagonists apart, but they were hampered by the frequent need to take evasive action in order to avoid flailing limbs and stiletto sharp fingernails.

Barbara and Jason stood and watched, slightly bemused, for a few seconds but with Jason groggy from the effects of the strong painkillers that had been recently administered to him and Barbara suffering from some kind of delayed shock, they seemed surprisingly unperturbed by what they were witnessing.

"Fat chance of getting any rest for the time being, I'd say…" Barbara observed, as Peter finally dragged a wriggling Lisa away from Miranda, who had been grabbed and held firmly in check by Trevor. Barbara steered Jason quickly and largely unobserved into the hotel foyer, where they were greeted by the night porter.

★ ★ ★

CHAPTER 6

Comings and Goings

Miranda hauled herself slowly and reluctantly out of bed. She had slept only fitfully at best and was dreading having to face the new day. The room felt cold this morning and she shivered as she left the warmth of her bed. She shuffled unwillingly over to the dressing table and switched on the light. Blinded by the sudden, glaring, infusion of brightness in an otherwise dark room, she switched it off again and settled instead to part the wooden shutters just a little, so that only a small, gentle shaft of watery light penetrated the room.

She tried to focus on her reflection in the mirror through half-closed eyes – it was as she feared. Her face was covered in small scratches, grazes and contusions. Here and there, there were traces of the previous day's make-up, which had run and smudged. Her eyelids and lips were red and swollen. Her normally sleek hair was crumpled, tangled and matted with spots of dried, congealed blood. With considerable reluctance, she examined her face in the mirror, as closely as she was able in the dim light, and swore quietly to herself. It was going to require a particularly substantial and creative cosmetic application to conceal the damage. She reached for a packet of pills, which was lying next to the mirror, removed two pills and placed them in her open palm. She stared thoughtfully at them for a moment before removing a third pill. She opened a half empty bottle of mineral water, left over from the previous day, and swilled the pills down. She swore quietly again and dragged herself slowly into the bathroom.

★ ★ ★

In the snug hotel dining room, members of the touring party had begun to file in to join the inevitable queue for breakfast. Although there was plenty of bustling activity around the tables on which the ample buffet breakfast had been carefully and attractively laid out, and some occasional whispered conversations, there was an unusually muted atmosphere, rather like a theatre audience waiting expectantly for the curtain to rise. Dave had decided to wear another of his colourful Hawaiian style shirts – purple and orange on this occasion. Susan had counselled against it, but he was in an ebullient mood – even if nobody else was – and was looking forward to the day's events with some relish. "Better than any soap opera," he enthused to Susan as he rubbed his hands together in anticipation.

As usual, Tony had arrived early for breakfast. This afforded him the usual opportunity to prepare the coach for the day's journey and load the luggage while everyone else was finishing their breakfast. Never effusive, he would, nevertheless, normally make a point of acknowledging people, if they caught his eye as they arrived but, this morning, he was sitting in a quiet corner of the room, with a steaming cup of black coffee, facing the wall and apparently engrossed in some papers and a well-thumbed road atlas, which were spread out on the table in front of him.

Most members of the party had already filled their plates when Barbara and Jason arrived, looking far less composed and more subdued than usual. Jason looked even paler than normal and his left shoulder was entombed in a large white sling. In the kerfuffle involving Miranda and Lisa the previous evening, few had noticed Jason arriving back from the hospital and, despite Miranda's indiscreet observations in the bar, not many people knew what had happened to him, so they were shocked and surprised at his appearance. Dave, of course, had made it his business to find out what had happened and, with an air of mock innocence, was the first to ask.

"Hello, Jason, what's happened to you?" he bellowed boisterously across the room.

Jason looked startled. He froze for several moments, as his pale cheeks turned pink with embarrassment.

"Oh, I had a bit of an accident last night… in the bedroom," he said, at last, evasively.

"Did you?" Dave gave a knowing wink. Peter was standing close by. Having seen, at first hand, the pain and distress that Jason had endured and, fully aware of the awkward and embarrassing circumstances surrounding his injury, he was keen to try and abort, or at least divert, Dave's line of questioning.

"Yes, I heard this crash and scream from the room next door. Apparently, the beds weren't properly secured and Jason fell awkwardly onto the floor."

"We were soooo very grateful for your help, Peter," Barbara was eager to assure him, having not had the opportunity to speak to him when they got back from the hospital. Suddenly, Frank's voice boomed out from close range.

"Well, I should sue someone if I were you – either the hotel or the tour operator, or both. Someone was negligent and you've suffered as a result. Mind you, some good has come out of it. At least you can cut short your holiday and go home."

"Oh, no," Jason protested, feeling his shoulder tenderly. "We're not cutting short our holiday. It was only a dislocation, like, which they fixed in the hospital – there are no breaks or anything – so as long as I'm careful and I can keep scrounging some ice to put on it, I should be fine to carry on…"

"But not in every sense by the look of you!" Dave leered as Susan dug a fleshy elbow into his equally fleshy ribs.

"Besides," Jason continued. "We've been enjoying it, like, and we badly want to see Italy."

"Enjoying it?" Frank asked, incredulously. "How can you be enjoying it? Poor lad! You must be suffering from delayed shock or something, or maybe you landed on your head. Or perhaps you like blood sports. You saw the end of the latest bloody conflict last night, didn't you?"

Before Jason could reply, Miranda, wearing her sunglasses and particularly heavily made up, strode slowly and dramatically into the room. Almost everyone stopped what they were doing and looked at her. The room fell deathly quiet. She walked straight over to where Tony was sitting. He had his back to her and had not seen her approach; nor had he sensed the sudden silence that had descended. Without warning, she reached in front of him, picked up his cup of coffee, shouted "Bastard!" and poured the coffee into his lap before storming off.

"What the…" Tony spluttered before suddenly becoming acutely aware of a damp and burning sensation in his groin. Grimacing with pain, he leapt to his feet and, while trying to hold the scalding hot front of his trousers away from the most delicate parts of his anatomy, lumbered over to the breakfast tables where a half full jug of cold fruit juice was standing. He picked up the jug, yanked his trousers forward at the waistband and poured most of the jug's contents into the front of them. The look on his face suggested that the relief was immediate and immense.

"Give the poor bloke some of your ice!" Dave yelled across the room to Jason.

After the previous evening's incident with the iron and the fire alarm, Brian and Valerie had not wanted to draw attention to themselves this morning. They had scuttled into the dining room, as unobtrusively as they could, quickly selected their food and had skulked away to a quiet table from where they had been staring open-mouthed at Tony's antics. So enthralled were they that, like Tony, they too failed to see or hear Miranda arrive behind them. She loomed over them, removed her sunglasses and coughed. Startled, they looked round.

Miranda stood with her feet apart, placed her hands on her hips, and tossed her hair back, dramatically. "I did warn you, didn't I?" she lectured, her voice quavering with emotion. "After the incident with the kettle, I did warn you but you took no notice, did you? You've been nothing but trouble right from the start. Now your iron has nearly caused a major fire, not to mention…"

Her sentence tailed off as she grappled with her emotions. She coughed again before adopting a more detached and formal tone.

"I have to advise you that I shall be contacting head office today to ask that you be banned from the rest of the tour, so you won't need to unpack when we get to Salzburg."

The dramas being played out in front of him exceeded even Dave's lofty expectations. He had observed the morning's proceedings with child-like delight, his eyes were sparkling and his lop-sided smile was becoming ever wider. Now, observing Miranda's increasingly absurd dramatics, he burst out laughing. Immediately, Miranda turned on him, narrowed her eyes and swooped, like a bird of prey sighting its next victim.

"And what are you laughing at?"

Before Dave had time to react, she reached out, grabbed his half full bowl of cereal and tipped the contents into his lap, before tossing her hair back again, replacing her sunglasses and striding off as dramatically as she had arrived. Dave gaped after her, motionless, with a spoonful of cereal poised halfway to his open mouth.

Whereas Dave had greatly appreciated the entertainment value of the dramas being enacted in front of him – at least until the final incident – Frank was appalled by what he had seen. Despite his own increasingly frequent public rebellions and cringe-making exhibitions, he could not tolerate the kind of drama queen histrionics that he had witnessed last night and again this morning.

"Bloody hell!" he exclaimed to no-one in particular. "We're going to have to do something about this!"

While Joyce sighed volubly, he reached inside his blazer pocket and produced a small notebook in a neat, mock leather binding, together with a ballpoint pen. He carefully opened up the notebook and began to write, carefully and methodically.

Dave meanwhile had leapt to his feet and was wiping the cereal remains from his trousers with his serviette. His lop-sided smile had vanished.

"Look what the bitch has done to my trousers!"

"Shame it wasn't your shirt!" Susan commented unsympathetically.

"Look what she's done to my breakfast!" added Dave with increasing indignation.

"Well now, that *is* serious," agreed Susan with more than a hint of sarcasm.

Tony was still trying to wring some of the fruit juice from his trousers as he walked carefully and uncomfortably over to sympathise with Dave. Like Dave, he got no sympathy from Susan.

"Look what she's done to *your* trousers! Mind you, after last night you had it coming. A bit of discomfort in the trousers is the least you could expect!"

Tony held his hands up in a gesture of supplication.

"I know, I know, I've got no excuses and I'm really very sorry about all of this. I don't want to mess up your holiday. I'll do my best to look after you and… you know…try and get things sorted. I'll have a word with head office, you know, to try and explain."

"Tony, lad, I've a feeling we might have to look after you!" Frank boomed from across the room. "Is anything swollen?"

★ ★ ★

Outside, it was a cool and overcast morning. The ground was damp from overnight rain and, although the air was drier now, a sullen sky gave warning of further rain to come. The sombre mood of the weather was reflected in the collective gloominess of the coach party as individuals straggled, mainly in ones and twos, towards the coach and slowly hauled themselves aboard. Tony had hastily changed into a clean pair of trousers and had just finished loading the final suitcases – those belonging to Brian and Valerie. Inside the coach, Frank went over to where Brian and Valerie were sitting morosely. Valerie was close to tears again; even Frank sensed it.

"Don't worry about what she said earlier. I promise you, if she tries to have you banned, she'll have a bloody riot on her hands!"

"In fact, I think she might have a riot on her hands anyway," Dave added, from across the aisle. "'Ello, watch out!"

Dave had caught sight of Miranda striding briskly towards the coach. Without any kind of acknowledgement to anyone, she slipped quietly onto the coach, proceeded quickly along the aisle to check, with fastidious care, that everyone was on board, returned to the front, sat down and stared fixedly out of the front window. Outside, Tony closed the luggage hold, climbed aboard without glancing at Miranda and started the engine. Everyone on board fell silent as the coach moved off, except for Valerie and Brian, who were having an intense whispered conversation and the two elderly ladies who launched into a long discussion about cake recipes.

As the coach set off on its morning journey, out of the hotel car park, down the road and onto the motorway out of Innsbruck, it would have been normal practice for Miranda to say a few introductory words – usually a polite greeting, perhaps an enquiry about how well everybody had slept, maybe a comment about the weather, usually a brief reminder about the day's itinerary and timings – but today, she said nothing. The coach travelled for some distance in an uncomfortable and tense silence. Some passengers fidgeted uneasily, others stared out of the window, as though suddenly deeply interested in the type and number of vehicles using the motorway.

The coach continued its journey deep into the Austrian Tyrol and the passengers' attention was gradually enlivened by increasingly impressive views of the mountain peaks and the small, pretty villages dotted haphazardly along the valleys. The elderly ladies began to argue over the right consistency of butter cream. Eventually, Miranda reached for the microphone and spoke. Her tone was distant and frosty, her voice harsh.

"Good morning, ladies and gentlemen."

She paused briefly, but there was a total, oppressive silence inside the coach, so she continued.

"This morning, as you may have noticed, we are heading into the Austrian Tyrol and will be stopping for a while in the pretty alpine town of Kitzbuhel. Then later we'll be heading north east for an afternoon visit to the city of Salzburg before we travel on to our overnight hotel."

Barbara rested her head comfortingly on Jason's right shoulder, squeezed his thigh gently and cooed encouragingly.

"Just think; we'll be in Venice tomorrow! I'm soooo looking forward to seeing Venice. Soooo romantic!"

Although she had spoken only softly, her comments, in the funereal silence of the coach, were overheard by Joyce, who turned towards her and whispered.

"Don't get your hopes up, dear. I reckon she'll have chucked half of us off the coach before then."

Miranda, meanwhile, was continuing with her stilted and unenthusiastic commentary.

"We do have a tight schedule today."

"As usual," Frank added, caustically and loudly.

"So perhaps I can remind you that you will all need to be back at the coach on time – we cannot afford to be late again. If anyone is not back on time, then I'm afraid we will have to leave without them."

Dave was feeling especially uncomfortable in the increasingly stifling and sullen atmosphere. It reminded him too much of being back at school, which were certainly not the happiest days of his life, and particularly of being in detention after school – an all too frequent experience. In an attempt to lighten the tension, he turned to Susan.

"Blimey, she nags more than you do!"

"Aye and with about as much effect, probably," Susan replied, with a hint of resignation in her voice.

The journey to Kitzbuhel was not especially long, just over 100 kilometres, nor especially complicated, following the quick motorway route most of the way, and, as a result, the coach made good time. As it pulled into the town's central coach park, Miranda issued her instructions, in the same cold, detached tone that she had used all morning, whenever forced to make an utterance.

"We're going to be here for two hours, so you have the choice of strolling around the town which is down the hill to my left, or you could take the cable car up the Hahnenkamm just across the railway line to my right. There are some spectacular views at the top but make sure you allow enough time to get back down and *please do not be late*!" There seemed to be more than just a hint of menace in her concluding remark.

Although noted primarily as a winter sports resort, with the famous Hahnenkammrennen downhill race, the town of Kitzbuhel has its attractions for the summer visitor; a compact and attractive centre with many old and colourful buildings, a couple of interesting churches and plenty of cafes, shops and boutiques. For the more adventurous, of course, the cable car ride to the top of the Hahnenkamm rewards their efforts with good walks and majestic views over the town and across the valleys. Not surprisingly, therefore, opinions were divided on how to make the best use of the time available. Gail, for one, had a clear preference. She turned to Peter and smiled her easy, persuasive smile.

"Shall we take Fred to the top of the mountain?"

"Oh, good idea," enthused Peter. He hadn't much fancied traipsing around the shops, though the churches might have been interesting, and a relaxing sit on the cable car was an attractive enough proposition. Besides, if he was going to be forced to take embarrassing pictures of a stuffed bear, he had less chance of being seen up a mountain than in the middle of the town. Moreover, there was a chance that the fresh, rarefied air at the top might help to unblock his heavily congested nose. As they made the short walk towards the cable car station, they were quickly joined by Trevor, who seemed a little more jaunty this morning.

Trevor's late evening phone call to Mike had been surprisingly illuminating and had clearly helped to lift his gloom. Contrary to what Julia had been told – or had told Trevor – Geoff Leggatt, it seemed, had not suffered any serious injury, was still in good physical health and had confirmed that he would be along to the conference centre this evening, as previously agreed, to fix the fire escape. So maybe, for whatever reason, Julia would not have found things quite as she expected when she got home late yesterday and Trevor was rather hoping that he might, at some stage, receive a contrite phone call or text message.

"Er... would you mind if I shared your cable car?" he asked, rather diffidently.

"Of course not, we'd be delighted," enthused Peter again, nasally. After all, Trevor had been very helpful in trying to break up last night's melée – the determined way in which he had dragged Miranda away from Lisa had been particularly impressive – and Peter and Gail wanted to thank him. In addition, here was someone, he thought, who could share the embarrassing burden of taking photographs of Fred, or even of being photographed with the ubiquitous quadruped.

The proximity of the mountains had given Barbara another adrenaline surge, but Jason had been quite quiet this morning and she wasn't sure how he was feeling or what he felt able to do.

"Can we go up the mountain?" She looked pleadingly at Jason, who could never resist the allure of her deep, limpid, brown eyes. He pointed nervously at his injured shoulder.

"OK, as long as you're not expecting me to ski down."

Delighted by Jason's positive response, Barbara raced excitedly ahead towards the cable car station, overtaking Gail, Peter and Trevor en route.

With his feet placed squarely and firmly on the tarmac of the car park, Frank stood and watched the cable cars ascending the steep incline and dangling precariously above the rugged terrain. He shook his head.

"I'm afraid you won't get me up in one of those things," he bellowed to anyone who was within earshot.

"Nor me," agreed Susan who was standing just behind him. "Come on, Dave, let's go and hit the shops." She strode off in the direction of the town with Dave following along, several reluctant paces behind.

For Brian and Valerie, it had been a particularly distressing morning. Following Miranda's bombshell announcement at breakfast, they had spent much of the journey in quiet, disjointed and often emotional conversation about what they should do next. Of course, it wasn't that they were enjoying the holiday especially, so the opportunity to return home early might have had its attractions but for Valerie's severe aversion to flying. They considered, briefly, booking themselves independently into a hotel somewhere to continue their holiday, but their money was running out and they would still have to find a way of getting home without flying. So, all in all, they decided they wanted, or rather needed, to stay on the tour. As a first step, therefore, they had resolved to plead their case with Miranda when they got to Kitzbuhel and had carefully rehearsed what they were going to say. In her present mood, they felt that it would not be productive to appear too confrontational or aggressive; a role that, in any event, neither of them was particularly good at. Threatening to report her to the company for her injudicious transgressions with Tony, her fight with Lisa and her out-of-control behaviour at breakfast might work, but it was a risky strategy and could easily backfire. Better, they felt, to be unreservedly contrite, to make an abject apology and to promise to be model holidaymakers from now on. With this in mind, they waited by the coach until all of the other passengers had disembarked and then tried to get back on board to speak to Miranda. Miranda, however, was having none of it. She saw them approaching and hastily kicked the coach door shut before they could climb aboard. They knocked loudly on the door a couple of times, but Miranda took no notice, wandering off up the aisle on the pretext of re-stocking the drinks machine, so, eventually, they gave up and walked slowly and despondently towards the town, deep in solemn conversation.

★ ★ ★

Freed, temporarily, from the smothering constraints of her family environment, Barbara was discovering a lot about herself on this holiday – her burgeoning sense of adventure, particularly in the bedroom, and the delight she took in being gently daring, almost provocative, especially in front of some of their more staid, elderly travelling companions – but, as the incident with Jason's shoulder had reminded her all too vividly, she could easily panic when faced with a crisis or predicament which she wasn't prepared for. She was also about to discover something else about herself.

She was sitting alone with, and extremely close to, Jason in the bright red cable car as it started to climb steeply up the side of the mountain, swaying gently from side to side, when she glanced out of the window and looked down. It was a big mistake. She was suddenly gripped by a paralysing fear. She clutched Jason's arm.

"Oooooh, I don't think I like this, Jace!"

"You didn't tell me you were scared of heights!" There was a hint of rebuke in Jason's voice.

"I didn't know I was. There aren't many high mountains in Birmingham!"

As a nauseous panic began to engulf her, she tried to bury her head, ostrich style, in Jason's shirt, but, in doing so, she accidentally butted his injured shoulder, causing him to cry out in pain, and her to offer a muffled apology.

As the cable car continued to ascend, it suddenly went quiet and slowed until it was virtually stationary. With her head still buried in Jason's shirt, Barbara yelled out.

"Oh my God, we've stopped! The cable car's broken!"

She began to sob hysterically, her stomach heaving in and out, and banged frantically on the window with her fist. The cable car was swaying appreciably in the gathering breeze.

"Help, get me out of here…"

Caught off guard by Barbara's unexpected and extreme reaction, Jason was unsure how to react. He had not experienced this kind of situation before and nobody had prepared him for it. His first instinct was to try and grab Barbara and place both arms around her in a protective embrace, but with only one available arm, it was impractical. He had begun to sense that his personal standing had fallen, in Barbara's eyes, since the accident with his shoulder and he desperately wanted to take decisive and heroic action; to be Barbara's knight in shining armour. Eventually, however, all he could manage was to say "Don't be silly, we're alright." It was a response so limp that he embarrassed himself. Barbara, meanwhile, had collapsed, still sobbing, face down on the floor.

"We're going to die!!" she screamed melodramatically, curling up into the foetal position, as the cable car began to move again.

Disappointed at his own lame performance so far, Jason decided to be firm. He bent down, placed his right arm securely under Barbara's chin and gently eased her head up from the floor.

"We are not going to die. Look the cable car's still moving. Look!!" His voice sounded stronger and more assertive than usual.

Barbara tried to turn her head away, but Jason kept a tight grip.

★ ★ ★

Down in the town, Susan and Dave had been sauntering along the attractive main street, doing some window shopping and watching the horses and carriages, laden with tourists, rattling their way past, when they bumped into a dejected looking Brian and Valerie. When Susan enquired, Brian tried to explain, without a great deal of coherence, how they had waited to speak to Miranda when they got off the coach but she had shut the door in their faces. Dave smiled warmly and placed an avuncular arm around Brian's drooping shoulders.

"Look, don't worry, Brian, my old mate. If she tries to throw you off the tour she'll have the rest of us to contend with. I reckon we've all got a few scores to settle with her one way and another – you should see the state of my trousers, for a start. Besides, as long as you're on the tour, you'll divert attention away from me and some of the others…"

Dave's attention was momentarily distracted by a gargantuan display of food in the window of a delicatessen. He paused briefly to look admiringly in the window, and Brian stopped and stood, rooted to the spot, behind him.

"Thanks, Dave. I hope you're right. I mean, I know we've had a few mishaps and that, but it's not as though we're accident prone or anything…"

Susan and Valerie had strolled on a few paces ahead but, sensing that their men had stopped, they turned round. Suddenly, Susan shouted "Look out!" as a horse and carriage came thundering down the street heading straight towards a statuesque Brian. To Valerie's own amazement, she found herself rushing forward and, with surprising athleticism, pulling Brian out of the path of the horse and carriage as they raced by.

★ ★ ★

In another part of town, Frank and Joyce were trudging along, as downcast in their own way as Valerie and Brian. The pessimistic side of Frank's nature was never far from the surface at the best of times and now, a kind of depressive gloom had descended. The holiday was proving to be the disaster he feared it would be and, for all her newfound confidence, Joyce knew that she would struggle to lift his mood. But, as they passed a souvenir shop, she made a desperate attempt to distract him.

"Do you think we should get some souvenirs?" she asked innocently.

"I don't think I want any reminders of this holiday, thank you."

"Maybe not, but we'll have to get something for the kids – and Bill and Angela."

"Oh… I suppose so, although it does seem a waste of money. Still, I'm not sure how much longer this shambles is going on for, so we'd better get them while we can. Do you suppose they speak English?"

"I'm sure they will if you shout loudly enough at them." Joyce clutched Frank's arm and dragged him inside.

★ ★ ★

At the top of the Hahnenkamm, a strong, persistent, cool breeze was blowing. Although it was unpleasant when walking directly into it, or when trying to hold a camera steady, it did at least ensure that the air was clear and there were splendid views down the valleys and across to the mountains, with scudding clouds obscuring some of the peaks in an ever changing kaleidoscope of light and shade. In the distance, however, some more ominous, darker clouds were beginning to gather.

Barbara and Jason stepped shakily from their cable car. Jason, paler than ever, and suddenly discovering that a thin cotton T-shirt offered very little protection or warmth in the face of a blustery mountain breeze, had placed his right arm protectively around Barbara who was quaking, sobbing and barely able to walk. He tried to comfort her.

"It's OK, we've made it. Dry land…"

Still badly shaken, Barbara was deeply ashamed of her antics in the cable car. Her sea-level bravado had rapidly turned into a cowering fear. She sniffed, wiped away a tear and looked up at him with moist, frightened eyes.

"I'm sooooo sorry. What an idiot!"

Any residual irritation that Jason may have felt about Barbara's histrionics melted away as he stared into her deep, brown, anxious eyes. For a fleeting moment, something about her expression reminded him of her father.

"Never mind! C'mon, let's go and see the views."

"OK, but slowly and not too near the edge, please."

Peter, Gail, Trevor and Fred had emerged, more confidently, from another cable car, just a little way behind Barbara and Jason. On the way up, they had been enjoying the ever-changing scenery and had seen nothing of the drama that Jason and Barbara had played out in a preceding car, but it was abundantly clear from their behaviour, as they walked unsteadily from the cable car station, leaning heavily on each other for support, that something was wrong. Peter strode up to them, deeply inhaling the mountain air as he did so.

"Hello! Everything OK?" he enquired genially. Jason would have preferred to have been left alone with Barbara at that particular moment but did not want to appear ungrateful at Peter's well-intentioned enquiry.

"Er, oh, oh, yes. We didn't enjoy the ride up here much, you know…?"

"I found it a bit scary, I'm afraid," Barbara volunteered. Peter nodded sagely.

"Yes, these cable car rides can be a bit scary can't they? You know, you'd be most welcome to share a car with us on the way down if you want. Might help to take your mind off things…"

"Oh, thanks," replied Jason uncertainly, not relishing the

prospect of Barbara putting on a repeat performance in front of other people. "We'll see how we go. I'm not sure quite how long we're going to be up here yet."

"Righto!" Peter nodded and walked back to where Gail was standing, posing with Fred, in front of an alpine backdrop. Jason and Barbara walked off in another direction.

"Funny bloke, that Peter," Jason mused, when he was sure that they were out of earshot. "Always offering to share; I'm surprised he hasn't offered to share his wife with anyone yet."

Barbara laughed, the sparkle slowly returning to her eyes.

"What are you suggesting?" she teased.

"Well you never know. Maybe he and Gail are "swingers". Maybe they have offered to join us so that we can have a "four in a car" romp on the way down".

Barbara laughed again.

"I think you've done enough romping for the time being. Mind you, that would certainly take my mind off things!"

★ ★ ★

Back at the coach, once the passengers had disembarked and dispersed, Tony wasted little time in making his excuses and leaving. Anxious to avoid damage to another pair of trousers, or to any particularly sensitive part of his anatomy, and largely on the pretext on finding some food, he quickly disappeared into town, leaving Miranda alone on the coach. On his reluctant return, some thirty minutes later, clutching a large bag of food and a can of drink, he found Miranda on the phone.

"Yes, yes, that's fine," she was saying. "I'll tell them when we get to Salzburg and explain how they can get from the hotel to the airport. Thank you very much for your help. Nobody wants to do this kind of thing, obviously, but it's all been very difficult, as I'm sure you can appreciate."

She ended her call and, although Tony's return had not gone unnoticed, she ignored him. Instead, she scribbled some hasty notes on a piece of paper attached to her clipboard and then continued to stare straight ahead out of the front window. Tony sat down in the driver's seat and began to open his bag of food. The purpose of her phone call had been all too evident.

"I don't believe you!" he exclaimed, before unwrapping and taking a bite out of a large ham and cheese roll. "You have, haven't you? You've got the Woods thrown off the tour."

"And why shouldn't I?" Miranda replied haughtily while continuing to look straight ahead. "They've been nothing but trouble since this tour started – you know that! And then after what they did last night…"

"Yes, but it was an accident. I'm sure they didn't mean any harm, and I expect they've learnt their lesson. Anyway, I thought we'd agreed that you were going to be a bit discreet. I mean they know what we've been up to. They're bound to report us to head office now!"

"Listen, dickhead! Practically everyone on this coach, it seems, knows what we've been up to, thanks to the bloody Woods. Face facts; after everything that's happened this week, we're probably finished with this company anyway. They'll be getting all kinds of reports of fights in the dining room, black-outs caused by our clients, fire alarms being set off by our clients, the Tour Director fighting with hotel bar staff, coffee and cereal being poured into people's laps – need I go on? Right now, I just want to get back at those who have done most of the damage."

"So, *we're* finished, are we? You mean *you're* finished, surely!"

"After what you did to me last night – or rather what you did to that bitch Lisa last night, don't expect any favours from me, sunshine. If I go, then I'll make damn sure you go as well."

With great ceremony, Miranda placed her sunglasses on her nose, somewhat incongruously as the weather was becoming extremely gloomy, flicked her hair theatrically, kicked the door open and stormed off the coach.

"Don't be late back or I'll leave without you!" Tony shouted after her. At least now Miranda was off the coach, he felt safe to open his can of drink.

★ ★ ★

In the town centre, Brian and Valerie had left Dave and Susan ensconced contentedly at a café and were ambling along, despondently and aimlessly, when Miranda flounced past them at speed, with her head in the air, looking neither to the right nor left of her. "Excuse me!" Valerie called, but she took no notice as she strode on.

"You'll have to have a word with her, Brian, when we get back to the coach." Valerie's suggestion sounded more like an instruction to Brian, though, in fairness, it was uttered in a more encouraging and supportive way than he had recently been used to.

"Yes, yes, I will, I will, but we don't know for sure that she is going to carry out her threat and get us thrown off the tour yet."

"No we don't, but by the look of her, I don't think her mood is improving. Let's try and get back to the coach a few minutes early for once and we can do a bit of apologising and pleading."

"Yes, yes, OK."

While continuing to walk, Brian turned his head and stared after Miranda as she disappeared rapidly down the street. He had only walked on a couple of paces when, almost inevitably, his foot sank firmly into a large, fresh pile of horse droppings.

"Oh, shit!" he exclaimed.

"Exactly!" Valerie agreed, a smile playing at the edges of her mouth.

★ ★ ★

At the top of the Hahnenkamm, Peter, Gail and Trevor had returned to the cable car station. They had spent a pleasant time strolling about, sniffing the air, savouring the views of the mountains with Kitzbuhel sheltering in the valley below, and taking various pictures of Fred, in a number of different poses against assorted alpine backdrops. As they were preparing to board the cable car to take them back down, Jason and Barbara arrived. Barbara was looking deeply troubled. She was trembling and had again tried to bury her head in Jason's scrawny chest.

"Come on, it'll be alright," Jason said, more in hope than expectation.

"Do you want to come in with us?" Peter offered. Recalling his earlier conversation with Barbara about Peter, Jason laughed nervously before looking down at Barbara, who was in an increasingly agitated and distressed state.

"Oh, OK, then," he agreed; anything was worth a try.

As an empty cable car arrived, they all scrambled aboard. Peter and Trevor wedged Barbara between them on one side of the car while Jason and Gail sat opposite. Gail was looking unusually pensive and was wearing a slight frown. After Peter had come to her aid so gallantly on the previous evening, Gail had drawn the conclusion, without evidence or justification, that Barbara's obvious admiration for Peter might turn into some kind of juvenile crush – after all, something similar had happened at his school before now – and was disapproving of their sitting in such close proximity.

As the car moved off, Peter and Trevor orchestrated a stilted dialogue in an attempt to distract Barbara.

"Well, that was certainly worth coming up for," suggested Peter in a staged, over-enthusiastic manner.

"Wonderful views," agreed Trevor, with equally artificial enthusiasm, as he clutched Fred.

"Mind you, it looks as though the weather's starting to close in. I reckon we timed that about right..." Peter tailed off as the cable car began to pick up speed and Barbara suddenly screamed loudly in his ear.

"Oh, no. I don't like this. I want to get out!"

Although he had helped Peter to part the warring factions on the previous evening, Trevor had been feeling increasingly worthless since Julia left. Instinctively an organiser – his job required it – he was feeling uncomfortably redundant now that he was on his own. But here, it seemed, was the perfect opportunity to seize control of the situation and prove his value.

"Look, I've had a bit of training in this sort of thing," he observed nonchalantly though, in truth, his basic first aid training at the conference centre hardly qualified him to deal with acute cases of vertigo. "The best thing for you to do is lie on the floor and shut your eyes." It was a confident sounding statement, even if it lacked any form of medical corroboration.

"Are you sure?" Peter queried. He didn't claim to be an expert, although, as an experienced teacher, he had encountered a great many adolescent ailments and symptoms – some more genuine than others – but he sensed that Trevor's approach might owe more to guesswork than conviction. Barbara, meanwhile, was continuing to shake and scream and, as she was screaming particularly loudly in Trevor's ear, he decided that firm action was needed. Ignoring Peter's question, he shouted at Barbara.

"Lie on the… Oh, never mind."

He handed Fred over to Jason who held him uncertainly and self-consciously by an ear. Placing his hands on Barbara's shoulders, Trevor tried to steer her gently onto the floor but when she instinctively resisted, he half-wrestled her to the floor. Confused and in a state of rising panic, Barbara screamed and struggled. As she felt the strength of Trevor's arms pinning her down, she kicked out wildly.

Peter had been shocked by Trevor's impulsive, strong-arm tactics – they seemed out of character and out of order – and he leant forward to try and ease Trevor's grip on Barbara, but Barbara's flailing foot caught him a superficial but painful blow to the chin. Recoiling, and anxious to prevent further damage to his facial features, Peter grabbed hold of Barbara's wildly swinging foot, but she was now struggling so violently that he had great difficulty in maintaining his grip, while trying, at the same time, to take frequent evasive action. As she kicked out again, Peter, still grimly holding onto her foot, fell forward on top of Trevor who, in turn, crumpled heavily on top of Barbara. Gail looked on with an increasingly heavy frown.

While these chaotic events were unfolding, another cable car, carrying a serious looking elderly couple, equipped with rucksacks and walking poles, slowly passed them on its way up the mountain. They gaped in obvious amazement at the spectacle that was taking place alongside, and the elderly man stood up and pressed his nose against the window for a better view. Anxious to assure them that all was well, Jason smiled weakly at them and, still holding Fred, waved in a limp, embarrassed sort of way. Suddenly realising that he had been holding Fred when he waved, he dropped him quickly onto the floor and wiped his hand, with some distaste, on his T-shirt.

Unable to assist much for fear of damaging his shoulder again, Jason could only watch as the melée developed and hope that Barbara would escape unscathed. But, when she did finally emerge from the bottom of the scrum, she was crying and gasping for air. As the cable car reached the lower station, Jason placed his good arm around her and tried to calm her.

"Jace, I'm sooooo sorry," Barbara sobbed, as they walked slowly out of the station. "I feel such a fool. Everything seems to be getting on top of me all of a sudden."

"You could say that!" he replied, looking angrily across at Trevor.

"Look, I honestly thought it would help if she lay on the floor and closed her eyes," Trevor pleaded. "That way she wouldn't be able to see anything and she'd relax a bit."

"Well, I wish you'd asked first before you started to manhandle her…"

Peter was about to offer his services as mediator when, from behind him, he heard Gail shriek.

"Has anyone got Fred?"

Everyone in the group stopped. They looked guiltily at each other and there was much shrugging and shaking of heads, but absolutely no sign of Fred.

"Oh no!" Gail wailed. "In all the confusion, we must have left him in the cable car."

"Don't worry," said Peter, suppressing his mounting irritation and trying to sound calm. "I'll go back up to the top, in case he's got handed in. You wait at the bottom in case he turns up there."

He turned to go back inside the cable car station but the exit gate had closed behind him. The only way for him to get back to the top was to go around to the entrance area and purchase another ticket. As he set off, fumbling in his pocket for the necessary money, Gail shrieked after him.

"But, Peter. By the time you've done that, we'll be late for the coach."

Peter turned and called back.

"Don't worry! Jason had better take Barbara somewhere quiet to calm down before they get on the coach. Perhaps Trevor could explain the situation to Miranda and Tony and I'm sure they'll wait. After last night she owes me a favour. I'll only be a few minutes!"

Trevor's already fragile morale had been badly dented by the sorry debacle in the cable car. He realised now that, in his overwhelming desire to be of some use to somebody, he had acted hastily and inappropriately. He was feeling ashamed and was desperate to make amends.

"Don't worry!" he added, echoing Peter. "I'll have a word with Miranda. I'm sure she'll be alright." He tried to sound reassuring.

"I wouldn't be too sure about that!" Gail called as Trevor set off back towards the coach, while trying to make his peace with Jason and Barbara.

"You'd better wait here in case Fred comes down by himself," Peter instructed Gail somewhat absurdly, before disappearing back inside the station.

★ ★ ★

At the coach, Miranda had returned from her peevish stomp around the town but, rather than climb aboard and sit down next to Tony, she had grabbed her ubiquitous clipboard and, with her sunglasses pushed up onto her forehead, was pacing around beside the coach as her "clients" began to return. As Dave and Susan walked past her and climbed aboard, Dave shouted: "Present, Miss!"

Frank had heard Dave and, as he and Joyce walked past Miranda to climb aboard, he also turned and shouted: "Present, Miss!"

Valerie and Brian had been hovering tentatively behind Miranda for a minute or two before Valerie pushed Brian forward.

He stopped beside the coach door, cleared his throat nervously and spoke with some hesitancy.

"Er, I was wondering if we might have a word."

Noticing Brian approach, and picking up a disconcerting whiff of horse manure from his direction, Miranda had started to study her clipboard with keener than usual intensity. As Brian waited for a response, she glanced quickly at her watch. "Not now!" she said, firmly, returning her gaze resolutely to the clipboard. Brian and Valerie tried to continue the discussion, but they were standing in the doorway and were obstructing the swell of people behind them who were trying to get on to the coach. With Miranda steadfastly refusing to budge, or even acknowledge them, they had little choice but to board the coach. After all, they consoled themselves, there'd be plenty of time to accost Miranda while they were travelling to Salzburg and she would have no alternative but to listen.

Jason and Barbara clambered unsteadily on board with Barbara still shaking from her ordeal. Trevor followed behind but, as he got close to Miranda, he paused and looked at her. Sensing his presence, Miranda glanced up from her clipboard and stared back at him. Distracted by Miranda's piercing gaze, he hesitated for a moment and ran his hand over his hair, before blurting out the news he had promised to convey.

"Er, there's been a bit of a problem at the cable cars, I'm afraid. You see, Peter and Gail, er, Mr and Mrs Edwards that is, have left Fred, er, that is, their teddy bear behind on the cable car and Peter, er Mr Edwards, has had to go back up to the top to try and retrieve it, so I'm afraid they're going to be a few minutes late. I said I'd pass on the message."

He did his best to smile reassuringly at Miranda but she just stared unblinkingly back at him.

"What is it with you lot?" she demanded at length. "Why is it that there's always someone late back, whenever we stop anywhere?"

★ ★ ★

Peter had purchased his ticket, boarded the first available cable car and was heading back to the top of the mountain. On the way up, he looked anxiously out of the window to see if he could spot the coach in the car park below, but without success. Somehow, the journey up the mountain felt much slower this time than last and he was growing increasingly restless, shuffling uneasily in his seat, leaping up periodically to look out of the window at the receding car park below or search vainly for any sign of Fred in the cable cars travelling past in the opposite direction.

As his car reached the top and the door slid open, he dashed out. The rarefied mountain air, which he had earlier found so refreshing, was now making him splutter and cough. He went over to where a disinterested looking attendant was sitting and there was a brief, stilted discussion, following which, the attendant shrugged and shook his head. Peter nodded a little dispiritedly, coughed several times, crossed over to the "down" side, waited for the first available cable car and got in.

★ ★ ★

Apart from Gail and Peter, all the passengers had safely returned to the coach on time and as they all waited, fidgeting in their seats and feeling increasingly uncomfortable in the pervasive atmosphere of hostility, recrimination and horse manure, Tony and Miranda were standing outside the coach arguing.

"I warned them," Miranda said aggressively. "I told them if anyone was late, we were going to go without them."

"Yes, I know you did," Tony reasoned. "But at least we know why they are late and we know they are on their way. They'll be here in a few minutes and we can soon make up that amount of time."

"That's not the point and you know it. We've got to assert our authority; you said so yourself. If we give in this time, it'll be someone else next time."

"Yes, but Mr and Mrs Edwards! They're no trouble, unlike some of the others. In fact, he's been doing his best to keep everyone else out of trouble, you included. I mean, them of all people!"

"It's no good. You can't start making exceptions."

"Well, I'm sorry but I think we should wait a few minutes."

* * *

Inside the lower cable car station, Gail had discovered, rather like Peter a few minutes earlier, that once the exit gate had closed behind her, the only way she could get close enough to the cable cars to scrutinise their contents, was to buy another ticket, stand on the "up" platform and peek quickly inside each car while its door was open, prior to beginning its ascent.

Having purchased her ticket, Gail positioned herself on the platform so that she could easily see inside each car as it moved slowly past, although, on several occasions, she had to stand quickly back to allow groups of people to climb aboard. Each cable car had a number and the name of a famous skier painted on the outside and Gail was trying hard to remember the number and the name of the one they had descended in. She was pretty sure it was number 45, the house number of her inquisitive neighbour Carol, and the skier's name was "Ludwig" something. After cursorily inspecting the inside of several cars, car number 45 bearing the name "Ludwig Leitner" came into view. Gail shrieked as its door opened to reveal Fred, lying face down on the floor. She dashed inside and, in her excitement, made two fumbled attempts to pick Fred up, before succeeding at the third go. By then, the door had closed and the car had begun its inexorable upward journey. Gail was now trapped and would have to stay in the car as it climbed slowly to the top and all the way back down to the bottom. As the car began its ponderous ascent, she carefully checked each car that passed her in the opposite direction. Eventually she saw a gloomy-looking Peter travelling slowly past. She leapt out of her seat, waved at him and held Fred aloft for him to see. Slightly puzzled to see Gail travelling past him in an upward direction, he waved back and smiled uncertainly. Once back at the bottom, he waited with increasing impatience for his wife and errant bruin to return. He was rapidly losing patience with Fred and tiring of his inscrutable company.

By the time Gail and Fred had completed their pointless and time-consuming round trip and were re-united with Peter outside the cable car station, the deadline for getting back to the coach had long since passed and Peter was uncharacteristically tetchy.

"Come on, come on, we'd getter get to the coach before it's too late!" he snapped at Gail and started to run towards where the coach had parked. It was just starting to rain; a cold, diagonal sort of rain that stung the flesh, and Peter and Gail kept their heads down as they raced towards the coach. As they got closer, they looked up and stopped. The coach had gone. They looked around the car park to check that it had not moved somewhere else but there was no sign of it, nor of any of its occupants. Peter stood motionless for a moment or two, his hands on his hips, his face bright red, squinting in the rain, as he tried to recover his breath and collect his thoughts.

"The cow!" he exclaimed, when he finally felt able to speak. Gail rebuked him.

"Peter!! I've never heard you talk like that before," she said, severely but not entirely truthfully. For all his calm phlegmatism, Peter had a temper to match the best when he was sufficiently provoked.

"I'm sorry but I'm afraid she is," he continued unrepentant. "She just couldn't wait, could she? She knew we were on our way. But oh no, she had to prove a point. And to think, I pulled Lisa off her last night. Maybe I should have stood back and let Lisa hammer seven bells out of her. She'd certainly have got more than just a few scratches and bruises if I'd let them carry on. And that's the thanks I get. Well, you just wait till I catch up with her."

"Absolutely! There is just one problem, though."

"I know; like what the hell do we do now?" he spluttered as the rain bombarded his face and balding pate.

Gail looked despairingly around her, hoping perhaps for some kind of divine intervention, while Peter had another coughing fit, and the rain fell harder. Then she saw, across the car park, what might be a glimmer of hope.

"Well, the railway station's just over there. Maybe we can get a train to Salzburg."

"Maybe we can, but we are not going to know whereabouts our coach is in Salzburg or what time it is due to leave."

"Have you got the address of tonight's hotel?"

"Well, yes, I think so." Peter patted his back trouser pocket reassuringly.

"Come on then." Gail's smile had returned. "We'll get by somehow. We might be able to find the coach park when we get to Salzburg or bump into somebody we know, but if not, we should be able to make our way to the hotel."

"No choice, I suppose," Peter agreed glumly as they marched off towards the station.

* * *

There was a brooding and venomous silence aboard the coach as it crossed briefly into Germany before heading north-east towards Salzburg. A silence, that is, apart from the two elderly ladies who had embarked on an energetic and opinionated debate about the increasing unreliability and infrequency of their local bus services.

Pestered once again by Valerie and Brian, from whom a discernible smell of horse manure still seemed to be emanating, and unable to escape, Miranda had tried to appease them by promising to speak to them later on, hopefully at a more opportune moment – perhaps one when she could break the news to them quietly and in confidence, and then beat a hasty retreat – but, sensing the unspoken hostility and hearing some sotto voce mutterings coming from the front of the coach, she had retreated to the back of the coach where she was unenthusiastically taking orders for refreshments, while Tony drove on silently, concentrating intently on the road ahead as his windscreen wipers swished remorselessly from side to side. While Miranda continued to occupy herself at the back of the coach, Frank leant forward and spoke softly, by his own standards, to Tony.

"You know, you might have done something to stop us

leaving without Peter and Gail. I mean you are the driver for God's sake!"

"Sorry, I did my best," Tony replied laconically. "But I just couldn't take the risk. She threatened to phone my wife and tell her about one or two things, you know, that I'd been up to."

"And is that the best you can do? At breakfast this morning, you said you were going to look after us. You said you'd try and get things sorted with head office."

"I know, I know, but she beat me to it, I'm afraid. Anyway, she is within her rights, you know, to leave at the agreed time, especially when warnings had been issued."

"Ah, I see," Frank said, with more than a hint of cynicism in his voice. "So you're frightened of her too! You know, this really won't do. Not Peacemaker Pete! Not leaving him behind!"

As the journey continued in an oppressive silence, Miranda began to feel intimidated. She could sense a kind of hostile tension around her and the journey ahead was a long one. She needed to do something to lighten the mood. She rummaged through the small and uninspired collection of CDs that the coach carried and, aware of the age range of most of the coach party, selected a disc containing hits of the 1950s and 1960s. She loaded it into the CD player, pressed the "play" button and waited. Nothing happened. She tried again. Still nothing.

"It's not been working properly for some time," Tony observed a little coldly. "I keep reporting it but nothing ever happens. It's probably buggered!"

"Oh well, thanks very much for telling me," Miranda replied with equal coldness. "I guess we'll just have to sit here in silence then."

★ ★ ★

At Kitzbuhel station, Gail stood in the booking hall, fretting and frowning, and clutching Fred tightly, while Peter went over to the ticket office. Outside, the rain was now falling remorselessly and the temperature had dropped dramatically. Gail shivered. After a couple of minutes of what seemed like an intense and complex discussion with much gesticulation, Peter returned smiling. He held up a couple of tickets.

"Well, they were damned expensive but it looks like we're in luck. I've got two tickets to Salzburg and there is a train. Unfortunately, it doesn't leave for nearly an hour." Gail's smile returned. She hugged him.

"Never mind! How long does it take to get there?"

"I'm not quite sure – bit of a language problem – about two and a half hours, I think, but I'll check with the guard on the train."

"Come on then, let's go and see the bits of Kitzbuhel we missed before we catch the train!" Gail's frown lifted as she strode, with renewed enthusiasm, out into the rain.

"OK, but no cable cars!" Peter called after her as he ventured, more reluctantly, outside.

* * *

During the journey from Kitzbuhel, Miranda had spent as much time as possible ponderously preparing and serving drinks and immersing herself in imaginary paperwork. Keen to avoid any further confrontation or public debate, she had deliberately refrained from making any announcements but, as the coach approached the outskirts of Salzburg, she had no choice. Her voice, when she finally spoke, was terse and frosty.

"We'll be arriving in Salzburg in about ten minutes. Unfortunately we cannot park in the city centre, so we are going to drop you in a coach lay-by. We are not allowed to wait, so you *must* be back there promptly at 5 o'clock and we will come and pick you up."

"Yes, miss," called Dave loudly.

"Oh, shit!" said Trevor quietly to himself. He had been banking on the coach remaining in a designated coach park, where Peter and Gail would have a good chance of finding it, if they managed to make their own way from Kitzbuhel. He ran his hand over his hair.

Ten minutes later, as predicted by Miranda, the coach pulled into a lay-by and the passengers began to step off onto the wet pavement. Brian had been so deep in thought, reflecting on what Miranda might be going to say to him and Valerie, when she was going to say it, and how he was going to react, that he had seemingly failed to notice that it was raining, in much the same way that he had failed to notice that Amsterdam was full of cyclists. Only as he stepped off the coach onto the pavement, immediately dunking his foot in a deep puddle – thereby washing the worst of the horse manure from it – did he realise that he had left his waterproof clothing in his rucksack on the coach. He swore quietly to himself and turned to get back on the coach but, as the last passengers got off, Miranda kicked the door closed and the coach sped away.

"Looks like you're going to get wet again, Brian!" Dave observed, unsympathetically. His remark alerted Valerie, who got off ahead of Brian and had not noticed his latest aberration. Putting her red umbrella up, the colour of which happened to match her shoes, she rounded on him.

"For God's sake, Brian! Must I do everything for you?"

"No need to Valerie," Dave said, helpfully. "He's quite capable of getting wet on his own."

★ ★ ★

Trevor made his way as quickly as possible to the heart of the old city and started to wander around the main squares – Kapitelplatz, Residenzplatz and Mozartplatz. With a diffidence befitting a British tourist, he tentatively approached a few individuals whom he judged might be locals – people wearing uniforms or business clothes – and, after much gesturing and pointing, he strode purposefully off.

After a few minutes, he came across a small shop selling maps and guidebooks. He went inside, purchased a map and, beneath a neighbouring awning, studied it carefully before he headed briskly away from the city centre, crossed the river Salzach, walked alongside the Mirabell gardens and eventually found himself at the entrance to the railway station. He ran inside, as much to get out of the driving rain as anything, looked slowly around him, ran his hand over his hair several times, carefully scrutinised the screens showing train arrivals, spoke briefly to a railway official, nodded, found a seat from where he could see most of the activity taking place in the station and sat down.

★ ★ ★

At a railway station of a different sort, Barbara and Jason were in the midst of a large crowd waiting to take the funicular train up to the Hohensalzburg fortress.

"Are you quite sure you want to do this?" Jason asked, with genuine concern and not a little apprehension.

"Jace, after what happened this morning, I need to," Barbara replied, without much conviction. "I've got to get used to these things. I'll be alright this time, honestly. This one doesn't leave the ground."

Unconvinced by Barbara's assurance, Jason was worried. He really couldn't face the embarrassment of her having another panic attack in the middle of all these people and, if she did, he wasn't sure that he would be able to cope any better than he had in Kitzbuhel.

"OK, if you're sure," he agreed reluctantly, still hoping that Barbara might change her mind. But she didn't.

"I'm sure!" she confirmed, punching him lightly.

By the time the small funicular train arrived, there were large numbers of people waiting to board and no obvious sign of any kind of queuing system. Determined not to injure his shoulder again, Jason decided to hang back as the doors opened, but he could not avoid being swept along by the crowd. As more and more people jostled and pushed their way into the limited standing space, and with only one elbow available to manoeuvre with, he became wedged into a corner of the carriage, his injured shoulder pressed hard against the wall. As more people piled up against him, he let out a cry of pain.

In the crush, Barbara had become separated from Jason, but

she heard his cry over the tumult and tried to push her way through the crowded carriage towards him. Being slightly built, she found it difficult to force a way through and her increasingly shrill requests to "excuse me" had little effect on the surrounding throng; she kept stumbling over bags, backpacks and rucksacks, which littered the floor, and inadvertently pushing her face into other people's damp waterproofs. As she slowly edged and stumbled her way towards him, the funicular started with a jolt and, with nothing substantial to hold on to, she was hurled forward. As she tried, in vain, to steady herself, she thrust out her hand, accidentally grabbed the back of Jason's sling and, as she stumbled and fell, pulled Jason down on top of her. As Jason fell awkwardly, emitting another cry of pain, he piled into other people, causing them to lose their balance and fall on top of him and Barbara in an undignified cosmopolitan and shrill, multi-lingual melée.

★ ★ ★

Getreidegasse is one of the longest and most famous streets in Old Salzburg. It also happened to be narrow and crowded and Dave and Susan were not enjoying themselves. As the rain continued to fall steadily, they repeatedly found themselves having to duck or jerk their heads to one side, in order to avoid being injured by the spokes of countless delinquent umbrellas, passing within inches of their eyes and ears. Rain dripped steadily from the overhanging awnings of the tall buildings that lined the street and the walkways quickly filled with large deep puddles. It was Dave who spotted their usual salvation – a café!

"C'mon, let's go in here, get some refreshments and dry off a bit," he urged. For once, Susan agreed with him.

In another part of the city, Frank and Joyce were trudging stoically across the square of Residenzplatz towards the cathedral. Frank was wearing a cloth cap and a heavy waterproof coat. He had his head down, which shielded him from the rain, but which also accentuated his hunched figure. Joyce, wearing a lightweight hooded jacket, glanced across at him. It didn't take much to sense that he was still in one of his brooding, depressive moods.

"You're very quiet, Frank," she observed.

"Mmmmm. I'm sorry, luv. I seem to have a lot on my mind."

"Like what?" She knew the answer, of course, but previous experience suggested that it was often better, in these situations, to try and get Frank talking.

"Well, I should have thought that was obvious," Frank snapped back. "Like… our so-called "tour director" is a bad-tempered, spiteful control freak with all the cuddly charm of a boa constrictor, who couldn't manage a piss-up in a brewery. Like… people are being thrown off the tour for various trivial reasons, others are being left behind; it's all so malicious. Like our driver seems more concerned with getting his leg over every night than he does about the welfare of his passengers…"

"I'm not sure you helped with your collective dispute yesterday, though. You might have scored a little victory, but it did rather get up Miranda's nose. You must remember you're not a shop steward any more."

"Yes. Maybe you're right. I promise I'll try and keep out of trouble from now on. I tell you what though, I've had enough of trudging round towns and cities trying to make myself understood, looking for something half-decent to eat and praying that we're going to find a public toilet before it's too late – and now it's sodding raining, my feet ache and I can't use my camcorder."

Desperately, Joyce tried to make light of the situation.

"Oh well, some good's come out of it then!"

"Yes, very funny. You wanted me to have a hobby when I retired, remember."

"Yes, but I had hoped that it would be one that you could actually do."

"Don't worry; I'll get the hang of it eventually. I tell you, we might have to do something drastic to salvage this holiday though."

As Joyce pondered how long Frank was actually going to stay out of trouble in the light of his last remark, he paused and glanced up at the still sombre, oppressive sky. They were standing close to the façade of the cathedral.

"C'mon, let's go in," Frank suggested. "It's dry in there, I can do some thinking and maybe offer up a prayer at the same time."

"So, on the whole, you're enjoying yourself then?" Joyce asked sardonically as she followed Frank inside, removing his cap for him as he entered.

★ ★ ★

Brian and Valerie had intended to visit the Mirabell gardens, which had been recommended to Valerie by one of her coffee morning friends. Unfortunately, Brian had forgotten to bring a map and they didn't really want to spend any of their increasingly limited funds on buying one. So, after wandering around for half an hour in the rain without finding the gardens or any directional signs pointing towards them, with Brian now soaking wet and with their minds distracted, they abandoned the idea and headed into the centre of town in search of some shelter.

"And to think we paid good money for this..." Valerie stopped herself as she realised she was starting to sound like Frank. "We've got virtually no money left, it's pouring with rain, you're soaked through – again – we've broken two cameras, lost or broken three watches and any time now we're probably going to be banned from the rest of the tour," she wailed as she tried to shield Brian, with her small red umbrella, from the worst of the rain.

"Might not be a bad idea if we're sent home, then," Brian added gloomily, rehearsing part of their earlier conversation, as more cold rainwater ricocheted off Valerie's umbrella, landed on his head and trickled down his forehead and into his eyes.

"And how do we get home? We haven't got much money left and you know what I think about flying...," Valerie added, rehearsing another part of their earlier conversation.

Brian nodded and shrugged as they spotted a souvenir shop and went inside to browse and dry off a little.

★ ★ ★

Once they had extricated themselves from their self-induced mayhem on the funicular, profusely apologised to those around them who had accidentally become embroiled in the melée, dusted themselves off and hastily fled the scene, Jason and Barbara had quite enjoyed their tour of the impressive Hohensalzburg fortress and the panoramic views over the rain-swept city and the cloud-covered peaks. Now, however, it was time to make the decision about how they were going to get back down to the old city, laid out spectacularly below them. Barbara was limping slightly, having twisted her ankle in the scrum. Jason's shoulder was already sore from his skirmish on the funicular and his clumsy efforts to protect it from the rain, by trying to wrap his waterproof cape over it, had only heightened the pain.

"How's your shoulder now?" Barbara asked as they approached the funicular station. Jason pulled a face.

"Not too great, I'm afraid; it's a bit sore, but no serious damage done, hopefully – just the pain killers wearing off a bit, I should imagine, and getting trapped in the funicular and…"

"I'm soooo sorry. I just tripped over and…"

"Don't worry, Ba," Jason soothed. "You didn't mean it. Anyway how are you now?"

"Oh, a few bumps and bruises; my ankle hurts a bit, but I'll be OK. I've managed to rip my jeans though."

She lifted up the hem of her waterproof jacket to reveal a jagged tear in the seat of her jeans, through which a small amount of flesh was protruding. Jason couldn't resist a closer look. With a mischievous smile, he bent down to examine the tear in more detail and poked his finger playfully through the hole.

"Mmmmm. So I see – better keep your jacket on then."

As they reached the entrance to the funicular, they encountered a large group of people waiting to board the train and, no doubt, impatient to get out of the continuous steady rain. Barbara thought she recognised some of the people that she had trampled on and fallen over on the way up. She started to feel uneasy and panicky, bringing back unpleasant memories of her cable car rides at Kitzbuhel.

"I think we'll walk down," she said with some conviction.

"Good idea," Jason agreed, rubbing his sore shoulder ruefully.

★ ★ ★

Trevor had been waiting at the station for what seemed like hours. There was a regular stream of people coming and going but, for Trevor, nothing of much interest was happening. He was an active, restless individual and he hated waiting around but he dare not risk wandering off for a while in case he somehow missed Peter and Gail's arrival. In any event, he was at least sheltered from the rain. From time to time, his mind wandered back to the events leading up to Julia's departure, and he would get up and pace up and down, going over the events in his mind, trying to excuse or justify his actions, attempting to alleviate the stress that those events had induced. Would she, as Trevor suspected, find that things were not quite what she expected when she got home and would she phone tonight? If she did, what would she say? Occasionally, he would glance at his watch, sigh heavily and fold his arms impatiently. As time went on, he glanced at his watch more often and paced up and down more frequently.

Eventually, the train that he had been waiting for arrived. It was on time. He got up and walked, apprehensively, along the platform towards it. He couldn't be sure, of course, that Peter and Gail would be on it but, after some moments of nervous anxiety, he spotted them getting off, towards the rear of the train. Smiling broadly he loped buoyantly towards them with his arms waving. Gail was the first to notice him. She too smiled broadly.

"Look, Peter, it's Trevor!"

Peter rushed towards Trevor, shook his hand warmly and thumped him heartily on the back, as Trevor almost skidded to a halt.

"Trevor, are we pleased to see you?" he cried exultantly. "How did you know we were on the train?"

Trevor looked embarrassed at the effusiveness of his welcome. "I didn't know. I guessed. I mean, I couldn't think how else you were going to get here."

"You mean you've been waiting for us to arrive?"

"Yes, for a little while. I mean I couldn't risk you getting left behind again. Not after the way you've helped me to… Anyway it's raining out there."

"We thought we might be too late," Gail said, slightly breathlessly.

"Not yet," replied Trevor as he turned and marched briskly towards the station exit. "But we haven't got that long to catch the coach, it's a bit of a walk and we really can't afford to be late again, so you'd better follow me," he called over his shoulder, as he strode off purposefully.

* * *

The rain continued to fall remorselessly and unremittingly out of a leaden sky, as members of the coach party, anxious not be late, began to assemble on the pavement beside the coach lay-by, with the appointed hour of five o'clock approaching. They were bedraggled, generally dispirited and very wet. Brian arrived, looking particularly wet, rather as though he had just stepped, fully clothed, from the shower. Valerie followed, umbrella aloft, trying, largely ineffectually, to shield him from the worst of the elements while, at the same time, struggling to avoid placing her fashionable high-heeled shoes in the many deepening puddles.

Frank, securely swaddled in his thick waterproof coat, looked at Brian with some dismay, from beneath his cloth cap.

"Good God! Look at the state of you!"

Dave eyed Brian up and down with mock repulsion.

"I do hope you're not going to upset the lovely Miranda again by dripping on her upholstery."

"To be honest, I'm past caring now," Brian shrugged as another torrent of cold water ran down the back of his neck.

Behind him, Jason and Barbara arrived. They had found the long, serpentine walk down from Hohensalzburg more arduous than they had anticipated, especially as some of the steep paths and cobbles were now wet and slippery. Barbara was limping more heavily now, wincing in pain every time her right foot touched the ground. Jason, in some discomfort himself, was doing his best to support her, using his uninjured arm, but their progress was slow, painful and ungainly. As they arrived, a pale, dejected Jason looked directly at Dave.

"Don't say a word. Just don't say a word!" he implored.

Dave opened his mouth to say something, but before he could utter a word, a loud and spontaneous cheer went up around him. Trevor had been sighted, smiling broadly, and approaching fast, with Gail and Peter in distant pursuit, struggling to keep pace with the taller and younger man.

"Look who I've found!" Trevor shouted as he got close to the assembled crowd.

"Well done, Trevor!" Frank called, breaking into exuberant applause. Pushing through the gathering crowd, he went over to Gail and Peter, who was standing with his hands on his knees, gasping for breath and coughing quite violently.

"We'd thought we'd seen the last of you!" Frank observed, slapping Peter heartily on his damp shoulder.

"Not yet," Gail gasped. "We came on the train and Trevor was kind enough to meet us at the station. I'll have something to say to Miranda about this. Why the hell did she leave without us?"

"Because she's an old…" Dave began, before Susan trod, heavily and deliberately, on his foot. "You'd better ask Tony."

"Yes, we will when we see him," Frank observed caustically. "Look at this. For once, we're all back on time. It's pissing down and where is the coach? Nowhere to be seen! I bet they're leaving us standing in the rain quite deliberately!"

It felt like several more miserable, damp minutes elapsed before the coach finally arrived, to ironic cheers, its doors opened and the passengers could begin to file aboard. Susan and Dave boarded just in front of Peter and Gail. As he passed Miranda, Dave unzipped his waterproof jacket and shook it violently in her direction. She flinched and recoiled with obvious displeasure. Feigning innocence, Dave smiled, turned and pointed at Peter and Gail.

"Look who we've found! I bet you're pleased to see them!" he said triumphantly.

Peter's normal amiable and tolerant mood had completely evaporated. Wet, tired and unwell, he remained vehemently outraged by what had happened to him and was determined to let Miranda know how he felt. He walked up to her, stared directly at her and shouted.

"Why didn't you wait for us back in Kitzbuhel? You knew where we were – Trevor told you – and you knew we wouldn't be long."

As usual, when under pressure, Miranda hid behind the rules.

"I thought I had made myself quite clear," she said haughtily, while brushing droplets of rainwater from her jacket. "If you weren't there on time, we were going to leave without you."

"Oh, come on. It's not as though you didn't know where we were and how long we were going to be!"

"You tell her, Pete!" Dave encouraged as he sat down, heavily. Seeing Tony sitting behind the wheel, looking disinterestedly out of the window and apparently ignoring the strident discussions taking place behind him, Peter rounded on him.

"And you, why didn't you refuse to go?" The effort of raising his voice was making Peter cough again.

Tony had been hoping to keep out of the increasingly heated debate raging around him. He had advised Miranda to exercise a bit of discretion back in Kitzbuhel but didn't want to be seen by her to be taking the "clients" side. In any event, he was presently more concerned about a coach-load of extremely wet people dripping onto his newly scrubbed floors and brushed upholstery. But he couldn't easily avoid Peter's direct question and, while his paroxysm of coughing continued, Tony sighed heavily and in a quiet, almost apologetic voice, tried to explain his action.

"Because she threatened to tell my wife about… you know… what's been going on."

Gail had been standing next to Peter, listening to the debate with rising anger and, while Peter continued to splutter, she took centre stage. Like her husband, she rarely became incensed but when she did, unlike Peter, she didn't shout. She just spoke slowly and firmly, giving each word more emphasis, and accentuating each point with flamboyant hand movements. Tony's abject, self-centred, almost off-hand response had infuriated her and she rounded on him.

"And don't you think your wife has a right to know what you've been up to. Oh, don't worry, she'll get to know anyway – bound to sometime – so in future, how about thinking less of yourself and more about those of us who have paid good money to come on this trip…" She stopped briefly realising that she was starting to sound like Frank. "Be in no doubt. I shall be writing to the company about this when we get back."

She sat down firmly in her seat, as a round of applause broke out around her. Her cheeks flushed, partly out of anger and partly out of embarrassment at making such an out-of-character public scene. It was at this moment that Brian and Valerie climbed aboard. Miranda couldn't be sure whether Brian deliberately brushed against her as he passed but, as she felt her sleeve turning damp, she took a deep breath and called to them. She couldn't defer the moment any longer. It was only a short drive to the hotel and once they had arrived there, it would be more difficult to say what she had to say.

"Ah, Mr and Mrs Wood. I thought you should know that I have spoken to head office and they have decided that you will leave the tour at the end of today. The hotel will help you arrange your journey back home in the morning!"

Though she had tried to speak as unemotionally as she could, there was a hint of triumph in her voice, which did not go unnoticed.

"Oh, for God's sake!" Frank exploded. He reached inside his blazer pocket and produced his pen and his small notebook in its neat, mock-leather binding.

Resigned to his fate, Brian had flopped wearily into his seat where he started to remove his sodden jumper. Valerie, however, was still standing in the aisle. She turned and advanced, slowly and menacingly, towards Miranda, until she was only inches from her. She was both angry and frightened.

"What? Are you serious? I can't fly. I simply can't fly!"

"And we've got no money left!" Brian added as he removed

258

his glasses and tried to wipe the soaked lenses on his less than pristine handkerchief.

In her high heels, Valerie was a few inches taller than Miranda, who felt a little intimidated by her close and imposing presence and slightly overcome by her strong perfume, so she retreated a pace to consider her response. Once again, under pressure, she hid behind the rules.

"Well, I'm sorry but that's head office's decision. You were warned…"

Valerie was fighting back the tears. The indignity of being humiliated in front of a coach-load of people was bad enough, but her fear of flying was such that she knew she would never be able to board a plane and that she and Brian would somehow have to make their way home across Europe by train and bus with very little money at their disposal. Trying hard to resist the temptation to slap Miranda around the face, she shrieked at her instead.

"Don't think you've heard the last of this. If we ever get home, I shall be writing to the company to make a formal complaint and demand compensation!" Another spontaneous round of applause broke out.

She sat down and burst into tears, as Frank glanced around him and spoke in one of his loud stage whispers to Joyce.

"No, no. This really won't do!"
He opened up his notebook, removed the cap from his pen and began writing, slowly and neatly. Whatever else he had or had not achieved in his life, nobody could accuse him of not being tidy and methodical.

Miranda, meanwhile, turned her back on everyone who had been shouting at her, kicked the door closed and sat down in her seat. As Tony started the engine, the hitherto dormant CD player suddenly burst noisily into life. With Miranda in desperate need of some good fortune, the first bars of "*Just Walking in the Rain*" blasted out.

For a moment or two, there was an incredulous silence before the howls of protest started. Having recovered from his latest coughing fit, Peter rose to his feet, a look of outrage on his face.

"If this is your twisted idea of a joke…" he thundered.

Flustered and confused, Miranda swore loudly, reached over to the obstinately disobedient machine and tried to stop it but, in her agitation, she succeeded only in replaying the offending track. As the volume of protests rose, she tried again and the same thing happened. Eventually, she swore again, even more loudly, thumped the machine and finally succeeded in switching it off.

"This won't do, this really won't do!" Frank reiterated, quietly, to Joyce.

He continued to write in his notebook, a little more briskly and less considered now. When he had finished writing, he carefully removed the page from the notebook and passed it surreptitiously across to Peter and Gail. They read it, nodded and passed it behind to Dave and Susan.

By the time the coach had reached its overnight destination, the Hotel Schutzberg, only a few miles from Salzburg, Frank's increasingly crumpled piece of paper had travelled right to the back of the coach on one side and back down to Frank on the other. Its content had provoked a low hum of discussion around the coach and, in doing so, had aroused Miranda's curiosity. But, despite trying hard, wandering up the coach and back on the pretext of replenishing the drinks machine, she had not been able to hear a word of what was being said and remained unaware of the content – or even the existence – of Frank's note. As the coach pulled into the hotel car park, she reached warily for the microphone.

"Just a couple of reminders before you leave the coach. Dinner this evening is at 7 o'clock. Breakfast tomorrow morning is from 7.30 and we leave at 8.15. Please make sure your suitcases are outside your rooms by 7.30. And after we have left here tomorrow morning, as we shall be travelling for quite a while before we get to Venice, I'll use the opportunity to collect the money for the optional excursions that you have signed up for. So please make sure you have your money ready."

Maybe she was becoming paranoid but Miranda thought she sensed a kind of conspiratorial silence as each of the passengers, even the two elderly ladies, left the coach without uttering a word. She was convinced that something was going on and suspected that Frank was behind it, whatever it was. So, she resolved to keep an especially close eye on things during the course of the evening.

The Hotel Schutzberg lacked the Tyrolean charm of the Ritzerbach Hotel. It was modern and impersonal and seemed, at first glance at least, to have been constructed out of square, grey, concrete blocks. Inside, however, there was an impressive, if superficial, display of pseudo baroque opulence. The entrance hall was unnecessarily vast with a mock marble floor, supporting mock marble columns, and surrounded by extensive troughs of florescent artificial plants. In one corner, there was a glimmering, white grand piano, probably never played, ostentatiously positioned beneath a mock crystal chandelier. Behind an excessively large mock-mahogany semi-circular reception desk, an earnest young man in an expensive looking red waistcoat was waiting expectantly, with a tray full of keys on the desk in front of him.

Frank and Joyce had, by tacit agreement of their fellow travellers, left the coach first in order to be at the head of the queue at reception. Behind them, they found Brian, still damp and crumpled from his earlier drenching, and Valerie, still damp from her tears. Brian was distraught. The holiday that he and Valerie had saved up so hard for, and had been looking forward to for so long, had turned out to be a disaster, largely through his own stupidity and clumsiness. As he stood in the queue, damp and dispirited, he began to brood. He began to see this holiday as somehow a microcosm of his life – much early promise, but ultimate failure and disappointment. He had some natural talent, he was certain of that, and, with a bit of luck, he might have been rich and famous – as Valerie had always desperately wanted him to be – but his lack of drive, his laziness and yes, maybe his stupidity meant that they lived tedious, trivial and unimportant lives in a small scruffy house in a small scruffy neighbourhood. As he pondered his predicament, he looked round and saw the white grand piano. His fingers began to curl and uncurl nervously.

Enough was enough. Perhaps it wasn't too late. He could accept his fate meekly, or he could fight. It was time to fight.

"Don't worry," Frank said, turning to address Valerie and Brian, and trying to sound soothing but actually sounding a bit aggressive. "We're not going to let her send you home. We'll sort it out for you."

From behind him, the young man behind the desk spoke with a heavy Germanic accent.

"Vot is your name, pliz?"

"Er, Armitage. Lance Corporal. Number 473…"

The young man ignored Frank's remarks.

"Ah, yes, here you are. Room 176."

Frank took the key, looked around, checked that Miranda was not within earshot, held the key above his head and loudly addressed the queue assembling behind him.

"Room 176. OK?"

Frank and Joyce moved away, allowing Brian and Valerie to confront the earnest young man behind the desk.

"And vot is your name?" the young man asked.

"Wood. Mr and Mrs Wood," Valerie replied. Brian was still deep in brooding thought.

The young man examined a piece of hand-written paper, positioned prominently on the desk in front of him.

"Ah, yes. Mr und Mrs Vood – I see you are leaving in the morning. Ve haf instructions to arrange to get you to the airport."

Frank, who had started to move off towards the gleaming mock-mahogany lift doors to the side of the mock-mahogany reception desk, overheard the conversation and dashed back. He spoke slowly and loudly to the young man, as he did to all foreigners.

"No, no, that won't be necessary now," he shouted. "There's been a change of plan. They'll be staying on the tour."

"Yes, yes. A change of plan?" Brian sounded confused. He hadn't been paying attention. His eyes were still focused on the white grand piano, across the entrance hall.

"You read my note, didn't you?" Frank asked. Brian nodded absently. "Well, I'll tell you more later," Frank continued conspiratorially. "We'll catch you at dinner."

But Brian didn't hear. He was already marching briskly towards the piano and flexing his fingers. He sat down heavily on the piano stool, lifted the lid and with only a moment's pause, began to play. The first soaring bars of Rachmaninov's Rhapsody on a Theme of Paganini, perfectly played, reverberated around the cavernous entrance hall. The queue of people waiting their turn at the reception desk stood, watched and listened, spellbound. There, at the beautiful, immaculate, gleaming, white grand piano, sat a dishevelled, damp, tramp-like, almost comic figure, eyes closed, his erstwhile clumsy fingers caressing the keys with unexpectedly sensitive dexterity as the powerful tune built to a melodic crescendo.

The young man at the reception desk, clearly affronted by Brian's unauthorised use of the piano and his shambolic appearance, and appearing neither to appreciate the quality of his playing, nor the music of Rachmaninov, called to him to stop, and when that failed to elicit a response, he began to move round from behind the desk towards him. Frank, however, held out a restraining hand and placed a reproachful finger over his pursed lips.

Her attention drawn by the unexpected sound of live piano music coming from the foyer and edgily suspicious of anything out of the ordinary, Miranda had dashed into the foyer to find out what was going on. The sight that confronted her stopped her dead in her tracks and she stood, mouth open, as Brian continued to enthral his fellow travellers in a way that she would not have believed possible.

Brian finished playing the muted ending to the piece. He sat motionless, head bent forward, eyes still closed, as though totally drained by his efforts. Behind him, every person in the queue burst into loud cheering and lengthy applause. There were some cries of "more" and "encore". Valerie watched motionless, with tears welling up in her eyes. She had heard him play many times over the years, but had never witnessed a performance as mesmeric, or an interpretation as sensitive as this one. Encouraged by the rapturous reaction to his impromptu concert, Brian suddenly jerked into life and, without warning, launched into the first dramatic notes of Grieg's First Piano Concerto.

Miranda, meanwhile, crept silently away, a look of thunder on her face.

* * *

The hotel dining room, like the foyer, was designed and decorated with a tacky kind of sham opulence. Like the foyer, the floor was made of mock marble. Around the edges of the room, there were more mock marble pillars with subdued up-lighters. The dining chairs were upholstered in a pink fabric within a framework of gilt painted wood. The colour of the cloths and napkins on the tables exactly matched the pink upholstery. Tables, spaced geometrically and precisely around the room between low tubs of plastic plants, were each set for eight places and, at dinner, Dave and Susan, Frank and Joyce and Barbara and Jason again found themselves on the same table. The other two seats were taken by Gail and Trevor, who had come into the room together. Looking round and seeing no sign of Peter, Jason nudged Barbara.

"There you are," he whispered. "I told you they were swingers!"

Barbara giggled but, to her credit, said nothing. Dave was of course much less discreet and much louder.

"Hello Gail, where's Pete? Does he know you're on a hot date with Trevor?"

"I'm afraid Peter's not very well tonight," Gail replied, her normally calm voice sounding strained, and her smile looking unusually forced. "He's been fighting a cold for several days now and I think the stresses and strains of the day combined with the wet weather have caught up with him a bit, so I've left him upstairs sound asleep."

"I think the stresses and strains of today have caught up with all of us in one way or another," Frank observed with customary gloominess.

At this moment, Valerie and Brian arrived. They had tried to slip unobtrusively into the room but everyone, it seemed, was looking out for them and, as they made their way to a table, they were greeted with more applause and cheering. After playing a section of Grieg's First Piano Concerto, for which he had received another standing ovation, Brian had performed an extract from Rhapsody in Blue, with great panache, and concluded his sparkling recital with some Chopin. His audience had been enraptured and were keen to show their appreciation for the obvious high-spot of an otherwise pretty grim day.

As the noise finally subsided and they settled into their seats, Susan went over to them.

"That playing earlier on was absolute magic," she enthused. "Nobody knew you had a talent like that, Brian."

"I've always said he was far too modest for his own good," Valerie cooed, basking in the reflected glory of Brian's bravura performance. Brian, of course, just looked embarrassed.

"The thing is," Susan continued, "I've just finished doing some temping for this guy who works in the entertainments business. I suppose you'd call him a kind of impresario. Anyway, he spends quite a lot of his time booking acts to perform on these big luxury cruise liners and I know he's always on the look-out for good new talent, especially musicians. You'd have to audition, of course, and, I hope you don't mind me saying so, you'd need to smarten yourself up a bit as well, but I reckon, Brian, that he could find you a load of work on these liners and, if you do well and get noticed, well, there's no knowing where it might lead. You'd probably only have to perform once or perhaps twice a day, plus maybe providing the background music during the captain's formal dinner so it would be a bit like a holiday for you and you'd be getting paid as well. It might make up a bit for this fiasco. Of course, it might be a bit of risk for you, being on a boat surrounded by all that water, but sometimes in life, you have to take a gamble, don't you? What do you think?"

Brian shot a nervous glance at Valerie.

"I wouldn't want to be away from home or from Val for too long," he whimpered.

"Oh, for God's sake, Brian!" Valerie sounded exasperated.

"It's the chance we've been waiting for all these years. Anyway, they might let me come with you from time to time."

She opened her pink handbag, which matched her shoes, and, from somewhere deep inside, produced a dog-eared business card. She handed it to Susan.

"Here you are. I had these business cards produced for Brian ages ago but, of course, we've never used them – never needed to till now. Anyway, there's all the contact details you need."

"Thank you, Valerie," Susan gushed before returning to her table. "I'll call my contact as soon as we get home and you can expect a phone call from him. And if you ever need an agent, well, I've got lots of contacts and can be very persuasive."

★ ★ ★

The first course, a simple egg mayonnaise, was placed firmly down in front of each guest by one of a small band of smartly suited waiters who flitted silently between tables as though on castors.

"Yes, I'm afraid Peter's found all this very tiring," Gail was continuing. "A different hotel every night; lots of travelling. He's not been sleeping well either what with his cough and the noises coming from other rooms." She shot a quick glance at Barbara and Jason who pretended they hadn't noticed but looked a little guilty as they continued to eat.

"You know, what he could really do with," Gail added, her smile returning, "is a few lazy days with no travelling; just relaxing and taking it easy, re-charging his batteries, with the sun on his back."

Frank began to look wistful. He gazed across the room, looking at nothing and no-one in particular.

"Yes, lying around on a beach somewhere, doing nothing much, just soaking up the hot sun…"

Dave, meanwhile, stabbed spitefully at his food with his fork, speared an unappetizing looking piece of yellow lettuce on a large stalk and held it aloft, with a look of disdain on his face.

"A bit of decent food wouldn't go amiss either."

Trevor had been poking unenthusiastically at his food, moving it around on his plate without showing any desire to eat any of it.

"Y'know," he said reflectively, "somewhere just to chill out, relax and take stock of things might be quite nice."

Barbara was shocked and dismayed at the lack of enterprise and adventure being displayed by her fellow diners. Having bolted down her egg mayonnaise, she pushed her plate to one side, leant forward and politely chided her companions.

"Oh, I don't know. This is all a bit of an adventure for us. We're sooooo looking forward to seeing Venice tomorrow – and I can practice my Italian a bit."

With his shoulder still swaddled in its sling, Jason had been trying to eat his food one-handed, using his fork as an all-purpose implement until it slipped from his grasp and clattered to the floor. Barbara reached under the table to retrieve it.

"Mind you, I'm not exactly firing on all cylinders," he said, looking sadly at his sling-encased arm, and, in his weakened state, beginning to feel cowed by Barbara's irrepressible enthusiasm. Beneath the table, on the pretext of retrieving Jason's fork, Barbara grabbed his crotch and squeezed it hard. He visibly winced.

"Sorry, just the shoulder giving me some trouble," he mumbled through clenched teeth. "A bit of time to rest it wouldn't be such a bad idea," he added, fidgeting in his seat as Barbara tightened her grip. Dave leered.

"Yes, remind us again Jason exactly how you did that …"

"Shut up, Dave!" Susan shouted down his ear with such ferocity that he too dropped his fork.

Joyce had been sitting quietly, carefully chewing her food, mulling things over and half listening to the conversation around her. She smiled contentedly. Joyce did not often approve of Frank's headstrong and occasionally hare-brained schemes but this time, she knew that he was right and that something drastic had to be done – and she was now much clearer about what needed to be done. If she had her way, it would no longer just be an angry protest meeting – it would be a meeting where some positive suggestions were made and some sensible, practical action would be taken. She would, of course, allow Frank to take the credit.

At the sound of Dave's fork clattering onto his plate, she started, looked up and glanced across the room. After their triumphal arrival and Susan's gushing and unexpected offer, Valerie and Brian were now sitting abjectly at a far table, sandwiched between Nigel and his insufferable mother on one side, and the two elderly ladies on the other. They had chosen the dinner table at which to begin a discussion on their various ailments and, in graphic detail, minor operations that they had recently suffered. Joyce turned and spoke quietly to Frank.

"I'm just going over there to have a quick word with Brian and Valerie and try and let them know what's happening and then perhaps we can have a brief word?"

She excused herself from the table and strode confidently towards Brian and Valerie.

★ ★ ★

The superficial, cosmetic opulence of the hotel did not extend beyond the ground floor and staircase. At first floor level, the bedroom floors were covered in well-worn linoleum tiles and the basic fittings in the modestly sized rooms were old and distressed. The beds were hard and uncomfortable and, in the bathrooms, the showers performed erratically, as did the supply of hot water.

Along the dingy first floor corridor, various members of the coach party were wandering, in dribs and drabs, towards room 176. As they arrived, they looked around furtively, knocked gently on the door, waited for it to open and then slid quickly inside.

Miranda had been suspicious that something odd, possibly sinister, was going on from the moment they arrived at the hotel. She still wasn't sure whether Brian's virtuoso performance at the piano had been some kind of pre-planned diversionary tactic and was determined to keep a very close eye on anything else unusual that happened. From her room, a little further down the corridor, she could hear rather more movement and chatter coming from the corridor than she would normally have expected at that time of the evening. She opened her door a tiny amount and peered out into the corridor, with growing puzzlement, as more and more people scuttled along the corridor before disappearing into room 176.

Inside the increasingly crowded room, Frank had removed his blazer and loosened his tie, but was still perspiring freely. He was standing, preening with self-importance, by the half-open window, clutching his notepad in its neat, mock-leather case. Dave, several inches shorter than Frank, was standing next to him, trying to see around and between the heads of the growing number of people congregating in the room. Some sat uncomfortably on the twin beds, others assembled around the sides of the room and two or three gathered in the bathroom doorway. Joyce had positioned herself by the door and, each time she heard a knock, she opened it quickly and stood aside as more and more people entered. Frank was issuing the orders, something he enjoyed, waving his arms around importantly and pointing, as much as he could within the increasingly cramped space.

"Try and budge up a bit more over there, there are more people trying to get in. Oi, watch what you're doing on those beds. We've got to sleep on them later!"

There was another tentative knock at the door. Joyce opened it and stood back as Brian and Valerie, looking apprehensive, followed by an unaccompanied Nigel entered. Somehow Dave spotted them through the crowd and shouted over to them.

"Brian and Valerie are here," he announced. There was an immediate ripple of applause, which was quickly shushed by Frank, who was anxious to avoid alerting Miranda.

"Brian and Val. Can you try and squeeze over here with us?" Dave asked as they tried to manoeuvre their way clumsily through the throng, still being followed by Nigel.

A moment or two later, Barbara and Jason arrived. Still feeling the effects of their earlier misadventures, and both a little sore from their accumulated injuries, they stared nervously at the crowd of people massing in front of them and began to back away towards the door. Joyce was quick to reassure them.

"Barbara and Jason. Welcome! Look, you needn't worry about trying to push your way through. We've got a special job for you two, which we think you are particularly well qualified for. Just stay here by the door and I'll tell you what to do!"

When the steady trickle of people entering the room finally stopped, Frank stood on a chair, his head almost touching the grubby ceiling, and began to count the number of people in the room. He tried two or three times to do so but, as people were moving around trying to secure a better vantage point or a more comfortable perch, he kept reaching a different figure. Disappointed that he did not have a precise total that he could write down, he decided, nevertheless, to make his opening announcement. It was getting extremely warm and uncomfortable in the room and he wanted to keep the meeting brief. He coughed loudly to attract everybody's attention.

"Now then, I think most people are here, so we'll make a start. As you know, our friends Peter and Gail were deliberately and wilfully left behind this morning. Now poor old Pete has got some of us out of a few scrapes this week, one way and another, and now, for his trouble, he is ill in bed and can't be with us. We think he's been treated very badly."

Cries of "hear, hear" and some clapping of hands reverberated around the room.

"And even worse in a way," Dave added from somewhere near Frank, "they are trying to throw our friends Brian and Val here off the tour. Now, we don't think that's fair. They should have to suffer the rest of this holiday like the rest of us!"

Dave's comments provoked some laughter and cries of "shame". Brian and Valerie, now standing beside Dave, looked self-conscious but managed a weak smile. Frank meanwhile was thoroughly relishing being in the limelight and addressing an apparently receptive audience. He was warming to his theme.

"They've had a lot of bad luck this week," he continued. "They haven't got much money left, Val hates flying and, on top of that, we now discover that Brian is a star talent in the making. So, do we agree that we need a battle plan to stop them having to go home?"

The question elicited nods of agreement and further cries of "hear, hear."

Suddenly Nigel, who was still standing next to Brian and Valerie, rather timidly raised his hand. Frank looked down at him with a mixture of shock and outrage. He was in full flow and wasn't expecting to be interrupted, least of all by Nigel.

"Oh, hello, Nigel! Does your mother know you're here?" Frank asked mockingly.

Nigel cleared his throat. "Yes, she does, thank you and she told me, er, rather she asked me to make sure that I told you her views. She said to tell you that she's got no time for people trying to take the law into their own hands and that if people are not happy about their holiday or the way they've been treated, then they should formally complain to the company when they get home."

There was a collective intake of breath and the room fell silent.

"Of course," Nigel continued, "speaking for myself, we all know that the best we'll get out of the company is a letter of apology and the offer of a few measly quid off our next holiday so, if you were planning to take matters into your own hands, then you'd have my support."

Cheering and clapping broke out around the room. If there had been any doubt about the likely level of support that Frank and his co-conspirators were going to receive, it had been dispelled with that one utterance from the unlikeliest of sources.

"Well said, Nigel," Frank beamed. "So here's what we thought we might do…" he continued before Joyce, standing by the door and peeping out into the corridor, interrupted him.

"Miranda's on her way," she called. "Quiet everyone until I give you the cue. OK, Jason and Barbara; you know what to do!"

Miranda had been unable to contain her curiosity any longer. The number of people entering room 176 and the cacophony of sounds coming from within, culminating in the loud ovation that greeted Nigel's comments, drew her inexorably towards the door. She slowly approached and was about to knock when she heard what sounded like pleasurable sighs and orgasmic groans of delight coming from just inside the door. She pressed her ear against the door. She then heard a female voice, Barbara's she thought, shouting "Yes, yes, yes, oh yes! Give it to me, big boy!" Almost immediately, she heard other similar passionate sounds coming from within the room and cries of delight and pleasure emanating from a variety of different voices, both male and female. She paused for a moment, considering what action she should take, then, as the sighs and groans started to build to their inevitable crescendo, she turned, dashed back to her own room, ran inside and firmly closed the door.

★ ★ ★

CHAPTER 7

Tour De Farce

They didn't bother to draw back the curtains. They just dragged themselves reluctantly out of bed, switched on the light, slowly got themselves ready and began, disconsolately, to pack. For all the encouraging things that had happened and the positive promises that had been made the previous evening, they shared a deep sense of foreboding this morning. However well intentioned and supportive their fellow travellers had been, something was bound to go wrong – it always did. Words were easy but they needed to be converted into actions and that was always the difficult bit, especially when the competence and efficiency of the ringleaders might be found wanting.

As usual, Brian gathered his possessions together in great, disorganised armfuls, threw them into a heap on the bed and stuffed them haphazardly into his suitcase. Valerie, on the other hand, folded all her considerable quantity of clothing neatly and placed each item carefully and precisely into her suitcase. They had nearly finished this increasingly well-practiced routine when they heard a knock at the door. Brian had his hands full and Valerie was nearer, so she opened it. Outside, in the dimly lit corridor, Trevor and Dave stood skulking, like a pair of naughty schoolboys. Trevor was carrying a dark blue travel bag, slung casually over one shoulder. Valerie quickly opened the door wide and her two visitors scurried furtively in. Eagerly, Trevor put his bag down on the dressing table, opened it and removed some food – bread rolls, ham, cheese and croissants – wrapped in paper serviettes, which they had obviously smuggled out of the breakfast room.

"Here you are," he announced chirpily. "Just a few things we acquired for you for breakfast. They should keep you going for a while, but you'd better keep them away from Dave here."

Valerie's emotions were in a delicate state this morning. She was encouraged by Trevor and Dave's timely arrival and the ebullient mood they were obviously in, but she still found herself fighting back the tears again. In truth, she wasn't feeling at all hungry, but didn't want to cause offence.

"Oh, that's very kind of you. Thank you so much!"

Dave, meanwhile, had been peering around the dark interior of the room.

"Now then, have you packed?" he asked, dubiously. Brian threw the final items into his suitcase and nodded. Dave and Trevor helped to zip their suitcases up – easier with Valerie's case than with Brian's – and tie the dog-eared string around them.

"OK, we'll take these," Dave said firmly. "Now remember what we said. Stay in your room and we'll come and collect you when the coast is clear."

"Enjoy your breakfast," Trevor added cheerfully, before he and Dave left the room, carrying a suitcase each.

★ ★ ★

The low cloud and rain of the previous day had cleared away overnight and there was a bright, fresh crispness to the morning air.

Frank emerged purposefully from the hotel, sniffed the air pleasurably, looked up at the cloudless, pale blue sky and rubbed his hands together with obvious glee. He brushed some imaginary dandruff from the shoulder of his blazer and looked over towards the coach, its freshly cleaned bodywork glinting proudly in the morning sunlight. As expected, Tony was there, fully occupied with loading suitcases into the hold, and a few members of the coach party were beginning to assemble, eager, it seemed, for the day's activities to begin. Followed closely by Joyce, Frank tried to look nonchalant as he strolled over to where Barbara and Jason were standing. He winked importantly at Jason, who offered a gentle nod and weak smile in return.

Frank, Joyce, Barbara and Jason formed themselves into what they hoped looked like a spontaneous and casual gathering, though their self-conscious mannerisms may have betrayed them to anyone who was watching. Fortunately, there was no sign yet of Miranda and Tony was so engrossed in loading the suitcases that he was unaware that he was being carefully observed. It wasn't long before Tony almost completely disappeared into the luggage hold, so that he could stack some cases at the back and, for a while, only his legs, protruding from the hold, were visible to the casual onlooker. Frank seized the opportunity and quickly boarded the coach. He was out of sight for only a couple of moments before he emerged, looking smugly triumphant. He went over to Jason, covertly removed a mobile phone from his blazer pocket and handed it to him with another knowing wink. Jason and Barbara moved quietly and quickly away to a safe distance, well away from the coach and their fellow travellers. After some painful experimentation, Jason found that he was able to hold the mobile phone in his left hand, as it rested in its sling, while he used his unencumbered right hand to press the buttons and keys with all the speed and dexterity expected of a techno-confident young man. Barbara stood next to him with a scruffy note pad and pen and, from time to time, made notes as Jason called out to her. Frank, meanwhile, stood by the luggage hold, waited for Tony to emerge and accosted him when he did.

"Er, excuse me Tony. Could I have a quick word?" he said, importantly.

Tony liked to focus on one task at a time and was clearly less than pleased to be interrupted. He was breathing heavily from the effort of loading the cases and, even though it was a cool morning, the usual beads of perspiration were forming on his forehead. He frowned, looked pointedly around at the large pile of suitcases still waiting to be loaded, scanned the environs of the car park in case Miranda was around and could be called in to assist and ostentatiously mopped his brow.

"Actually, it's not really very convenient at the moment."

"Oh, I am sure the suitcases can wait a minute or two. We don't mind if we are a few minutes late leaving – we're quite used to it by now – but it is very important that we have a quick word, I promise you. It won't take long."

Frank placed an avuncular but firm arm around Tony's muscular shoulders and steered him away from the pile of suitcases. Tony looked anxiously over his shoulder at his unfinished task and tried gently to extricate himself from Frank's embrace, but Frank tightened his grip and marched him away.

"Don't worry, Tony," Joyce called after him. "I'll keep an eye on the suitcases for you."

When Frank was sure that they were far enough away not to be overheard or interrupted, he stopped and, while still clasping Tony's shoulders, spoke slowly and precisely.

"You see, the thing is, Tony, old lad. Well, how can I put this? You know you mentioned that Miranda was threatening to tell your wife about – well, you know – your little indiscretions?"

"Yes," Tony replied suspiciously. He was stronger and younger than Frank and, no doubt, could have broken free from Frank's bear hug and walked away from him if he'd really wanted to, but there was something in the tone of Frank's voice, a kind of sinister persuasiveness, that kept him rooted to the spot.

"Well, as Gail said yesterday, your wife is bound to find out sooner or later. Somebody's going to spill the beans. Now, if Miranda tells her, there's a fair chance you might be able to blag your way out it. You know the sort of thing – she had a crush on you, wanted to get your wife out of the way, no truth in what she says, she has a vivid imagination, always making things up, is well known for this sort of thing, has a bit of a reputation – that kind of thing. But, on the other hand, if some of the passengers were to inform your wife and then, a bit later, some more – quite independently – were to corroborate the story, well then that would be a bit harder for you to explain away, wouldn't it?"

Tony's unease was increasing. He had a lot more cases to load and couldn't really see the point of Frank's observations. But there was something going on, of that he was sure.

"Maybe," he replied, "but why would anyone want to do that? Anyway, even if some of you did want to, you don't know her and you don't know where we live, so there's no way you can get in touch with her."

"Ah – now then, that's where you're wrong, I'm afraid,"

Frank replied with a sardonic smile and a hint of smugness in his voice. He turned round and pointed towards the distant figure of Jason who was still studying the mobile phone intently and regularly calling out to Barbara who was equally frequently jotting in her note pad.

"You see," Frank continued. "You really shouldn't leave your phone lying around. Young Jason may be a bit clumsy but he is something of a technical wizard – I taught him all he knows, of course – and he will have found all your stored numbers, which Barbara is making a note of. No doubt your wife's number is there somewhere, along with some others that maybe you'd prefer we, and she, didn't know about!"

"Oi, give me that back!" Tony shouted. He broke free from Frank's clutches and started to run towards Jason and Barbara, but they saw him coming and ran off across the car park and into the street, still holding the phone. For all their combined injuries, their young legs moved at a speed that Tony's greater bulk and maturity of years couldn't compete with and, realising that his pursuit was hopeless, he stopped and glowered at them as they disappeared out of sight. While Tony stood there, breathing heavily and unable to decide quite what to do, or quite what was going on, Frank caught up with him.

"As I was saying…," he continued, re-placing his arm around Tony's heaving shoulders. Apparently casually, he steered Tony around to the back of the coach where he could no longer see the luggage hold and the open door. When Joyce was satisfied that Tony had been escorted safely out of sight, she waved enthusiastically towards the hotel entrance. Seeing the wave, Dave and Trevor emerged from the hotel and, carrying a suitcase each, dashed as quickly as they could across the car park and loaded them hurriedly into the luggage hold, hiding them behind some more cases which they threw in. A few moments later, Susan emerged from the hotel with Brian and Valerie who ran, as best they could, towards the coach.

Trevor had been rather quicker across the ground than the more corpulent Dave and, having completed his task, was stealing quietly away from the coach as Brian and Valerie approached.

Dave, however, had only just loaded his suitcase and, as he stepped back from the hold, without looking, he collided with the onrushing Brian and Valerie. Despite her high-heeled shoes, Valerie managed to step nimbly aside, but the more ungainly Brian, his balance already imperilled by the weight of the heavy rucksack on his back, took the full force of the impact and tumbled backwards into the stack of suitcases still waiting to be loaded, scattering them in a broad, untidy arc. Joyce rushed over to help him up and, while he was still getting his breath, bundled him onto the coach behind Valerie.

While this ungainly subterfuge was being played out on one side of the coach, Frank was continuing to talk to Tony as he guided him slowly around the other side.

"Of course, what might make things even worse would be if the passengers informed the company of some of the things you've been up to. I mean, it's not just Miranda is it? There was that girl Lisa the other night and I'm sure if we started ringing some of the numbers stored on your mobile, we'd find some more. It's against company rules, all of these shenanigans, I imagine…"

★ ★ ★

Frank and Tony concluded their discussions around the far side of the coach, unseen and unheard by others. Frank shook Tony's clammy hand, smiled his slightly sinister smile and escorted him back to the near side of the coach where, ashen-faced, he continued to load the suitcases which Brian had spread-eagled for him, before he headed off into the hotel to make an urgent phone call. Once he was out of sight, Jason and Barbara returned to the car park, looking pleased with themselves, and handed Tony's mobile phone to Frank. He placed it in his pocket and had begun to stroll nonchalantly towards the coach when he spotted Nigel approaching, with his mother, making laboured progress, some distance behind. He beckoned urgently to him.

"Morning, Nigel. I do hope your mother isn't going to put a spanner in the works today. Only I know she doesn't approve of what we're doing and from where she's sitting on the coach…"

Nigel chuckled. "I don't think she'll be a problem. I seem accidentally to have given her a couple of her sleeping pills this morning, instead of her usual medication. Ooops, silly me!" He chuckled again and winked at Frank.

Miranda arrived much later than normal, looking unusually pale behind the ubiquitous sunglasses. Though she was still puzzled about the precise purpose and nature of yesterday evening's bizarre gathering in room 176 and, despite one or two other distinctly strange occurrences, their stay at the hotel had been less eventful than she feared and she was determined, this morning, to re-assert her authority. As a result, she bustled about, rounding everyone up and counting them onto the coach. There was a strange acquiescence about the passengers this morning. As the coach pulled away, more or less on time despite Frank's "little chat" with Tony, Miranda stood up, noted, with quiet satisfaction, the two unoccupied seats where Brian and Valerie had previously sat, sat down again and reached for her microphone. Though outwardly calm, she sounded more guarded than usual.

"Good morning!" She spoke in a detached, formal manner and was not prepared for the rousing chorus of "Good Morning, Miranda" that assailed her from all parts of the coach. She jumped, looked nervously behind her, and paused for a moment before continuing.

"This morning we will be heading south out of Austria into Italy and making our way down to Venice. We have quite a long journey ahead of us so, in a little while, when we are on the motorway, I'll come and collect your payments for the optional excursions that you have chosen, if you could have your money ready, please."

As the coach travelled swiftly along in bright, clear conditions, with just a hint of white cloud floating above some of the distant mountain peaks, there seemed to be more of a buzz of excitement on board than of late. Miranda was vaguely aware of an increased level of chatter and what seemed like a more upbeat mood, which she ascribed to the improved weather, the pleasant alpine scenery and the anticipation of going to Venice, but she paid little attention as she busied herself with the task of collecting money from all the "clients" who had previously indicated that they were interested in some or all of the additional options available to them. This was no easy task. Apart from the trips already undertaken in Amsterdam, there were options for a gondola ride in Venice, evening tours of Rome and Paris, a trip up a mountain in Lucerne, a boat trip on Lake Lucerne and a visit to Versailles. Everyone had, in theory at least, already filled in a form indicating which options they wanted to participate in, but they would not necessarily remember which ones they had marked and, after due reflection, they might also want to change their minds. So Miranda was expecting that the task of confirming choices and collecting money could take some time and not a little patience.

She began at the back of the coach where a number of pre-planned delaying tactics were put into operation. Questions, often irrelevant or fatuous, were asked about some of the excursions – how long would they last? Could they decide on the day of the option when they saw what the weather was going to be like? Was lunch included? What alternatives were there for those who chose not to go on the options? Money was "accidentally" dropped on the floor from where it seemed to take an inordinately long time to retrieve, incorrect amounts of money in an unhelpful mixture of sterling and Euros were handed over, and the actual amounts to be paid were challenged, as was Miranda's patience.

While Miranda was being detained by the orchestrated campaign of procrastination at the back of the coach, Trevor rose quietly from his seat and tiptoed down the aisle, past Nigel's mother who was sound asleep, to the toilet, where he gently pulled open the door. Checking that Miranda's back was still turned, he beckoned to Brian and Valerie. It had been an uncomfortable journey for them so far. In the cramped confines of the toilet, Valerie had been forced to sit on Brian's lap, supporting his weighty and lumpy rucksack on hers, while, at the same time, holding the door closed, since the lock no longer worked. They were, therefore, relieved to be relieved and they crept stealthily – or as stealthily as Brian could manage – up the aisle and slid quickly and quietly into their usual seats. Their triumphant arrival was greeted with some silent giggling, gestures of support and nods of approbation from passengers near the front.

As the delaying tactics continued, it took Miranda a considerable time to progress gradually down the aisle, carefully placing all the money she received in a large zip-up wallet and neatly filing the completed and signed forms in a pink folder. Eventually, she arrived at the seats only recently re-occupied by Brian and Valerie. She had begun to fumble in her folder for the correct form before the chilling realisation suddenly dawned.

"What the f…! How did you get here? What the hell are you doing here?" she demanded, incredulously, her voice cracking with emotion. "You are supposed to be on your way home. I told you yesterday that you were banned from the rest of the tour and I asked the hotel to make arrangements to get you to the airport and…"

During Miranda's outraged and befuddled invective, Dave and Frank had slowly and silently risen from their seats and were now standing in the aisle, with Frank's height and Dave's width completely blocking Miranda's passage back to the front of the coach. Trevor, meanwhile, had slipped unnoticed into the aisle behind Miranda, cutting off any possible retreat that she might want to make to the back of the coach or the rear exit door. She was trapped.

Frank coughed loudly, alerting Miranda to the manoeuvres that had taken place, and, as she looked up, gave her a particularly sinister smile.

"Well, you see, my dear, there's been a bit of a change of plan. This is, after all, our holiday, which we have paid good money for. So we all had a meeting last night, you may have heard us, and we decided, democratically, that we wanted our friends Brian and Val to stay with us, so I'm afraid we were very naughty and we smuggled them on board. They've been hiding in the toilet. The lock doesn't work properly, by the way…"

It was the scenario that Miranda had always dreaded. Within a few dramatic seconds, her authority had been flagrantly flouted and the balance of power had dramatically shifted. There wasn't much that she could do about it immediately. She was trapped and she was flustered. Her brow furrowed, her throat became dry, her neck turned pink and the hand clutching her folder began to quiver slightly.

"But you can't do that. It's a company decision…" Her voice lacked its usual authority. It quavered as it betrayed the fear and vulnerability she was suddenly feeling.

"Ah, but we have," Dave interjected. "I think it's what used to be called a mutiny." Doing an appallingly hammy imitation of Charles Laughton in "*Mutiny on the Bounty*" he rolled his eyes and shouted "this is mutiny Mr Christian!" Then, returning to his normal voice, he yelled "the crew are taking over the ship!"

The announcement was greeted with a tumultuous outbreak of cheering and applause throughout the coach, though almost certainly not in appreciation of Dave's limited acting abilities. Nigel's mother stirred briefly but went back to sleep. Miranda looked round in some panic, noticing Trevor standing behind her and watching her intently, while she tried desperately to find a way to regain control of the situation.

"What do you mean? You can't do this! You can't do this! Tony, you're not going to let them do this, are you?"

Tony did not turn round. He kept his firm hands on the steering wheel and eyes focused on the road ahead. There was, however, just a hint of a smile on his lips.

"Sorry, luv, I'm with them," he shouted, over his shoulder.

"Oh, are you indeed? Well, then, you leave me no choice. If you don't help me out of this mess, stop the coach, phone for help or something, then I'm afraid your wife's going to hear all about your little indiscretions."

"Too late, I'm afraid, luv," Tony replied, calmly. "I phoned her from the hotel before we left this morning. I warned her you might be in touch and to take no notice of your vivid imagination."

Frank smiled again at Miranda. It was an eerie smile and it made Miranda shudder. He gestured towards the now empty pair of seats, where Trevor had been sitting.

"Have a seat for a moment," he said, trying to sound pleasant but, to Miranda at least, there was more than a hint of menace in his voice. Sensing that she had little choice, and with Frank, Dave and Trevor gradually closing in around her, she sat down in the seat by the window, looking bewildered and upset. Her eyes, no longer hidden behind her sunglasses, were red and watery. Joyce handed Frank a copy of the company's holiday brochure and, as Trevor sat down next to Miranda, he looked sternly down at her.

"You see, it says in the brochure here: *"your friendly and informative tour director will ensure that you have an enjoyable holiday."* Now you haven't done that have you? I mean, you tried to get poor old Brian and Val here banned from the rest of their holiday; the holiday that they've been saving up for all year. You left Gail and Peter behind yesterday on the flimsiest of pretexts – and after Peter had saved you from being beaten up, too. God alone knows what he had done to upset you! And he's not been feeling well. You were very unpleasant to Dave here over his.. er.. little accidents."

"Very unpleasant!" Dave agreed, nodding vigorously.

"In fact," Frank continued, with more than a little exaggeration, "you've been very rude and unpleasant to most of us at some stage or other."

Miranda started to sob violently, her whole body shaking. "I've got my job to do. I'm only doing my job," she spluttered through the tears.

"Not very well, I'm afraid," Frank said, almost apologetically, before standing upright, straightening his tie and adopting an official sounding voice. "So we've decided to remove you from your position – you are no longer our tour director."

Miranda stood up and tried to move towards Frank but Trevor raised his knees, dug them firmly into the back of the seat in front of him and refused to budge. With Frank and Dave still blocking the aisle, she had nowhere to go, so she sat down again.

"But that's absurd," she sobbed. "I mean, I *am* the tour director; everyone knows I'm the tour director. The company is paying me to be tour director. The hotels we are going to – they all know me. They know I'm the tour director…"

Up until now, Dave had been content to leave most of the talking to Frank; he was, after all, quite good at it in an overbearing, pompous kind of way and Dave was not noted for his eloquence. Nevertheless, he was thoroughly enjoying the thrill of the adventure, just as he was enjoying being one of the ringleaders of the rebellion, thrust into an unaccustomed position of power, influence and responsibility. The adrenaline had begun to pump through his body and, suddenly and quite unexpectedly, he started to feel the kind of stirring in his loins that he had not experienced for a long time.

"Ah, well, that's the other thing," he said, turning awkwardly away from Miranda's gaze in order to avoid giving her an embarrassingly close-up view of the prominent swelling developing in his trousers. "We've decided to make a few changes to the itinerary. I mean, just look at the state we're in. We're all knackered. It looks as though Trevor's marriage is on the rocks. Poor old Jason over there is all strapped up and needs some time to recover. Peter is quite poorly with a heavy cold that he can't shake off – not helped by being left behind in the pouring rain yesterday – Val and Brian have suffered enough traumas these last few days to last a lifetime, Frank and Joyce are missing the seaside and I haven't had a decent meal since we left England. So after we've been to Venice today, we've decided that we are going to find somewhere warm and sunny, preferably by the sea, where we can all relax and chill out for a few days. Of course, there is one problem."

"Only one? And what's that?" Miranda asked, shaking her head in disbelief at the increasing lunacy of the situation. Dave pointed to Miranda's wallet.

"We're going to need some money to book hotels, buy some food, that kind of thing. So I'm afraid we're going to have to have our money back!"

Dave reached across Trevor to try and snatch the wallet that Miranda was still holding, but she reacted too quickly and pulled it away. Instinctively, she held the wallet in her right hand and raised it aloft out of his reach. In the seats behind her, the two elderly ladies had been unusually quiet this morning. Maybe they had finally run out of topics of conversation, maybe the arduous daily schedule was beginning to sap their energy, or maybe the journey was proving to be more entertaining than usual this morning. Surprisingly, they had attended Frank's meeting the previous evening and knew what was being planned. As soon as Miranda's hand holding the wallet shot up into the air, one of the ladies, with surprising speed and dexterity, leant forward, snatched it out of Miranda's hand and, amidst a ripple of applause, handed it quickly over to Dave.

"That's stealing; you can't do that!" Miranda shrieked.

"Well, it's not exactly stealing is it?" Frank reasoned. "We aren't going to go on most of the optional tours that we've just paid you for and, besides, after all we've been through, I do think we're entitled to some money back, don't you?"

"This is outrageous," Miranda blustered. "I've had enough of this!"

She pulled her mobile phone out of her jacket pocket but, as she started to activate it, Trevor reached forward and snatched it out of her hand. Miranda screamed.

"You can't get away with this you know!" she screeched, hysterically. "All the hotels will be expecting us. If we don't arrive…"

"We've thought of that," Frank interrupted, calmly. "Allow us to introduce our new multi-lingual tour director – Barbara!" He turned away from Miranda and gestured towards Barbara.

Barbara stood up, a little nervously at first, but the combination of applause, cheering and whistles that greeted Frank's announcement, encouraged her. Spurred on by her burgeoning spirit of adventure, she smiled broadly, took an extravagant bow and blew kisses enthusiastically down the coach.

Dave, meanwhile, stared down at Miranda and leered lopsidedly at her.

"Of course, there is another problem. If Barbara here is going to take over as our tour guide, she's going to need your uniform. Now, I'm no expert but she's about your size, I'd say."

"Oh no! Oh no!" Cringing in her seat, Miranda held up her hands in horror.

"So if you'd just like to slip out of your uniform," Dave continued, with obvious lascivious delight. Indeed, it felt as though his trousers were about to burst open.

"Get lost!"

"Look, I don't want to belabour the point," Frank observed caustically, still wearing a menacing smile. "But, I don't really think you have too many choices. Now, we can either forcibly remove your uniform, or you can slip out of it here in front of everyone, or Joyce and Susan will escort you to the toilet and you can change in there. I believe Barbara has brought a change of clothes for you."

On cue, Barbara produced a carrier bag, containing some nondescript casual clothes, which she flourished dramatically above her head. In the increasingly forlorn hope of finding some allies, Miranda looked desperately around her, but all she heard was a couple of cries of "Get 'em off!" from somewhere near the back of the coach. Seeing no way out, she sighed heavily, brushed some tears from her reddening eyes and slowly stood up. Trevor stood up and moved into the aisle to allow her to pass.

"If you think I'm changing here…" she wailed, treading heavily and deliberately on Trevor's foot before flouncing off towards the toilet with Susan in bustling pursuit, squeezing past Trevor and accidentally treading heavily on his other foot as she passed, followed, at a more leisurely and careful pace, by Joyce, carrying Barbara's carrier bag. Grimacing, Trevor quickly returned to his seat, where he removed his shoes and rubbed both feet thoughtfully.

As the coach continued on its way, raised but indistinct female voices could be heard coming from the toilet. After a delay of some minutes, Miranda eventually emerged, slowly and sulkily, wearing Barbara's spare clothes and carrying her discarded uniform under her arm. Escorted by Joyce, to the front of her, and Susan, to the rear, she made her reluctant way back down the coach. As she ran the gauntlet of gibes and jeers from both sides of the aisle, a vivid image flashed into her mind of the ship's captain, humiliated by his mutinous crew and consigned to walk the plank. She stopped next to Trevor's seat and closed her eyes in embarrassment and trepidation. While her eyes were still closed, Dave prised her uniform from under her arm and handed it to Barbara.

"Here you are Babs; pop into the loo and change into these," he chortled.

As Barbara sashayed her way eagerly to the toilet, and as Trevor stood up to allow Miranda to return to her seat, she confronted Dave.

"There's a hole in the bottom of these jeans!"

They were the ones Barbara had torn on the previous day's eventful excursion to Salzburg. Dave stared impatiently at Miranda for a moment and then bent down to examine the hole in more detail. He felt more gentle stirrings in his loins.

"So I see!"

"Alright, I get the picture," Miranda huffed before sliding past Trevor and sitting down next to the window.

"So did I," leered Dave.

It wasn't long before Barbara emerged from the toilet sporting Miranda's uniform and carrying her discarded clothes in a carrier bag. The uniform was a good, if snug, fit and she vamped slowly and coquettishly down the aisle, playfully pouting at the men that she passed and drawing cheers and whistles as she did so. Jason turned and looked admiringly at her. So did Susan.

"Wow, I've always, like, fancied girls in uniform," Jason drooled.

Joyce turned round in her seat and started to tease him.

"Sorry, no fraternising with the tour guide – it's against the rules. Besides, looking at the state you're in, fancying from afar is about as good as it's going to get."

As Barbara finally reached the front of the coach, Frank stood up and greeted her eagerly, shaking her hand warmly.

"Now then, Barbara," he said, sounding a little patronising. "You know what you've got to do? Get on the phone to all the hotels we are due to stay at over the next few days. Explain that there has been a nasty outbreak of food poisoning. Half the passengers, including Miranda, are very ill and we are having to return home. Say something vague about the company being in touch soon to sort out the necessary compensation. You'd better start with the one we were due to stay in tonight; the Hotel Fortezza or whatever it's called. And you had better try to contact the gondola people in Venice and tell them that we won't be making a booking today."

"Righto." Barbara sat down and started to burrow in the papers that Miranda had left in her brief case at the front of the coach.

Suddenly, Miranda rose swiftly to her feet, brushed her hair away from her face and tried to clamber across Trevor. But her progress was summarily halted by Trevor, who quickly stood up, and Frank and Dave, who resumed their blockade positions, solidly and threateningly, in the aisle.

"This is just ridiculous," Miranda exploded. "I'll report you all to the company!"

"The thing is, Miranda," Frank replied, still sounding condescending. "The company is almost certainly going to get twenty or thirty letters of complaint about you when we get home, so I don't think one complaint from you is going to make much difference, do you? Even Tony will support us."

"Too bloody right, I will!" Tony affirmed.

"Now then," Dave said, beginning to tire of Miranda's histrionics. "Are you going to cooperate and sit quietly here next to Trevor, or not?"

Miranda placed her hands on her hips and stood her ground, defiantly eyeballing Dave. "If you think I'm going to cooperate…" she began.

"Very well, you leave us with no choice," Dave interrupted. He turned away from Miranda and addressed the rest of the party. "Has anyone got any suggestions about how we can keep Miranda in her seat and stop her making a nuisance of herself?"

Barbara had become highly excited by the adventure and was desperately anxious to play her part to the full. She was still supposed to be rummaging through Miranda's papers but, on hearing Dave's plea, she leapt, unthinking, to her feet and called to him.

"I've got some handcuffs in my bag!" she blurted out.

"Oh no!" Jason groaned to himself and tried to bury his head in his one free hand as gales of laughter and cheering reverberated around the coach. Suitably chagrined by her impetuous confession, Barbara cringed and crept quietly back into her seat.

★ ★ ★

The elderly ladies had now embarked upon a new discussion, this time concerning National Health waiting lists for hearing aids, but, around them, there was an abnormally high level of excited and nervous chatter, making it difficult for them to hear what each other was saying. The morning's actions, though largely pre-meditated, had had a de-stabilising effect on events. No longer was there a detailed and carefully planned itinerary – nobody knew where they would be tomorrow, or even tonight – and it was hard to predict how the leaders of the coup were going to behave now that they were in control, or how Miranda was going to respond to her enforced captivity. For the moment, at least, she was sitting quietly, if moodily, next to Trevor to whom she was handcuffed by the left wrist. In the tour director's seat at the front, Barbara had been making a number of phone calls, assisted by the occasional prompt from Tony.

When she began making the calls, Barbara had been apprehensive, almost jittery, not sure what kind of response she would get on the other end of the phone and knowing that any kind of slip on her part might give the game away. But, by the time she made her final call, she had become the epitome of confidence. "Merci, monsieur. Au revoir," she said, with calm assurance before putting the phone down and turning round to address Frank.

"Well, that's the last of our stop-over hotels cancelled."

"Well done, Barbara. Now all we have to do is find somewhere nice to stay for the next five nights!"

Fully recovered from her initial panic and the embarrassment of admitting she possessed a pair of handcuffs and triumphant after the apparent success of her phone calls, Barbara's confidence was rising again and she was determined to fulfil all of the responsibilities of an official "Tour Director" in a proper and professional manner. With complete assurance, she reached for the microphone and switched it on.

"Buon giorno, ladies and gentlemen. As you probably realise, we are now in Italy and heading towards Venice, which we hope to reach in…"

She turned and looked questioningly at Tony.

"An hour and a half," Tony said quietly.

"Which we hope to reach in another hour and a half or so," she affirmed confidently.

The responsive cheering and cries of encouragement that followed Barbara's announcement prompted her to embellish her new role. She reached for her guidebook to Italy, thumbed through several pages and then began to quote diligently from it.

"Italy has a population of nearly 60 million people and occupies an area of just under 120,000 square miles. It has a wide variety of landscapes and a unique architectural and artistic heritage…"

By the time the coach arrived, more or less at the predicted time, at the Tronchetto coach park outside Venice, Barbara had tirelessly covered several chapters of her guidebook, covering Italian history, culture and cuisine, and had just completed a detailed history of the Doge's Palace.

"We're just going to park the coach," she continued, rather obviously but with unabated gusto. "And from here we are going to get the waterbus into Venice."

Except for Nigel's mother, who had to be vigorously prodded into reluctant, sleepy life, the passengers seemed especially keen to leave the coach; maybe it was the anticipation of visiting Venice, maybe it was a reaction to the long and eventful journey, maybe it was the sun shining, maybe they simply couldn't take any more commentary on the history and culture of the place. But, as they began to stand up and gather their possessions from the overhead racks, Susan suddenly swung round and pointed towards the still sullen figure of Miranda.

"Hang on a minute, what are we going to do with her?"

"Oh, sod it – we've forgotten that!" Frank admitted. He was angry with himself.

"Well, we can't take her with us." Dave observed, with his usual penetrating insight. "She might look a bit conspicuous being handcuffed to Trevor like that. Maybe we should lock her in the luggage hold!"

At this point, Trevor raised his unfettered hand.

"Woa, woa. Hang on a minute! I don't mind staying on the coach to keep an eye on her if you like. I've got two sore feet and anyway Venice loses its romance a bit when you're on your own. Especially as it's where Julia had her honeymoon with her ex that she's now gone back home to be with!"

Trevor's voice was heavy with pathos and everyone fell silent for a moment, unsure what to say or do. The silence was broken by Tony.

"Yeah, you go off and enjoy yourselves. We'd be delighted to look after her. Me and Trev – we'll cope!"

Gail wandered down the coach towards Trevor with that all too familiar look of well-intentioned concern on her face.

"Are you sure you'll be alright, Trevor?" she fretted. "I'm sure we can think of something if you want to come?"

Trevor waved his arm in an airy, almost contemptuous gesture.

"No, you go on, I'll be alright. But just remember, you owe me another favour! That's two so far, I make it!"

The passengers disembarked. Tony followed them, kicking the coach door shut behind him, and raced ahead to ensure that the waterbus was waiting for them and to confirm all the necessary arrangements, including timings for the return trip, with the skipper. Having satisfied himself that all was well, he spoke briefly to Barbara, Dave and Joyce – Frank was nowhere to be seen – before he left the rest of the party snaking its way towards the waterbus and returned, at a much slower pace, to the coach. He climbed aboard, kicking the door closed behind him, walked down the aisle and sat in Brian's seat, inspecting it carefully before he did so, next to Trevor and Miranda. A gloomy and edgy silence descended.

From the Tronchetto coach park, it was a short walk along the quayside to where the waterbus was waiting. As Frank was the first to leave the coach, he had spent a few brief moments hurriedly using his camcorder to film the distant lagoon, although the jewel of Venice itself was well hidden behind the scruffy and dilapidated dockyard in the foreground. While he was concentrating on his filming, he felt a firm tap on his shoulder. Irritated at the interruption, he tutted and looked round, forgetting to turn the camcorder off, to find Joyce gesturing to one of the buildings behind them.

"Frank, if you need to go to the toilet, you'd better go now before the waterbus is ready to leave. We haven't got long and there may not be many toilets in Venice."

"Yes, right," Frank agreed and he dashed off to the toilets with his camcorder dangling from the cord around his neck, pointing downwards and still recording. It continued to record as Frank dashed inside the toilet, cursed as he paid the obligatory fee and made prolonged and productive use of the urinal, before completing the process with a couple of robust shakes. He had just zipped himself up and was washing his hands with his usual pernickety thoroughness, when he heard Dave shouting at him from the doorway.

"Come on, Frank. We're getting ready to leave."

He dashed from the toilets, his camcorder still swaying gently from its cord, rushed after Dave and scrambled on board the waterbus with the rest of the party.

★ ★ ★

On the coach, meanwhile, with all the passengers, apart from Trevor, having left, Miranda, now virtually alone and with plenty of time to sit and brood, was suddenly overwhelmed by a sense of emptiness and desolation. She tried to hold back the tears that she felt welling up and, in her frustration, she thumped the back of the seat in front of her with her fist.

"I don't believe this is happening! It's all so ridiculous! Do you know what they're going to do when they get back?"

Trevor scratched his head thoughtfully.

"I don't really know and, to be honest, I'm not sure they know. But they're not violent people. They are just ordinary folk who desperately want to have a good holiday. But there's no doubt they are angry at the way they feel they've been treated, so you need to be careful."

There followed a strained silence as Miranda brushed away a tear from her cheek. Needing a tissue, she looked around in vain for her travel bag.

"My bag, my bag," she wailed. "Where's my bag?"

Tony sighed, got up, walked slowly to the front of the coach and retrieved it from the floor. He handed it to Miranda and hastily returned to Brian's seat. Miranda opened her bag and reached inside for a tissue, with which she wiped her cheek and blew her nose with such ear-splitting gusto, that Trevor recoiled in his seat. She then reached inside her bag again, pulled out a small packet of pills, emptied two of them onto her hand and swallowed them.

Not for the first time, Trevor was watching her intently. Although the close, captive proximity to Miranda was not without its attractions, he found himself worrying again. He was worrying whether Miranda might be planning some kind of escape bid or violent revenge. Perhaps the company trained her for such eventualities. Maybe she had another phone secreted in her bag or, worse still, maybe she was going to produce a knife or some other potentially dangerous weapon and start threatening him with it. Maybe she would start thumping on the window just as a policeman walked by. He was starting to feel as vulnerable as she was.

"What are those for?" he asked, nervously, pointing to the packet of pills. Miranda peered carefully at the label.

"Oh, I'm not sure. Something the doctor prescribed to calm me down, I think. Or maybe it was to pick me up. I dunno really but I expect they're doing me some good."

Another prolonged and uncomfortable silence followed, before Miranda suddenly thumped the back of the seat in front of her again.

"Oh, I hate this sodding job!"

"Then, why are you doing it?" Trevor ventured tentatively.

"Dunno really." Miranda began to sob again. "I broke up

with my boyfriend a couple of years ago – we'd been together for five years, we were planning to get married and … and anyway it hit me hard at the time. I was in a boring dead-end office job, with lots of boring, dead-end people, I was very depressed and I just felt I wanted a change – you know, do a bit of travelling, get away from it all; a bit of escapism. My mother's family are Italian so I'm used to travelling around Europe – I used to quite enjoy it."

"Funny thing is, though, I always thought I was quite good with people till I took this job. But then, you just end up dragging coach-loads of tossers around Europe with a clipboard in one hand and a stopwatch in the other – same old dreadful hotels, miles of motorway driving – a quick stop here then back in the coach. You do your best, you really do! You try to tell them something interesting about the places they are going to see, but all most of them want to do is eat, drink or go shopping. And they're always complaining about something – the hotels, the food, the coach, the weather. Then there's all the paperwork! I tell you, I just can't handle it any more. I probably would've given it up last year, but I'd met Tony on one of our tours. I mean, I knew he was married and everything, but I thought we had something a bit special, you know. I really used to look forward to the tours that Tony was on. And now look what the bastard's done to me!"

Tony stood up and looked across apologetically at Miranda. He felt that there was a lot that he should be saying by way of explanation and apology, but words, especially the right words, didn't come easily to him.

"I think I'll go and sit at the front for a while," was all he could manage.

He wandered slowly off, leaving Miranda and Trevor alone together with their thoughts, their vulnerabilities and their fears.

★ ★ ★

The waterbus made its way steadily across the sparkling lagoon and along the Canale della Guidecca, passing the Piazzetta San

Marco and the Doge's Palace, before arriving at the jetty adjoining Riva degli Schiavoni. The sun, now very hot, was shining out of a cloudless azure sky. The group disembarked in an expectant mood and gathered together in a close circle to await further instructions. As a gesture to the heat, Frank had removed his tie and had placed a battered straw hat on his head. It was the same straw hat that he had sported when playing bowls on hot summer days for at least the last twenty years. He stepped forward, looked at his watch and began to address the group with the kind of bombastic authority at which he excelled.

"Now, we're going to need a bit of time to sort out a hotel for tonight and we don't know yet how far we are going to have to travel. So I gather we've made arrangements with the waterbus people for you to be back here in four hours. I hope that's OK!"

Suddenly Barbara stepped forward from the crowd.

"Excuse me, but I'm the Tour Director now, you know."

"Of course you are, Barbara, I'm so sorry!" Frank acknowledged with mock deference.

"Thank you." She turned to address the group. "Can we be back here in four hours, please?"

There were nods of agreement as the group began to disperse. Frank, meanwhile, gestured to Barbara and Jason.

"Right, Jason and Barbara; you know what you've got to do?"

Barbara and Jason nodded eagerly and sped off in the direction of St. Mark's Square. Frank, meanwhile, had intercepted Peter, Gail, Valerie and Brian as they began to wander off at a more leisurely pace.

"Gail, do try and cheer Peter up a bit," he urged. "And keep that blasted bear of yours under control. And, Val, if you could keep Brian away from the water for a change, we'd all be very grateful."

"I'll do my best," Valerie affirmed with a smile that contained more warmth than he could remember seeing before. The battle on their behalf had been worthwhile. Playfully, she pulled Brian away from the waterside amid some laughter from the dispersing party.

Frank looked around beaming with pleasure. Somehow,

things seemed to be improving already. Then he felt a tap on his shoulder. He turned round to find Nigel's mother, looking formidably stern and glowering at him.

"Excuse me!" she boomed. "I don't really know what's been going on this morning – I've been very drowsy for some reason – but Nigel started to put me in the picture as we came over on the boat. I want you to know that I disapprove most strongly of your antics. Everyone else, from what I can gather, seems happy enough for some reason so there's nothing much I can do for the moment, but when we get back I shall most certainly be complaining to the company and you may very well be hearing from my solicitors."

Frank stood his ground. He tried to smile disarmingly at her but succeeded only in looking menacing again.

"Well, I'm very sorry you're not happy," he oozed. "But we had the support of everyone at the meeting last night, including Nigel here."

"Er, come along mummy," Nigel stuttered, looking flustered. "I think we need to have a word." He took his mother's arm and led her away. Joyce led Frank away in the opposite direction.

★ ★ ★

On the coach, after another long and tortuous silence, Trevor and Miranda had resumed their conversation.

"So, will you resign?" Trevor asked.

"Well, let's put it this way. There aren't too many tour directors around who have had their coach and the tour itinerary hi-jacked by the passengers, had their money stolen by the same passengers, been forced to strip off on the coach, got held captive on their own coach, handcuffed to a passenger, and kept their job. Not to mention fighting with hotel staff and deliberately pouring hot coffee into the driver's lap!"

"No, I suppose not, if you put it like that."

Trevor was about to say something more, when Miranda suddenly raised her handcuffed arm in frustration, yanking Trevor's arm upwards.

"Who's got the key to these things?" she demanded. "I need a pee!"

Trevor shrugged.

"I haven't." He called down the coach. "Tony, have you got the key to these handcuffs?"

"No, mate. They didn't give me the key. They must have gone off with it."

"Oh, bloody brilliant!" Miranda complained, thumping the back of the seat in front of her again.

★ ★ ★

For some members of the tour party, this was their first visit to Venice and, with only four hours at their disposal, in energy-sapping heat and with jostling crowds to contend with, they needed to be very selective and purposeful in what they chose to do. Most began by making the short walk along the waterfront to St Mark's Square, where some joined the long queue to visit St Mark's Basilica, others bravely ascended the Campanile for spectacular views over the city and the lagoon beyond, and a handful ventured inside the relative cool of the Doge's Palace. One or two paid a lot of money for a gondola ride, while others were simply content to wander around the labyrinthine back streets, over the narrow canals, pausing occasionally to look in the window of a souvenir shop – or even step inside – before almost inevitably emerging somewhere along the Grand Canal with stunning views towards the Rialto Bridge and the magnificent pastel-coloured palazzi lining both sides of the shimmering water.

Frank and Joyce made for the middle of St Mark's Square where they were surrounded by tourists and pigeons in more or less equal numbers. Unbeknown to Frank, his camcorder had been switched on and recording ever since they left the Tronchetto coach park. But now he wanted to record the scenes around him, so he carefully raised his camcorder, lined up the view and pressed the "on/off" button, thus turning it off. Thinking he had turned it on, Frank was at a loss to understand why the infernal machine was apparently refusing to record. While Joyce waited impatiently, sweltering beneath her expansive straw hat and shaking her head in exasperation, he studied the camcorder closely and shook it gently.

"Damned foreign cameras," he muttered, pressing the "on/off" button repeatedly. When he had given sufficient vent to his feelings, he glanced down at his doggedly hostile camcorder and noticed, to his surprise, that it was now switched on and recording. Setting aside his frustration for the moment, he concentrated on capturing a visual masterpiece for posterity. At least he was, until a pigeon flew low overhead and did what pigeons often do, onto Frank's straw hat and down the front of his blazer.

Not far away, in a small side street, Dave and Susan emerged from one of the proliferation of take-away food shops, each clutching a large pizza, which they devoured voraciously, as they walked on.

Elsewhere, after several abortive enquiries, Barbara and Jason had located an Information Centre with an Internet café attached and strode determinedly inside.

★ ★ ★

Still handcuffed to Trevor, Miranda had stumbled her way to the coach toilet. The toilet door, which opened outwards, was slightly ajar and Trevor was standing just outside, on the steps that led down to the rear door, with his handcuffed right arm stretching inside the doorway. He kept trying to avert his gaze from what was going on inside the toilet, but he was finding it difficult to resist the occasional surreptitious glance. After one glance that was clearly less than surreptitious, Miranda shouted at him.

"Oi, no peeking!"

Instinctively, Trevor hastily looked the other way. As he did so, there was a sudden, violent tug at his handcuffed arm and he lurched sideways, slipping on the step, losing his balance, crashing into the open door and ending up half inside the toilet.

"Oi, be careful!" he shouted. "You nearly had my arm off!"

"Oh, do come in," shouted Miranda sarcastically from within. "Take a good look, why don't you!"

Deeply flustered, Trevor quickly closed his eyes.

"I'm not looking, I'm not looking. Will you please just hurry up!" he pleaded.

"No, you're not looking, are you?" Miranda confirmed with more than a hint of surprise.

"Go on, Trev, take a look!" Tony yelled from the front of the coach. "You won't be the first!"

"Shut up, tosspot!" Miranda yelled back, nearly deafening Trevor in the process. "I'm beginning to think that Trevor might actually be a gentleman, unlike you and most of the other men on this coach!"

This outburst prompted a hiatus in conversation, during which all that could be heard was Miranda adjusting her clothing and flushing the toilet.

"Sorry Trevor, I've just got to wash my hands!" she said, apologetically.

There followed another sharp tug on Trevor's arm and he found himself being pulled, still with his eyes shut, further into the confined space of the toilet, where he stumbled into Miranda, accidentally jamming her up against the wall. In order to support herself, she instinctively held out her unfettered arm and flung it around Trevor's waist. They remained locked in their unintentional embrace for several seconds.

★ ★ ★

The heat of the sun had clearly been therapeutic and, although Peter was still feeling a bit under the weather, he had greatly enjoyed promenading around Venice with Gail. Despite the queue, he was glad to have seen the interior of St. Mark's Basilica and had savoured their leisurely stroll around some of the colourful back streets. Alongside the Grand Canal, almost under the shadow of the Rialto Bridge, they had purchased some ice creams and found a vantage point on the water's edge, where they could sit and watch the heavily populated vaporetti and gondolas continually weaving glistening paths across the water as they traversed the canal. They had meandered sedately over the Rialto Bridge, peering casually in the windows of some of the small, exclusive and expensive shops that lined the route and had followed the signs that led them back to St Mark's Square and out onto the waterfront. Peter looked at his watch.

"Ah well, it's been very nice but we'll have to be getting back soon."

Much of the natural, relaxed radiance had returned to Gail's smile.

"And are you feeling a bit better now?" she enquired.

"Yes, I am! Much better," Peter replied contentedly.

As they ambled their way along the wide waterfront back towards the Riva degli Schiavoni, carefully negotiating the market stalls and souvenir sellers, they passed the Doge's Palace on their left and arrived at the Ponte Della Paglia, from where some of the best and most famous views of the Bridge of Sighs, a little further down the canal, could be enjoyed. For once, the bridge was relatively uncrowded. Gail stopped.

"Would you be able to take a picture of me and Fred on the bridge?" Gail asked, smiling as winsomely as she could.

"I see now why they call it Bridge of Sighs," Peter muttered, but he returned Gail's smile and dutifully removed his camera from its case.

"Oh, alright, but be quick!" He tried not to sound snappy.

As they approached the parapet of the bridge, they noticed Valerie and Brian, leaning casually against it and gazing vaguely down the canal. Anxious to avoid the risk of being late again, they had returned early and were killing a bit of time. Brian was perspiring freely. He was not built for heat.

"Hello Brian," Peter greeted him cheerfully, if a little nervously. "Still dry?"

"Yes thanks, more or less, and that's the way I intend to stay!" He raised a bottle of mineral water to his lips and quaffed liberally from it.

Valerie and Brian watched intently as Gail carefully placed Fred on the parapet, placed a restraining hand behind him and posed for Peter to take the photograph. As Peter completed his unenviable task, watched by a growing number of bystanders, and put his camera away, Brian bent down, picked up his rucksack and slid the bottle, with what remained of the mineral water, into a side pocket. Brian didn't often bring his rucksack with him – it had in the past proved something of an expensive liability when swung around carelessly in small souvenir shops – but Valerie was taking no chances after he had left it, with his waterproofs inside, on the coach in Salzburg and had insisted that, in future, he always took it with him. Today, of course, in hot and increasingly humid conditions, he hadn't needed his waterproofs and he had become rather resentful at having to lug his cumbersome and largely redundant rucksack around Venice all day.

Having picked it up, he slung it grudgingly and clumsily over his shoulder and half turned. In doing so, the side of his rucksack, made wider by the recent insertion of the mineral water bottle, caught Fred a glancing blow, spun him out of Gail's reach and knocked him off the parapet, sending him plummeting into the canal below, where he landed, with a gentle plop, inelegantly on his back.

"Oh, my God, look what you've done!" Gail shrieked.

"Oh, not again! Not that bloody bear again!" Peter rushed across and looked down over the parapet to see Fred, still on his back, starting to float gently away along the canal. Though part of him wished never to see the troublesome animal again, he knew what he had to do. "Don't worry, I'll get him back!" he promised, with little conviction.

He looked around in desperation, unsure what to do, before rushing over to the quayside where gondolas were being offered for hire. Brian, meanwhile, turned apologetically towards Gail and struck Valerie heavily on the shoulder with his rucksack.

"I'm terribly sorry. If there's anything I can do…?"

"Just stay out of the way!" Gail shouted, her normal unruffled calm quickly turning to something approaching unbridled hysteria.

Peter, meanwhile, had found a gondolier, whose grasp of

English seemed disappointingly basic, and was trying hard to explain the situation to him. Despite the urgency of the predicament, he was having to talk very slowly and enunciate his words in a ponderous, deliberate way. It was at times like this that he wished he taught languages rather than history.

"You see," he tried to explain. "My wife's bear has fallen in the water over there and she's very upset. I need to hire a gondola so that we can go and get it back?"

The gondolier was a swarthy, tanned and healthy looking man, probably in his mid-forties, with a wide midriff and a round jovial face. He seemed confused by Peter's explanation at first but then, as he slowly reflected on Peter's words, a kind of realisation seemed to dawn and a broad smile spread across his face.

"Your wife, she is bare in the water, on her back?" he asked in very broken English. Then he whistled and made an exaggerated egg-timer shape with his hands before smiling again, even more broadly than before.

"We go to her – you sit in here please!"

He gestured to a gondola, which he held steady as Peter scrambled aboard.

"You must hurry!" Peter urged.

"Si, we will hurry," the gondolier agreed, still smiling broadly, as he lugubriously hauled himself into the gondola and slowly pushed it into life.

Gail, Brian and Valerie were still on the Ponte Della Paglia, gazing over the parapet helplessly as Fred, still bobbing up and down on the water, began to drift away from the shadow of the bridge. Then, a gondola containing an expensively dressed couple of indeterminate age, passed close by. It was difficult to guess the nationality of the couple, but they had an olive-skinned Mediterranean complexion partly hidden behind expensive matching sunglasses. As they passed Fred, the woman let out a cry of pleasure, reached out an immaculately manicured hand, plucked him out of the water and held him close to her.

"Hey, that's our bear!" Gail shouted excitedly, hoping that the woman was on a rescue mission but, although she looked up briefly and flashed a highly polished, cosmetically enhanced smile at those on the bridge, she appeared not to understand, or not to have heard what Gail had said, and the gondola carried on smoothly down the canal.

"I'll head round the back and try to catch them up," Brian called, anxious to make amends.

"You'll do no such thing," Valerie ordered, sensing another imminent disaster. "You'll only end up getting lost or falling in the water again. You wait here. I'll go!" With that, Valerie set off in pursuit, but her high-heeled shoes were not designed for high-speed mercy missions and her progress was laboured and tottery.

Beneath the bridge, from the bows of his recently commissioned gondola, Peter had observed Fred's capture. "Follow that gondola!" he bellowed at the gondolier who, by now, was looking more than a little puzzled at a scenario that was certainly not turning out quite the way he had imagined. On the bridge, Brian stood and watched the drama unfolding slowly below him. His fingers curled and uncurled nervously. He turned and saw Valerie wobbling slowly out of sight. "Oh, bugger this!" he muttered to himself and, securing his rucksack to his back, he lolloped off in pursuit.

Further down the canal, the two gondolas, one still pursuing the other in a kind of serene, slow motion chase, passed under another bridge. Seconds later, Valerie appeared, panting, breathless and lacking her usual gracefulness, on the bridge. She looked quickly down the canal, realised that she had just missed the gondolas, ran a sweaty hand across her sweaty brow and ran off in pursuit. Almost immediately, Brian did the same thing.

★ ★ ★

At the agreed assembly point on the Riva degli Schiavoni, an animated gaggle of coach party members was beginning to assemble. Many carried bags bulging with souvenirs and mementos and their spirits, already buoyed by the mutinous adventure they had embarked upon, were high. With the residue of dried pigeon droppings still prominently displayed on his hat and the lapel of his blazer, Frank stepped forward importantly to greet each new arrival effusively, although his welcome for Nigel was noticeably warmer than the one he reserved for his mother.

"How are you both?" Frank ventured hesitantly.

"Nothing to worry about," Nigel assured him in a whisper. "She's due for some more medication when we get back to the coach!" He winked mischievously.

As the agreed rendezvous time approached, the numbers had swelled encouragingly. Positioning himself prominently in the centre of the gathering throng, Frank addressed them.

"Right, are we all here?"

Behind him, Barbara coughed loudly and pointedly.

"Whoops! Sorry, Barbara!" Frank apologised.

"That's alright!" she admonished, playfully. "Right, are we all here?"

Dave and Susan had been looking round anxiously. "It doesn't look as though Brian and Val are here yet," Dave said, fearing yet another disaster had befallen them. "Nor are Peter and Gail," added Susan, concerned that Peter's fragile health may have taken a turn for the worse in the increasingly oppressive heat.

"Oh, God, I might have known." Frank's deeply ingrained pessimism caused him to run all kinds of potential, though improbable, disaster scenarios over in his mind. As a brief distraction from his gloomy premonitions, he turned to Jason, who was standing close by, looking pleased with himself and clutching a small bundle of papers.

"And how did you get on?" Frank asked.

"Quite well, I think, actually." Jason replied in a voice that exuded more confidence than usual. He wanted to say more but Frank cut him off.

"Excellent! Tell us about it when we are all together. Now then, what are we going to do about our absent friends?"

★ ★ ★

Further along the canal, the gondolier's determined, rhythmical and muscular efforts had brought his comparatively lightly laden gondola virtually alongside the one containing the elegant woman, her equally elegant companion and a waterlogged and less than elegant bear. The woman was still clutching Fred in a loving embrace. As his gondola drew alongside, Peter leaned across, as far as he safely could, and began to remonstrate with her.

"Please can I have the bear back? He belongs to me, er, that is to say, he belongs to my wife!"

Whether or not the woman understood what Peter was saying, she just laughed and held Fred triumphantly aloft as though he was some kind of trophy that she had just won.

While Peter continued to plead with her, without success, Valerie arrived at the side of the canal, panting heavily. There were some narrow, well-worn, stone steps, with metal railings on either side, leading down to the water's edge. Valerie tottered unsteadily down the steps and, with the limited amount of breath that she still had available, she shouted loudly at the woman in the gondola, who turned round to see where the raucous noise was coming from. It was Peter's opportunity. He rose unsteadily in his gondola and, while the woman was still staring at Valerie, made a desperate lunge for Fred. To his surprise and delight, he managed to snatch the wayward bear out of the woman's grasp but, with one foot now in the woman's gondola and one foot still in his own, he began to teeter violently and, as he started to lose his balance, he hurled Fred desperately towards where Valerie was standing. As Fred sailed through the air, Peter fell backwards, somehow slithering into the canal in the narrow gap between the two gondolas. Valerie was not noted for her sporting prowess and, seeing Fred hurtling through the air towards her, she closed her eyes and held out her arms limply in front of her. Peter had been a skilful rugby player in his youth and his "pass" was inch perfect. As Fred descended, softly if damply, into Valerie's soft, if damp, bosom, she wrapped her arms around him in triumph.

"I got him, Pete!" she yelled triumphantly, as her high heels wobbled precariously beneath her on the worn and uneven steps. At this, her moment of glory, Brian came galloping up behind.

"Oh, well done, Val!" he shouted and rushed over to embrace

her. Unfortunately, a combination of Brian's momentum, the additional impact generated by his heavy rucksack, Valerie's unsteady footwear and the unevenness of the stone steps, caused Valerie to fall backwards and, still locked in Brian's strong embrace, they toppled, spectacularly and inelegantly, into the canal with a resounding splash.

For Peter's perplexed gondolier, it had not proved to be the expedition that he had anticipated. But he was not disappointed; he would not have missed this little escapade for the world. To begin with, he tried hard to suppress his mirth but his violently wobbling stomach eventually betrayed him and he was laughing out loud by the time he hauled a waterlogged Peter back into the gondola. Brian, meanwhile, had managed to grab hold of the railings and, assisted by some willing members of the crowd, who had assembled to watch the free entertainment, succeeded in pulling himself, Valerie and Fred out of the water, to generous applause from the appreciative bystanders.

* * *

On the coach, Miranda was crying again. She had been for some time. She looked very vulnerable and Trevor desperately wanted to help in some way but, after his recent contretemps with Julia, his confidence was low and he was terrified that anything he might say or do could end up making matters worse. What's more, being handcuffed to someone whose moods were so volatile filled him with anxiety. He remained silent, withdrawn and thoughtful for a while but the sound of Miranda continually crying and the sight of her red eyes, damp cheeks and smudged mascara was more than he could take. Gradually, an embryonic idea began to form.

"So what will you do when you get back home?" he ventured, innocently.

Miranda sighed.

"Dunno!"

Another uncomfortable pause followed before Miranda

spoke, the words suddenly gushing out as her tears had been, moments earlier.

"Oh, look at me! What a joke! I'm nearly 30. I'm hopeless at my job. I've got no chance of getting another job with the kind of references they'll give me. Every relationship I've ever had has been a disaster. I live in a squalid little flat and I'm broke!"

Another pause followed. Trevor stroked his hair with his free hand.

"I see," he said, at last.

"Oh well, that's alright then!" Miranda replied sarcastically.

Trevor opened his mouth to say something, hesitated, thought better of it and closed it again. But, on reflection, there was something he really did need to say. He took a deep breath and tried again.

"Look, I don't know whether this is any help or not, but I run a conference centre in Surrey. We're doing quite well – you know, business seminars, team building courses, residential weekends. We've got a good restaurant, some nice grounds, heated swimming pool, lots of decent overnight accommodation. And being quite near to Heathrow and Gatwick, we get quite a lot of bookings from foreign businesses on fact-finding visits, that sort of thing. Anyway, I've just had a resignation and we need to take on someone new for "front of house" duties. You know the sort of thing, taking bookings on the phone, meeting and greeting, checking that all is well with the guests, keeping a discreet eye on them during the day, but also making sure they don't take any liberties while they're with us; someone who is polite but can be firm when necessary. Now we'd have to work on some of your people skills a bit – you'd need to be a bit more flexible and helpful and a bit less confrontational – but I reckon you could do it with the right training, if you wanted to. You're smart, attractive, got a lovely smile – when you want to use it – you can use your language skills with some of our overseas visitors and you can certainly be firm enough when you have to be! I think we'd need to take you on, on a temporary basis to start with, to see how it goes, but if it goes well and you settle in, we could make it permanent.

We'd match your present salary, including tips, of course. What do you think?"

"Oh, yeah, very funny!"

"No, no, I'm serious!"

"Oh, yeah, so what do I have to do to get the job then, as if I didn't bloody know?"

"Nothing. I've just offered it to you. We'd have to train you for a little while first, of course."

"Hang on a minute. You're in Surrey, right?"

"Yes."

"One of the most expensive parts of the country, right?"

"Yes."

"And I'm renting a pokey flat in one of the cheaper parts of Kent and I've got no money."

"Yes."

"So where am I going to live – a bloody dog kennel?"

"Ah, I didn't mention that I wanted you to live on site did I? Be the point of contact in an emergency. Be on hand in case the fire alarm goes off in the middle of the night, or there are any serious problems with our overnight guests. We've got a small flat on site you can have for a nominal rent; fully furnished, with a nice view over the grounds. Free use of the swimming pool and subsidised use of the restaurant."

"Are you serious?"

"Couldn't be more serious!"

"You know, you're a lovely man, Trevor!"

"I've heard that before!"

Miranda sniffed, dabbed her eyes, smiled, albeit a little uncertainly, and reached across to try and hug Trevor. Unfortunately, they got entangled with the handcuffs and, unwittingly, Miranda's manacled hand ended up resting in Trevor's lap. She held it there for a moment or two and then smiled again; this time it was a full, generous, flirtatious smile.

"Hello! I think you're quite enjoying all of this, aren't you?"

★ ★ ★

Along the Riva degli Schiavoni, the bedraggled quintet of Gail, Peter, Brian, Valerie and Fred were making their way towards the rendezvous point. They knew they were late and were trying to hurry, but rapid progress wasn't easy. Though Gail herself had avoiding a ducking in the canal, her intimate travelling companion, Fred, had lost most of his erstwhile photogenic charm with his fur tangled, grubby and very wet. Soaked through, Peter was shivering despite the intense afternoon sunshine. His cold, wet trousers and shirt were clinging uncomfortably to his chilled flesh. But Brian's appearance, somehow, was altogether baggier and more waterlogged. His wet matted hair had stuck to his forehead, water was trickling down onto his glasses and into his eyes and his clothes, shoes and rucksack were each leaving a trail of dripping water behind him as he stumbled along. In the kerfuffle, the heel of one of Valerie's shoes had broken off. As a result, she had removed both shoes and was walking with extreme discomfort, barefoot, on the hot pavement, trying to move into the limited shade whenever she could. Her normally neatly coiffured hair was now straight, dirty and unkempt. Her saturated, thin cotton top was clinging tightly to her contours and was now so transparent that she looked like an entrant in a wet T-shirt competition. At first, she felt dreadfully self-conscious but, after a while, she began to quite enjoy the obvious attention of the men that she passed. And as she walked painfully alongside her dripping spouse, pondering on the manifold disasters of the holiday, she began to reflect on life and fate and fortune. There was, she knew, something more to life than working on the cosmetics counter in her local department store and having vacuous coffee mornings on her day off. If Susan could be believed, then maybe Brian's musical career was about to take off at last, so perhaps it was time that their lives began to change in other directions as well. She smiled mischievously.

As they reached the rendezvous point, they stopped and looked around for some friendly faces, but saw none. There were plenty of people about, but they could see no-one from their party.

"What the… I don't believe it!!" Gail wailed, clinging tightly to Fred.

"But, they can't have left without us again, surely!" Peter groaned. Then, seemingly from nowhere, a hand tapped him on the shoulder. He wheeled round to see Dave grinning stupidly at him.

"And where have you lot been, you naughty children?" Dave greeted them.

Peter breathed a visible sigh of relief as the rest of the party began to emerge, laughing, from behind the corners of buildings and vendors' stalls. Frank studied the new arrivals with disbelief.

"Bloody hell! It's the water babies! Don't tell me, you couldn't decide whose turn it was to fall in the canal, so you all went in!"

"Something like that, you see…" Peter began before Barbara bustled them along.

"Yes, yes, you'll have to fill us in later," she said, pointing to the waterside. "The waterbus has been here, waiting for you for some time now and we've got to get back to the coach."

"Oi, don't get too bossy!" Frank chided Barbara. "You know what we do to bossy tour directors."

"Sorry, Frank!"

Members of the group edged through the crowds of tourists towards the waterbus and began to board it.

★ ★ ★

Miranda looked impatiently at her watch.

"They're late!"

Trevor yawned and stretched.

"Well, you know this lot for timekeeping."

Miranda tugged frantically on the handcuffs as Trevor had stretched his arms so far above his head that he had almost lifted her out of her seat. He quickly lowered his arms.

"How do you think I should play this when they come back?" Miranda sounded agitated.

"Like I say, they're only interested in having a good holiday and I suspect they'll have some plans to do that, but, as I said earlier, they are quite angry, so you'll need to keep calm, be quiet and, above all, don't get stroppy – even if they try and wind you up, which I am sure they will. I'll offer to keep an eye on you – look after you, stop you trying to sabotage things – but you've got to make sure that you don't do anything silly or provocative, otherwise they might make life very difficult for you – for us both." He thought it diplomatic not to mention that one of the more radical ideas mooted at yesterday evening's meeting, was to throw Miranda off the coach in some remote part of Northern Italy, without any money or luggage.

Miranda smiled reassuringly at him.

"I'll do what you say, Trevor, I promise. I just want to get out of this mess!"

She placed a hand on his knee and stroked it comfortingly. Trevor wriggled.

★ ★ ★

It was nearly thirty minutes later when the first members of the tour party began to climb aboard the coach, after what had obviously been, for most, a highly enjoyable trip. People were carrying bags of souvenirs and chattering excitedly about what they had done, where they had been and what they had seen. The exceptions, of course, were the two elderly ladies who were in the middle of a discussion about the best plants to grow up against a north facing wall, Nigel's mother who marched, stony-faced and truculently to her seat, and Gail, Peter, Brian and Valerie, who climbed gingerly aboard and settled, rather sheepishly, into their seats.

In the midst of the growing hubbub, Trevor called out to no-one in particular.

"Where the hell have you all been?"

Dave turned round apologetically.

"Sorry, Trev. No prizes for guessing who was late, again!"

"And who fell in the water again!" Susan added.

"Never mind about that just now." Trevor sounded unusually

impatient. He called out again to no-one in particular: "Who's got the key to these bloody handcuffs? I need the toilet and it is rather urgent!"

Barbara, standing at the front of the coach, looked guilty.

"Oh hell! Sorry, Trevor, I forgot."

She reached into her bag, rummaged around until she found the key and handed it to Trevor. Miranda went to say something, but Trevor tapped her, gently but firmly, on the ankle with his foot and she remained silent. Trevor unlocked the handcuffs and disappeared rapidly towards the toilet. Dave waited until Trevor was safely inside the toilet before turning round again and addressing Miranda.

"And how have you been, my dear?"

"I am not your dear, as it happens, but I've been OK – no thanks to you." Miranda was sounding too haughty and she knew it. She cursed silently to herself.

"And have you been plotting and scheming while we've been away?" Dave persisted. Miranda recalled Trevor's words, gripped the arms of the seat as hard as she could and gritted her teeth.

"No, I haven't. Trevor and I have been having a chat…" She was sounding calmer now.

"And?"

"And… Obviously, I can't approve of what you are doing but there doesn't seem any point in trying to stop you. I am a bit outnumbered, so you just get on with your plan – whatever it is – and I'll just sit here and keep quiet for the time being."

"And you expect me to believe that?"

Miranda was gripping the arms of her seat so hard that her fingers began to hurt. She could feel her short temper rising but, remembering Trevor's words, was determined not to be provoked. She looked anxiously around in the hope that Trevor was on his way back, but he wasn't. The speed of his departure suggested that he might be gone for some time. She took a deep breath and spoke as calmly as she could.

"Why don't you ask Trevor when he comes back? He'll tell you!"

"Right, I will!"

Seriously flummoxed by the effort of controlling her natural inclination to throttle the life out of Dave, Miranda quietly reached into her bag, slipped two more pills into her hand and swallowed them in one movement.

At the front of the coach, Jason and Frank had been having an earnest discussion. Frank was writing something carefully in his notebook. Eventually, their discussion ended and Frank neatly removed a sheet of paper from his notebook and handed it with great ceremony to Tony.

"Tony, we've got ourselves some accommodation for the next five nights. But I'm afraid it's going to be quite a bit more driving for you today."

Tony studied the note and frowned.

"Strewth, so I see. That must be about two hundred miles or so. It'll probably take four or five hours and I'll need to have a rest break, otherwise I'll be breaking the law."

"No problem. We'll be stopping for a meal en route. But we'll need your help to find somewhere."

"And will you be needing me or the coach after we arrive? You see, I really should be having a day off. I'd normally take a day off when we're in Rome, but…" Tony was sounding tired.

"Well, we might want to arrange an excursion to Milan or Lugano or one of the lakes, if there's enough interest, so you'll need to keep in touch with Barbara, but most of us will probably just want to chill out, so I imagine most of your time will be free until next Tuesday."

"That's good. Only, I think I'll give the missus another call when we stop. If my sister will have the kids, I'll see if I can get her out here for a few days. We need a break – I don't usually get one in the summer – and I think there are a few things I need to discuss with her if you know what I mean."

"Seems like a good idea to me," Joyce affirmed. "And what will you do when you get back home? I can't imagine the company approving of all these shenanigans."

"No, you're right, but I don't know how much longer the company will keep going anyway. There are rumours that it's in serious financial trouble. But there are always plenty of jobs

313

around for drivers and this is no life for a married man with kids – there are too many temptations. Anyway, I need to be spending more time with my family."

"You're starting to sound like a disgraced politician."

"Disgraced, certainly. That's why I want to talk to my missus. I've let her down badly."

By now, Trevor had returned from the toilet, a greatly relieved man, and everyone else had taken their seats. Frank leaned across and whispered loudly to Barbara.

"OK, Barbara, Trevor's back. Tony's OK. Tell 'em what's in store."

Tony switched on the ignition, the coached purred into life and the last, long journey of the day got underway, as the sky overhead grew darker and more threatening. Barbara reached for the microphone and switched it on.

"Good afternoon, ladies and gentlemen," she announced, exuding cheery confidence. "On behalf of Jolly Roger Tours, we hope you enjoyed your trip to Venice this afternoon. As you know, there has been an agreed change to the itinerary for the rest of our holiday. Unfortunately, we are in the middle of the high season so it has not been easy. We haven't been able to find enough accommodation for you all round here and the Italian Riviera is a bit too far away. But I am pleased to announce that my partner, Jolly Rogers, and I have secured accommodation for us all on beautiful Lake Maggiore at Stresa, where the temperature is currently 34 degrees!"

Her announcement drew a noisy, animated response. There was some laughter, there were some shouts of approval, some people cheered and some applauded. It prompted Dave to turn round and look at Miranda again.

"I bet it's a long time since you heard these sounds coming from one of your tour parties."

Miranda stared at him, but feeling Trevor's foot sharply tapping at her ankle again, she pursed her lips and said nothing. Barbara, meanwhile, continued with her announcement.

"For those of you who want to take it easy and relax for the next few days, there are plenty of opportunities to do so in Stresa.

There are lakeside gardens, the old town, a small beach, even a cable car up the mountain. You can also get a boat to the beautiful Borromean islands, across the lake to Pallanza and Villa Taranto and even to Locarno in Switzerland. But, if any of you want to go further afield and see places like Milan or Lugano or Lake Como, there is a railway station in Stresa, we are told that some local excursions are available, or, if we ask Tony nicely, and there is sufficient demand, we might be able to arrange our own. And if you don't like the hotel or the lake, then we can always move on again to somewhere else; maybe get to Rome and Florence after all!"

Barbara paused again, as more cheers echoed around the coach, before continuing.

"Unfortunately, because we are in the middle of summer, we haven't been able to find enough rooms for everyone at the same hotel, so we are going to be using three different hotels which are quite close to each other. In a minute, we are going to circulate the details of the hotels and give you a chance to tell us which one you would prefer to stay at, if you have the choice. You'll see that a couple have swimming pools and one of them is a little bit out of town, for those who prefer a quieter location. Now, I'm afraid we've got a lot of travelling to do this evening so it will be quite late when we arrive but the good news is we do not have to get up early tomorrow…"

"If at all!" Dave interrupted loudly.

"And we will stop en route for a meal tonight," Barbara continued.

"An edible one for a change?" Dave interrupted again.

Susan clamped her hand over Dave's mouth.

Jason, meanwhile, leant forward and tapped Frank on the shoulder.

"We do have one small problem with the accommodation we've booked," Jason confided, a little sheepishly. "I don't know what we're going to do about Miranda and Trevor. We've got enough family, double and twin-bedded rooms to accommodate everyone who needs one, we've found two adjoining single rooms for Nigel and his mother, and we've got one single room for Tony, but we couldn't get any more single rooms, you see. They're all booked."

Frank raised his eyebrows.

"This'll be interesting; wish me luck!"

Frank got up and walked slowly over to where Trevor and Miranda were sitting. His angular frame towered over them as he leant forward. He smiled in a smug, patronising sort of way.

"Now then, I don't know what we are going to do with you two," he began in his usual bluff way.

"How do you mean?" Trevor looked puzzled and felt a little intimidated by Frank's looming presence.

"I mean, for a start, that we are going to have to keep a very close eye on our friend Miranda here. We don't want her blowing the whistle on our little jaunt."

Miranda felt Trevor's foot gently nudging her ankle again. She looked earnestly up at Frank.

"Look, I just want to get this nightmare over with, as soon as possible. You'll get your comeuppance soon enough. Have your five days in Stresa, or whatever, if that's what you want and then just get me home. I'll have to make my report then, though; the company will expect it. Meanwhile, Trevor will look after me ... you'll keep me out of mischief, won't you Trev?"

"I guess." Trevor was still puzzled and a little unnerved.

"And secondly," Frank continued. "We couldn't get enough single rooms, so it's double and twin-bedded rooms only."

Miranda knew what was coming next. She needed to look shocked.

"You mean...!"

"Well, we can't let you have a room to yourself. We haven't got enough rooms and anyway there's no knowing what you might get up to in your own room, on your own. So..."

Miranda had not honestly expected that she would be allowed the luxury of a single room when she was effectively under escort and had not been relishing the prospect of sharing with Susan or Joyce or any of the other solicitous women on the tour. Susan, in particular, had looked at her strangely on more than one occasion. Compared with the alternatives, therefore, she

found the prospect of sharing a room with Trevor not unattractive
– it could be a very enjoyable and interesting way of getting to
know her new employer – but she knew she needed to appear
outraged.

"What do you take me for, some kind of tart?" she protested.

Frank went to say something, changed his mind and just
shrugged. Miranda, meanwhile, continued with her protest.

"God, this just gets worse!"

"We can offer you both a twin bedded room, but that's the
best we can do," Frank emphasised without sounding especially
apologetic.

"Oh, God! It just gets worse," she repeated. "Well, as long as
it's single beds, and there's a lock on the bathroom door, I guess
I'll have to put up with it. Trevor is, after all, a gentleman, unlike
some others I could mention!"

"And don't forget I'm a married man. I don't want word
getting back to my wife that, you know…" Trevor felt that he
ought at least to offer a token protest – after all, he hadn't been
consulted about the proposed sleeping arrangements – although,
in all honesty, he found the prospect of sharing a room with
Miranda no less attractive than she did.

Frank was unusually discomfited. He recognised, belatedly,
that he was rather taking Trevor for granted and wanted to make
amends, particularly in view of Trevor's unselfish act in foregoing
his trip to Venice to act as Miranda's minder. He decided to
change the subject.

"By the way, Trevor. I did a bit of filming while we were in
Venice. It's a bit amateur, like – I'm still getting used to this
wretched machine – but as you did us all a huge favour by
offering to look after Miranda here, I thought you might be
interested in having a look at it. Not the same as being there
obviously, but it might, you know, give you a flavour…"

He removed the camera from around his neck and handed it
eagerly to Trevor. Trevor could think of nothing worse than
being forced to look at Frank's amateur video but he didn't want
to cause offence, so he did his best to appear keen.

"That's very kind of you, Frank. I'm sure I'll enjoy it," he replied disingenuously. Encouraged by Trevor's apparently positive response, Frank tried to sound knowledgeable about the workings of his camera and spent several minutes on a patronising, and not entirely accurate, explanation of how the various buttons worked.

"There," he said at last, "it should be set up for you now, so all you have to do is press the *play* button here and you'll see Venice in all its glory on the little screen! And if you press this *pause* button here, you can stop it and start it again whenever you want to."

Frank smiled in a way that was intended to be reassuring, but which actually looked faintly deranged, and returned to his seat. Trevor exchanged looks of bewilderment with Miranda before effecting a mock yawn. With obvious reluctance, he operated the camcorder as instructed and then glanced disinterestedly at the small screen, with Miranda looking on from the side. For the first thirty seconds or so, there were some fairly nondescript, shaky and not entirely focused shots of Venice's unattractive dockland area, but then, unexpectedly, the film began to take on a more intriguing aspect and Trevor began to peer at the screen more intently. Frank had clearly left the camcorder dangling from his neck and still recording as he started to walk somewhere – there were unsteady pictures of the ground with Frank's feet moving quickly in and out of the shot. After a short time, Frank stopped walking, briefly, and then the light changed and the floor became tiled. The distant, barely audible sound of a toilet being flushed gave a clue as to where Frank might be and then, suddenly, there was a close-up shot of a porcelain urinal followed, in glorious, uncensored detail, by the sight of Frank undoing his flies and peeing. Trevor chuckled, played back the key piece of action again and then handed it across to Miranda, who played it again while giggling loudly.

"Frank!" Trevor shouted. "Have you looked at what you've recorded?" This time it was his turn to be kicked firmly in the ankle.

"Shhh," Miranda whispered. "You should let a few others enjoy this!"

Frank had heard Trevor call him and turned round. Momentarily flustered, Trevor ran his hand over his hair before a thought occurred to him.

"Frank," he called, holding up the camcorder. "This is really very good. When I've finished with it, would you mind if a few others had a look?"

"Be my guest!" Frank was overjoyed; someone was at last appreciating his camera skills. He sat back in his seat basking in the warm glow of contented appreciation.

While Miranda tried hard to suppress an extended bout of giggling, Trevor played the film back to the relevant section and passed it across the aisle to a still damp, cold and dispirited Brian and Valerie. Valerie took charge of the camcorder, firmly declining Brian's offer to operate the controls, and they viewed the offending section with muted amusement. This contrasted sharply with the uninhibited pleasure that Susan and Dave displayed when their turn to view arrived. Susan, in particular, couldn't help laughing out loud.

"Bloody hell, you can see why there is so much water in Venice!" she exclaimed between snorts of laughter.

"Yes and all from such a small source," Dave exploded, his stomach vibrating with mirth.

Initially proud and delighted that his camera-work was causing so much pleasure, Frank became puzzled by Susan and Dave's raucous reaction. He turned round.

"Here, what's all the laughter about?" he asked, suspiciously. Dave held the camcorder aloft before replying.

"Nothing, Frank. We were just commenting on your equipment. Do you know, it's amazing what you can produce these days from something so small. Maybe you should zoom in a bit more next time, though?"

As more ribald laughter followed, Frank stood up, stiff, bristling and formal.

"It might be a good idea if you gave it back, then," he said with typical pomposity.

"Certainly, Frank," Dave acquiesced graciously, handing the camcorder back. "I must say you've captured some really unusual sights! You don't see many of these in the travel guides!"

Almost snatching the camcorder out of Dave's grasp, Frank went back, frowning, to his seat and nervously started playing his film back. He soon came to the section that had caused so much merriment. He stared, gaping at the screen, momentarily lost for words.

"What the…" he said at last. "Oh, no, oh, shit. I don't……"

Dave was savouring every moment of Frank's acute and obvious discomfort. Still chuckling profusely, he leant across with some words of advice.

"What a fuss to make over a little thing like that! But don't delete it, Frank. You should send it to one of those television programmes, you know, that feature funny clips from home videos. They'd pay you a few quid for that one. Mind you, they'd have to show it after the nine o'clock watershed!"

Joyce had been looking over Frank's shoulder and had been watching his pictorial disaster with much the same amusement as the few others who had been privileged enough to witness it. Eventually she leaned across and deliberately whispered to Frank so loudly that her remarks could be clearly heard by the occupants of neighbouring seats.

"You know, somehow, Frank, you've just about captured the essence of our holiday there; a complete and total piss-up!"

★ ★ ★

The much-vaunted stop for a meal break turned out to be a chaotic affair. Tony didn't really know the route from Venice to Stresa – it did not feature on the company's normal itinerary – and couldn't really recommend anywhere to stop, so the motorway services which he chose, were selected, more or less, at random. The services had a pleasant looking restaurant area and, ostensibly, a reasonably priced and varied menu, but it had obviously been a quiet evening and the duty staff were clearly not prepared for the sudden arrival of a coach party of ravenous British tourists. There were, in fact, few staff on duty and even fewer available dishes. Some members of the group made the best of it, selecting what they could from the menu and waiting patiently, while the clearly disgruntled staff prepared the food in a slapdash fashion. Others headed for the adjoining shop where a limited range of slightly stale sandwiches, baguettes and other snacks was available. Nigel's mother, meanwhile, remained on the coach, sound asleep, her medication having taken the effect that Nigel expected.

Also on the coach, Trevor and Miranda both complained that they had not had any lunch, though Miranda did so more vehemently than perhaps she should, and made it clear that they did not intend to forego another meal, however indifferent it might turn out to be. Although Miranda had been calm and quiet on the journey, apart from when she was viewing Frank's cinematic masterpiece, nobody was prepared to risk letting her off the coach, so, while Tony and a number of passengers stood guard, Trevor was allowed to disembark, make a mental note of the selection available in the shop, report back to Miranda for her to make her choice, return to the shop to make the necessary purchases, carry them back on the coach, discover that Miranda had changed her mind and disappear into the shop again.

The relative disappointment of the meal break had not done much to dampen spirits, however, and – Nigel's mother apart – there was a cheerful enough atmosphere on board as the coach finally pulled away on the last leg of its marathon journey. Barbara, still revelling in her new role, reached for the microphone.

"OK, holiday makers. Another two hours or so and we will all be at our hotels," she announced cheerfully.

"And just to make the time go quicker," Dave announced, standing up and reaching into a couple of large carrier bags, "I've got some refreshments for you."

During the protracted meal break, he and Susan had slipped into the shop and purchased a substantial quantity of beer, together with a few token soft drinks, which he began to hand round enthusiastically. As he passed Miranda and Trevor on his way to the back of the coach, Miranda went to say something but again felt Trevor's foot pressing gently into her ankle. Dave, however, had noticed Miranda start to open her mouth and he paused.

"Yes, Miranda, my pet – something wrong?"

"No, no. I…I…don't suppose I could have one, could I?"

Dave raised his eyebrows and chuckled.

"A bottle of beer, I mean!"

"Oh, so it's alright to drink beer on the coach now, is it? Oh alright, go on then. But don't spill any on the floor!"

He removed the top from a bottle and handed it to her. Trevor looked concerned.

"Are you sure that's wise after those pills you took?"

"Who cares!" Miranda said dismissively and took a large swig from the bottle.

★ ★ ★

As darkness descended, the pace of the journey seemed to slow. There was no longer much that could be seen out of the windows, the seats were beginning to feel hard and uncomfortable, it was getting late and fatigue, after a long, emotional day, was setting in. For the more lubricated passengers, however, none of this seemed to be much of a problem. Some joined in with Dave's ad-hoc sing-along though the content of the songs became increasingly more dubious and the quality of performance deteriorated as the level of alcoholic intake rose.

It was very late into the evening when the coach finally arrived in Stresa and began its slow procession around town, with Tony having to stop several times to ask for directions to each of the three hotels that had been booked, dropping the designated people and their luggage off at each one. The necessary farewells at each hotel, together with the issuing of instructions for keeping in touch, mainly by text, were undertaken against a background sound of increasingly raucous and tuneless singing coming from within the coach. Somehow, the level of noise did not seem noticeably to decrease as each group of passengers left the coach, although it stopped altogether when it was finally Dave's turn to leave.

It was difficult to form an impression of the Hotel Gallinara in the dark. It was not quite as modern as some of the hotels they had visited, four storeys high, ostensibly well maintained and with a hint of Italianate Art Noveau about its design. The tourists disembarked, rather stiffly, from the coach, collected their luggage and made their way into the spacious foyer.

Having made the booking, Jason led the way into the hotel, followed by Barbara. They were joined by Gail, Peter, Brian, Valerie, Trevor, Miranda, Frank, Joyce, Dave, Susan and Nigel and his mother.

After a long and, at times, demanding day, Jason was pale, tired and in some pain. His arm was still swaddled in its sling, though the bandaging lacked its original pure crispness and was looking grey and grubby. Peter, Valerie and Brian's clothes, although virtually dry now, were crumpled and badly stained from their earlier immersing in the Venetian canal network. Brian's hair was bedraggled and bespattered and Valerie was still carrying her battered and broken shoes. Dave was displaying all the characteristic symptoms of excessive alcohol consumption and was swaying gently from side to side with an oafish, vacant, lopsided grin on his face. Miranda, meanwhile, had succumbed to the combined effects of strong alcohol and an excess dose of her pills. She was barely awake, mumbling incoherently to herself, and was leaning heavily for support on Trevor, their handcuffed wrists carefully hidden beneath a strategically placed coat. Nigel's mother had also succumbed, in her case to a surfeit of sleeping pills, and, as soon as they entered the hotel, had to be found a chair, on which she sat and dozed, occasionally snoring loudly.

The receptionist, a small balding man, with heavily greased hair, dark stubble and bad breath, surveyed the scene in front of him with ill-concealed disdain. Jason stepped forward, rather hesitantly, clutching a handful of papers.

"The, er, party booked in the name of, er, Rogers earlier today?" he ventured awkwardly, almost stammering over his words. The receptionist's expression brightened a little.

"Ah yes, sir," he acknowledged in broken English. "I have your room keys here. You will need to fill in some forms and we will need to check your passports."

Gail tapped Peter on the shoulder and whispered conspiratorially in his ear. "Try and make sure we don't get a room next to Barbara and Jason this time. We could do with some sleep." Peter nodded obediently, although he doubted, somehow, that Jason was capable of quite the same gymnastic performances that had graced the earlier part of their holiday.

The receptionist, meanwhile, studied the new arrivals for a second time, more closely now, before concluding that maybe the forms and the passports could wait until the morning. He spread a number of keys out on the desk in front of him, together with a quantity of blank forms. His eyes ran along the faces in front of him for a third time – he seemed especially interested in Miranda's disconcerting appearance.

"Excuse me, sir," he addressed Trevor, who visibly jumped, took a step back and rapidly began to turn pink. Was there something wrong? Had the receptionist been tipped off? Did he perhaps recognise Miranda from somewhere, or had he spotted the handcuffs?

"Er, yes?" Trevor replied trying not to sound as guilty as he felt.

"Your wife; she does not look too good?"

"My wife? Ah, no, you don't understand. She's not… ah, yes, she's rather tired. She's had a long journey and she's on some powerful medication. But, I ah… I'm sure she'll be alright in the morning."

At that moment, Peter sneezed loudly and without warning.

"And my husband will be alright in the morning too, although he's not on any medication!" Gail added quickly and unnecessarily, sounding defensive, but smiling as reassuringly as she could.

"What timesh breakfasht?" Dave asked, slurring his words slightly and steadying himself against the reception desk.

"From 7.30 until 9.30, sir. Enjoy your stay!"

★ ★ ★

In a dark, unoccupied hotel room, on the top floor, a key turned in the door. It creaked open slowly, allowing Trevor to stumble in while still propping up a stupefied and disorientated Miranda. He fumbled around for the light switch and turned it on. Without really taking much notice of his new clean, spacious and comfortable surroundings, complete with balcony overlooking the lake, he half dragged Miranda towards the nearer of the two beds, picked her up and laid her, untidily, face up, on the bed. She didn't stir. He reached into his pocket, found the key to the handcuffs, undid them and went back outside the room to collect their cases. As soon as his back was turned, Miranda, apparently still asleep, began to slide, slowly and gently, off the bed and onto the hard, wooden floor, where she lay, sprawled and motionless.

Trevor dropped the suitcases quickly onto the floor and ran back over to the side of the bed where Miranda lay. He gently placed his hands and arms underneath her and carefully lifted her back onto the bed. Before he had chance to remove his hands and arms, however, Miranda reached out with both arms, embraced him tightly and, while apparently still asleep, pulled him down on top of her and began to sigh heavily.

It was at this point that Trevor's mobile phone began to ring. While still locked in Miranda's determined embrace, he managed to extricate it from his pocket and had just answered it when Miranda let out another loud sigh.

"Hello… Julia? What a nice surprise. What's that? You thought you heard someone making a noise? No, no, I don't think so. It's a very hot and humid night here so I've got the window open. There are some people outside making a bit of a noise down by the pool. No, no. I'll put the air conditioning on when we go, er, that is when I go to bed."

After some furious fidgeting, wriggling and a little gentle wrestling, Trevor managed to prize himself out of Miranda's grasp and he continued his conversation with Julia as he made his way to the bathroom.

"Yes, it's been an exhausting day. We have had to drive to a different hotel – there was a last minute change of plan, something to do with food poisoning, I think – a massive cock-up somewhere…"

He disappeared into the bathroom while still talking and closed the door firmly behind him. On the bed, Miranda half stirred, briefly, from her stupor and muttered "a massive cock up – that sounds nice," before drifting back to sleep.

★ ★ ★

Further along the corridor, in another similar, pleasant, almost elegant room, Brian and Valerie were, yet again, assessing the damage resulting from their latest dunking.

Valerie had removed her top, skirt and, finally, her coordinated designer underwear, throwing them angrily onto the bed.

"They're all ruined; I won't be able to wear them again," she protested.

It was a hot, sultry evening and she felt somehow more comfortable naked. She walked over to the dark wooden dressing table, sat down on a dark wooden chair and looked in the large, square mirror with its dark wooden surround.

"Good God! Look at the state of my hair," she complained. "I don't know what I'm going to do with that."

Brian had removed his besmirched shirt and trousers and, now wearing only a scruffy pair of boxer shorts, had thrown them dismissively onto the floor.

"Still, at least we are still on holiday with a few relaxing days to look forward to and I'm sure things will get better…" His voice, lacking assurance, tailed off altogether, as he studied the condition of his rucksack. "Mmm, this is going to have to dry out for a day or two."

He unzipped the main compartment, turned it upside down and shook the damp contents out onto the bed. Out tumbled a crumpled jumper, a cagoule, some waterproof trousers, several melted chocolate bars, a bag of crisps, the official pack of now soggy holiday documents, some batteries for the camera that got broken a few days ago, several sweet wrappers, a half-drunk bottle of water of indeterminate vintage, some tissues and, as Brian continued to shake the rucksack vigorously, from its deepest, darkest recess, a key-ring holding the keys to their suitcase padlocks, plopped neatly onto the bed. Brian looked startled, guiltily gathered it up swiftly and threw it back into the rucksack before Valerie had time to notice.

But Valerie wasn't looking. She was studying herself closely in the mirror. For all the ravages of time, her breasts were still firm and pert and her body had retained, for the most part, its youthful shapeliness. As she studied herself, admiringly, her thoughts returned to her modelling days and the buzz she got from knowing that all those eyes were studying every contour of her naked body. She recalled their evening in Amsterdam's Red Light District and the raw excitement and erotic tension that pervaded the place; she reflected on her recent damp walk through Venice and the many admiring glances she got as her firm nipples pushed against her wet, transparent top. Maybe, she thought to herself as she continued to gaze intently into the mirror, she might be able to resurrect her modelling career – there was still time before she got too old and gravity took its inevitable toll. Brian wouldn't approve, of course, but then, he didn't need to know. If his musical career was about to take off at last, then she could undertake some discreet modelling assignments when he was away. She still had a lot of her old contacts, after all. As she reflected on the possibility, she became increasingly excited. Now was the time to share another thought with Brian.

"You know, Brian," she announced at last. "I've been giving a lot of thought to this holiday and what has gone wrong so far."

"I bet you have!" Brian mumbled.

"Apart from the fact that I don't think we're really suited to these kind of organised coach tours, one of the main problems is that you keep getting soaked to the skin and ruining all your clothes; you've hardly got any left for the next few days. Now unless we avoid water altogether in the future, which isn't really practical, unless they run a coach trip to the Sahara Desert, I don't think I can guarantee that you're not going to get another soaking at some stage. So what we need to do is make sure that you're not wearing much at the time."

"What the hell do you mean?" Brian was puzzled.

"I mean we ought to try a beach holiday somewhere warm

where all you need to wear is some shorts. Or if we're really feeling daring, possibly even one of those naturist holidays…"

"You mean lying around on a beach somewhere, in the nude, with everyone staring at us?"

"Of course, we don't have to go the whole hog if you don't like the idea, but we'd make sure we go somewhere where nobody knows us and if anyone is staring, they'll be staring at me, not you. These places are full of fat middle-aged men, so I'm told! Anyway, let's go somewhere hot and at least keep our clothing to the bare minimum. I'm sure we can get to some of these places without flying. What do you say?"

"Well, thanks for the compliment!" Brian's mind was in turmoil. He thought he knew Valerie so well after so much time together but now, somehow, he didn't feel he knew her at all. This racy, exhibitionist kind of talk was not at all what he had come to expect from her. Normally, these days, when she wasn't nagging him, she was more focussed on mundane and material things – the latest gossip from her coffee mornings or the new range of cosmetics that had just come in – not exciting, perhaps, but it made him feel comfortable and secure. But now, suddenly, he felt uneasy and threatened. Part of him was genuinely shocked by what she had just said, but, he had to admit, part of him was also quite excited.

"I think I'd better take a cold shower and think things over," he announced, stepping out of his boxer shorts and striding towards the bathroom. Valerie could see he was excited. She smiled.

* * *

In another room on another floor, at Susan's insistence, Dave had also just partaken of a cold shower. In his case, it was to try and shake off the worst excesses of his alcoholic over-indulgence. When he stepped, shivering, out of the shower, therefore, he was surprised and delighted to discover that the stirring of the sinews that he had felt earlier on in the day had survived both the alcoholic onslaught and the icy water and was very prominently on display.

He strode proudly and naked into the bedroom, thrusting his erect manhood ahead of him and grinning with devilment. Susan was lying quietly in bed reading.

"What do you think of this, Sue?" Dave bellowed proudly. "Look at that – you could hang your hat on that!"

Susan looked up and stared with amazement. "Good God! I wondered what it was for. Well, it's a long time since I saw one of those, I must say! But, I hope you're not planning to bring it anywhere near me!"

"Come on, Sue, you can't leave me like this," Dave pleaded. "It would be such a shame to waste it and I don't know when it's going to happen again."

Susan looked at him, upright, perky, expectant, and still a little tipsy, and smiled tolerantly at him. "Oh alright, come on then. Bring it over here!" She tossed her book onto the floor and pushed the duvet down, inviting Dave to join her in bed.

To her considerable surprise, she found herself enjoying Dave's all too rare and surprisingly nimble athleticism. Gradually, she too began to experience feelings she had not experienced for some time, deep and satisfying, and as they built to an orgasmic crescendo, she cried "encore" and leapt on top of Dave, determined to take full advantage of his rediscovered attribute.

In the next room, through a thin wall, Peter and Gail could hear Dave and Susan's noisy, robust bedroom antics only too clearly. Peter coughed gently and looked dolefully across at Gail.

"Well, don't blame me. You only said you didn't want to be next to Barbara and Jason again."

Gail smiled, placed an affectionate arm around Peter's shoulders and pecked him lightly on the cheek.

"Night, night," she whispered and reached out and turned off the light.

★ ★ ★

CHAPTER 8

The End of the Road

The warm sun rose in a clear azure sky. Its golden rays shimmered on the opalescent ripples of the tranquil lake as they lapped gently on the serpentine shoreline. Dave scratched his crotch, vacantly. His bloodshot eyes were hurting in the glaring light of the breakfast room and he was having to squint, but there was a new inner contentment about him this morning as he scoured the room for fresh morsels to pile onto his already heavily congested breakfast plate. Wearing the last in his collection of flamboyant Hawaiian shirts – primarily an iridescent floral array of crimson and orange – there was an unusually sprightly spring in his step as he went over to the table where Frank and Joyce were sitting and enthusiastically plonked his laden plate down in front of him.

"Now that's something like a breakfast!" he oozed, with saliva almost visibly dribbling down the side of his chin, as he surveyed the gargantuan feast spread before him.

Joyce looked up from her more modest but, nevertheless, ample breakfast, her face an embodiment of mock horror.

"Good God, I don't know what's worse. That plate of food or your shirt!"

Susan sat down beside Dave, an unusual hint of pinkness around her face and neck and a faint sparkle in her eyes, just in time to hear Joyce's familiar-sounding remark. Though her own plate was more than adequately stocked, she surveyed Dave's plate rather as a novice mountaineer might survey the north face of the Eiger.

"You know, if you're very lucky, some of that food will be on that shirt in a minute; that should tone it down a bit," she smiled benignly. "So what are you planning to do today?"

Joyce fell silent for a moment. The dramatic events of this holiday, her many new experiences, the friends she had made and her growing confidence meant that her former obsequious relationship with Frank was coming to an end. In the future, she was determined that their partnership would be more one of equals. She well knew, of course, that Frank's traditional, almost Victorian attitudes and his intransigence would be difficult to overcome and there were going to be emotionally difficult times ahead, but she was not prepared to return to the way things had always been in the past and she was ready to do whatever was necessary. Meanwhile, she was going to enjoy the next few days.

"We're going to pretend we're by the sea, back home," she said, at last. "You know, take a walk along the prom, sit and watch the world go by, find somewhere for a mid-morning coffee. Check out the local toilets. Maybe take a boat trip. What about you?"

Susan's reply was surprisingly resigned.

"If the bar's open all day, I doubt that we'll get much further than the hotel and the pool!"

Suddenly, from somewhere close behind them, there was a loud crash and the sound of breaking crockery. Frank continued to eat without even looking round.

"Sounds as though Brian's arrived," he observed sardonically.

His dining companions turned and looked in the direction of the noise. Sure enough, Brian was standing forlornly over a pile of broken china on the floor, apologising profusely to one of the hotel staff, who had come rushing over.

"You know," Frank continued. "It's a good job Miranda's not here or she'd have them chucked out again!"

"Yes and where are Miranda and Trevor, by the way?" Susan enquired.

★ ★ ★

Trevor had been sound asleep. He hadn't stirred when the antiquated plumbing began to creak noisily under the strain of early morning ablutions in neighbouring bathrooms. Nor had he stirred when, along the corridor, doors were slamming and animated conversations, in several different languages, were being struck up, as people made their way loudly to breakfast. He stirred briefly when he heard a mobile phone ringing somewhere close by, but he had started to doze again when the realisation suddenly dawned that the phone in question was his own. Barely awake, he threw the duvet back, leapt naked out of bed and began to move, as quickly as he could, in the direction of the dressing table, where he had abandoned his phone the previous evening.

He had taken no more than half a step, however, when his progress was violently arrested by a sharp jerk on his right arm. Confused, he turned around sharply to find that his right wrist was handcuffed to an unclothed alien arm, which was protruding from beneath the lumpy duvet. As his brain gradually unscrambled the events of the previous evening, he shouted "phone, phone" and pulled Miranda, naked and drowsy, out of bed, by her manacled wrist. Badly hung-over and struggling to comprehend what was happening, Miranda found herself being dragged, unwillingly and indignantly, across the wooden floor towards the ringing phone.

"What the hell is going on?" she protested, checking her bottom for grazes and splinters, as Trevor warily answered the phone.

"Hello?… Julia! This is a nice surprise. Hang on a minute; I'm just wrestling with some baggage."

He covered the phone with his hand and whispered to Miranda who, in a state of dazed confusion, was struggling to get to her feet.

"It's the wife! The key, where's the key?"

He pointed to the handcuffs, but Miranda just blinked uncomprehendingly at him. He pointed to them again and, this time, Miranda's face registered an inkling of understanding. She began to fumble among a jumble of objects randomly scattered on the dressing table, found the key to the handcuffs and began to unlock them as Trevor continued to talk into the phone.

"Sorry, dear, as you know, we arrived at the hotel very late and very tired last night and we, ah, I just crashed out. I was just looking for the key to the suitcase when you phoned. Yes, of course I can leave that for the moment. You sound agitated. Are you alright?"

Trevor listened to what seemed like a long, shrill diatribe on the other end of the phone as he walked into the bathroom and closed the door behind him. Miranda sat on the bed, massaging some life back into her recently manacled wrist and looking anxiously towards the bathroom door. After a moment or two, she rested her head in her hands, trying hard to unravel in her pained mind, the tumultuous events of the previous day that had resulted in her waking up naked in bed, with a hangover, in a strange hotel room, handcuffed to a member of the coach party who was also naked and who was now talking to his wife on the phone.

"Oh, my head," she moaned trying, in vain, to recall what had happened. She groaned as some vague, hazy recollections began to form in her befuddled mind.

* * *

In the bright but slightly faded elegance of the hotel breakfast room, Peter and Gail had helped themselves to modest, nutritious breakfasts of fruit and yoghurt and sat down at the large square table which already accommodated Dave, Susan, Joyce and Frank. Peter smiled weakly at them and then quickly looked down at his breakfast. Somehow he was finding it unusually difficult to look Dave and Susan in the in the eye this morning.

"Morning, Peter, and how are you today?" Dave asked affably. Peter went to say something, but Gail spoke first.

"He's much better now, thank you." She smiled reassuringly.

Peter nodded. "I must say, it was nice to be able to unpack our suitcases properly for once and I'm looking forward to getting out there in the sun somewhere and taking it easy for a while. No more dashing about. No more missing coaches. No more falling in the water."

At that point, Barbara and Jason came into the room. Barbara led the way, looking assured and smiling confidently. She was wearing a low-cut turquoise top and high-cut denim shorts. Jason was, as usual, wearing a creased t-shirt and jeans. Looking pale and uncertain, he followed a little way behind.

"Hey, there they are!" Dave shouted exuberantly. Their small group burst into applause, which elicited looks of stern disapproval from some of their fellow diners and caused Jason to study the floor in some discomfiture.

"You stars!" Susan called, adding to Jason's embarrassment. "You certainly found us a good hotel here! And just look at the weather outside!"

"And how were the beds – nice and soft I hope?" Frank asked in his usual toe-curling way.

"Shut up Frank!" Joyce snapped. "You're embarrassing them!" Frank ignored her.

"I hope you're going out in the sun later. No offence, but you still look very pale – well, you do, Jason. I mean you're not pale, obviously, Barbara. But no-one will believe you've been on holiday unless you get a nice tanning, er, sorry, tan."

Smiling smugly at his mischief making, and ignoring Joyce's increasingly desperate proddings, Frank picked up his cup of coffee. Barbara, however, was unfazed. Putting on her best vampish walk, she sashayed over to Frank, stood provocatively with her bosom close to his face, leaned forward and pouted.

"Yes, Frank you're quite right," she said, trying to sound sultry and seductive. "We shall be out by the pool soon and, you never know, I might be doing a bit of topless bathing."

"Don't even think about it!" Joyce said sharply but it was clearly too late as Frank's hand started to shake, spilling some coffee onto the freshly laundered tablecloth. He was just starting to mop the spillage up, as best he could, when he felt a tap on his shoulder. He turned round to find Nigel, hopping up and down, looking anxious.

"I'm glad I've found you here. I thought you ought to know," he blurted out, "that mother has been trying to phone Conn Tours to tell them all about what you've been up to. So far, she's only been able to get some kind of recorded message and we're going out now – she'll be down in a moment – but she's determined to try and contact them when we get back. I'm sorry, but I thought you ought to know." He looked nervously around.

"Oh well, that's that then!" Frank prophesied with characteristic gloom.

"Not necessarily!" Joyce interjected. She turned to Nigel. "Have you decided what you're doing today, yet?"

"Nnnno, not yet. I haven't been told what I've decided!"

"Well then, what you need to do is pamper your mother. Take her out into the sun. Take her on a boat trip across the lake to somewhere nice – the islands, maybe – find a pleasant pavement café where you can buy her a coffee or maybe an ice cream, treat her to a good lunch and if she needs a rest, find her a pretty spot in the shade where she can sit and watch the world go by. Give her a brilliant day, do what she wants, and then, before you come back to the hotel, ask her if she still wants to phone head office and risk losing the next three or four days of her holiday. And if none of that works, come and find me when you get back and I'll have a word with her."

"Yes, that's right," Frank added. "We'll work on her."

"You'll do no such thing, Frank," Joyce snapped. "You can stay out of it. You'll do more harm than good. No, no, I'll have a word with her, woman to woman."

Frank was taken aback at Joyce's unexpected display of independence and none too keen to encourage it.

"And if that doesn't work?" he asked, scornfully.

Joyce laughed. "Well, then me and the girls here will beat her up and throw her in the lake!" For the second time in a couple of minutes, Frank spilled some coffee.

★ ★ ★

As she gradually began to recall more of the momentous events of the previous day, Miranda started to shake quite violently. Instinctively, she wrapped the duvet around her, for comfort as much as for warmth. She could hear Trevor's voice in the bathroom. He sounded quite agitated but she couldn't quite make out what he was saying. She looked across to the door of the bedroom and momentarily considered the possibility of escape but she wasn't even dressed, she didn't know how long Trevor was going to be and, in truth, didn't have the remotest idea what she would do – or could do – once she got out of the hotel. She was in no doubt that she needed Trevor, both now and, in all probability, for some time to come. She was sitting on the bed, wrapped demurely in the duvet and shaking rather less obviously, when Trevor emerged, clutching his mobile phone. She looked up. Her face looked haunted and vulnerable.

"Well?" she asked nervously.

Trevor looked thoughtful. He ran his hand over his hair and sat down on the bed beside her.

"That was Julia – my wife!"

"Yes, I know who she is!" Miranda couldn't help sounding impatient and somewhat sarcastic. She needed to know what was going on. She was starting to shake more violently again.

"I don't think you were aware at the time – you were, ah, well, you were a bit unwell I think – but she phoned me last night, soon after we arrived. She phoned to say, ah well, that, ah, when she got home to Mark, that's her son, and Geoff, that's her ex, she realised she had been tricked by both of them. They really wanted to try and get her back – to be a family again... But there was nothing wrong with the cat, or Geoff – never had been. It was all just a pack of lies to get her back home. Obviously, she was very angry with them both, especially Geoff. And believe me, when she gets angry... She said she was going off to sort him out. She phoned to apologise for leaving me the way she did and asked me if we could kiss and make up."

"And?"

"And I said I thought we should meet up and talk about it when I get home in a few days. I think she was expecting something more from me and I don't think it went down too well. She hung up on me. God, she's got such a temper on her sometimes, I worry."

There was a long pause, during which Trevor ran his hand several times over his hair. He too looked haunted and vulnerable and Miranda wanted to reach out and touch him, but he had not made any attempt to cover himself up and she was disconcerted by his unashamed nakedness.

"And then just now," Trevor continued, beginning to pace the room and clearly struggling with his emotions. "Just now, she phoned to say that she had done something very foolish after she slammed the phone down on me last night and that she would have to lie low for a while. She started to say something else but my battery packed up – very mysterious!"

"You know," he continued after another uncomfortable pause. "Once she'd gone back home, I missed her, of course, but somehow not as much as I thought I would and it's sets you thinking. If that's the case, then maybe there's something wrong with our relationship anyway and it's perhaps for the best if we don't get back together again… at least until we've all had time to calm down and take stock for a while…"

Miranda could not disguise her delight. "Oh, Trevor!" she cried as she threw back the duvet, stood up, ran towards Trevor and threw herself at him with such force that he fell back onto the spare bed, pulling Miranda down on top of him.

★ ★ ★

South East of Stresa, Tony was driving the empty coach along the motorway towards Milan, where, a little later, his wife was due to fly in to the airport. She had been lucky to get a flight at such short notice and Tony was looking forward to seeing her. But he felt ill at ease and restless this morning and his mouth felt unusually dry. It was bad enough driving what was effectively a stolen coach on the open road but, at the end of it, he knew that the meeting with his wife would be emotionally difficult. Taking a swig from a bottle of lukewarm mineral water, he reflected on the events of the last few days and what he was going to say to his wife when they met, trying hard to compose the words he would use carefully in his mind; he wasn't very good at spontaneous communication and, if he wasn't very careful, he could make a mess of things. He knew he was going to have to be honest with her; more honest, at least, than he had been recently. He also knew that what he had to say could put their relationship under such strain that even his pleas for forgiveness and his promise to work closer to home in future and to come home every night might be insufficient to repair the damage. Still it had to be done; it would be better coming from him now than someone else later – time to be brave. He took another swig of water.

★ ★ ★

Returning to their light, airy hotel room after a leisurely breakfast, Peter and Gail opened the French window and stepped out onto their small balcony, sniffing the warm clean air appreciatively. Beyond the swimming pool and through the trees, they could see the tranquil blue waters of the lake.

"Ah, this is better!" Peter opined with obvious enjoyment. Gail smiled her relaxed smile and gently squeezed his hand. She leant on the balcony rail and looked down at the swimming pool below.

"Oh, look! There's some of our group down by the pool." She waved cheerfully at them.

As Susan had predicted, Dave had got no further than the side of the pool and he and Susan were relaxing on sun beds with some iced drinks beside them on a small white plastic table. Still wearing his patterned shirt, Dave had now donned a shapeless pair of khaki shorts and a faded baseball cap. Susan was wearing a loose-fitting T-shirt and cool billowy cotton skirt.

As they looked up and waved back to Gail, Jason and Barbara walked past. Apart from his sling, Jason was stripped to the waist revealing a pale, skeletal torso above some baggy bathing shorts. Barbara was wearing a skimpy white bikini. Dave watched open mouthed as Barbara glided slowly and provocatively past and settled onto a sun bed, next to Jason, and just a few feet away. She reached into her shoulder bag for a bottle of sunscreen and looked mischievously around her.

"Where's Frank?" she asked, sounding disappointed. Dave chuckled.

"Frank and Joyce have gone off to find the bandstand and a branch of Harry Ramsden's. Very continental!"

"Blimey, you can talk!" Susan mocked. "And I suppose you're suddenly the great cosmopolitan man about town!"

"Alright, alright. Point taken! But I might just have pizza for my lunch today, as it happens."

Dave stretched out a lazy, flabby arm to reach for his drink but was momentarily distracted by the sight of Brian and Valerie ambling towards them along the raised edge of the pool. Valerie looked elegant as usual in the striking one-piece, powder blue, designer bathing costume that she had decided to pack at the last minute and Brian, anything but elegant, in his voluminous faded grey shorts, black socks and a pair of grubby sandals. Dave waved at them in acknowledgment.

Barbara, meanwhile, had leaned forward on her sun bed.

"Oh, well, if Frank's not here, it's his loss!"

With that, she reached behind her, undid her bikini bra, removed it and lay back on her sun bed, proudly exposing a pair of firm breasts. Jason leapt to his feet.

"Barbara what do you think you're doing!" he chastised.

Barbara looked cross. Not only had she discovered a lot about herself on this holiday, she was also discovering quite a bit about Jason. As she had become more confident, outgoing and uninhibited, he seemed to her to be growing more cautious and reserved. The bedroom accident hadn't been his fault, of course, but he seemed to be using it as an excuse to become less adventurous and more disapproving. In some ways, he was starting to behave like her father. Barbara sighed.

"Come on, Jace!" she chided. "I don't exactly get much chance to do this kind of thing at home!"

"That's right, you tell him," Valerie encouraged, as she walked serenely past, with Brian in her wake. "As a matter of fact, I think it's an excellent idea."

She moved across to a vacant sun bed, not far from Barbara, sat down, undid the halter neck of her costume and rolled it down to her waist so that she too was topless. She lay back on the sun bed, closed her eyes and sighed contentedly.

Brian stopped in front of Dave and stared open-mouthed at Valerie.

"What the hell do you think you're doing?" he protested, but Valerie ignored him.

Dave had been staring open-mouthed at Barbara and he now started to gawp at Valerie in much the same way. He was beginning to feel the same vague stirring in his loins that he had felt yesterday. He mopped his perspiring brow.

"Blimey, is it me or is it getting hot? I think I might have to go back to our room soon to cool off," he muttered through a film of saliva. Susan completed the trio of those staring open mouthed at the impressive and entirely unexpected mammarian display. "Me too!" she mouthed, beginning to squirm awkwardly on her sun bed.

In an attempt to cool down and slake his dry throat, Dave made another attempt to reach for his drink. But he was still staring, unblinking, at Barbara and Valerie and wasn't concentrating on what he was doing. His outstretched hand knocked the glass onto the tiled floor surrounding the swimming pool, where it broke into a number of jagged pieces. Alerted by the nearby sound of breaking glass, Brian looked down to see sharp, shimmering shards of glass on the ground immediately in front of him. He tried to take last-minute evasive action, but his sandals slipped on the wet tiles, he lost his balance and fell, with a satisfying splash into the pool, showering Dave, Susan, Barbara, Jason, and Valerie with cold water.

Up on the balcony, laughing heartily, Gail and Peter moved slowly back into their room.

"Well I'm certainly feeling much better now!" Peter chuckled.

"Come on, let's get out of here before they make this topless bathing compulsory," Gail said, still laughing. "We'll go and explore the town and find somewhere quiet to relax a bit later."

Peter smiled. It was ironic in a way that Barbara and Valerie, both of whom, at one time or another, Gail thought might have fancied him, were lying topless just a few feet below their balcony, and taking no notice of him whatsoever. But then, over the years, Gail had erroneously thought a number of women had fancied him. It was strange, therefore, that his clandestine liaisons with Jenny, the geography teacher, appeared to have gone totally unnoticed. It never meant much, of course and it was over now, anyway. Maybe Peter would confess one of these days but then, on the other hand, perhaps it was better if nothing was said and the past was quietly buried.

For her part, Gail would probably have tolerated Peter's brief affair if she had known about it. After all, it would have gone someway to assuaging her conscience after her ill-considered fling with Doctor Penfold a year or two ago. It never meant much, of course and it was over now, anyway. Maybe Gail would confess one of these days but then, on the other hand, perhaps it was better if nothing was said and the past was quietly buried.

Nodding his agreement to Gail's suggestion, Peter grabbed their door key and they stepped eagerly out into the narrow corridor and marched briskly towards the lift. During the last couple of days, Peter had made a number of increasingly impolite suggestions as to what he would like to do to Fred, including some form of ritual execution, but Gail was keen to see the maligned bear safely returned to Carol's ample bosom, so it was agreed that it would be best all round if Fred stayed behind, relaxing quietly on the bed and keeping out of trouble.

★ ★ ★

Bed was also very much on Miranda's mind. She knew that she was, for the time being at least, heavily dependent on Trevor. Clearly, she no longer featured in Tony's life – he had gone off to meet his wife – and, without Trevor's help, she would return to England jobless and broke. For her part, she now needed to make Trevor as dependent on her as she was on him and his marital difficulties had given her the opportunity she needed. She knew what to do and how to do it.

While Miranda partook of a long refreshing bath by way of preparation, Trevor, temporarily relieved of his guard duties, found the time and opportunity to tune the television to an English-speaking service, currently broadcasting a news bulletin.

He could never quite bring himself to sever all links with home when he was on holiday and liked to keep in touch with the news. But he was only able to concentrate on it for a few minutes before Miranda emerged from the bathroom, refreshed, glowing and naked, and threw herself uninhibitedly at him.

On a small, flickering screen, a news bulletin was being broadcast. The words, read with authority, but little feeling, by a young female broadcaster, echoed around the room largely unheeded by its two occupants, who were lying on the bed, indulging in increasingly intimate activity, the hot sun shining through the open balcony door onto Trevor's naked and, for the moment, pale buttocks, as they moved rhythmically up and down.

"Some breaking news; it has just been announced," the newsreader said, "that the British-based coach tour operator, "Conn Tours" has gone into immediate liquidation leaving hundreds of holiday-makers stranded in various locations throughout Europe. More news as we get it."

"Severe thunder storms have badly affected the city of Venice overnight. St. Marks Square and the surrounding area are reported to be heavily flooded. We understand that a lightning strike and subsequent fire has caused severe damage to the Hotel Fortezza and minor damage to several adjoining buildings. We hope to have a more detailed report in the next few minutes."

"Meanwhile, some other news: police are still investigating a mysterious fire, which has destroyed much of a Conference Centre in Surrey overnight. It is known that one man, named as Geoffrey Leggatt, a self-employed handyman, lost his life in the blaze, but it is feared that others may have been trapped in the badly damaged accommodation wing. Police are regarding both the fire and the death of Mr Leggatt as suspicious at this stage and, it is understood, are anxious to interview Mr Leggatt's former wife, Mrs Julia Cockrell, who apparently returned home early from holiday two days ago but has now disappeared. They are also trying to contact the manager of the Centre who, it is believed, is currently on a coach holiday somewhere in Europe…"

★ ★ ★